Desert
Run

Also by Betty Webb
Desert Noir
Desert Wives
Desert Shadows

Desert Run

Run

A Lena Jones Mystery

Betty Webb

Poisoned Pen Press

Library of Congress Catalog Card Number: 2005934982

ISBN: 1-59058-234-9 Hardcover

Poisoned Pen Press
6962 E. First Ave., Ste. 103
Scottsdale, AZ 85251
www.poisonedpenpress.com
info@poisonedpenpress.com

Printed in the United States of America

For Paul

Acknowledgments

The author gratefully acknowledges her many debts to: the granddaddy of all books about Arizona's Great Escape, *The Faustball Tunnel: German POWs in America and Their Great Escape,* by John Hammond Moore, Random House, 1978; John Leptich, at the *Scottsdale Tribune,* for sparking her interest in this story; Elizabeth Bruening Lewis, for details about the escape; Larry Jorgensen, former guard at Camp Papago, for firsthand information; former Camp Papago POW Rolf Koenigs, now a resident of Glendale, Arizona, for insights on camp life; the Papago Trackers and the Arizona National Guard Historical Society; U.S. Senator John Kyl's office for information on Ethiopian immigration patterns; Tom Bonsall, for information on car productivity during World War II; the Phoenix Studebaker Club, for information on Golden Hawks; Steve Ralls, Director of Communications for the Servicemembers Legal Defense Network, for information on the treatment of gay World War II veterans; the Superstition Mountains Museum in Apache Junction, Arizona, for information on the legend of the Lost Dutchman Gold Mine and topographical information on the Superstitions Wilderness; Kathleen Cady, for information about SSI payments and practices; the Sheridan Street Irregulars for their vigorous critiques; Toni Laxson, of the Scottsdale and East Valley *Tribune* newspapers for information on crime reporting techniques; and last but certainly not least, Marge Purcell and Debra McCarthy for manuscript troubleshooting.

Chapter One

December 24, 1944

At 1:36 a.m. on Christmas Eve, Gunter Hoenig, crewman on German U-boat 237, ate Arizona dirt.

The gunnery mechanic didn't mind. Dirt was better than mud, and at least the narrow, one hundred and seventy-eight foot tunnel he and his comrades had dug underneath the prison camp fence remained as arid as the desert above before last night's rain began to fall. Taking heart from the encouraging shouts behind him, Gunter spit the dirt out of his mouth and crawled on. Less than thirty feet left to go and they would all be free. Once out of the tunnel, he and the other twenty-seven German prisoners of war would make their way to Mexico, where supporters of the Reich would smuggle them back to Germany.

Gunter smiled. The Americans had outsmarted themselves, believing they could outwit members of the Reich's great navy merely by caging its sailors on this inland sea of sand. As Kapitan zur See Erik Ernst pointed out, where humans live there will always be water, and Arizona had proved no exception. The maps smuggled into camp showed that this seemingly arid country was criss-crossed by manmade canals which fed into great rivers. Oh, German sailors understood rivers! And rafts! The raft Das Kapitan had designed and he and his friend Josef had built would navigate those rivers all the way to the sea. What difficulty would riding a mere river prove to men who had conquered the mighty Atlantic? As for their less adventurous comrades behind them in the tunnel, Mexico was less than two hundred miles away, and their feet would be sufficient.

"Schnell, schnell!" *Kapitan Ernst, right behind him, barked.* "Quickly, quickly!" *He followed up his words with a blow across Gunter's buttocks.*

Did Das Kapitan think he wasn't already hurrying? Not for the first time Gunter ground his teeth in fury at his commander. Perhaps once he and Josef reached the canal, they would make their own plans.

That final freedom must wait. First, escape through this narrow tunnel (not much narrower than U-237!), then a sprint to the high brush by the canal. Then he would tell Josef his thoughts and they would slip away from Kapitan to navigate Arizona's waters on their own. Perhaps their commander had managed to save them when the U-boat caught fire, but he had abandoned so many others. Fifteen men dead, and all because of his cowardice.

Gunter could still hear his shipmates' screams.

Ach, *no time to think of that now. Just hands and knees churning up dirt, but good, all good, because the end of the tunnel was less than twelve feet ahead. He could already see the velvet night.*

Above him, in the camp itself, the remaining German prisoners drank home-made schnapps and sang Stille Nacht *to cover any noise their escaping comrades might make. They had grown fat and happy and preferred the comforts of camp to the unknown dangers of the desert. Well, good luck to them. But for him, the taste of freedom was sweeter than any Christmas pudding.*

Only ten feet more. Five. Three...

Hands reached down to pull him out into the mesquite-scented air.

Freedom. Danke Gott!

Chapter Two

It was a good day to film, but a bad day to die.

The elderly star of *Escape Across the Desert* sat slumped in his wheelchair, blood ruining his white shirt and every other surface in the small kitchen. I'd seen neater slaughterhouses.

Knowing it was pointless but praying it wasn't, I knelt beside him and put my finger on his neck, hoping a tell-tale throb would prove he hadn't yet bled out. "Kapitan Ernst?"

Dead men seldom answer. The former U-boat commander's flesh was cool and rigor well-established, meaning that he had died long before sunup. Duct tape sealed both arms to the wheelchair, almost as if the killer feared that the ninety-one-year-old double amputee might put up a fight. I doubted he had, so why the overkill, why so many disfiguring blows? Why had the killer beaten Ernst to death, taking his good sweet time?

Him? Violence like this usually pointed to a male perpetrator. Then again, women were getting meaner these days.

The police would want to know the exact time I discovered the body, so I checked my Timex. Seven twenty-six a.m. I took one final look at Ernst, then backed out of the kitchen. Retracing my footsteps as closely as possible, I exited the house the same way I had entered, leaving the door open behind me. When I reached the curb, I fished my cell out of my carry-all and called 911. Then I called Warren Quinn, director of *Escape Across the Desert*, and told him that Das Kapitan would never be ready for his closeup.

Up and down the street of the quiet Scottsdale neighborhood, men and women were backing BMWs and Mercedes out of their driveways, some of them clutching travel mugs in one hand and cell phones in the other, leaving them to steer with their knees. I winced as one of these suburban Kamikazes came perilously close to my restored 1945 Jeep. When the driver passed by with at least a half-inch to spare, I gave her the finger, but she didn't even notice—she was too busy applying eye-liner. Nearby, someone was cooking bacon and its fatty scent drifted away on the crisp breeze humming through the Papago Buttes. From one house I could hear a blender, and from another, the yapping of a small dog. Birds sang, children laughed.

Until the news helicopters thundered in.

The film crew of Living History Productions was working out of Papago Park, the site of an old World War II German POW camp. The thousand-acre desert park dividing the city of Phoenix from Scottsdale was only a quarter-mile west, so along with the news copters, Warren and his assistant director Lindsey Reynolds beat Scottsdale PD to the murder scene by a good three minutes. Lindsey looked her usual cool self, but Warren was in such a state it took all my strength to keep him from running into Ernst's house.

"He can't be dead, Lena! I need him for my last scene!"

If Ernst had been murdered at the beginning of the shoot, I would have been shocked at Warren's seeming heartlessness, but after being around movie people for several weeks, I was getting used to the Hollywood credo: film first, feel later.

"Believe me, Warren, he's dead."

"But…" The director stopped and took a deep breath. During the pause, his usual compassion overrode his business concerns. "Poor old guy. What happened? Heart failure?"

"Kind of." Not really a lie, because when you come right down to it, all deaths are ultimately the result of heart failure. Drown, your heart stops. Take a bullet to the brain, your heart stops. Get the holy living hell beat out of you while you sit duct-taped to your wheelchair, your heart stops.

Warren stared at the house, no longer anxious to enter, maybe because he'd noticed the blood on my shirt. He ran trembling fingers through his beach-blond hair. In his early forties, he still had a clean, farm-boy face, only slightly hardened by his sharp eyes. "Does he have relatives? Kids?"

"Not that I know of."

When he swallowed hard, I began to regret not closing the front door behind me, because the scent of death was beginning to mingle with the odor of frying bacon. It was an unfortunate combination, but I'd smelled worse.

Warren pulled himself together. "Lindsey, we have to let everyone on the set know we're closing down for the day. Out of respect."

Lindsey shook her perfectly coiffed head and when she spoke, her voice was calm. "No need. We'll just shoot around him."

One by one front doors opened along the street, and by the time several Scottsdale PD cars came screaming up, the sidewalk in front of Ernst's house was filling up with not only Ernst's neighbors, but the gaggle of film buffs the shoot always attracted. The area bustled with a frenzy it probably hadn't experienced since that Christmas Eve night in 1944 when twenty-eight German POWs, Kapitan zur See Erik Ernst among them, dug under the Camp Papago fence and fled into the desert. Some crowd control was in order, so I was happy to see Captain Kryzinski, my old boss from my days at Scottsdale PD, exiting an unmarked cruiser. Whenever a crime involved—however peripherally—someone of Warren Quinn's stature, the brass wanted to cover their collective butts.

While detectives and crime-scene techs trooped past him and a couple of uniformed officers began to cordon off Ernst's property, Kryzinski gave me a grim look. "Great, another high-profile murder. The Chamber of Commerce will be thrilled. So what are you doing, Lena, messing around with these film types? You got some piddly little security gig going with them or something?"

"Hardly piddly." I explained that after some expensive camera equipment had disappeared a month earlier, Living History Productions hired Desert Investigations to run background checks on a few gaffers. After I fingered the culprit, Warren kept me on to act as a go-between his company, the Arizona Film Commission, and over-friendly locals. The money was more than double my usual fee, and the job's relatively tame duties made a nice respite from the dark cases I normally worked. Until today.

Kryzinski flicked his eyes toward Warren, who despite his distress was as handsome as half the actors in Hollywood. "You finally give up on Dusty?"

How quickly gossip travels in the desert. After several years of pseudo-intimacy, my boyfriend Dusty began disappearing for weeks at a time. Despite several bouts in rehab, where each time he swore to turn over a new leaf, he had disappeared again. This time I wasn't waiting for him to come back. Not that my love life, or lack thereof, was any of Kryzinski's business. Besides, Warren and I enjoyed only a professional relationship.

"Forget about Dusty, Captain. I have."

"Whatever you say." He turned away from Warren and studied Ernst's house, a stucco ranch half-hidden behind several twisted olive trees. "It's weird, don't you think, a former POW living right across the street from his old prison camp?"

"Ernst was a weird guy." But Kryzinski was right. The neighborhood was an odd place for a U-boat captain to end up, but as I'd learned from my work on the documentary, Camp Papago hadn't exactly been Devil's Island. Also, the view from Ernst's picture window must have been spectacular. On a clear day—and most Arizona days were clear—he would have been able to see the red-mauve Papago Buttes rising in the distance, the muted greens of tall saguaros thrusting up through the scrub and the vivid red blooms of prickly pear cactus attracting rainbow hummingbirds. But with careful scrutiny, he would also see the leveled ground where the prison camp's barracks once stood, and in some places, the deep impressions in the earth from the weight of stockade towers.

Kryzinski followed my gaze, but didn't find the view all that interesting. "How come you were the one to discover the body? You acting as his chauffeur or something?"

I shook my head. "I decided to watch some filming before I went to my office, so I was hanging around the set. Lindsey usually took care of picking up Ernst whenever he was needed, but she had something else to do this morning so yesterday she asked his care-giver to bring him over. When Ernst didn't arrive by eight and nobody answered his phone, Warren asked me to drive over and see what the holdup was." I glanced around to make certain no children or tender-eared grannies were within hearing distance. Closest were Warren, Lindsey, and the pesky, whippet-sized salesman from the autoplex down the street who had driven them over in the '57 Studebaker Golden Hawk he was trying to sell Warren. I kept my voice low anyway. "When I knocked, the door swung open. I called Ernst's name, but I knew before I went in. Death has an odor."

Kryzinski narrowed his eyes. "Yet you continued on inside the house. I'm disappointed in you, Lena. An experienced detective like yourself should know better."

Up above, a red-tailed hawk wheeled through the cloudless sky, its lonely *keee-rrr* announcing that it hadn't eaten in a while. A tough life, for all its seeming freedom, but a life I envied at moments like this, when I wanted to be elsewhere, doing anything other that what I was doing, even dealing with ground kill rather than people.

"Lena?"

The hawk drifted behind the Papago Buttes so I had to look at Kryzinski again. "I knew something was wrong so I continued into the house to render aid."

He wouldn't let it go. "Since you could smell what you smelled, what made you think you could 'render aid'? Were you planning to give him last rites?"

Lucky hawk, who never had to explain his actions. "Okay, so I was pretty sure Ernst was dead, but I...Oh, who the hell knows why I went in. I'm human, and I just wanted to help." What was with my old boss? Maybe it was his age. Since I'd seen him last, his formerly glossy black hair had turned as flat and gray as cement.

"Sorry. It's just that so much has been going on down at the department lately, what with the new Police Chief and all. I need to make sure my detectives are dotting their i's and crossing their t's."

There was no point in reminding him that I hadn't been one of his detectives for three years. Old habits die hard. So did my affection for him, and it softened my answer. "Actually, Captain, I was worried about Ernst before I reached the house. He'd been acting weirder than usual the last few days, always dropping hints about some big secret he was going to reveal in the film's final interview. He said the secret was 'like gold.'"

"Interview? I thought this was a movie?"

I passed on Warren's explanation of how his documentaries worked. "Besides the re-enactments of various aspects of the escape, Warren planned to do a series of interviews with some of the original people involved with the camp. He's lined up a couple of historians, some of the camp's surviving guards, and Fay Harris. You know, the reporter for the *Scottsdale Journal*. I think you two used to go out." He neither confirmed or denied. "Okay, so maybe I was wrong. She's the one who wrote the book, *Escape Across the Desert*, which Warren optioned for the documentary. The pivotal interviews were to be with Ernst, since he was the only escapee Warren could get. There are a few more POWs still alive back in Germany, but from what I hear, their health is too fragile for them to make the trip. And one over on the west side of Glendale, but he didn't want to be involved in the project. So as far as the German side of the story goes, Ernst was Warren's 'star,' as he liked to call himself."

Kryzinki frowned as a young police officer staggered out Ernst's door and vomited under an olive tree. "That's all very interesting, but what kind of 'big secret' was Ernst hinting about? Do you think he meant gold, the metal? Or was that just a manner of speech?"

"Nobody knows. Warren doubted that Ernst had anything new to add to the information already known about the escape, but he humored him anyway. Anything to keep him happy."

Kryzinski glanced over at Warren again. More or less recovered from his shock, he was leaning against the fender of the Golden Hawk with Lindsey. The adoring glances from the looky-loos reminded me that he was probably the closest thing to a Hollywood celebrity this South Scottsdale neighborhood was likely to see, although they were treated from time to time to glimpses of the Oakland Athletics baseball team, which had a practice field in the park.

"This Warren guy, he any good?"

"Supposed to be. He won the Best Documentary Oscar a couple of years ago for *Native Peoples, Foreign Chains.*"

"I didn't see that." Kryzinski's movie tastes ran to Clint Eastwood and James Cameron.

"It was about the Colonial practice of enslaving Native Americans and shipping them to work on sugar cane plantations in the Caribbean."

"I didn't know we did that, sold Native Americas out of the country as slaves."

"Most people don't." I changed the subject. "*Escape Across the Desert* was due to wrap next week, but now that Ernst is dead, I don't know what will happen."

"Wrap?"

"Finish filming."

One side of Kryzinski's lip lifted in a sneer. "Look who's gone Hollywood. Gonna buy yourself a Shitzer, now, or whatever those little dogs are called, and tool around in two-hundred-dollar sunglasses?"

"Come off it, Captain." Just like old times, with Kryzinski sniping at me, me sniping back. Fortunately, Detective Kyle

McKindroe, a friend from my own days in the department, emerged from the house and walked up to us.

Although middle-age, with years of experience under his belt, McKindroe looked green around the gills himself. "It's pretty bad in there, Captain. I'd say whoever did it wanted to get up front and personal."

My thoughts exactly. The level of violence directed against Ernst hinted at a personal relationship between killer and victim. But while still in Ernst's kitchen, I had noticed several drawers pulled out, and it was possible that Ernst merely interrupted an intruder, someone high on drugs. Addicts' crimes tended to be messy. Visualizing the kitchen again, I remembered something. By rights, Rada Tesema, the Ethiopian care-giver who visited Ernst several days a week, should have discovered the body when he came over to cook breakfast before bringing Ernst to the set, as he'd promised. But Tesema was a no-show. Where was he?

While I stood there in thought, McKindroe went back in the house, leaving Kryzinski staring at me. "What?"

I liked Tesema, whom I'd met on several occasions, and doubted if he had any violence in him. "What do you mean, 'what'?"

"I know that look of yours, Lena. What are you thinking about? That care-giver who never brought Ernst over to the set? Where the hell is he, anyway?"

I glanced toward the curb. Unless I was mistaken, the autoplex guy had resumed his badly timed sales pitch. As he slid hands along the Golden Hawk's sleek hood, I heard snatches of spiel. "...highly collectible classic gold-and-white two-tone...T85 three-speed with overdrive manual...two-hundred-seventy-five horsepower..." Beyond him and hurrying toward us was Fay Harris, reporter's notebook in hand.

"Here comes Fay, Captain, closing fast."

Kryzinski wouldn't allow me my evasions. "Where's the care-giver?"

"Sorry. I don't know."

He frowned. "Okay, let's try it this way. Did Ernst have any enemies that you know of?"

Probably more than I could count. It would be hard to have a history of torpedoing American warships without incurring a few grudges. From what I had heard, Ernst had been unusually ruthless, even for a U-boat commander. The ugly rumor going around the set was that Ernst had a habit of shooting survivors out of the water, which was a war crime under the Geneva Conventions. But I wasn't ready to tell Kryzinski yet.

"Enemies? Why would an old man—an amputee, no less—have enemies? Look, Captain, if you want to know more about Ernst, talk to the people who worked with him." I gestured toward Lindsey, who was staring at the car salesman as if he'd lost his mind. "Ask Lindsey. She interacted with Ernst more than anyone."

As much as Kryzinski wanted to stay and question me further, his own professionalism dictated he do otherwise. After telling me to leave the homicide investigation to the Scottsdale PD, he asked me to come into the station later that afternoon and make a full statement. When I promised I would, he walked over to question Lindsey, the *Journal* reporter hot on his heels.

While we'd been talking, the uniformed officers had finished sealing off the perimeter, but that didn't stop one neighborhood looky-loo from ducking under the bright yellow crime tape and swiping a handful of gravel from Ernst's desert landscaping. Apparently he felt that Death was a celebrity, too. The man's efforts went for naught when a nearby cop made him toss his treasure, then ordered him away. Grumbling, the man faded into the crowd.

"You a movie star, honey? You look awful familiar." I turned to see an elderly woman, her back bent almost into an "L" as she leaned on her cane. She might have been pretty once, but now her skin sagged from her cheeks and chin, and her varicosed legs appeared too thin to support her body.

I shook my head. "No, ma'am, just a private detective."

She cocked her head and stared at me through thick bifocals. "I remember now. You're Lena Jones. You were on TV a couple of months ago when you saved some woman from burning alive."

That case, which involved the death of a Scottsdale publisher, still bothered me, so I changed the subject. "Did you see anything suspicious last night?" Experience had taught me that the elderly, for all their physical problems, could be excellent observers.

"You could say that."

At that point I should probably have directed her to Kryzinski or one of the detectives, but my curiosity trumped my willingness to follow orders. "Why don't you tell me about it, Mrs…"

She limped closer. "I'm Carol Hillman, dear. I live right next door to the Kraut and I always sleep with my window open. Before you start to lecture me, let me reassure you there's bars on the window, so it's safe enough. Anyway, around two this morning, a woman started banging on his door and the racket woke me up. She was a redhead, almost as pretty as you, but she dressed, well, cheap. Tight miniskirt, tiny bodice top. Implants."

Kraut? Deciding she might have lost a family member overseas during WWII, I didn't comment on her use of a pejorative term you almost didn't hear any more. However, I also doubted that this myopic woman could see whether someone had implants at a distance of twenty-five feet, especially in the wee hours of the morning. "You are very observant, Mrs. Hillman."

She frowned. "Don't condescend to me, young lady. The porch light was on and those implants were real bazookas. A blind man couldn't miss them, not that he'd want to."

Properly chastised, I apologized. "You should tell one of the detectives about this. I'm not part of the investigation."

"I'm telling *you*. After the Kraut—we weren't on first-name terms, and I'll be damned before I ever call him *Das Kapitan* like he wanted everyone to—after the Kraut let the woman in, things were pretty quiet for a while, so I started drifting back to sleep. But all at once I heard yelling, most of it from her, something about him being responsible for everything."

"You heard all this?"

The frown again. "Didn't I just tell you I sleep with the windows open? So did the Kraut. Difference is, he didn't have any bars. It's a wonder the idiot wasn't murdered long before now."

An interesting thing for her to say. The memory of Ernst's body, duct-taped to his wheelchair, flashed through my mind. Yes, a woman could have killed him. Maybe even an elderly woman if she'd been able to get enough leverage. And hated him enough. "Did you hear exactly what this 'everything' was?"

Mrs. Hillman shook her head. "Not all of it. Just some stuff about her reputation, although why she should care, dressed the way she was, is beyond me. And I didn't hear what he said about it, either, because he kept his own voice down. Until the end, that is, when he lost his temper and started yelling back at her in Kraut."

German, I guessed she meant. It wasn't beyond the realm of possibility that a ninety-one-year-old man had a thing for hookers, and it wouldn't be the first time a hooker had killed a john, but those incidents were almost always spur-of-the-moment killings. The duct tape around Ernst hinted of premeditation. "Had you seen the woman before?"

"Never. The Kraut lived next door to me for more than twenty years, and other than you, that sweet black care-giver of his, and Little Ms. Skinny over there..." Here she pointed to Lindsey. "...the redhead was his only visitor. Bastard had no friends."

I studied her for a moment, watched her eyes narrow every time she said "Kraut," and went ahead and asked the question. "Mrs. Hillman, did you lose anyone in the war?"

"My husband. Two uncles. My son-in-law lost his entire family. Jewish, you know." A combination of rage and grief swept across her face.

Sensitive to Mrs. Hillman's old sorrows, I softened my voice. "You really need to talk to the detectives in charge of the case. They'll want to find that woman and question her."

She gave me a hard look. "Don't want to get involved, huh? I guess I was wrong about you. You're just like the rest of your generation, you don't care about anyone except yourself." With a sniff, she walked away, leaving me staring at *Das Kapitan*'s house.

Thus put in my place, I started toward my Jeep, then stopped as a thought struck me.

Where *was* Rada Tesema?

I didn't know Ernst's care-giver well, having met him only a couple of times, but judging from our few encounters he seemed like a nice enough man. Even the hardly PC Mrs. Hillman liked him. A licensed practical nurse, he worked for one of Scottsdale's many home care agencies, which were enjoying high times as the city's population aged. From what I knew, he arrived at Ernst's house at six o'clock, three days a week, to cook breakfast and do what needed to be done. And he really seemed to care about his charge. Once, when I had volunteered to take Ernst home from a location shot—Warren had kept him late to film him silhouetted against the sunset—I'd found Tesema standing on Ernst's doorstep, fumbling through a jangly mess of house keys. His car, a battered blue Nissan, hissed in the driveway.

Relief covered Tesema's face when he saw Ernst in my Jeep. "*Kapitan Ernst*, please call when you be late! I worry you hurt in there!"

Ernst hadn't bothered to answer. After Tesema helped him out of the Jeep and into his wheelchair, he rolled past the Ethiopian with a barely audible grunt.

So where was Tesema now? Chauffeuring Ernst around wasn't in his job description, Lindsey usually took care of that, but since he had promised to do so this morning his absence was odd. Could he have been murdered, too, and his body hidden somewhere? Or had Tesema himself…? No, I refused to consider that possibility. Something must have happened to keep him from his regular rounds. But whatever the reason, I needed to alert Kryzinski.

Even a man like Das Kapitan deserved justice.

Chapter Three

After tipping off Kryzinski about Tesema, I had no time to feel guilty. I left Warren to inform the rest of the film crew of Ernst's death and Lindsey to figure out a way to "shoot around" the problem, then headed to my office at Desert Investigations. When I arrived, my partner, Jimmy Sisiwan, was pulling into the parking lot.

"Morning, Lena." Balancing several case files in one hand and a large Starbucks in the other, he struggled out of his pickup. He refused to meet my eyes and I knew it had little to do with his ever-polite Pima Indian heritage.

"Jimmy, we have to talk about that bombshell you dropped on me yesterday."

He hurried to the office door, shaking his head all the way, rippling his long black hair across his shoulders. "We've already talked it over, and I'm sorry, but my mind's made up."

No good deed goes unpunished. The client whose thirteen-year-old daughter I rescued from a forced marriage in a polygamy compound was now returning the favor by making off with my business partner. Esther didn't want to live on the Salt River Pima-Maricopa Reservation with Jimmy and his large, extended family. She wanted a traditionally employed husband and a house in the 'burbs. While part of me sympathized with her struggle toward an Apple Pie existence after living in a cult for so many years, the other part resented her implied criticism of my partner's life. Granted, I was hardly neutral on the subject, because Esther had also talked him into accepting a job with Southwest MicroSystems, Inc., the state's largest technology firm—and Desert Investigations' biggest client.

"We didn't talk it over, Jimmy. You delivered the news and I sat there and took it."

He shot me a look as he settled in front of his computer. "That's not how I remember the conversation."

"You're right. I'm sorry I said those things about Esther. They were uncalled for."

Here's the thing about Jimmy and me. He is the gentle yin to my fierce yang, and yet because we are both orphans, we have more in common than not. Shortly after Jimmy was born, his parents died of diabetes, a disease so common on the reservation that it's called the Pima Plague. It was still permissible then for non-Native Americans to raise Indian children, so he was adopted by a Mormon couple in Utah. As for myself, I was orphaned at the age of four when I was found lying in a Phoenix street with a bullet in my head. Since the bullet destroyed my memory and no one arrived to claim me, I was turned over to Child Protective Services, where I was shuttled from one foster home to another.

Guess who got the better end of the deal? Jimmy spent his childhood having birthday parties and going to church. I considered it a good year when I wasn't raped.

Now my best friend and business partner was mad at me because of the harsh things I'd said about his fiancée. "Lena, it's not that Esther's become so—and I'll quote you here—'disgustingly middle class.' It's just that she…she…" He drifted off, his eyes fixed on his computer screen. After keying in a few strokes, he turned back to me. "She wants to put the past behind her and live a normal life. Get married, raise a family, and all the rest of it. I fail to see what's so contemptible about that."

I duly apologized, but couldn't give up without adding a question. "And you, Jimmy? What do you want?"

His smile faded. "I know what I'm doing. Now excuse me, but I need to get to work." With that, he logged onto one of those quasi-legal data bases he used to run background checks on some of Southwest MicroSystems' prospective employees. Another sore spot. The company had been so impressed with his last checks that they'd made him an offer he couldn't refuse, and when he left, he'd take a large chunk of Desert Investigations' revenues with him. If he didn't kick some back my way, Desert Investigations would be in serious financial trouble.

In order to hang on after Jimmy left, I needed to change my way of doing business. Not only would I have to stop taking so many pro bono cases, but I would also have to hire another online research expert, since my own computer skills were south of zero. Somehow I had to talk Jimmy into staying. And Ernst's murder might make the perfect vehicle.

While formulating my plan of attack, I went over to the small refrigerator and took out a Tab. Soon after gulping a slug of pure caffeine, I felt the rush. I would save my agency. True, my Main Street office, in the center of Scottsdale's Art District, wasn't as fancy as its neighbors, just two rooms—one furnished with a couple of bleached pine desks, four matching chairs with some generic Indian-print upholstery, and several filing cabinets lining Navajo White walls. The smaller room in back allowed for private consultations, but in the way of conference rooms everywhere, it was seldom used and served as a repository for old case files. But best of all, my apartment was right upstairs.

I peered at Jimmy over the top of my Tab. "Did you know that Erik Ernst was murdered last night?"

He spun around in his chair. "The U-boat guy?"

"Someone duct-taped him to his wheelchair and beat him to death. How about running Ernst's name through the system to see what you come up with?"

"I'm really busy. Besides, the police should handle this. We have no client in the case."

"Consider it a parting gift to me."

His wince distorted the edges of the curved tribal tattoo on his temple. I'd touched the guilt nerve. "Oh, all right. Are you looking for anything in particular?"

Gratified, I chugged the rest of my Tab and threw the empty can in the trash. "The documentary covers the war years, so focus on Ernst's life afterwards. All I know is that after he processed out, he went back to Germany. Then a few years later, he immigrated to the U.S. and settled in Connecticut. I seem to remember him telling Warren that he worked as a nautical engineer for a design firm there. After he lost both legs in a boating accident, he moved to Arizona."

Jimmy looked doubtful. "You think the boating accident could be tied to his murder?"

"Stranger things have happened." At least I'd tricked him into working with me again, for however brief a time.

"Sounds far-fetched, but I'll try."

Dusty had said the same thing to me the last time he checked into rehab.

Love wounds us all. It's what we do with those wounds that determines the direction of our lives. Do we travel in circles, or do we struggle on ahead? After wasting five years on an alcoholic boyfriend, I had finally let go, and now the future yawned ahead of me, unformed and unlived. Some people would have found such a vast terrain of possibilities exciting. I worried that I might repeat my old mistakes.

Maybe it was time for me to find that new direction. During a working dinner the night before, Warren had put his hand upon mine, indicating interest in something beyond business. But the gesture spooked me so I leaned away and casually withdrew my hand, talking security all the while. The threat to my emotional equilibrium wasn't over. When he walked me out to the parking lot, he leaned forward to give me a peck on the cheek. I jerked my head back just in time. This morning, on the drive over to Ernst's, I'd been wondering if I'd acted foolishly.

Now it all seemed so petty.

Shortly before noon the phone rang, but it wasn't a client. Since I was standing near the microwave eating my lunch of ramen noodles, Jimmy answered. After clicking on HOLD, he said, "It's Warren."

I carried the ramen to my desk and picked up the extension. "Terrible morning, right? Have you figured out what to do about the final scene now that Ernst is, uh, not available?"

Warren no longer sounded frantic, just sad. "Lindsey says a Frank Oberle interview can substitute for Ernst's." Oberle was a former prison guard at Camp Papago, the only one left who was spry enough to walk over the park's rough terrain while yakking into a mike. "He can talk about the camaraderie that grew up between the Germans and the Americans, about how many of them became such close friends that they wrote to each other after the war. She think it'll be effective."

It sounded saccharine to me, but I didn't say so.

"Listen, Lena, I didn't call to talk about the project. I've been thinking about dinner yesterday. You seemed uneasy when, well…I'm sorry about that. No offense intended."

The apology should have made me happy. It didn't.

He wasn't finished. "Still, I believe in being up front about these things, so I'll come right out and say it. I'm attracted to you, but if you don't feel the same tell me now and I'll keep my distance. It's all up to you."

Here it was. The invitation to an unformed future. I took a deep breath and told the truth. "I'm coming out of a bad relationship so I'm a little gun-shy."

"Aren't we all? But we could take it slow, have dinner again. What do you say?"

I closed my eyes and took a chance. "Okay. When?" My face felt as if it was on fire.

"Tomorrow night at seven. I'll pick you up at your place." The director, directing.

Thrown off balance, I almost changed my mind, but then remembered my safety net. After filming finished in a couple of weeks, Warren would return to California. Anyone, even me, could survive a two-week relationship. "Seven it is."

"I'm very pleased." I expected him to hang up, but he didn't. "Say, from the buzz going around after you took off this morning, the cops suspect Ernst was killed by someone who knew him. You're the detective. Does that sound right to you?"

This was more comfortable ground, but not being certain how much information he needed to have, I hedged. "Anything's possible. Ernst wasn't the world's greatest guy, remember."

"He sure had a mouth on him. I was offended by the way he talked to what's-his-name, the Ethiopian guy who takes care of him."

"You mean Rada Tesema."

"Yeah. One day last week when Lindsey was out on location, Tesema came to pick Ernst up, and I've got to tell you, having grown up in the film business I've seen some abusive types, but I never heard anything like Ernst before. He had Tesema almost in tears."

I frowned. "Do you remember why?"

"Afraid not. We were having trouble with the boom and most of my attention was on that."

Maybe I was wrong about Tesema. Maybe he'd taken all the abuse from Ernst he was about to. Maybe he used his keys, crept into the house during the night, and beat his misery-maker to death. But there was another possible scenario. He could have arrived for work at his regular time, found Ernst's body, and fled. What was Tesema's immigration status? Probably green card. Permanent legal residents usually went to great lengths to avoid being caught up in police-type trouble, especially big police-type trouble like murder.

Oblivious to my musings about Tesema, Warren continued, "Part of me wishes I felt more upset about the old guy, but I don't, other than the fact that his death sure screwed up our shooting schedule. For that matter, what about that promise he made to give us some big revelation about the escape for our final scene? If he knew something, why didn't he tell us last week, when the cameras were rolling? Why hold out until we were about to wrap?"

I didn't attempt to answer his flurry of questions. "Scottsdale PD will sort it all out." I had a theory about the "revelation," though. Ernst had impressed me as a man with a highly developed sense of self-importance, not above resorting to trickery and outright lies to increase his screen time in *Escape Across the Desert*. One of the sound men on the set told me that Ernst had even demanded screen silence from the German-speaking actor who portrayed him as a young U-boat captain, insisting that the only "Kapitan zur See Erik Ernst" voice heard in the film be his own. The actor had been furious, Ernst adamant, leaving Warren to negotiate his way through a minefield of egos.

Warren appeared satisfied with my non-answer. "Let's hope Scottsdale PD is better than LAPD, then. By the way, I couldn't help but notice the dust-up this morning between you and Captain Kryzinski. Is that the bad relationship you were talking about?"

I laughed. "Me and Kryzinski? Hardly. He's my ex-boss from my days on the force. Since I opened up shop as a PI he's helped me with some of my cases and I've helped him with some of his. There's no doubt in my mind that he'll find Ernst's killer."

Which shows how badly I'd misread Kryzinski.

While watching the local news as I dressed for work the next morning, I saw two Scottsdale PD detectives shoving a handcuffed Rada Tesema into their car. Although the grim-faced detectives refused comment and Tesema was too frightened to speak, the blond-on-blond newscaster filled in the blanks.

"Yet another Hollywood tragedy unfolded yesterday, only this time in Scottsdale, where the filming of Oscar-winning documentarian Warren Quinn's new project had to be shut down for the morning when it was discovered that one of its principals had been murdered during the night." She took a deep breath, then continued. "Erik Ernst, who during World War II was held prisoner at the German POW camp in Papago Park and took part in the famous 1944 Christmas Eve escape, was found dead in his home yesterday morning. After a brief investigation, Scottsdale detectives arrested Rada Tesema, an Ethiopian national who served as Mr. Ernst's care-giver. More at five."

She pasted a smile on her face. "In other news, little Holly Granger got the shock of her life when her Labrador Retriever, Slick, came home with…" I clicked off the TV.

Brief investigation, indeed. What about the mysterious woman who brawled with Ernst in the middle of the night? Uneasy, I threw my clothes on and ran downstairs to the office, where Jimmy was already running more background checks for Southwest MicroSystems.

"The police made an arrest in the Ernst case."

When he turned around, I noticed how tired he looked. "Let me guess. The Ethiopian." At my nod, he gave me a cynical smile. "The more things change, the more they remain the same."

Recently, Jimmy's own cousin had narrowly escaped being tried for murder, so he could hardly be blamed for viewing the justice system with a jaundiced eye. I felt the same way, and wondered why the police hadn't followed up on Ernst's late-night visitor. Or perhaps they had, and found no connection to the crime. Ernst could have been a dirty old man and his visitor merely catering to his needs. As for the shouting the neighbor heard, sex could be a noisy number for some folks.

For the next couple of hours, Jimmy and I concentrated on our separate tasks, avoiding any mention of his imminent departure. I finalized the paperwork on several cases and began sending out invoices. Despite the glamorous image of television PIs, most of a real private detective's days verged on dull, entailing everything from skip-tracing deadbeats to background checks on errant or prospective spouses. For instance, Beth Osman, a wealthy Scottsdale widow descended from one of Arizona's original copper mining families, had met Jack Sherwood, a shop-ping center developer who was relocating to Scottsdale from Mississippi. They had been dating for little more than a month but he was already talking marriage. Beth professed strong feel-ings for the man, but wanted Desert Investigations to give him a once-over. We had, and found him clean—on paper, at least. No wants, no warrants.

When I called to relate my preliminary findings, she sounded unsatisfied. "Lena, I...I just feel that there's something..." Her voice caught. "He *is* from out of state."

"Unlike yourself, Beth, most people here *are* from out of state. People move here from other places. Of course, most go back to where they came from after their first Arizona summer."

"Ha ha." Her laugh held little amusement. "You said, 'on paper.' What's the next step up?"

Remembering my own fear of commitment, I felt for her. "A more comprehensive investigation. I could run surveillance on him for a few days and check a few out-of-state-sources."

A trembly sigh. Obviously, she hated what she was doing. "Yes. Do what you have to. I'll pay you for another ten, no, make that twenty hours. I want to make certain before I..."

I could have finished her sentence for her. *Before I fall so hard there's no return.* I simply reiterated my fee. "Plus expenses."

Another sigh. "Right."

In total sympathy with her relationship paranoia, I hung up. The first man in my life, a fellow student in the ASU Criminal Justice program, dumped me for another girl ("I need someone less complicated."). A few years later, a fellow police officer in Scottsdale PD demanded I give up my career for him ("I want a wife, not a colleague."). More recently, Dusty had vanished and reappeared in my life depending on his sobriety status, frequently trailed by the women he'd romanced while on his bender. One of them had tried to kill me.

Considering everything, I was tempted to ask Jimmy to run a background check on Warren before tonight's date, then decided against it. Anyone with Warren's high profile would have little to hide.

"Hey, Jimmy, I'll be shadowing Jack Sherwood for the next few days, possibly longer. Would you mind holding down the fort?"

"No problem." He looked so relieved to have me out of the office that I figured his conscience had been bothering him. We had started Desert Investigations together and I'd been foolish enough to believe we'd continue running it together until…well, until. Now "until" was here.

I rummaged through the supply closet for the items I'd need on the Sherwood surveillance. Camera with zoom lens, tape recorder with long-distance mike, two wigs: one brunette, one auburn. From past experience I knew that the wigs, along with the help of makeup, various sunglasses, and extreme wardrobe changes could make me look like three different women. I also needed to rent a couple of cars less noticeable than my customized Jeep. A Neon, perhaps, and some kind of generic Ford? No. Jack Sherwood was a high-flier and the places he frequented would call for something more upscale than Neon-and-Ford territory, such as a Beemer and a Lexus. As I picked up the phone to punch in the number for Hertz, it rang in my hand.

"Desert Investigations. Good morning." Unless the caller was a new client with a fat wallet, I was determined to get him—or her—off the line quickly.

"Is Miss Lena Jones?" An Ethiopian accent, hollowed by the echoes of other men's voices. In the background, one man cursed loudly while another wept.

My stomach clenched. "Yes, Mr. Tesema, this is Lena Jones. But before you get started, I need to tell you that my fee…"

He didn't wait for me to finish. "I call you from jail. You will help me, please. I not murder Kapitan Ernst but they going to kill me for it anyway."

Kill him? Even if Tesema was eventually found guilty, why did he believe he'd wind up on Death Row? Sure, Arizona still had capital punishment, but only for extreme situations, such as the child rapist who had killed both his two-year-old victim *and* her mother, then dumped their bodies in a canal. "Oh, Mr. Tesema, that won't hap…"

"They stick needle in my arm and I die. Then my family starve. You help me, please."

Why wouldn't he listen? "I'm sure your public defender…"

"I have wife, four sons, two daughters back in Ethiopia. I make family's only money. If I die, they starve. If I not work, they starve."

I knew little about current Ethiopian economic conditions and hoped they weren't as extreme as Tesema painted them. But in the end his fear—which impressed me as being more for his family than himself—swayed me. Desert Investigations could at least look into his situation and perhaps steer him toward the appropriate government agencies to help his family while his case snailed its way through the court system. "I'll come down to the jail this afternoon and we'll talk. But I can't make any promises."

"You are blessed woman."

Regardless of the extremity of Tesema's situation, I smiled. Men had frequently used a "B" word to describe me, but "blessed" wasn't it.

Chapter Four

"I not kill Kapitan."

The black-and-white-and-pink jumpsuit should have made Rada Tesema look foolish, as was its apparent intent, but Tesema's innate dignity won out. While only of average height, his delicate features and straight carriage even in shackles lent him a nobility seldom seen in the Fourth Avenue Jail. He didn't look like a murderer, but few murderers did.

"My wife, my children…" He swallowed, then tried again. "You must help them!"

A spate of cursing rang through the corridor outside, mingling with a woman's answering please-baby-don't-be-like-that-I-just-sucked-him-not-fucked-him. Although relatively new, the jail already reeked of damaged dreams and lost hope.

Tesema didn't belong here.

I leaned across the table. "Mr. Tesema, did you or didn't you show up at Ernst's house yesterday morning? If you did, why didn't you call the police immediately? And if you didn't, why not?"

A flicker in his eyes, a quick look away. Here came the lies. "I told police I busy with other Loving Care client that morning. I call Kapitan Ernst, say I come later in day. He say is fine."

"Loving Care?"

"Name of agency I work for. Have many clients, not just Kapitan."

"Did you give the police the other client's name?"

He looked down at the floor. "Name not important."

There had been no other client. Maybe the police were right and Tesema had snapped. But when I recalled the murder scene, the duct tape tying Ernst to his wheelchair, it didn't make sense. Tesema had a practical nurse's well-developed arm muscles formed by lifting people in and out of beds and wheelchairs. He wouldn't need to tape an old man down in order to beat him to death.

A woman might, though.

The cursing and crying outside started up again even worse than before, so I fired off my next question to get Tesema's mind off it. "Did Ernst have any female visitors?"

"Women?" He glanced at the door leading to the corridor. "He too helpless for…" A flush darkened his already ebony skin. Then he recovered himself. "The Kapitan once talk to me about crazy woman, how she bother him. But I never see her."

Could this have been the same woman Ernst's neighbor saw banging on his door the night of the murder? "Did Ernst say why this 'crazy woman' was bothering him?"

He started to spread his hands, but the shackles around his wrists prevented the I-don't-know gesture. "He say she call and call. He very angry."

"Did he give a name?"

"No. He just call her bad word." Deeply uncomfortable, he looked away again, tried not to listen to the shrieks outside.

Mrs. Hillman had described the woman as skimpily clad. "This bad word, was it 'whore'?"

Tesema seemed ready to faint from embarrassment. "You nice lady. Please not to talk like that."

"But was that the word he used?"

"Yes," he whispered, unable to meet my eyes.

The woman finally stopped her caterwauling, but the man continued to curse. From what I could make out, he'd gutted the man they were arguing about. But at last Tesema had given me something concrete to go on. There would be a record of the calls to and from Ernst's house. In the meantime, Tesema was doing himself no favors by sticking to his improbable story.

"If there was no other client, and if you did show up for your regular appointment at Ernst's house yesterday morning, you probably got some of his blood on you. Innocently, of course." As had I. Last night, when I undressed for bed, I discovered blood smears on my Reeboks. I threw them in the garbage with my bloodied shirt.

Someone in the jail had been coaching him, because he admitted to nothing. "Police took shoes and all clothes I wear."

That didn't sound good. It was my guess that he had arrived on schedule, found Ernst, checked to see if he was still alive—bloodying himself in the meantime—then fled. "Mr. Tesema, if there is one spot of blood anywhere on your clothes, they will be able to determine exactly whose it is through DNA typing. Do you understand?"

"They can do this?" His words were little more than a mumble.

Didn't he have a television set? On most cop shows, which I couldn't bear to watch, crime labs processed DNA samples within minutes. "Oh, yes. The police can also pull Ernst's phone records to see who called him in the past few weeks. For instance, when he didn't show up on set, Warren called him twice from his cell before asking me to check on him. There'll be a record of those calls. If you, as you said you did, phoned to tell him you were too busy to show up for work, there'll be a record of that call, too. If you didn't…" Home care agencies preferred their caregivers to call them to report any cancellations, not the client: that way they could send out a replacement. His story stunk. "How long have you been Ernst's care-giver?"

"Seven…no, eight months. Man before me, he quit. Said Kapitan Ernst too mean."

Which begged the question of why Tesema was still hanging around. "During your time with him, how often did you miss your regular appointment?"

When he looked back up at me, his eyes were filled with outrage. "Never! I not do that! He need my help!"

I gave him a grim smile. "Do you see, Mr. Tesema, how easy it is to find out if a person is lying? You told the police that you were 'too busy' to show up yesterday, but you just admitted to me that you never missed an appointment."

He hung his head. "I not kill Kapitan Ernst."

That part I believed, not that my opinion made any difference. Tesema's utter transparency made him a prosecutor's wet dream. He needed a good criminal defense attorney, but with his lack of funds would probably wind up with the usual public defender: young, inexperienced, overwhelmed. "My advice is to stop listening to your cell mates and tell your lawyer the truth. That's the only way he can help you."

"Only rich men have lawyer."

"This is America, Mr. Tesema. The court will appoint one for you."

Tesema shook his head. "Cell mates, they tell me about these free lawyers. They say I be lucky if lawyer remembers my name."

Having observed the often less-than-scintillating performances of some public defenders, I didn't argue his point. Still, I tried to sound optimistic. "Don't give up so fast. For all we know, you might get lucky and draw someone good."

"I not that lucky."

Another sad truth. "Have you called your wife yet? Does she know about your situation?"

The visiting room was close and muggy, but the large drop of moisture on his cheek resembled a tear more than it did perspiration. "I try, but jail not allow call to Addis Ababa. Cousin there have phone, not wife."

I wondered if there was an Ethiopian consulate in Arizona. Probably not, and for the same reason we didn't have a Chad consulate nor a Moravian one: not enough Chads or Moravians in town to make the cost outlay worthwhile. We used to have what passed for a Swedish consulate down at the Volvo dealership, but the car salesman/diplomat moved to Oregon after suffering through his first one-hundred-and-fifteen-degree Scottsdale summer.

"I'll call the Ethiopian consulate in New York, Mr. Tesema, and see what they can do for you. And I'll..." I would what? Make sure his wife and children were fed? "I'll talk to someone about her situation and find out how much she needs..." I trailed off. Why was talking about money so embarrassing?

Not for Tesema. "She need my money. I get paycheck yesterday but not wire home before police arrest me. Paycheck in my room, on dresser. It already signed. Roommates show you where I keep. You cash and send to her, but not to tell her I in jail. That make her worry."

"I can't cash your check!"

"Then my babies starve."

Getting my hands on his check might be more of a problem than Tesema realized, since the police had probably sealed off his room during their search for evidence. It was a good thing I still had contacts at Scottsdale PD. With a growing sense of unease, I took down the address of Tesema's apartment, where he lived with three other Ethiopian nationals, as well as instructions on how to wire money to his wife in Addis Ababa. "Write a note authorizing me to act on your behalf and I'll see what I can do."

"That mean I your client now?"

I fought off the impulse to pull out my hair. With Jimmy leaving, I needed clients with money, not sad stories. But then the woman down the corridor started up again, screaming that I-loved-him-more-than-your-lazy-ass-and-he-was-bigger-than-you-anyway, and for some reason, when I opened my mouth to tell Tesema no, the word that emerged was, "Yes."

His gloom vanished and he gave me a blinding smile. "You an OK woman."

First he'd called me blessed, now I was just OK. At least he was becoming more realistic.

Upon my arrival back at Desert Investigations, I called Reverend Melvin Giblin, my ninth or tenth foster father—I'd had so many during my childhood I'd lost count—and after the usual how-are-you's, told him about Tesema's situation and his family's needs. As soon as the Rev promised to look into the matter, I thanked him and rang off. Then, switching over to the Beth Osmon/Jack Sherwood case, I phoned Hertz and reserved a BMW for tomorrow, a Lexus for the next day. That accomplished, I punched in the number for Scottsdale PD and left a message on Captain Kryzinski's voice mail. Then I stared at my partner's back and tried to figure out what I could say to keep him from leaving me.

To my relief, Kryzinski returned my call immediately and asked me to come to the station. Happy to escape from the tension in my own office, I jumped into my Jeep and headed up Hayden Road for Scottsdale North.

T. S. Eliot might have said April was the cruelest month, but he didn't live here. For us desert rats, April is by far the kindest month, the last breezy, balmy time before the temperature began its inexorable climb into triple digits. In appreciation of this perfect day, I had stripped off the Jeep's bikini top and drove no more than ten miles over the speed limit. The landscaping bracketing Hayden Road was a riot of color, with pink oleander blooming alongside Mojave goldenbush. Sage and honeysuckle scented the air, which was only slightly tainted by the exhaust of the big, fat Hummer ahead of me which bore the bumper sticker, ADMIT IT—YOU'RE JEALOUS.

Fighting down the urge to ram the Hummer, I concentrated on the problem at hand, which was to pump as much information as possible out of Kryzinski. Perhaps he would tell me why his detectives zeroed in on Tesema so soon, ignoring Mrs. Hillman's statement about a big-bazookaed redhead.

By the time I arrived at Scottsdale North, I had inhaled enough carbon monoxide to make me queasy so I did little more than wave to the officer at the front desk, an old friend. He buzzed me through and I rode the elevator up to the third floor, where Captain Kryzinski sat in his glassed-in office, wearing a gray suit as subdued as his face. The new police chief had swept the department clean of all expressions of style or originality, such as the Western-cut suits Kryzinski had once flaunted, and I knew that most of the cops were unhappy with the changes. So I paid little attention to Kryzinski's dour expression.

I didn't bother with the basic pleasantries, but started right in, careful to keep my voice down so that passing brass couldn't hear me. "Okay, so Rada Tesema lied about his whereabouts. Big deal. What makes you think he's a good candidate for the Ernst murder? Why not Ms. Big Tits? You know, the silicone sister who showed up in the middle of the night and screamed the house down?"

Usually Kryzinski kept his voice low, too, but not today. As if unconcerned who heard him, he fairly boomed his answers. "You must be talking about MaryEllen Bollinger, that's B-O-L-L-I-N-G-E-R, lives in Scottsdale at 8175 East El Cordobes, Unit 220-A. For starters, her alibi's a lot tighter than Tesema's. At the time Ernst was getting his brains bashed in, she caught a speeding ticket way the hell up in Anthem, that planned-up-the-ass community off I-17, where she was headed to see her boyfriend. The DPS officer who wrote her up said she didn't have a speck of blood anywhere on her, and considering the way she was dressed, he could see pretty much everything. Oh, and we found a neighbor—not your adorable Mrs. Hillman—who heard Ernst yelling at her when she ran back out to her car and took off like a bat out of hell. So he was still alive when she left."

"Who is this neighbor?"

"Guy on the other side of Ernst's house. A deacon in the Scottsdale Baptist Chuch."

I bared my teeth at him. "And deacons never lie."

"Don't start. But your friend Tesema? He's a whole different story. First, our same witness saw that old blue car of his pull into Ernst's driveway not long after Ms. Bollinger left. And regardless of what Tesema may have told you, he spent a good deal of time in the house, too. Secondly, we matched Tesema's shoes to some bloody footprints in Ernst's bedroom. That and the kitchen both looked like they had been ransacked. And guess whose bloody fingerprints we found on all the drawers?"

He didn't give me time to answer. "Your precious Mr. Tesema's, that's whose. Thirdly, MaryEllen Bollinger, the 'silicon sister' you're so snippy about, wasn't the only person known to have had a screaming fight with Ernst. Our witness told the detectives that Tesema and Ernst went at it a couple of days ago, too, with Ernst yelling 'You *Schwarzer*' this and 'You *Schwarzer*' that."

"*Schwarzer?*" I knew what it meant but wanted to see how he'd say it.

Kryzinski's face twisted in distaste. "The German equivalent of the 'N' word. Nice guy, your Mr. Ernst. Anyway, according to the neighbor, Mr. Tesema didn't take the insult kindly and yelled back something to the effect that if Ernst kept using the 'S' word, he, Tesema, that is, would cut out Ernst's tongue and feed it to the jackals. I guess he hasn't been here long enough to learn that we don't have jackals, just pit bulls and coyotes."

"That's one bright spot for my guy, then. Ernst was beaten to death, not cut."

"Maybe Tesema was so pissed off he didn't bother to choose the right cutlery."

It was my turn to scowl. "You're saying he was in too big a hurry to grab a knife, but took time to gag and hogtie his victim?"

"C'mon, Lena. You know as well as I do that most murderers are irrational, otherwise they'd figure some way out of their problem that doesn't entail prison time."

True, but Tesema had never struck me as irrational, just a stranger in a strange land. Yet his behavior when he discovered Ernst's body was troublesome. Why had he gone through Ernst's drawers? I didn't want to believe he was a thief, but with a whole family to feed back home, he might have been tempted to supplement his Loving Care paycheck by a little pilfering. And if the unforgiving Ernst caught him…"Was anything missing from Ernst's house? Money? Jewelry? Credit cards?"

Kryzinski shook his head. "Not that we know of. His wallet was still in his pants, along with a full complement of plastic and forty-two dollars in cash. As to jewelry, he was wearing a watch and one ring, a clunky-looking thing with an Iron Cross. Before you ask, we didn't find a cache of diamonds and rubies anywhere, but that doesn't mean he didn't have them and that they weren't stolen."

"Just because Tesema's prints were all over the house doesn't mean he was the person who tossed the place."

A chuckle from Kryzinski. "Maybe it was elves."

"Why would Tesema steal from his employer? If caught, he'd lose his job." The minute the question was out of my mouth, I realized how silly it sounded. It wasn't all that unusual for hired help to filch from employers they hated.

But Kryzinski took the question seriously. "Tesema admitted that Ernst had cut back on his hours, so maybe he felt he had nothing to lose."

I raised my eyebrows. Ernst had cut back on his care-giver's hours? It didn't seem sensible to me that an elderly amputee wouldn't take advantage of all the health care he could afford. Ernst wasn't poverty-stricken, because his house, while not quite *Architectural Digest* cover material, was stuffed with the standard Scottsdale luxuries. On my way into the kitchen, I'd seen a Bose stereo system, a big-screen plasma TV, and a salt-water aquarium that took up most of one wall. Even the car Ernst no longer drove, yet which remained parked in his garage for Tesema to chauffeur him around in, was upscale: a Mercedes-Benz S Class retrofitted for hand controls, about ten years old.

Since there was nothing else to learn, Kryzinski and I spent the next few minutes commiserating over what had happened to the Arizona Diamondbacks, but the team's fall from grace didn't seem to bother him as much as it did me. Which was odd, because he was the bigger fan. In fact, nothing much did seem to interest him, not even my news that his favorite Western wear shop had gone out of business. "You feeling all right, Captain?" His ruddy complexion was wan, and he'd lost weight. And all that gray hair…

"I'm fine."

"You don't look fine."

"I've just got a lot on my mind these days. Look, I'm due at a meeting in just a couple of minutes, so if you're done…"

"I can take a hint." Before leaving, I showed him the note Tesema had written granting me permission to retrieve his paycheck. After a phone call to smooth my way, he said, "The detectives have finished going over Tesema's room. I advise picking up his check as soon as possible. After that, you never know. I might not always be here to run interference."

I started to ask what he'd meant by that, but before I could, he hustled me out the door and closed it between us.

Tesema's apartment was in Mesa, a city of approximately a half-million people. To get there from Scottsdale, you have two choices: the always crowded freeway or down Pima Road to McDowell, the recently widened six-lane highway through the narrow end of the Salt River Pima-Maricopa Indian Reservation. The day being so beautiful, I opted for the latter.

Although the reservation did not share Scottsdale's manicured elegance, the wild, wide-open spaces were a respite from the city's ever-increasing skyline. Thanks to the casinos that opened several years back, the Pima Indians, whose fortunes hovered near the poverty line for decades, were enjoying boom times. Houses had replaced the old shacks, and new pickup trucks sat in their driveways. The raven-haired children who played in front of the day care center wore new clothing emblazoned with the logos of rap groups and action film stars, but horses still grazed under the mesquite trees and wild javelina still drank from the irrigation canals. There was little traffic along McDowell other than a few gravel trucks from the local quarries. Once, out of habit, I mistakenly took the dirt turn-off toward Jimmy's trailer, the one he'd bought when he moved back from Utah five years earlier in search of his Native American roots. I realized my error as I pulled into the gravel drive.

I had always liked Jimmy's trailer, an old Airstream. His uncle, who owned a body shop, had decorated its exterior with paintings of Earth Doctor, the father-god who had created the world and everything in it; and his adversary, Elder Brother, from whom he'd fled into a labyrinth beneath the earth. Between them, Spider Woman tried to make peace. Strife was a constant, the trailer told me. In your time here, walk gently upon the earth, respect the animals, and leave your descendants a name that can be spoken with pride.

In the back, rooting around the prayer lodge Jimmy had constructed out of mesquite branches and native grasses, were a javelina sow and her three piglets. I watched them for a while, enjoying the wind as it swept across the mesquite-dappled fields, listening to the piglets' grunts as they dug in the soil for tasty roots. When the little family finally moved away, annoyed by the two laughing Pima teenagers who galloped their horses through the brush toward them, I turned the Jeep around.

How could Jimmy could abandon such riches?

The Ethiopians lived near the Mormon Temple in a one-bedroom apartment so decrepit it should have been condemned. The walls looked like they hadn't been painted since Ernst was a U-boat captain, but layers of paint still managed to cement the windows shut so that the small living room was hot and stuffy. Cheap linoleum designed to look like bricks covered the floor, but was so thin in some areas you could see the black backing. The few pieces of furniture were limited to a wobbly kitchen table and chairs, and a ratty brown sofa the men had probably recycled from a nearby alley. The apartment wasn't completely bleak. Rada and his roommates had livened up the place by thumb-tacking brightly colored African folk art posters on one wall and several hand-carved crosses to the other.

A man introducing himself as Goula Hadaradi, the only Ethiopian not yet at work, greeted me with a polite gravity. After I showed him Rada's note, he led me into a tiny bedroom and gestured toward the bottom level of one of the two bunk beds. "This where Rada sleep." Then he tapped on a plastic storage container pushed against the opposite wall. "This where he keep clothing." He crossed the room to a scuffed chest and opened one of the drawers. "This is drawer for his papers. When police take him, I put paycheck here, keep safe." Before handing the check over, he read Rada's note again. "Yes, he says to give to you. That Rada's signing, I recognize from back of check. So I give. But you send to wife. She *need.*"

The passion in his voice hinted of yet another family left behind, so I assured him I would wire the money to Addis Ababa immediately. "By the way, Mr. Hadaradi, why didn't Rada bring his family with him when he immigrated?"

Hadaradi looked away for a brief moment, but not before I saw sadness slip over his face. "Like rest of us, Rada only have money for one person to come. Before coming, we all move families from north, where is still fighting, and now we save up to bring families over."

"Fighting?"

Anger replaced sadness. "Is big war over border. Many die. My father, my uncle, two brothers, all dead. Like Rada's father and brothers."

I vaguely remembered a CNN report about Ethiopia's border war with Eritrea. Not being personally affected by other than a brief stab of pity for everyone concerned, it had then slipped from my mind. "You guys are political refugees?"

"U.S. not worry about our war. We win lottery for green cards. Now all make big money. Can afford to bring family soon, be happy. Family is life. Without family, life is nothing."

Not being able to remember my own family, I wouldn't know. But "big money"? Judging from the looks of the Ethiopians' apartment, they didn't even make medium money, and what little they did, they never spent on themselves. But that's the immigrant life. Years of toil and sacrifice for their children, who, when they grew up, were ashamed of their parents' accents. I wondered about my own family and what they might have sacrificed for me. But whatever they had done or not done was blurred forever behind the scar tissue on my forehead. My parents only emerged at night, in pieces of memory-nightmares.

I wondered if all the Ethiopians had immigrated together. "Mr. Hadaradi, did you know Rada in Addis Ababa?"

"No. I come here two years ago from little village to south. Rada comes later. I meet him at Ethiopian Church, at what they call Social Evening. Rada not go to church but that OK."

"I didn't know there was an Ethiopian church in Mesa."

Hadaradi shook his head. "Phoenix. I think we are only Ethiopians in Mesa. Some Sudanese here, some Somalians. Many Mormons." He gave me his first smile.

I appreciated his attempt at levity, but needed to find out what, if anything, Tesema had said to his roommates about Ernst. "When Rada…"

He interrupted me by taking keys out of his pocket and walking toward the door. "No time. I only home to watch policemen look around, keep our things safe. Now I due at other job."

"Other job?"

"Need three. All of us, even Rada. He help take care of four people. Almost never sleep. You go now, please. Have to lock apartment."

Unlike Tesema, Hadaradi didn't have a car, so I dropped him off in front of the Burger King where he worked. From there, I went to Tesema's bank, where a bank officer helped me through the laborious process of international wire transfers. Good deed accomplished, I drove back to Desert Investigations, thinking hard all the way. Four clients and little sleep. I wondered how irritable I might feel if I were exhausted, yet had to care for so many people, one of them a foul-mouthed U-boat captain.

Irritable enough to commit murder?

At five, I pronounced Desert Investigations closed for the day. After a few final taps on his keyboard, Jimmy headed out to spend the evening with his fiancée, leaving me to lock up. This accomplished, I clenched my teeth and climbed the stairs to my apartment.

"No problem, no problem," I muttered, as with my snub-nosed .38 drawn and ready, I unlocked my triple-locks, let myself in, triple-locked the door behind me, and began my routine search for an intruder. So much for therapy. But as Dr. Gomez had so astutely pointed out, a few months of court-ordered anger management couldn't erase a childhood filled with abuse. And they did nothing to soften the memory of the foster father who had hidden himself in my bedroom closet, the better to rape me when I arrived home from school.

I'd been nine years old at the time.

My search revealed no rapist in any of the closets. No rapist under the bed. No rapist hiding in the bathroom or the kitchen cupboards. Relieved, I put my .38 down on the clothes hamper, stripped, and showered. Thirty minutes later, after scrubbing my skin raw, I still felt dirty.

Warren arrived promptly at seven, not the least taken aback that I eyed him for a long time through the peephole before beginning the complicated unlocking process.

"You look beautiful," he said, stepping into the apartment. "I've never seen you in a dress before."

Although I'd purchased my all-purpose black dress off the sale rack at Robinson's-May, Warren's Armani suit had a loftier pedigree and his aftershave probably cost more than the dress. "You look beautiful, too."

He glanced around the living room. "Did you just move in?"

"About four years ago, but I'm not much on decorating." An understatement if there ever was one. The room was basic, since the only items I had added after leasing it fully furnished were a Kachina doll, a Navajo rug, a couple of toss pillows, and an oil painting done by an Apache artist. Seeing the apartment through Warren's eyes—and remembering Jimmy's colorful trailer—I realized my home sweet home had the personality of a motel room.

Outside in the rapidly cooling spring air—did I smell magnolia blossoms, already?—Warren helped me into the passenger seat of his leased Land Rover as though I were some frail creature who couldn't manage the climb, and I didn't know whether to be charmed or insulted. I decided on charmed. "Where are we going?" Someplace dark, I hoped, where no one I knew would see us in case dinner ended badly.

He pulled away from the curb and headed off into the night. "How about that three-star restaurant at the Phoenician?"

The chance of my not being recognized at one of the city's premiere resorts was slim. Not only was I on a first-name basis with the maître d' because I'd once helped him find his runaway daughter, but I would probably also know half the diners, too. In these litigious days, private detectives get around. But Warren was trying to make an impression, so I tried not to let my disappointment show. "That's nice."

Stopping at a crosswalk, where a gaggle of Bermuda shorts-wearing tourists were crossing, he gave me a look. "Too public? Then you recommend a place."

He could read moods, a good sign. A man who paid attention to people. Relieved, I directed him to Pasta Brioni, a nice little Italian restaurant tucked discreetly into a shopping center. The place was quiet, dimly lit, and the owner/chef served original dishes rivaling the Phoenician's. Best of all, the clientele didn't blab.

The evening wasn't as uncomfortable as I had feared. Not at first, anyway. It was refreshing to sit in a romantic restaurant with a handsome man again, pleasant to be asked what I suggested on the menu, and a relief not to monitor my date's alcohol intake. Although Warren ordered a glass of white wine, he never touched it. I, as usual, ordered tea. In between bites of his chicken piccata, he told me about Jaheese, the Arab mare he stabled in an equestrian complex near Griffith Park, and I told him about Lady, the bay mare I kept in Cave Creek. We made tentative plans to go riding together sometime, but I doubted either of us would follow through. When his schedule lightened, he'd be gone. And why take a flight to Los Angeles just to go horseback riding in Griffith Park?

Then he told me about his classic car collection, which he'd started when his father gave him a 1937 Buick sedan for his sixteenth birthday. "It was midnight black and looked like something that Al Capone would drive. Man, I felt tough in that thing! It scared the crap out of all the kids at Hollywood High."

Most of the rich kids in Scottsdale got Beemers for their birthdays, so I had to applaud his father's creativity. The Buick was probably safer for a teenager than a snot-nosed import, too. "Your dad must be an unusual guy."

"You could say that." He looked over to the bar, where despite my assertion that Pasta Brioni was a quiet place, one of the bartenders had just launched into a surprisingly good rendition of *One for My Baby*, backed by a customer on the piano. When the bartender finished, he got a big round of applause, then everyone went back to eating.

Warren picked up where he'd left off. "And for my eighteenth birthday, I got a 1959 Edsel Ranger. Turd brown, butt ugly, and in terrible condition, but by then I'd learned enough to restore it myself."

"Um, tell me about your dad." Not having one of my own, I always liked hearing about other peoples' families. "And your mom. What was it like growing up in Hollywood? Were your folks in the business?"

When he smiled, he looked like a California beach boy. The restaurant's warm lighting erased the lines at the corner of his eyes, and softened the creases that ran from the corner of his mouth to his almost too-perfect nose. "Let's talk about you, instead. I notice that you don't drink."

Talk about a segue.

But there was no point in being secretive about my background—most of it had aired on the local news a year earlier when I solved a high-profile murder case—so I gave him the same sanitized version I gave everyone, leaving out the beatings and rapes. "Since I don't know who my parents are, I don't know what kind of addictive genes I might be carrying around. So I don't indulge."

He put his fork down. "Let me get this straight. You can't remember who your parents are, why you were shot, or who shot you?"

I smiled, shook my head, and shoveled more Shrimp Brioni into my mouth. "Nothing before the age of four." A small lie there. I remembered the bus I was riding in just before I was shot, the gun itself, a red-headed man standing in a forest clearing. But those things I only discussed with Dr. Gomez.

Warren looked down at his chicken piccata, then said something unexpected. "If you ask me, memory can be overrated."

In light of some of my memories, I agreed with him. But I was determined to keep the conversation as light as possible. "Hey, everything turned out fine. I received a scholarship to ASU, became a police officer, and when I left the Force, opened Desert Investigations." I left out the part where I'd been shot in a drug raid. "Now I'm working for a famous Hollywood director! Lots of foster kids do worse." Most of them, in fact. A study I once read revealed that only one of five ex-foster kids were mentally healthy and/or regularly employed. Few graduated from high school, went on to college, or led lives that could be considered remotely normal. The rehab clinics and prisons teemed with my less fortunate brethren. I left that part out, too.

When he looked back up at me, his expression was puzzling. There was gentleness around his mouth, but his blue eyes had darkened with an emotion I couldn't readily identify. "Jesus, Lena. You've managed to accomplish so much with so little, while I...never mind. My films should tell you all you need to know about me. The part that matters, anyway."

Then he smiled again and the darkness in his eyes lifted. His tone became flirtatious. "Do you know why I decided I had to know you better?"

I flirted right back, in my own PI kind of way. "Because I made you sign a two-month contract instead of a day-to-day agreement?"

He threw back his head and laughed. "Now *that* was a dart from Cupid! But, no. That's not the reason. The very *second* you pulled onto the set with that '45 Jeep I knew you were the woman for me."

I didn't know whether to be thrilled or to run like hell. But when he leaned over and give me a quick kiss on the cheek, I didn't flinch. Yes, I was making progress. So much so that for the rest of the evening I was able to push all my worries away, including those about Rada Tesema and Beth Osmon.

As a wise man once said, sufficient unto the day is the evil thereof.

Chapter Five

6:10 p.m. December 25, 1944

Hidden in a deep ravine a few miles east of the prison camp, Gunter Hoenig watched the sun slip behind a mesa. Soon the cold night would descend, but they did not dare light a fire to warm themselves. They would shiver, once again, wishing they were back in Camp Papago with their companions, enjoying Christmas dinner. Nothing had gone right for him and his friend Josef since the escape, not their attempt to join up with the more even-tempered Kapitan Daanitz, nor their plan to float down the Gila River to Mexico...

River!

If their situation hadn't been so desperate, they could have enjoyed a big laugh at the joke. What were the American cartographers thinking, labeling that dry gully a river? Rivers had water! Yet when they reached it, they discovered that their so-called river was nothing but sand, sand, and more sand stretching away for miles—just like the Cross Cut Canal that ran alongside the prison camp. All dreams of floating to Mexico had vanished. Oh, how Kapitan Ernst had cursed when he realized their mistake, but as usual, Kapitan Daanitz had handled his disappointment with dignity.

"Mexico is little more than a hundred kilometers away and do not we have feet?" Daanitz had said with his philosophical smile. "We look 'American,' and if we split up into small groups of two or three, we can reach the border unmolested. Food will pose no problem as long as we develop a taste for rattlesnake stew."

"Better than U-boat food!" Josef had joked.

But Kapitan Ernst, who hated Daanitz as much as the other submariners loathed Ernst, put forth another idea. Why should they kill themselves attempting to make the border when they could double back and walk a few kilometers into the Superstition Mountains. There they could find shelter in one of the old mines marked on their map and hole up until the end of the war. Perhaps they would even find gold!

"The Fatherland will be victorious soon," Kapitan assured them. "If we do not run, we will be in place to join our brave comrades when they arrive, and then we can play our part in founding the American Reich. There is yet great glory awaiting us!"

"Great glory?" Daanitz's face contorted with something that, if Gunter had not known better, looked like disgust. "Do not be so certain, Kapitan Ernst. I have heard stories…" He looked up at the sky, from which a fine drizzle had begun to fall, but not the downpour they needed to make the dry riverbed flow. "If those stories I hear are true, I would not wish for any of us to be in America when the war ends."

Kapitan Ernst sneered. "Who will care what happened to a few Jews and gypsies? One German is worth ten thousand of each." With that, he had ordered the two remaining members of his crew to follow him into the mountains. Being good Germans, Gunter and Josef followed orders, even when given by their despised Kapitan.

Now look at them, Gunter mused, as he huddled in the ravine next to Josef, pooling their body warmth. They were cold, hungry, scavenging food like alley rats from grapefruit orchards and trash heaps. So much for the great glory of the Kapitan Ernst's American Reich. At least the rain was letting up. Perhaps this night, unlike the last, would not be so cold.

"The Kapitan has been gone a long time," Josef whispered. "Do you think something happened to him?" He sounded hopeful.

Gunter did not bother to hide his smile. "Past events have proven that we are not so fortunate. I am certain he will return soon, bringing more grapefruit and curses."

His words proved prophetic. As night folded the desert in its chilly embrace, Gunter heard footsteps scrambling across the rocks above. Then Kapitan Ernst's wolfish face peered down at them.

"Come up, come up, lazy schweine! *We will eat well tonight!" Kapitan motioned them from their cover. "I have found a farmhouse just over that rise. A cow, chickens, a vegetable garden. And inside, tins of food and piles of warm blankets. We will take what we need, then continue east into the mountains."*

Fear clenched Gunter's heart. "There will be a farmer, maybe, with a gun. We have nothing, not even a knife." A farm boy from the same Bavarian village as Josef, he knew it improbable that a working farm would remain unprotected. "Perhaps either Josef or I should reconnoiter?"

He didn't like the smile that crept across Kapitan's face. "I guarantee there will be no resistance. Now, schnell, *hurry. A Christmas feast awaits us!"*

With the inky sky darkening their faces and the birds silenced under the burden of night, they crept through the brush toward the house. When they reached the edge of the farmyard where the golden light from a window spilled across the sand, Gunter bit his lip in consternation. Where were the sounds of laughing children, the contented murmurs of husband and wife discussing the fruits of the day, the friendly rumblings of dogs? All he could hear was the pained lowing of a cow, as if its bag was full to bursting. His misgivings increased. It was late, almost eight o'clock. Why had the cow not yet been milked? What sort of farmer would allow his animal to suffer, allow good milk to go to waste?

As they emerged from the brush and sprinted across the farmyard, the answer floated toward them on a soft desert breeze.

The smell of Death.

Chapter Six

Wearing a red wig and the yuppiefied suit I'd purchased from a Scottsdale resale shop, I picked up a dark blue BMW from Hertz the next morning and set about tailing Jack Sherwood. It wasn't hard to see why Beth Osmon had fallen for him. Even from this distance I could see that he was as tall, dark, and handsome as the cliché. His Southern manners put smiles on the faces of everyone he came in contact with: the desk clerk at his residence hotel, the caddy at the golf course, the waitress at the expensive watering hole where he drawled through a business lunch with local bigwigs, one of them a former state senator known as much for his honesty as his inability to win re-election. I observed no suspicious behavior, and yet by the end of the day, I'd become convinced something was wrong.

Sherwood was too slick.

As I dropped off the Beemer at the Hertz lot near Desert Investigations and switched to my Jeep, I made a mental note to ask Jimmy to initiate an in-depth background search on Sherwood. While he had no police record in Mississippi or anywhere else—a dip into the AFIS database proved that—it might prove informative to find out the names of his Southern associates. Or maybe Jimmy would turn up an ex-wife or two. Exes frequently had interesting tales to tell.

A glance at my watch told me it was now past six, but evenings were good for home visits. Kryzinski had given me MaryEllen Bollinger's address, so I pulled off the red wig, threw it into the back, and pointed the Jeep north for a ten-mile battle through the remnants of rush hour to North Scottsdale.

El Cordobes Luxury Condominiums was typical of the area, with storybook architecture and anal compulsive landscaping. Perfectly cared-for pink and purple petunias lined the narrow cement walk that curved around a cream-colored adobe complex designed to look like an Indian pueblo. Discreet ceramic signs decorated with Hopi symbols identified each of the fifteen build-ings, but regardless of the community's good looks and signage, the massive development was a hopeless maze. I wandered in increasing exasperation until I found Unit 220-A hiding on the second floor of the sixth building. The woman who answered the door studied my PI license carefully. An attractive, if rather plastic blonde, she stood in the center of the doorway as if loathe to invite me inside, but behind her I could see a sea of white: white carpeting, white walls, white leather sofas—the whole Marilyn Monroe deal. She identified herself as MaryEllen's roommate and told me I was five minutes too late, that MaryEllen had already left for work.

"She just *left* for work?"

The woman bared perfectly capped teeth. "She hardly keeps banker's hours."

Implants, white apartment, non-banker's hours. I was begin-ning to get it. "Perhaps you could tell me where she, ah, does what she does."

The teeth again. "MaryEllen does the same thing I do. You say you're a detective, go detect."

I offered a smile of my own. "Cute. But why not help me out here?"

More teeth. "Oh, you're no fun. She's at The Skin Factory, on Scottsdale Road."

Too bad I hadn't known this before my trip north. The Skin Factory was less than a mile south of my office. A topless bar, it was the latest addition in a long line of so-called gentlemen's clubs, massage parlors, and outright bordellos that were turning South Scottsdale into a sexual combat zone. The Scottsdale City Council, its tunnel vision focused on the glittering developments of the upscale northern section of the city, appeared content to let the southern end rot, ignoring the pleas of the neighborhood's hard-working blue-collar families who resented the horny drunks driving down their streets looking for action.

I thanked MaryEllen's roommate for her help. As I started down the stairs she called out, "Tell MaryEllen that Clay called right after she left. And to be careful. He might show up." Before I could ask who Clay was, she closed the door.

Rush hour was over, so I made good time and pulled into the parking lot of the Skin Factory a mere fifteen minutes later. With its landscaping of Italian poplars and neo-Tuscan facade, the bar was trying for tasteful, but that's always a losing proposition when the front of your building features a ten-foot-high pink neon sign of a naked woman in a pose similar to those found on the mud flaps of pickup trucks. The name SKIN FACTORY blinking on and off in purple neon did help, either. After parking the Jeep between a rickety Ford pickup and a sun-bleached Nissan, I made my way to the bouncer stationed outside the entrance.

"You looking for work, honey?" Mr. Bouncer was about the same size as my Jeep and probably every bit as tough, so I didn't crack wise while his eyes expertly tracked every line of my body. "Jim generally likes them a little younger, but I say, hey, a few miles on a gal can be awful sexy when she's built like you."

Uncertain whether to feel flattered or insulted, I flashed my PI license. "Thanks for the compliment, but I was hoping to have a few words with MaryEllen Bollinger before she..." Before she does what? Clocks in? Goes onstage? Gets down butt-naked?

Mr. Bouncer narrowed his eyes, not that it took much; they were already at half-mast. "You want to talk to her, you make an appointment."

I thought fast. "It's about, uh, Clay. And the trouble she's been having with him."

He grunted. "That mope. Go on back, then. The dressing room's on the left side of the stage, behind the pillar that says EMPLOYEES ONLY. Tell her not to worry, that Otto's got her back."

Once through the door, I was stopped by yet another bouncer who—my PI license notwithstanding—made me fork over the twenty-dollar guest admission. Eyes stunned by the dimly lit room, I stumbled through a fug of cigarettes and soured beer toward the brightly lit stage, trying to evade the hands that reached for me. The dancer, a brunette sporting a matched set of double-D's, gyrated against a pole, her hips out of sync with the beat of a Nine Inch Nails soundtrack. Well, if I were as top-heavy and stoned as her eyes told me she was, I'd probably flub a few dance steps, too. Another bouncer, this one larger than Otto, stood by the dressing room door, but when I flashed my ID and mentioned Clay, he opened the door for me, muttering, "Don't know why she needs a PI. I'll take care of the asshole for free."

MaryEllen Bollinger sat facing the makeup mirror. When she turned around, I could see why Clay was on a first-name basis with the club's bouncers. A startlingly beautiful redhead, she sported a shiner almost the same size and color as the maroon aureole around her nipples, although the concealer she'd applied did a masterful job of disguising the damage. "You the new girl?" she asked, her voice as high and soft as a child's. "You're not due on for another hour."

With her looks, it was hard to understand why she worked in a cheezy South Scottsdale topless bar, not Hollywood. Maybe she couldn't act. Then again, most starlets not half as beautiful as she couldn't act, yet they still headed up sit-coms and rode around in limos. But MaryEllen's career decisions—or lack thereof—were irrelevant to my mission so I handed over my ID and told her why I'd come. "Other than the killer, you were probably the last person to talk to Mr. Ernst the night of the murder."

So flat was her affect that at first I thought she hadn't heard me. She kept staring at my ID card while her foot tapped to the music leaking through the door. Finally she shrugged, making her perfect nipples bounce up and down. "The cops have already checked my alibi. Besides, Ernst is dead now, so what does it matter?"

An odd remark, considering that Ernst was dead and that *was* the matter. "What was your connection to Ernst?"

"None of your business." With that, she faced the mirror and began applying more concealer to her eye. Her back didn't bear bra strap marks, but with implants like hers, who needed a bra? The rest of her was real enough.

"You're a suspect in a murder case. Wouldn't you like to clear your name?"

The mirror reflected her smile. "The name 'Bollinger' will never be cleared. The damned Nazi saw to that sixty years ago. Now, you'll have to excuse me, Miss Jones. My public awaits." The eye now looked as perfect as the rest of her. She put the concealer away in her makeup kit, then stood up, her almost impossibly long legs lengthened even further by five-inch stiletto pumps. Her matching silver thong was tiny enough to prove that she was a natural redhead.

It never hurt to appeal to someone's good nature, even a topless dancer's. "Please, MaryEllen. An innocent man has been arrested for Ernst's murder, an Ethiopian immigrant named Rada Tesema. He has a wife and children back home who depend on him for financial support."

When she blinked, silver eyeliner sparkled. "Ethiopia?"

"Border wars, famine, the whole bit. Tesema is his family's only ticket out."

She closed her eyes long enough to give me hope, so I pushed it further. "He has four sons, two daughters. All hungry."

Her eyes were a vivid blue, unclouded by drugs. "Does he love his daughters as much as he loves his sons?"

The question caught me off guard.. "I...I didn't ask."

"Lots of men don't, you know. Especially in those Third World countries. Women don't count for much over there."

"Judging from that shiner you're sporting, they don't always count for much here, either."

She surprised me again by leaning forward and gently touching the scar above my own eye. "No, they don't, do they?"

The expression on my face must have been all the answer she needed, because she straightened and said, "I'm dancing a four-hour shift tonight. You want to talk, call me sometime Sunday afternoon. That's my day off. Until then, why don't you do a little research? If you really are a private detective, it should be a piece of cake. Bollinger. Scottsdale. Christmas Day. 1944."

With that, she left me staring at my own scarred face in the dressing room mirror.

If there was such a thing as a wasted day, Saturday was it. I picked up a Lexus at Hertz, tucked my blond hair into a brunette wig, and again followed Jack Sherwood back and forth across the city, from shopping center to spa, from business lunch to business dinner. Everywhere he went, he left a trail of smiles and big tips. Yet I couldn't get over my feeling that something was seriously out of kilter with the man.

By the time I returned the Lexus and made it to the office, Jimmy, who had dropped in for a while, was gone. A search through the papers he left on my desk revealed no new information on Sherwood's dealings in Mississippi. But private cases paid less than corporate ones, and Southwest MicroSystems' background checks paid even more than the usual, so those came first. Still, I put a sticky note on his computer screen, reminding him to run the Sherwood file first thing Monday morning. From the conversation I'd had with Beth Osman on the way back from Hertz, I feared that she—despite her suspicions about Sherwood —was falling more deeply in love with him.

Women were so crazy.

My office voice mail was clogged with messages. My own relationship anxiety spiked when I came across a message from Warren asking me for another dinner date.

Should I, or shouldn't I?

I considered it carefully before making up my mind, then punched in Warren's number. He didn't pick up on his cell, so

I left my own message. Dinner sounds great, I purred into his machine. Seven o'clock, too. I'll be waiting. As soon as the words were out of my mouth, I wanted to recall them.

Embarrassed by my own craziness, I didn't.

It was pointless to open Desert Investigations on Sunday morning, especially since I'd worked all day Saturday, so as soon as the sun was up, I put on some running clothes and took my usual six-miler down to Papago Park and around the Buttes. The film set was deserted, with all the camera, sound and light equipment locked securely in the trailers. The only person present was the security guard I'd hired, and he waved to me as I jogged by. A few blocks on, I passed Erik Ernst's house, where a few pieces of yellow tape still fluttered in the morning breeze. I averted my eyes. Once back at my apartment, I took a long shower, but it didn't wash my restlessness away. Rada Tesema's face still haunted me.

Around ten, I heard a knock at the door, and looked through the peephole to see a delivery man standing there with a huge bouquet of deep red roses. On Sunday? Discarding my usual caution, I opened the door and signed for them. After I'd whisked them inside, I opened the card and read:

> For the most amazing woman I've ever met.
> W.
> P.S. Her Jeep's cool, too.

I filled an empty Trader Joe's coffee can with water and arranged the roses as best I could. Then I carried them over to my faux pine coffee table and stared at them, inhaling their sweet aroma as it drifted through my apartment.

Dusty had never sent me roses.

Once the novelty of the roses wore off, I flipped through my old blues albums, finally settling on Robert "Washboard Sam" Brown's *Rockin' My Blues Away*. This was one of my favorite anthologies since it included contributions by Memphis Slim and Roosevelt Sykes on piano, and Brown's half-brother Big Bill

Broonzy on guitar. Although one of the best singer/composers in the business, Brown's recording career was cut short during World War II, when royalty disputes broke out between the American Federation of Musicians, the record labels, and the radio stations that wanted to play their music. By the time the dispute was settled in November 1944, Brown's career had waned, which made his pre-WWII recordings even more valuable. After making myself as comfortable as possible on my lumpy sofa, I listened to all twenty-two cuts on *Rockin' My Blues Away*. As the last cut ended, I realized that at the same time Washboard Sam and his friends were wailing away in Chicago blues bars instead of recording in studios, German POWs were streaming into Camp Papago.

There it was. Sunday or not, I simply couldn't keep my mind off the Erik Ernst case.

Giving up my attempt to celebrate a day of rest, I headed for the Scottsdale Public Library and its impressive periodical files. The library sat behind a swan-filled lagoon on the big Civic Center complex, nestled between City Hall and Scottsdale South Police Station. The doors opened just as I arrived, and I joined the line of patrons streaming through the big glass doors.

The *Scottsdale Journal* had long stopped allowing non-reporters access to their morgue, but the library had archived the entire eighty-eight years of *Journal* issues onto microfilm. With the aid of a helpful librarian, it didn't take long for me to find what MaryEllen Bollinger had been hinting at. No Bollinger was listed in the December 25, 1944, edition, but the next day's issue told me everything I needed to know.

FAMILY FOUND MURDERED

Scottsdale—Christmas ushered in tragedy for one Scottsdale family. Late Christmas night, Edward Bollinger, 40, his wife Joyce, 32, daughter Jennifer, 12, and sons Robert and Scott, 10 and 8, were found dead by a relative in

their remote farmhouse. Edward Bollinger was shot to death near the barn
with his own shotgun. His wife and
children were found in the kitchen,
beaten about their heads. The house
was ransacked and the family's cream-
colored 1939 Oldsmobile convertible
was missing.

"If anyone has any information as to
the whereabouts of Chester Bollinger,
15, the family's oldest son, please let
the Maricopa County Sheriff's Office
know," said Sheriff Leroy Jeakins.

When asked if it was possible if
Chester Bollinger himself might have
some knowledge about the murders,
Sheriff Jeakins refused further comment.

The killing of the Bollinger family
came amid rumors that numerous German
POWs, who were stockaded at Papago
Park, have somehow managed to escape.
At press time, this could not be
confirmed, although there have been
complaints in the past about Camp
Papago's lax security.

Neither Sheriff Jeakins nor Camp
Papago officials would comment whether
there was any connection between the
Germans' reputed escape and the Bollinger murders. However, Scottsdale
residents are advised to lock their
doors and to report anyone acting
suspiciously, especially if he speaks
with a German accent.

I sat back from the microfilm reader and began to think.

"The name 'Bollinger' will never be cleared," MaryEllen
had said. "The damned Nazi saw to that sixty years ago." Was
this what she meant? She was, at the most, in her late twenties,
not born when the Bollinger family was slaughtered, although
given her last name she was no doubt related to them. Had

the escaped POWs been connected to the murders? And if so, why was no mention of the murders being made in Warren's documentary?

As I continued to read through the Journal's old issues, I discovered the answers.

DECEMBER 27, 1944

GERMAN ESCAPEES NOT MURDERERS, FBI SAYS

Scottsdale—In a meeting held yesterday in downtown Phoenix, FBI Special Agent Ronald Adlow and Maricopa Country Sheriff Leroy Jeakins issued a joint statement saying that the German POWs who escaped on Christmas Eve from the stockade in Papago Park were not involved in the murders of the Bollinger family.

"While we understand the community's fears, be assured that none of the twenty-eight men who tunneled out of Camp Papago on Christmas Eve killed the Bollinger family," said Sheriff Jeakins.

"The evidence we've gathered points away from the Germans. A single pair of bloody footprints leading away from the bodies show that the killer was a small-statured person, perhaps a teenager. We have reliable information that a teenage boy was seen driving a car resembling the Bollingers' Oldsmobile through the outskirts of Scottsdale during the late hours of Christmas night.

"Camp Papago has given the Sheriff's Department complete physical descriptions of the escapees, and all twenty-eight were large men who wore shoe sizes much larger than the

```
footprints we found. I would like to
point out that Chester Bollinger is
small in stature, and he has not yet
come forward to tell us what, if any-
thing, he knows about the murders. If
anyone has knowledge of young Mr. Bol-
linger's whereabouts, they are urged to
contact the police immediately. But do
not attempt to apprehend him. According
to those who know him, he once attacked
his father with a hammer."
    FBI Special Agent Ronald Adlow said
that it was possible the Germans came
across the farmhouse either before or
after the Bollinger family had been
killed, but if so, all the Germans did
was remove food, some clothing, and a
few blankets.
    "We have assurances from Camp Papago
officials that none of the POWs has a
reputation for violence," Adlow said.
```

That last quote made me shake my head in disbelief. The Germans didn't have a reputation for violence? Why in the world did Agent Adlow think that the U-boat crews had been imprisoned at Camp Papago in the first place?

Another thing about the article bothered me. Sheriff Jeakins had come so close to accusing Chester Bollinger of the murders that it bordered on libel. Same for the *Scottsdale Journal* itself. Granted, in the past sixty years there had been curbs put on the information law enforcement agencies could release about juveniles, and even more curbs on the way newspapers could report crime. But the inflammatory language used in the article still bothered me.

My eyes tired from the glare of the microfilm reader, I stood up and walked into the ladies' room to splash some water on them. While I leaned across the sink, a major Scottsdale celebrity came in, clutching a big stack of books on eighteenth-century England. Diana Gabaldon, silk scarf fluttering, hip-length brunette hair swinging as she walked. Her time-travel adventure novels had put her on the *New York Times* best-seller list several times. I'd read them all. We'd exchanged pleasantries: I'd once helped rid her of a stalker. Eyes refreshed, I returned to the microfilm reader.

The next few issues of the *Scottsdale Journal* reported the capture of several Germans, three near the Mexican border, one in Mesa, one in Tempe, and a couple on nearby Indian reservations. But a week after the escape twenty-two of them remained at large, including Kapitan Ernst and two members of his U-boat crew. In one article, the unknown reporter—at the time, newspapers apparently didn't identify an article's writer by name—called the search for the POWs "the greatest manhunt in Arizona's history." Photographs of the remaining escapees were printed over the fold, with the headline, "$25 reward per Nazi!" I stared at the young Ernst, who was almost unrecognizable from the shrunken, wheelchair-bound man he'd become. He glared at the camera from underneath a thick thatch of pale hair, and the cold look in his eyes made me believe that he was perfectly capable of murder. The *Journal* reporter seemed to believe so, too, because he included the following paragraphs at the bottom of his article.

> One of the most notorious of the escapees is Kapitan zur See Erik Ernst, who was one of the POWs originally implicated in the murder of fellow POW Werner Dreschler. Dreschler, who had been suspected of giving the Allies information about U-boat deployment, was found hanged in a shower stall March 12 at Camp Papago mere hours after his arrival in the camp. His body bore the marks of more than 100 cigarette burns and knife wounds, all inflicted before death. In the following inquiry, Ernst was cleared of the charges.
>
> Also troubling are the persistent rumors that a month before Ernst's capture in the Mediterranean, his

```
U-boat torpedoed a civilian ship bound
for Palestine from Europe. However,
this was never proved and all non-German
witnesses to the events are dead.
```

I let out my breath in a slow whistle, causing several nearby library patrons to raise their fingers to their lips in protest. I ignored them. Torpedoing civilian craft was against international law, even in wartime. Furthermore, judging from the ship's destination, there was a good chance it had been filled with Jews fleeing the Holocaust. I'm not much of a believer in coincidence, and I felt deeply uncomfortable about Ernst's connections to so many crimes within such a short period: the civilian boat sinking, the torture-death of a fellow Camp Papago inmate, and the fact that he had been on the loose in the same area where an entire family was slaughtered. But after searching through the microfilm for a few more minutes, another article led my suspicions in a different direction.

JANUARY 6, 1945

MURDER SUSPECT CAPTURED

Scottsdale——The last surviving member of the murdered Bollinger family was discovered last night, hiding in the attic of a friend's house only two miles away from the murder scene.

When taken into custody, 15-year-old Chester Bollinger told sheriff's deputy Harry Caulfield that after a family argument early Christmas morning, he left home to go to a friend's house and therefore knew nothing about the murders which took place later that day. The teenager was charged with his family's murder.

"The community can rest easy now because we believe we've solved this heinous crime," said Maricopa County Sheriff Leroy Jeakins.

I stared at the headline. MURDER SUSPECT CAPTURED. No "alleged" to soften the accusation. How times had changed.

Further *Journal* articles stated that by the end of January 1945, twenty-five of the German POWs had been caught and returned to Camp Papago. Three of them—Ernst and two of his former crewmen, Gunter Hoenig and Josef Braun—remained at large. Fast-forwarding the microfilm to early March, I found the article celebrating Ernst's capture by the two Apache Junction farm workers who had walked in on him while he was stealing food from the shed where they'd been bunking. But nowhere could I find anything on the subsequent capture of Gunter Hoenig and Josef Braun. The two had been swallowed up in the Arizona desert.

Chester Bollinger's trial for the murder of his family was covered extensively by all the Arizona newspapers. He was found not guilty. A neighboring farmer testified that he had seen the Bollinger family alive on Christmas Day, hours *after* Chess turned up at his friend's house. A school friend of his further drove a stake through the prosecution's heart by testifying that for the entire day and night of the murder, the two had been playing card games in the friend's attic. The jury accepted this unlikely alibi, but it hadn't been good enough for the *Scottsdale Journal.* The day after the "Not guilty" verdict was handed down, the newspaper ran the following editorial:

JUNE 12, 1945

Scottsdale—In what appears to many to be an astounding miscarriage of justice, 15-year-old Chester Bollinger, known as Chess, was released from jail today and sent to live with a cousin. Although acquitted of the murder of his family, most Scottsdalians—especially those who know the young man personally—bemoaned the fact that he was once more free to continue his violent career.

"I don't know what this country is

coming to when decent people can be murdered in their beds by young punks like Chess," said elderly Horace Stanton, who owns a grapefruit orchard not far from the Bollinger farm. "I can bet you that his father was too lenient with him, and that's why he's turned out like this. It goes to show you the Bible knows what it's talking about: spare the rod and spoil the child."

Not everyone agrees with Stanton's assessment. One of the teenager's staunchest defenders has been Deputy Harry Caulfield, Chess' arresting officer.

"Chess is no angel but the jury found him innocent and we have to accept their verdict," said Caulfield. "As for the talk that the boy was undisciplined, it simply isn't true. The story I hear is that the kid frequently showed up at school covered with bruises from beatings administered by his father. We should let young Chess get on his with life. If he commits more crimes in the future, we will deal with them then."

Other *Scottsdale Journal* articles showed that Chess Bollinger's troubles did not end with his not guilty verdict. At the age of seventeen, he served four months in jail for beating a grocery clerk. At nineteen, he knifed a man on a downtown Scottsdale street and pulled a deuce at Arizona State Prison. After his release, he married a woman who had been writing to him while he was in prison, and for several years he vanished from the *Scottsdale Journal's* pages. The honeymoon ended in 1963, when the *Journal* reported that Chess was arrested for breaking his wife's arm because she undercooked the Thanksgiving turkey. At that point Chess' former pen pal divorced him. Two weeks after being released from jail on the domestic violence charge, he was arrested again, this time for car theft. He served three more years in prison.

None of this stopped him from re-marrying or beating more women. Once he'd done his time for the car theft, his arrests for domestic violence began again. The worst incident happened in 1988, when he was sent back to Arizona State Prison for battering his second wife and their ten-year-old daughter. The wife escaped with a few bruises and scalp lacerations, but the daughter was hospitalized with two broken ribs.

The daughter. After looking at the dates again, I finally figured out MaryEllen Bollinger's connection to the Bollinger family. And to Erik Ernst.

She was Chess Bollinger's daughter.

The last time Chess made the pages of the *Scottsdale Journal* was in 1993, when he was arrested once more for domestic violence. This article, written by my friend Fay Harris—the paper had started printing its reporters' names—stated that Bollinger's wife refused to press charges. Chess went home, where the family supposedly lived happily ever after.

It did not escape my notice that on the occasion of each of Chess Bollinger's arrests, the *Scottsdale Journal* always made reference to the 1944 murders of his family and his subsequent trial. The newspaper's disclaimer that Chess had been found innocent always sounded less than convincing.

"The name 'Bollinger' will never be cleared. The damned Nazi saw to that sixty years ago."

Did MaryEllen believe Ernst held information that could clear her father's name? I thought about the possibility for a while, eventually coming up with a more intriguing question. Was it possible that MaryEllen suspected that *Ernst* killed the Bollingers?

While returning the boxes of microfilm to the librarian, I began to wonder why MaryEllen believed that Kapitan Ernst 'ssupposed crimes were the only things tarnishing the Bollinger name.

Why didn't she hold her father responsible, too?

Chapter Seven

Continuing to break my vow not to work today (hanging out in the library didn't count) I drove to back Desert Investigations and let myself in. I hit the light switch to kill the gloom empty offices always have, and crossed to my desk. Many of the art galleries along Main Street opened on Sundays, and as tourists wandered by, some of them stopped to peek through my glass office door. I ignored them and punched in MaryEllen Bollinger's number. Although it was early afternoon, MaryEllen sounded like she'd just crawled out of bed, her sweet soprano deepened to a rasp. Working the night shift can do that to you.

"Christmas Day, 1944," I said. "Your grandparents and your aunt and two uncles are killed. Later, your father stands trial for murder, but thanks to a neighboring farmer and a friend who alibis him, he gets off. How am I doing?"

She coughed and cleared her throat. Then I heard something that sounded like the click of a Bic, and seconds later, a deep inhale. The real reason for the rasp. "You did your homework, Ms. Jones. Now we're ready to talk."

"First question. How did you know Erik Ernst was living in Scottsdale?"

Another inhale, another cough. "I didn't. At least not until they started filming that documentary in Papago Park. The *Journal* ran an article about it and actually mentioned him. I started dropping by and hanging out in back with the other film groupies, knowing that he'd have to turn up sooner or later, and he did, about a week ago. I made sure he didn't see me, and later, I followed him home, but I didn't try to talk to him then because I was too shook up. I only confronted him the night he, uh, died."

The night he, uh, was murdered. I didn't believe her. Rada Tesema had told me that Ernst complained about a "crazy lady," and I was certain he'd meant MaryEllen Bollinger. I said as much.

"Oh, all right. I called him a few times. So what?"

So plenty. "Why? What was the point?"

Inhale. Exhale. Cough. She really should stop smoking. "Because I wanted to make him confess. I thought if I told him how much he'd hurt my father, how much he'd damaged my family, that he'd finally tell the truth, go with me to the police and confess."

Somehow I refrained from laughing. MaryEllen was abysmally ignorant about human behavior. Getting a murderer to confess his crimes out of the goodness of his heart seldom worked, which is why we have trials. "Ernst denied killing your grandparents, didn't he?"

"Yeah. When I went to his house that night and asked him to clear our family name, he laughed in my face."

I tried to put myself in her place: late at night, alone in a house with the man she believed had destroyed her family. What would I have done? "MaryEllen, did you search his house to see if he'd hidden some kind of proof?"

"No." More coughing, a real fit this time. Maybe she had searched his house, maybe she hadn't. Probably not. Like most people trying to get information on their own, she could only go so far and no farther, which is why God created private investigators.

A tap at the door made me start. A man in a pink golf shirt and madras shorts. "Hold on, MaryEllen. I'll be right back." I set the phone down and opened the door. "We're closed on Sundays. Come back tomorrow."

"I'm looking for the mystery bookstore," the man said in a Minnesota accent. "It used to be here."

"Not for years." Irritated, I directed him to Poisoned Pen's new location and closed the door. Then I killed the lights and closed the door blind so no one else could see in. Fortunately MaryEllen was still on the phone, puffing away at her cigarette. "Sorry about that," I told her. "Just a tourist. But back to your visit at Ernst's. What did you think would happen even if Ernst confessed everything to you?"

"My poor father would be vindicated."

Ah, yes. Poor Chess, the father who beat his wives and shattered his little girl's ribs. Why should she care how the thug felt? I was so curious, I asked.

"You don't understand. Nobody does."

"Try me."

"Ms. Jones, please believe me when I say that Daddy isn't a bad man. He's had a rough life and he never got any good breaks. After his whole family was murdered, he was forced to go live with some older cousin of his who already had seven children, and resented him being there. Her husband beat him every time he opened his mouth, so he ran away when he was seventeen. Not that it made any difference. Maybe he was found innocent at the trial, but no one ever believed it. His…his problems later weren't his fault. Things just kind of happened."

"Beating a child until she suffers broken bones doesn't 'just kind of happen.'"

"You don't understand."

"You already said that."

Her voice dropped so low I could hardly hear her over the laugher of tourists passing by on the sidewalk outside. She'd said something about "reasons."

"You'll have to speak up, MaryEllen."

"I said, 'Daddy had his reasons.' He said I was a real handful as a kid."

I considered her reply, then put two and two together. As softly as I could, I asked, "MaryEllen, does Clay say you're a real handful, too?"

She hung up on me.

As long as I was in the office, I decided to make a few more calls. I knew that former Maricopa County Sheriff Leroy Jeakins was dead, because I had pulled traffic duty at his funeral during my first year at Scottsdale PD. And even if the FBI agent in charge of the Bollinger case was still alive, well, the Feds were notorious for not cooperating with PIs. Or anybody, for that matter. This left then-sheriff's deputy Harry Caulfield. Although he had to be in his eighties, I decided to give him a try anyway.

Sometimes, although not often, life gets easy, and this was one of those times. The first Harry Caulfield in the Phoenix phone book turned out to be Deputy Caulfield's son. Without coaxing, he gave me his father's phone number. "Dad has a lot of time on his hands and he loves to talk about the old days," Caulfield Jr. said. "Especially the Bollinger case. He gave a long interview about it to a reporter a few years back, you know, the same woman who wrote about those German POWs in that book, *Escape Across the Desert.* I guess she's kinda famous now, 'cause they're turning it into a movie. Let me warn you, once Dad gets started on the Bollingers, there's no stopping him."

A garrulous subject would make for a nice change, so I punched in Caulfield Sr.'s number.

"Harry's Bar and Brothel."

What a card. "Deputy Caulfield?"

"If you're sellin', I'm not buyin'. But if you're giving it away, what the hey." A snicker.

"Deputy Caulfield, my name's Lena Jones. I'm a private investigator working on the Erik Ernst murder, which I'm sure you've read about, and I've begun to suspect that the Bollinger case might be connected. Could you spare me some time?"

The snicker grew into a guffaw. "Are you good-looking, PI Jones? If you are, hustle yourself over here tomorrow and I'll tell you anything you need to know. Come to think of it, I'll tell you even if you're only medium-looking!"

For a moment I wondered how fast Deputy Caulfield could run, then took comfort in the fact that I could probably run faster. "I'm booked tomorrow, Deputy Caul…"

"Call me Harry. I retired twenty years ago."

"Okay, Harry. How about right now? Or at least as soon as I can get there from Scottsdale."

"It's a date, sweet thing. Leave your chastity belt at home."

God help me.

Apache Junction, only twenty-five miles due east of downtown Phoenix, had originally been an Apache Indian hunting grounds, but in the mid-eighteen hundreds, the Apaches were edged out by prospectors mining for gold in the nearby Superstition Mountains. Local legend held that one of those mines, the Lost Dutchman, still contained untapped reserves of gold, but the word "Lost" wasn't a mere romantic term, it was descriptive. Jacob Waltz, the man who supposedly discovered the rich vein in the mountains, died in 1891 without revealing its location. Apache Junction now played host to retirees instead of gold miners and Indians, but from time to time, you could still see twenty-first-century prospectors leading their pack mules into the Superstitions in search of the Lost Dutchman.

Deputy Harry Caulfield lived in Sundown Sam's Retirement Village, a small mobile home park huddled against the foothills of the mountains. The park was typical of Arizona's many retirement communities: about five acres of concrete pads with hookups for trailers and RVs, an over-chlorinated pool, and a rec center that offered card games and crafts. A purple shuttle bus was parked in front of the rec center to haul the residents off to Barry Manilow concerts in downtown Phoenix. As I drove along the narrow lane looking for Caulfield's pad, I noticed numerous elderly women walking in groups or tending to the flowers that grew in pots in front of their trailers. I saw almost no men.

The exterior of Caulfield's double-wide reflected the local legend. Life-sized decals of miner's tools decorated the white sides of his trailer, and a plaster statue of an old prospector and his burro stood on his concrete porch. Affixed to the trailer door was an incongruous bit of whimsy: a sign reading IF THE

DOUBLE-WIDE'S A-ROCKIN', DON'T COME A-KNOCKIN'. I took a moment to make certain the double-wide wasn't a-rockin,' then rapped on the door. It opened immediately.

An elderly pirate look-alike—wolfish grin, black eyepatch—faced me. What little hair the man had left was white and slicked back with something that smelled like Old Spice. "Pretty Miss Lena, I take it! We been waiting for you!"

We? He stepped aside to usher me into a living room crammed with a large sofa, two recliners, a gun cabinet stocked with a large assortment of rifles, and several oak tables weighted down with U.S. Navy memorabilia and award plaques from the Maricopa Sheriff's Department. As he made his way to one recliner, he limped badly. The man sitting on the sofa clutching his cane was easily as old as Harry, and his bald pate was speckled with age spots. He looked vaguely familiar, but for the moment I couldn't quite place him.

"Pardon the hobble, but my arthritis is acting up," Harry explained, as he lowered himself into the recliner and motioned me into the other. "I shouldn't complain. Here I am, eighty-two years and my cholesterol count's damn near perfect, unlike my buddy's there, whose blood could butter pancakes. In case you're wondering, after we hung up I called him and told him to get his butt over here. He moved to Sundown Sam's a year ago. Imagine my surprise when I discovered that my new neighbor used to guard those Nazis over at Camp Papago."

Now I recognized the man. Warren had hired him to tell his story in *Escape Across the Desert*. He'd been chauffeured to the set one morning while I was finalizing the pilfering investigation, but when it had started to rain, his scene was rescheduled and he was taken back home. During that brief time, we hadn't said a word to each other.

He waggled his fingers at me. "I'd be pleased ta meetcha if Harry'd perform the formalities." His voice sounded as young and elastic as a teenager's.

Harry chuckled. "If it's formalities you want, then formalities you'll get. Private investigator Lena Jones, meet former U.S.

Army Corporal Frank Oberle, once stationed at U. S. Service Command Unit Number Eighty-Four, also known as Camp Papago. Now he's going to be a big movie star. Say, anyone want some iced tea? It's already made."

Amazed to be offered anything weaker than moonshine in this hyper-male lair, I opted for a glass. When seconds later Harry handed us glasses of mango-flavored tea complimented by a sprig of fresh mint, I was further amazed. Harry was good at reading faces. "The wife domesticated me before she died," he explained, his tough-guy image only slightly marred by the sudden tremble in his voice. "She said I'd starve to death if I didn't learn to do things for myself."

Oberle nodded. "She was took by the cancer, just like my wife. Same year, too."

After Harry cleared his throat, the wolfish leer left his face and his brash manner gentled. "I hope you don't hold my smart mouth on the phone against me. When you first called I assumed you were one of the broa…women from around here. I'm one of the only, ah, relatively healthy men left, and they…." He flushed.

Oberle cackled. "Oh, come on, Harry. The ladies have elected you Official Trailer Park Stud. Now quit with the apologies and let's get on with the show."

Apology duly rendered, Harry settled down to the basics. "What did you want to know about the Bollinger case? If you've done any research at all, you must be aware that I never believed Chess Bollinger killed his family. He was a punk then and he's probably a punk now—if he's still alive—but he's not a murderer."

Oberle rolled his eyes. I ignored him. "You're sure of that, Harry?"

"As sure as a one-eyed detective can be." Pleased by my startled expression, he gestured to his eyepatch. "Shrapnel at Pearl Harbor. After the Navy patched me up, I couldn't see well enough to fight but as it turned out, the Maricopa County Sheriff's Department was glad to have me because so many of the county's able-bodied men were overseas scrapping with Hitler and Tojo. By the time the Bollingers were killed I'd been with the Department almost three years, and by then, I'd learned a thing or two about bad guys."

I took another sip of Harry's mango tea. "You seem to be the only person who believes in his innocence."

"You're right. These days, every serial killer caught in the act gets 'the alleged killer' treatment. It never used to be like that. Back in the days when the Bollinger killings went down, Arvis Spaulding, the *Journal's* publisher back then, was Edward Bollinger's very own drinking buddy, so he wasn't inclined to be neutral. Long before the murders he'd heard enough about Chess from Edward to make him think the kid was the spawn of Satan. Before, during and after the trial, Arvis printed screeds that would get his newspaper sued to blue blazes today. The public, which was as prejudiced as he was, ate it up. Arvis didn't give a rat's ass about child psychology—if he knew such a subject existed—but over the years I took a few courses at ASU, courtesy of the G.I. Bill, and was able to figure a few things out about Chess. Edward had elected him as the family scapegoat. Anything that went wrong, Chess was blamed for. Sick cow? Chess' fault. Bad weather? Chess' fault. Plague? Chess' fault. Locusts? Chess' fault. World War II? Chess' fault."

He stared out the trailer's tiny window for a moment, but I knew he was really looking sixty years back. "Okay, the kid liked to fight. He even went after his father once and broke the bastard's nose. I never blamed him for that. Edward Bollinger drank *real* heavy—today he'd be called an alcoholic—and he was pretty fast with his fists when he got drunk. So every time something bad happened around the place, he beat the snot out of Chess just on principle. You ask me, it's no wonder the kid went bad. And he did go bad, make no mistake about that. Turned out more vicious than his daddy."

A sordid tale, but not unusual. I wondered aloud what had happened to Chess after he'd dropped off the *Scottsdale Journal's* radar.

"No clue," Harry said, his voice deepening with regret. "Maybe I should have kept tabs on him, but I didn't. Too depressing."

Harry still believed someone other than Chess killed the Bollingers. I wondered if he was simply in deep denial, a condition which sometimes happened to detectives when they got too close to a case. Against all proof to the contrary, they'd become convinced that a suspect was innocent, and would start ignoring proof to the contrary. Sometimes their denial got them killed.

Unaware of my line of thinking, Harry continued. "I'm not saying that at some point Chess might not have beat somebody 'til they died and then didn't get caught, but I'm telling you he didn't murder his family. Certainly not his mother or sister. That little girl…Chess was crazy about her. You shoulda heard him carry on when I drove him out to her grave."

Yeah. Deep denial. "That was a kind thing to do."

He shrugged. "The family was already buried when we caught up with him, and I felt it was kind of a shame that he never got to say goodbye. So, yeah, I drove him out to the cemetery. The kid totally fell apart." He paused, then added, "Not that a bucket of tears prove anything."

At least Harry realized that some of the worst murderers were the biggest criers at their victims' funerals. "If Chess didn't kill his family, who do you think did? One of the Germans?"

Harry started to answer, but Frank Oberle, who all this while had been sitting quietly if impatiently, jumped in. "Not the Germans! Say what you will about them boys, they wasn't dumb enough to get themselves mixed up in that kind of trouble. As soon as they crawled out of that tunnel, they put as much distance as possible between themselves and Camp Papago. 'Sides, none of them, other than Ernst, was a stone cold killer. When I found out we was both going to be in the same place at the same time again, I just about chucked up my Raisin Bran. Why, I almost backed outta the movie! Thank God I was able to control myself, 'cause that check the film folks is givin' me will buy an awful lot of Twilight Specials down at Denny's."

After sixty years, Oberle still hated Ernst. How many people who'd been around Camp Papago in those days felt the same way about him? As soon as the question surfaced, I remembered how Ernst had died: just like the Bollingers—gagged and beaten to death in his kitchen. Could he have been killed by someone who had loved them and all these years had nursed thoughts of revenge? I floated my unlikely theory to Harry. A retired deputy, he would have seen his share of revenge killings over the years.

Harry rubbed his bad leg for a moment, then leaned back in the recliner. "The psychology's wrong. From what Frank here has told me about Ernst—and he never shuts up about him—Ernst always ordered other people to do his dirty work, like he did with that new prisoner, Werner Dreschler."

The *Scottsdale Journal* article had gone into great length about the Dreschler torture killing, but I was surprised that Harry had heard about it. "You knew about Dreschler?"

"Everybody in Arizona knew about the Werner Dreschler case. Prison camps, Nazis, torture and murder? If it happened today, it'd be a prime time TV movie before Dreschler was buried. If you ask me..."

Oberle interrupted again. "Yeah, talk about your entertainment value. Speaking of, I was surprised when I found out that the Dreschler thing wasn't going to be part of the documentary, 'specially since there was a whole chapter about it in that reporter's book. Say, come to think of it, you're working for that director guy, too. Did you ever ask him why he isn't doing something on poor old Werner?"

I shook my head. "I just found out about him, but I'll ask Warren next time I see him."

"A waste of time, if you ask me," Harry said. "The Germans saw him as a spy, and they did what service people always do to spies. Just a little more so." Then, turning to Oberle, he said, "You know, old son, I'm beginning to come around to your way of thinking. Maybe Ernst did order those two crewmen of his to kill the Bollingers. It sure sounds like him."

Oberle shook his head furiously. "But not like *them*! I knew both Gunter and Josef, and they was real good guys, even if they was German. Especially Josef. That big kid had all them rabbits around camp eatin' outta his hand! Nah, Josef wouldn't hurt a fly. And his buddy Gunter, all that ol' boy wanted to do was draw pictures. I never could figure out how either of them wound up on a U-boat. They shoulda been home raisin' chickens or something."

"Conscripted," Harry broke in. "Toward the end of the war, the Germans were grabbing little kids off the street and sending them to fight."

Oberle waved his hand. "Whatever. But neither of those boys would murder anybody, not even under orders from their slimy Kapitan. Pah! Talk about your worst of the worst. If there was any justice in the world, somebody woulda killed Ernst a long time ago."

Harry gave his friend a pirate smile. "Did you try, Frank? I hear somebody nearly did him in when he was still living back East, too. Sure you didn't fly out there for a little vacation?"

Oberle snorted. "Me in Connecticut? Too cold. 'Sides, if that'd been me, Ernst would a been missing a head, not his legs. But what the hell. He was pure evil. It's nice to know that in the end he died slow. I hope he was conscious all the way to his last breath."

So much for age mellowing a person. This case had already taught me that regardless of their age, people were people. Harry and Oberle were not at all unusual in that they were both still consumed by the same loves and hates as they had been sixty years earlier. Harry grieved for the Bollingers; Oberle for Werner Dreschler; Ernst's neighbor for the husband and uncles lost in World War II. The common stereotype of addled seniors shuffling around with nothing on their minds but their cats and Social Security checks was a deeply flawed one.

"Mr. Oberle, what exactly did you mean when you called Ernst pure evil?" Remembering the documentaries I'd seen about the Nazi death camps, I had other candidates for the title.

His answer echoed my own thoughts. "As some of them politicians say today, I musta mis-spoke myself. Hitler was sure no saint and neither was Eichmann or Dr. Mengele with his creepy human experiments. But if Das Kapitan woulda had the same power, he'd a pulled the same shit, pardon my French. I had me a cousin in the Navy, stationed back East, and he kept an eye on Ernst for me. After the war and we shipped ol' Ernst back to the pit of Hell he'd come from, he started cozying up to the U.S. officials, tryin' to get some work. Couple a years later, they brought him over here to help the Navy with some submarine stuff. That didn't work out all too well, 'cause the way I heard it, he started treating them Navy engineers like he treated his U-boat crew. Us Americans don't go for that.

"Anyway, the Navy gave old Ernst his walking papers, but by then he was a U.S. citizen, so they couldn't forcibly ship his Nazi ass back to Deuschland Über Alles. He got hired by one of those fancy-dancy yacht-designing firms in Connecticut, and sure as shootin', history started repeatin' itself. Ernst bullied everybody so bad they was going to let him go when he had his little boating 'accident.'" Oberle gave a satisfied snort. "That's when the sonofabitch decided to move here, to leave his co-workers at the boatyard safely behind."

Harry winced as he crossed his arthritic leg. "Still a weird thing for an old sea dog to do, if you ask me. Move to the desert. Why not back to Germany?"

Oberle had a quick answer. "Because Ernst was mean, and meanness don't necessarily translate to brave. He wasn't exactly the Man of the Hour in Germany, remember. He got too many of his crew killed, and I'm bettin' there was plenty a grudges there. And then he blew it in Connecticut. So if both those places was gettin' too hot for him, why not Arizona? We treated them Germans pretty good while they was Uncle Sam's guests and a lot of them came back for visits. A couple a them even moved out here. Besides, I hear those Deuschland winters are real bearcats, especially when you're missing your legs. Cold hurts a stump something awful. I should know." Here he shocked me by rolling up his pants leg, revealing an artificial leg attached a couple of inches below the knee. "If there was any justice in this crappy world…"

"More tea?" Before I could answer, Harry stood up, grabbed our half-full glasses and limped into the kitchen with them. I followed, effectively ending Oberle's tirade.

"Sorry about that," Harry said, filling the glasses to the brim. "Frank lost two brothers in the war, both Navy, and I think in his mind Ernst himself torpedoed them out of the water. The only reason Frank didn't join the Navy himself was because of some inner ear thing he has, makes him seasick as hell. That's how he wound up in the Army. They transferred him to Camp Papago after he was wounded in North Africa."

There were all kinds of wounds. The ones you could see, and the ones inside. Frank Oberle truly hated Erik Ernst. And knew where he lived.

Once Harry and I resettled ourselves, I asked him if there was anything more he could tell me about the Bollinger murders that never made the papers.

He shifted around in the recliner, trying to find a more comfortable position. "I always believed we should have followed up on reports of thefts out there in the sticks around that time, but once the sheriff fingered Chess…" His unpatched eye unfocused for a moment, tracking the years, the pain. "Some farmhouses were broken into, and there'd been a lot of vandalizing in town. And don't forget Edward Bollinger's convertible. The car went missing the day of the murders. Edward kept it out back in the barn so his precious cream puff wouldn't get rained on. In those days, half the people in town kept their keys in the ignition, which would have made it easy to steal, and I suppose Edward did, too. But maybe I'm wrong. Why kill a whole family just for a car?"

I knew enough about World War II to find something odd about Harry's story. "Wasn't an Oldsmobile convertible an unusual car for a farmer to be driving around in? Especially since the government instituted gas rationing during the war, except for farm and defense-related vehicles. I would have thought that Edward Bollinger would have that car up on cement blocks for the duration, not sitting there with a tank of gas."

The pirate smile again. "Give the lady an A in American History! Sure, Edward had a pickup and a tractor, all the usual farm stuff, but he was a heavy drinker and skirt-chaser, too, so I imagine that convertible helped with the ladies. I'm betting he saved a little extra gas for it."

"Was the car ever recovered?"

"Nope. My best guess is that it wound up in Mexico."

"Even back then?" I knew that running stolen cars across the border was big business now, but in 1944?

Both men laughed, but Harry, the ex-cop, was the one who answered. "Pretty Miss Lena, thieves have been smuggling cars across the border ever since cars were invented. Mexicans like a nice, shiny ride as much as the rest of us. Who knows? Maybe as we speak that old convertible is sitting in some papacito's shed right now or is pulling taxi duty down in Nogales."

Or rusting away in an Arizona arroyo.

Chapter Eight

Gunter Hoenig stood in the small farmhouse kitchen, momentarily paralyzed by the horror of the scene. The near-decapitated man by the barn had been bad enough, but this abattoir! In front of him were a woman and three children sitting in chairs, arms tied behind their backs, beaten so badly they hardly appeared human.

What kind of beast would do such a thing?

"Do not step in any blood," Kapitan Ernst warned, while he shoveled food into a sack he had made from tied-up blankets. "We must leave no footprints."

Gunter hardly heard him. Out of a pity he could no longer control, he stepped forward and touched the cheek of the youngest child, a boy of around eight. To his shock, the cheek was still warm. Praying to a god who had seemed absent these past few years, he dropped his hand to the boy's neck, feeling for the carotid artery. No, the poor child was dead.

Ignoring Ernst's shouted orders, Gunter avoided the pools of blood as he bent over the other bodies, hoping for signs of life. The other boy, around ten, was dead. The little girl, also. The woman, oh, she had once been so beautiful, with hair of flame.

"Mein Gott!" A flutter underneath his fingers, softer than a butterfly's wing against a cloud, but the woman still lived.

Gunter looked around. Where did these people keep their telephone? His own situation—the escape from Camp Papago—no longer mattered. He would call the operator, and in his rough prison camp English, relate what had happened here. The operator would send help…

"Schweinehunt!"

A blow to the side of his head stunned him for a moment and he only just ducked in time to avoid another closed-fist slap from Kapitan Ernst, whose face was almost as red as the blood in the kitchen. "Pig dog! Quit mooning over that American whore and help us load supplies into these blankets!"

"But Kapitan, she breathes! We must summon a doctor imme-diately!" *Ignoring an order for the first time since the beginning of the war, Gunter grabbed a dish towel from the sink and pressed it to the woman's head. If he could only stop the bleeding…*

Another blow from Ernst, this time so strong that Gunter almost fell. "Idiot! She is not your concern."

Josef, who had been weeping in the corner, finally found his voice. "Kapitan, Gunter is right. We have no quarrel with civilians. It is our duty to help these people, for decency's sake."

Gunter did not think it was possible, but Kapitan's face grew even redder. "Your only duty is to follow me, you Mama's milksops! What do Bavarian farm boys know of war?" *He picked up the bloodied tire iron lying on the floor.* "Ah. We can use this! You, Josef, go into the bedroom and bring us many blankets! The nights here are too cold."

Like an automaton, Josef—his eyes still glassy with shock—left the kitchen.

Ignoring Das Kapitan's orders, Gunter started in search of a telephone, but was brought up short by a whisper. He looked behind him to find that the woman had opened her eyes—they were such a pale blue that looking into them was like falling into the sky—and was trying to speak. His heart nearly torn in two from grief, he placed a gentle hand on her matted hair, leaned over and brought his ear to her ruined lips. "What, Frau?"

The woman's moan turned into a whisper.

"Tommy…why?"

Before Gunter could move to shield her, Das Kapitan brought the tire iron down and silenced her forever.

Chapter Nine

When I arrived at the set Monday morning, the rising sun was spreading its golden glow over the Papago Buttes. In the hon-eyed light, the buttes glowed as if they were on fire, cooled only slightly by the muted greens of sage and mesquite on the flat plain below. After parking my Jeep, I threaded my way through the half-dozen trailers that by day provided shelter for *Escape's* cast and crew, and by night kept the expensive film equipment locked up safely. The usual contingent of onlookers was already in attendance, kept from edging into camera range by a thin strip of barrier tape and the ever-present guard.

If I remembered correctly from the shooting schedule, my reporter friend Fay Harris was due to film her scene early this morning before she went in to work at the *Scottsdale Journal*. By now familiar with the fits and starts of film-making, I planned to catch her between takes. It was becoming increasingly obvious to me that the Bollinger and Ernst cases were connected, and I was curious why the Bollingers weren't mentioned in her book.

I ducked under the tape barrier and walked toward the replica of one of the original officer's quarters, a small, wooden shack outside of which were gathered several actors dressed as German POWs. Warren was nowhere in evidence, but I spotted Fay immediately. She was dressed in a safari-flavored pantsuit, and was tromping across the site of the old prison camp toward a faux camp tower, trailed by a sound man and a Steadicam-wielding cameraman. Her chestnut hair stood out in wild curls around her face, and even from a distance of around twenty yards, I could see that her eyes were frantic. Lindsey, looking more like a runway model than an assistant director, followed close behind her, bawling orders for everyone to do this, do that. The whole thing looked so comical that one of the spectators behind me began to laugh.

Lindsey turned and stood with hands on her hips. "Who did that?"

The looky-loo shut up.

Casting a final glare around, Lindsey yelled, "Quiet on the set!" Then she turned and snapped her fingers at Fay as if the reporter was no more than her trained terrier. "For the fifth time, Fay, do it like I told you to. Walk straight ahead toward that guard tower and recite your lines. Walk and talk, talk and walk. Or can't you do both?"

From the expression on Fay's face, I feared there might be another murder. Where was Warren, and what in the world did he think he was doing, allowing the always-abrasive Lindsey to direct this scene? Up until this point, he'd only used her for off-set location shots; scenery, not people.

At the words, "Roll camera!" Fay walked forward yet again, trying desperately to avoid a patch of cholla cactus which threatened to spike her shins. "The German POWs were very clever," she said, as she huffed along. "Before they began digging their tunnel, they obtained permission from camp commandant Colonel William A. Holden to build a sports field for a game they called "faustball," which is similar to soccer. Therefore, the guards didn't suspect a thing when they saw wheelbarrows full of dirt being piled on the field, then leveled. By the time the Germans were through digging their one-hundred-and-seventy-eight-foot tunnel, it is estimated that more than.... *SHIT!*" Fay hopped back and forth on one foot.

"Cut!" Lindsey's face grew red. "We were rolling, you idiot! Don't you know film costs money?"

"I'll idiot your skinny ass as soon as I get these cactus spines out of my leg." With a dark look at Lindsey, Fay limped over to a rock, sat down and began to de-spine herself.

Lindsey started for her. "Listen, bitch, you…"

I was about to insert myself between the two when from the corner of my eye, I heard a door creak open from one of the trailers. When I turned to look, I saw Warren standing there with a beautiful blond woman. As soon as he saw what was going on, he ran toward us. "That'll be enough, Lindsey!" he called, as he ran. Usually a neat man, his shirt flapped out of his pants and his collar was crooked. "Fay, are you okay? I can get the first aid kit…"

Fay waved him away, muttering something about being a native Arizonan and knowing how to deal with fucking cactus spines. "But it would have been nice if I hadn't been directed to walk straight through the damned cactus patch!"

Lindsey was quick to defend herself. "It was picturesque!"

Warren gave her an exasperated look. "That's enough, Lindsey. Go get yourself a cup of coffee while I attend to this." Then he turned his back on her and leaned over Fay, holding out his hand. "Come on, kiddo, let me help you over to the first aid trailer to get that leg fixed up."

Fay looked mollified, but refused his help. "You know, Warren, this thing took more time than I ever dreamed it would, and I have to get to the paper. The mayor's holding a news conference this morning and I need to cover it. Tell you what. Let me know what day you want me to come back and I'll try, but promise I won't be working with that…that crazy assistant of yours. Otherwise, you can count me out of this production." She made "assistant" sound like a curse.

"But…" He noticed me for the first time. "Oh, hi, Lena."

"Hi yourself." Hyper-aware of Warren's disheveled condition and its probable cause, I couldn't bring myself to sound friendlier. Instead, I followed the limping Fay toward the parking lot. "Hold on, Fay. I need to talk to you about the Bollinger case."

She stopped dead. "Edward Bollinger and his family?"

So she did know about them. "Yes. I want to know why…"

After looking around, she lowered her voice. "Interesting you should bring the Bollingers up, what with old Ernst getting his brains bashed in the other day just like they did. Yeah, we can talk, but you need to know that this is something I'm following up on my own. In the meantime, I wasn't lying to Warren. I have to head over to City Hall. Drop by the paper tomorrow and we'll talk."

Disappointed, I walked with her to her car, a dust-covered Nissan. As she opened the door, maps and clipboards slid onto the asphalt. "Oh, crap. What a perfect day." I helped her shovel everything back in. Nissan re-packed, she straightened up and smoothed her unruly hair. "Remember, anything I tell you has to be off the record. We may be buds, Lena, but I'm not about to let you nose me out of a scoop."

She sped off as the car salesman from the autoplex cruised up in the Studebaker Golden Hawk that Warren had his eye on. "Say, it's Lena, isn't it? Aren't you some kind of private investigator?"

When he got out of the Golden Hawk, I shook his offered hand. "Yep, that's me, Lena Jones, some kind of detective."

He was in his forties, and despite his lack of height, with his silver hair graying at the temples, he looked almost as distinguished as Warren. Unlike Warren, he'd gone soft around the middle, but then again, he probably didn't get as much exercise as Warren did. Especially not with beautiful blondes in trailers.

Oblivious to my foul mood, he beamed an insincere salesman's smile. "We've never actually met. I'm Mark Schank, of Schank Classic Cars."

I decided to get my own back. "Oh. *That* Mark Schank. I used to laugh at your car commercials. Especially the one where you wore the huge cowboy hat and sat on a burro with a monkey perched on your shoulder. Your dad, who had the good sense to wear a hat that fit and ride a real horse, called you 'My Little Buddy.'"

His smile grew pained. "Thank you for that memory. I only did it because at the time I was naive enough to think it might lead to a career in Hollywood. When that didn't pan out, I followed Dad into the business. Now I satisfy my film jones by watching Warren work."

Actually, Schank wasn't just any car salesman. In addition to their large fleet of Cadillacs and Hummers, he and his father hosted an annual collectible car auction, a spectacular event that had begun to rival the success of the legendary Barrett-Jackson Classic Car Auction in North Scottsdale. Every May high rollers flew in from all over the world to bid on the Schanks' Deusenbergs, Cords, and Ferraris. The auction was so popular that, like the Barrett-Jackson, it had turned into a ticketed arts festival, with rock bands, crafts booths, and gourmet food vendors. For the non-billionaires, the father-son team also sold less expensive collectibles, such as the sleek Golden Hawk and muscle cars from the Seventies and Eighties.

Ever the salesman, he gestured toward my Jeep. "A '45, right? Bet I could get some good money on that for you, especially with that custom paint job. Think about it."

When I bought the Jeep from a desert tours company five years back, it had been painted hot pink, and a set of steer horns did duty as a hood ornament. Then Jimmy's uncle, the owner of Pima Paint and Collision, repainted the Jeep a beautiful sandstone color and covered it with many of the same Pima mythological figures as he'd painted on Jimmy's trailer: Earth Doctor, Elder Brother, Coyote, Night Singing Bird, and Spider Woman. As one of the Jeep's many fans once pointed out, my ride was a rolling petroglyph.

"I'll never sell my baby," I told Schank.

His smile didn't diminish. "First time I talked to him, that's exactly what the Golden Hawk's owner said. But life can throw curve balls. Wouldn't matching his-and-hers Mercedes look great in your garage? We sell those, too."

"Sorry, not interested." I didn't own a garage, and a Mercedes would look stupid covered with petroglyphs. As for matching "his and hers" cars, first you have to have a "his," and I didn't.

Alert to the edge in my voice, Schank dropped the sales pitch. "Well, it's been pleasant talking to you, Lena, but I promised I'd bring the Golden Hawk over for a test drive."

I watched him head toward Warren, who had taken Lindsey aside and was talking to her quietly, pausing every now and then to pat her on the shoulder. My, my. Quite the ladies' man. Then I looked at my watch and saw that the morning was slipping away and I had yet to accomplish a thing, so I climbed into my Jeep and headed for Desert Investigations. Before I pulled out of the parking lot, I saw Warren head back to his trailer. When he opened the door, I caught a quick glimpse of the tall blond woman who'd remained inside.

I wondered if he'd send her roses, too.

"The info on Jack Sherwood's on your desk," Jimmy said, as I entered Desert Investigations.

Still furious with myself for being taken in by Warren, I shuffled through the readouts. Somehow Jimmy had managed to access Sherwood's cell phone records (illegal, yes, but show me a private eye who stays within legal limits and I'll show you an inept private investigator). Within the past two months, Beth Osmon's boyfriend had placed seventy-six calls to a number registered to Jack Rinn, in Hamilton, Alabama. I punched in the number and when a drawl-voiced woman answered, asked for Mr. Jack Rinn.

"I'm sorry, my husband's in Phoenix on business." She sounded young. Children chattered and laughed in the background.

Oh, Jack Rinn, you dog. "Ah, yes, Mrs. Rinn, I'm calling from Phoenix and I haven't been able to reach him at his office. An emergency's come up and I have to reach him within the next couple of hours or we're..." Or we're what? "Or we're going to lose considerable money. I've lost his cell..."

Without any more prompting, Mrs. Rinn gave me Jack Rinn's cell phone number, which just happened to be the same as Jack Sherwood's. I thanked her and hung up.

There was little doubt that Rinn was Sherwood, and the alias meant that he was probably a grifter, after Beth Osmon's money. When I called and told her, she sounded less than happy at the news. After ironing out the quaver in her voice, she said, "There could be an innocent explanation, Lena. Maybe Mr. Rinn is Jack's cousin or something. You know those Southern families, they tend to do a lot of business together. It wouldn't be odd at all for cousins to give each other's phone numbers as emergency contacts. And the same first names run in families all the time. We...In my family, there are three Beths. We're all named for the same great-aunt."

Probably a great-aunt with money. "Anything's possible." I didn't worry about her knee-jerk defense of the man. Women reacted that way all the time when first confronted with proof of their men's infidelities. Once the news settled in, though, everything changed.

When she next spoke, her voice was firm. "I want you to find out exactly who Jack Rinn is. I don't care if you have to fly to Alabama and interview his dog!"

That's my girl. "It probably won't be necessary. I'll contact an Alabama private investigator I've dealt with in the past and have him take over from that end. With your approval, of course. It'll cost you a lot less than paying me to fly out there." Alabama was said to be particularly pretty in April, but so was Arizona and I had other cases here that needed my direct attention. Especially Rada Tesema's.

"You have my approval to do whatever you need to do. Just get to the bottom of this."

"Will do. And Beth?"

A sniffle. Now her emotions were swinging back the other way. That, too, was normal considering the circumstances. I felt like sniffling myself. "What?"

"Under no circumstances should you confront Mr. Sherwood about this. It could be dangerous."

There was such a long pause on the other end of the phone that I thought I'd lost her. But at last she spoke. "I'm not stupid, Lena. Just in love." Then she hung up.

Stupid. Love. Two different words for the same damned thing.

❦

I'd barely finished giving Alabama PI Eddy Joe Hughey the details on the Sherwood/Rinn case when the other line rang.

"I'm sorry I missed you this morning, but there was a problem on the set that I had to see to." Warren. "Did you get the flowers I sent?"

"They're beautiful. Ah, we need to get together." Although I'd told Beth not to indulge in any confrontation, I felt ripe for one of my own. I needed to keep it civilized, however, because the checks coming in from Living History Productions were more necessary than ever now that Jimmy was leaving. Besides, I'd only gone out with the man once, so whatever woman he wanted to mess around with in his trailer was none of my business. "Let's get together this evening, if you have the time." *So you can hear my speech on the dangers of mixing business with pleasure.*

The pleasure in his voice almost made me feel guilty. "I'll pick you up at seven again. But let's try a different place this time, bigger. There's something…"

Something I want to tell you? No problem. I'm a big girl. I forced a laugh. "How about India Palace, on McDowell?" *Bigger and brighter.*

"I'll make the reservations."

When I hung up, I noticed Jimmy looking at me with pity. Did I look as depressed as I felt?

Warren picked me up in his leased Range Rover on the dot of seven, and as we drove along McDowell Road where it wound its way through the Papago Buttes, he inserted a CD of Mozart's *Eine Kleine Nachtmusik* into the CD player. I would have preferred a little Hound Dog Taylor, but at least he wasn't playing something as overt as *Bolero*. Considering the circumstances, that would have been unforgivable.

The Mozart little more than a cricket's chirp in the background, I seized my chance to pump him for information before our relationship went south. "Warren, why aren't you doing anything about the murder of Werner Dreschler in your film? That was quite the big case in its day, and there was a rumor that Erik Ernst was involved."

"I know."

His answer took me aback. "You *knew?*"

He stomped on the brake to avoid hitting a coyote that decided at the last minute to cross the road. As he accelerated again, he resumed the conversation as if nothing had happened. "Sure I knew. I do my research. The major problem is that if I attempted to tell the Werner Dreschler story, it would take over the whole documentary. One of the first things you learn in film school is *focus*, to not get so caught up in side issues that you lose the narrative thread. So I'm limiting *Escape Across the Desert* to the escape itself. But I'm already making notes to include the Dreschler case in my next film, the one I'm making about capital punishment. Did you know that the six POWs hanged for Dreschler's murder were the victims of the last mass execution in the United States?"

No, I hadn't known that, although if I had, I doubted if I would have used the word "victims" to describe the men, remembering that Dreschler had suffered scores of cigarette burns before the six POWs, possibly egged on by Das Kapitan, mercifully hanged him from a shower. But at least Warren had answered the question to my satisfaction.

When we arrived at India Palace, the turbaned maître d' ushered us toward a small private dining room at the back. I'd planned a business discussion, not an intimate tête à tête, so I balked at the glass-beaded entrance, but Warren slipped his arm around my waist and hustled me through. "There's someone I want you to meet."

Sitting at a table waiting for us was the blond woman I'd briefly glimpsed at Warren's trailer this morning, wearing a silk dress that probably cost more than my Jeep and who closely resembled the famous movie star Angelique Grey. The twin girls with her, who appeared to be around six years old, were her spitting image. The moment they spotted Warren, they gave twin squeals of "Daddy!" and ran toward him. Within seconds, he looked as if he'd been blown backward through a wind tunnel—collar askew, shirt-tail out of his pants, hair mussed.

Just like he'd looked when he emerged from the trailer this morning.

When he finally peeled the girls off him and sent them back to their seats, he repaired himself as best he could. "What a perfect evening, surrounded by beautiful women!" Then he introduced me to his ex-wife, who really *was* the famous Angelique Grey, and their two daughters, Star and Moon. Not quite knowing how to handle the situation, I gave everyone a weak smile.

Warren didn't notice my discomfort. "Angel flew in this morning..." The little girls laughed so hard he had to start again. "Angel flew in by *airplane* this morning and was kind enough to stop by the set."

The twins cheered.

He blew them a kiss and continued. "She's starting a fashion line with some Scottsdale designer, and to make a long story short, I told her all about you, Lena. She's dying to pump you for information."

What information could a famous movie star possibly need from me? "I'll be glad to answer, if I can. But I need to warn you that I don't know anything about fashion." Probably an unnecessary warning, because anyone could tell that just by looking at me. Clean jeans were my idea of dress-up.

But Angelique's smile looked genuine. "Last week I inked a deal on an upcoming NBC crime drama where I play a private investigator who's set up business with an escaped convict. When I called Warren yesterday to tell him the twins and I were on the way out here, he said you know everything there is to know about being a PI. I was hoping you could give me tips that might help bring some reality to the role."

Reality, indeed. The idea of a private investigator setting up shop with an escaped convict was about as realistic as sitting down to dinner with your movie star ex-wife, your twin daughters, and the woman you were currently dating. People certainly did business differently in Hollywood. "For starters, an escaped convict would have trouble getting a private investigator's license."

"That's what I told the writers, too, but the project has already been green-lighted as written and my partner's already been cast, so we're stuck with it, which is another reason I want to at least get the other details right. Do you carry a gun?"

"Uh…" I fiddled with my napkin.

Warren beamed. "She sure does! She's got this big .57 Magnum stashed in her carry-all right now."

Although he had said it loudly enough for everyone in the main dining room to hear, I doubted if anyone reacted. After all, this was Arizona and chances were good that at least half the women in the restaurant were packing. Angelique seemed alarmed, but the little girls looked thrilled and I could already guess what they'd ask Santa for Christmas. In the interests of accuracy, I set the record straight. "I think Warren means a .357 Magnum. My own gun's a revolver, a snub-nosed Colt .38."

Warren looked disappointed. "But you've used it, right?"

Yes, I had, but I preferred not to dwell on that aspect of my career. I smiled at Angelique. "In my business, the whole point of carrying a gun is not having to use it. What kind of weapon are they giving you for your sit-com?" I took a sip of water.

"A .50 caliber Desert Eagle."

When I choked, Warren gave me a concerned look. "You okay, Lena?"

There was no point in telling him that a woman toting a .50 caliber Desert Eagle had recently tried to shoot me, and my memories of that monstrous automatic were *not* rosy. I took another sip of water. "The Desert Eagle is a nice weapon, but perhaps a little expensive for the average PI. Despite all the PR, we don't make a lot. Remember those old Sam Spade movies? The poor guy could hardly pay his rent." I didn't mention my own looming financial difficulties.

She frowned. "There's nothing we can do about the gun, either, because it ties into the name of the show—*Desert Eagle.*

My character's name is Tiffany Eagle, and she's half-Cherokee. The show's set in Santa Fe, which is where the desert part comes in."

Dare I tell her that if there were a Cherokee woman to be found in Santa Fe, she would probably have moved there from either Oklahoma or North Carolina? And that a half-Cherokee would probably not have Angelique's ivory skin, platinum hair and azure eyes? "Perhaps you'd like me to look at that script?" I knew there was little chance she would take me up on my offer.

She reached down and opened the suitcase-sized Nuovedive handbag nestled next to her Tommy Choos. "What a coincidence. I just happened to bring a copy."

I shot Warren a dirty look. While he manufactured an air of injured innocence, Angelique passed the script across the table. I took it and stashed it next to my non-glamorous revolver in my cheap canvas carry-all.

"Any chance you could have it finished by tomorrow, Lena? The girls and I are returning to L.A. on an early flight, and I'd like to take it back with me. Shooting starts next week, and I told the writers I'd probably have a few suggestions."

Warren wouldn't meet my eyes.

Silencing a groan, I gave Angel a nod. She beamed back at me. So did the girls. I wondered if they were as smart as their mother.

After Warren walked me to the top of the stairs at my apartment, he gave me a kiss that chased away my irritation and woke up my dormant hormones. Then he stroked the hair away from my flushed face. "You know the real reason I invited Angel and the s to have dinner with us?"

"Free editing services. Which reminds me. If I'm going to ad that script, I'd better get started." I backed away from him efore things got too hot. I wasn't ready yet.

But he closed the distance between us and caressed my cheek with the back of his hand. "That was part of it. But I also wanted you to see how well Angel and I get along."

I brushed his hand away and began unlocking my door. "And that matters because…?"

"You can tell a lot about a man from the way he gets along with his ex-wife."

"And that matters because…?" I knew I sounded like a broken record, but given the state I was in, there was little I could do about it.

He turned me to face him and before I could protest, gave me another hot kiss. It could have lasted thirty seconds or thirty minutes, time got away from me. When we finally came up for air, he answered my question with one of his own. "Why do you think, Lena?"

I took a cold shower, wrapped myself in a robe, and propped myself up in bed to read Angel's script. Other than a few technical problems, such as blue-eyed Indians and revolvers that ejected bullets, the script wasn't too bad. Weirdly enough, I could almost see the high-cheeked Angelique Grey in the role of Tiffany Eagle, although I imagined her with full body makeup, dyed black hair and brown contact lenses. I finished the script around three, and after penciling some final comments on the back, I laid it on my night stand, turned off the light, and tried to sleep.

It didn't work. I kept thinking about the dinner with Warren, Angel, Star and Moon. With such an unusual post-marital relationship, how could everyone seem so relaxed? Granted, Angel was an actress and could probably put on a convincing act of bliss while being strapped into the electric chair. But her children were, as they say in Hollywood, civilians. And the uncomplicated happiness in the girls' eyes appeared genuine.

An Oscar-winning film director. A movie star. Twin girls. A laughably inept script.

What the hell was I getting myself into?

Chapter Ten

Around eight the next morning I dropped off the marked-up script at the front desk of the Sheraton, where Angel was staying. On my way back to the office, I stopped by the *Scottsdale Journal* in hopes that my timing would be better than yesterday's. To my disappointment, Fay Harris was on her way out the door.

"Sorry, Lena, but today's a mess. I need to get back down to City Hall and talk to the mayor. The aide she fired last month just filed suit for sexual harassment."

I raised my eyebrows. The city's politics tended to be no more corrupt than the average city of its size, but sexual harassment in the mayor's office was a new wrinkle. The vision of the prim grandmother—for some reason most of Scottsdale's recent mayors had been women—copping a feel from some hunky young aide tickled me. "This aide, does he have any proof? Or is it a 'he said, she said' thing."

Fay chuckled. "More like a 'she said, she said.' If you want to know the juicy details, read the *Journal* tomorrow."

As she trotted toward the *Journal*'s parking lot, I followed. "I'll do that. But do you think you have time to talk to me then, maybe meet me for lunch? You promised to tell me something about your suspicions that Erik Ernst was connected to the Bollingers. Off the record, of course."

Since the front seat of her Nissan looked every bit as cluttered as it had yesterday, I guessed that she used the car as an on-the-go extension of her office filing cabinet. "Yeah, There's a lot I can tell you about the old bastard that didn't make it into my book." She took a Kleenex out of her purse and wiped away bird droppings from the Nissan's window. "Something about the Bollinger case doesn't make sense to me, so I drew a diagram of the area surrounding their farm, and that started me looking at other crimes in the area during the same time period. There were some real surprises, too, so I wrote them up. I wanted to put all my discoveries into the book, but the publisher's attorney blue-pencilled everything. Same with some of the interviews, because he said some of the quotes bordered on libel. For instance, a source told that me Edward Bollinger had been bragging that…"

She flicked a look at her watch. "Oh, hell, gotta get down to City Hall before the mayor lawyers up." Before she drove off, she stuck her head out of the window and made a date to meet me at a nearby restaurant. "Noon tomorrow, at First Watch."

It was a date she wouldn't keep.

When I made it back to Desert Investigations, Esther was sitting on Jimmy's lap, blowing into his ear. They immediately sprang apart, Esther with a guiltier look on her face than the situation called for. Maybe she felt bad about luring my partner away. I hoped so.

I dumped my carry-all on the desk. "You guys find a house yet?"

Recovering from her embarrassment, Esther threw me a blinding smile. "We're in negotiations for one." She named a subdivision in central Scottsdale known for its Wisconsin-green lawns and rigorous rules. "It isn't large, only two bedrooms and one bath. The yard's pretty small, too, but it's a start. If we make a big enough down payment, the realtor says we could close in three weeks."

Had her teeth been whitened? How different Esther now looked from the terrified woman who had escaped from one of Arizona's most notorious polygamy compounds. I wondered if her daughter Rebecca, whom I had later smuggled out of the same compound, would grow up looking so sleek. But, she was a fresh-faced teenager, not Hollywood royalty. Not that there was anything wrong with that.

I feigned enthusiasm. "Two bedrooms and a yard! Maybe we can all get together for lunch some time." When I was a kid, Reverend Giblin used to take me and his other foster children camping in the area, which used to be at the northern boundary of Scottsdale. This was before the bulldozers ripped out the native fauna and replaced the cactus and mesquite with Bermuda grass. Try as I might, I couldn't see Jimmy living up there amid the yuppies and retirees. "Hey, Jimmy. You looking forward to joining the great American middle class?"

He wouldn't meet my eyes, and I noticed that the tribal tattoo on his forehead had darkened, which it tended to do when he blushed. "I guess."

I found his own seeming lack of enthusiasm interesting. Jimmy might live in a trailer in the middle of the nearby reservation, but it was a nice trailer with the entire reservation as his back yard. Then again, maybe leaving his prayer lodge behind was what made him sound so subdued. Chances weren't good that his new homeowner's association would allow him to build one in his backyard.

"Boy, a new house in three weeks! Bye-bye reservation, eh? And you start your job at Southwest MicroSystems when?" I sounded so chipper I hated myself.

"That's in three weeks, too." I could barely hear him. "But I wanted to take some time off before I start, to regroup."

"A new house *and* a new job! Fantastic!" Please, someone stop me. "You going to get your tattoo removed, too?" I was kidding but the bereft look on his face told me I'd inadvertently hit the mark. Esther planned to give Jimmy the same kind of make-over she gave her customers in the cosmetics aisle. How long would it take, I wondered, before she talked him out of attending tribal pow-wows? For a brief moment I was tempted to ask her why she didn't marry a man who was already white and save herself the trouble.

But a late-arriving wave of common sense kept my mouth shut.

After Jimmy and Esther left for lunch, I went to the cupboard and picked up a container of ramen, splashed in some hot water from the tap, then gobbled it down. For health's sake, I ate an apple. Not exactly a gourmet meal, perhaps, but it did the trick.

Belly full, I shoved the ramen container out of the way and placed a call to Reverend Giblin. I was gratified to hear that the prison ministry group from his church had already started visiting Tesema and, at his request, had put together a package of clothing and other items to send to his family back in Ethiopia. "We'll make sure his family is cared for and that he doesn't feel abandoned," the Rev finished. "The rest is up to you."

With that load off my shoulders, I called Captain Kryzinski at Scottsdale North, who—if his pattern held—would be working through lunch. Old dogs not known for learning new tricks, he picked right up.

After sharing a few pleasantries, we began to discuss the case. "C'mon, Lena. Don't tell me you still believe Tesema's innocent." From the slurping noise he then made, I figured he was eating his usual lunch of Whopper, super-sized fries, and chocolate shake. A health nut he wasn't.

"Tesema didn't do it, Captain. Trust me. Ernst had more enemies than the mayor has scandals."

A laugh. "You've heard about the latest, I take it. I'm not saying Ernst was in the running for the Humanitarian of the Year award, but there are too many things tying Tesema to the killing for us to ignore. His lies, his fingerprints…"

"He lied because he was scared. And since he was over there all the time taking care of the old bastard, his fingerprints mean nothing unless you found them on the bloody club or whatever it was you think he beat Ernst to death with."

"No, we haven't found the murder weapon yet, but…."

"Of course you haven't. The real murderer took it away with him." Or her. I still wasn't convinced MaryEllen Bollinger was one hundred percent innocent. She carried a grudge against the old man, and those bouncer friends of hers at The Skin Factory seemed loyal. I suspected that if she asked them to kill someone for her, they would comply in a heartbeat.

"Be that as it may…"

"I'm telling you, Tesema didn't do it!" Frustrated, I changed the subject. "Has an attorney been assigned to him yet?"

Kryzinski rattled off a name I knew about from an earlier case. Gary Bridger had let a perfectly innocent man be convicted for murder, and when his family then appealed to me to prove their son innocent, it had taken less than a week for me to find the evidence that overturned his conviction. "Oh, for Pete's sake, Captain. Bridger's the bottom of the heap. Literally. They say he finished dead last in his law school graduating class."

"Beggars can't be choosers. You know how the legal system works."

Yeah, I did. And it creeped me out. "It's a good thing the Rev's church ladies are around to keep Tesemea's spirits up."

For a moment, his silence was so deep that I thought I could hear him splash his fries into his ketchup. Then, "The Rev's church ladies, did you say? Are you talking about Reverend Giblin?"

"Of course. His group is already visiting him and sending care packages to his family. You know the Rev started that prison ministry last year because you helped grease the bureaucratic wheels."

"The Rev's doing good work, no doubt about it. It's just that Tesema's rabbi is probably already helping him with that."

I stared at the phone. "Did you say *rabbi*?"

"Sure, Tesema being Jewish and all. Then again, maybe he hasn't been attending synagogue regularly. I'm Catholic but it's been so long since I've been to Mass my priest probably wouldn't recognize me if I fell on him."

"Wait a minute. What makes you think Tesema is Jewish? He's from Ethiopia. Aren't they mainly, well, Christian?" I remembered the crosses on the wall of his apartment. "Or Muslim?"

"And Jewish. Not all of them went to Israel during that airlift a few years ago. Some stayed, some came here. When my detectives were going through Ernst's house, they found Tesema's Star of David hidden in the coffee cannister, so they booked it into evidence. There's no doubt it's Tesema's, what with that nice thumb print on the back."

"Whoa! What do you mean, his Star of David?"

More munching, more slurps. "Lena, you ought to start your day by reading the newspapers, because that Star of David is mentioned in today's front page *Scottsdale Journal* article, although we're down below the fold now. Apparently the chain broke at some point while Tesema was over there doing his thing. It's our guess that Ernst found it, and being more Nazi than American, got all shook up at the prospect of a Jew daring to touch a member of the glorious Master Race. Tesema said he called him a Jew *schwarzer* and refused to give the necklace back."

Jew schwarzer. Mrs. Hillman, Ernst's next door neighbor, had believed Ernst yelled "You *schwarzer*" to Tesema, but she misheard. Why, oh why, had Tesema blabbed all this to the police? Hadn't his attorney told him to keep his mouth shut? Then I remembered who his attorney was: Gary Bridger, boy wonder.

Kryzinski was still talking. "The way we figure it, being called a Jew *schwarzer* set Tesema off. He brooded about the insult for a while and eventually realized that if he lost his caretaker's job, his family back home would be in the deep brown stuff. So the night of the murder he jumped in his car and went over there, determined to try to smooth things over or at least get his Star of David back. We don't think he planned to kill Ernst, but one thing probably led to another and..." He stopped for another slurp, then continued. "And, well, Tesema beat him to death. With a little luck, Bridger might be able to swing a deal for involuntary manslaughter."

Which would be fine if Rada Tesema had actually murdered Ernst. But regardless of the provocation, I still couldn't see Tesema tying up an old man, however reprehensible, and beating him to death. How could I allow a man I believed innocent man to "swing a deal" for a crime he didn't commit? Before I said this to Kryzinski, I remembered the rumors that Ernst's U-boat had torpedoed civilian ships attempting to carry European Jews to Palestine. Could Tesema have killed Ernst as an act of vengeance for them? I was still mulling over this remote possibility when Kryzinski delivered the death blow to an already miserable day.

"Lena, there's something else you should know."

"Don't tell me Tesema's confessed."

"We should be so lucky. No, it's about me."

My spine straightened, as it always does when I'm about to receive bad news. "Are you sick?" Remembering how pale he had been looking, I had a vision of him on his deathbed, wasting away from some terrible disease.

The answer he gave was only slightly less terrible. "I'm tired of the Scottsdale bureaucracy, kid. I'm moving back to Brooklyn."

Now it was official. Everyone I loved was leaving me.

Hadn't that been the pattern for my entire life? Thirty-one years ago, my father left me when he died in a forest clearing, and shortly afterwards, my mother left me to die on a Phoenix street. Then Child Protective Services shuttled me from foster home to foster home, until I found one where Madeline—my fourth or fifth foster mother—could deal with my depressions and fits of violence. But after a year Madeline left me, too. True, she'd contracted breast cancer and the battle for her life had left her unable to cope with the rigors of raising a disturbed child, but her desertion was no less real for that. By the time she'd completed chemotherapy and her tests were clear, I'd disappeared back into the system, ending up in the horrific household where rape was a weekly occurrence.

That "mother" and "father" had left me when I stabbed the family rapist. Next up on the Let's-Leave-Lena list came Reverend Giblin, where once again I was foolish enough to relax, to believe I was safe with a decent, loving family. Wrong. Right around the time I started to act more like a normal human being than the animal I'd become, Mrs. Giblin suffered a stroke and died, and the geniuses at Child Protective Services decided that a widower shouldn't take care of foster children without a woman's presence. Although he protested all the way, the Rev ultimately left me, too.

Now Jimmy was leaving me.

And Captain Kryzinski.

Was the Universe trying to tell me something?

Maybe the Universe was trying to tell Kryzinski something, too. As we talked, it appeared that the new Scottsdale police chief had decided to "upgrade the department's image" and start handling everything by the rule book. This meant, Kryzinski groused, that management should immediately cease what had been a cozy relationship with outside sources. No more judicious leaking of information in order to receive better information, no *quid pro quo,* no unhealthy fraternization with PIs such as myself.

"The world's changing, Lena," Kryzinski said. "Individualism's out, bureaucracy's in, and Big Brother's watching us all. The other night I was talking to Steve, my son-in-law who just quit NYPD to start his own PI agency. He says it's like this back there on the Force now, too, rules and regs up the ass. Hell, it's so bad that most of those new college cops have science degrees. Private work is the only place left now where an old cop can do things the way he wants to do them. So I'm going back to Brooklyn and work for Steve. *With* him, actually. We'll be full partners, like you and Jimmy."

"Wait a minute, wait a minute. Did I hear that right? You're going to turn PI?" My mind was churning.

"It's either that or retire, and I'm not ready to hang 'em up yet."

"Jesus, boss. I've got an opening right here at Desert Investigations. Jimmy's leaving to make big bucks with Southwest MicroSystems."

A long, long silence. Then he broke my heart all over again. "It wouldn't work, kid."

"Yes it would!" It was all I could do to keep from screaming, please don't leave me, please don't leave me.

He broke through my misery with a chuckle. "I appreciate the offer, but don't you see? I'm too used to telling you what to do, and to start flipping that around would get real uncomfortable real fast. Nah, my mind's made up. There'll be no problem working with Steve 'cause we worked different precincts when I was back there. Besides, I miss my grandkids. All my family's there, you know."

There it was, the "F" word again. Family.

Everybody had one but me.

Chapter Eleven

I couldn't stand it, I simply couldn't stand it.

With a quick glance outside, I saw that the skies were still blue and the sun was still shining. Life would go on. Nevertheless, I shoved away from my desk, hit the lights, and locked up. When Jimmy returned from lunch, he could answer the phones. For now, I was getting the hell out of the office.

I dashed upstairs to change into something more upscale than my Wal-Mart turtleneck and jeans, then headed for Papago Park. After parking the Jeep next to the Studebaker Golden Hawk—it looked prettier every day—I ambled slowly onto the set trying to act casual. No point in letting Warren realize how desperately I needed to be with someone who still had feelings for me. Irrational, perhaps, but I didn't care. I stationed myself between Harry Caulfield, looking more like a pirate than ever with his crooked grin and eyepatch, and Mark Schank, who was here either as a film buff or to make a buck off the Golden Hawk. Given his avaricious expression, my betting was on the latter. At the time, though, both men were intently watching Warren direct Frank Oberle, who looked thrilled to be taking over Ernst's place.

I felt better just listening to Warren's soothing voice. "Now, Frank, what I want you to do is sort of meander around underneath the guard tower where you used to be stationed, and say whatever comes into your mind. Talk about the Germans, how nice they were, how well you guards got along with them. And don't worry about anything, you'll be great. If you flub up, which I doubt you'll do because you're a natural, we'll just do it again."

Oberle ingnored Warren's flattery. "Them Germans weren't all nice. Kapitan Ernst…"

Warren interrupted with a pained smile. "This scene's the film's emotional payoff, so let's try to stay positive."

"Listen, son, if you'd a lived through World War II like me, you'd know what to do with all that positivity crap. Das Kapitan was a thug and I'm glad he's in hell." But he did as Warren directed, hobbling on his false leg across the rocky ground, stopping once to prod his cane at a rusted beer can, talking all the while. The camera and sound crew followed, skipping nimbly over the cactus.

Oberle's voice carried toward us on the soft April breeze. "I remember the night of the escape like it was yesterday, especially the Christmas carol those Germans was singin'. *Stille Nacht.* It made everybody feel warm and fuzzy-like, you know, two nations, one faith, Baby Jesus gettin' born and all that rot. Some of us guards sang along with them. Course, what we didn't know was that the Germans was just usin' all that commotion to cover the sounds their buddies was makin' as they crawled on their bellies like snakes through the tunnel. The sneaky bastards."

Harry chuckled and Warren rolled his eyes, but kept the cameras rolling.

Oberle pointed up at the reconstructed guard tower. "There's where I was stationed that night, in Guard Tower Two, over-lookin' Compound 1A, where they escaped from," Oberle said. Then he squatted down and slapped his hand on the ground. Warren was right: Oberle was a natural. "You can still see here how the ground's all sunk in from the tower's weight." Using his cane for leverage, he stood up. "Problem was, there's a blind spot here, all the way from Guard Towers Two and Three, and us guards could never see everything that was goin' on with those German boys. Captain Parshall, the camp's provost marshal, warned the high mucky-mucks about the blind spot, but they ignored him. So guess where the Germans dug, huh? Unlike our pointy-headed brass, they wasn't fools."

Beside me, Harry chuckled again. I knew he'd heard it all before, but the tale his buddy spun about the 'pointy-headed' brass' screw-ups warmed the cockles of his old enlisted-man's heart. Near us, several extras stood smiling and nodding. Most were tall, blond-haired and blue-eyed, cast for their resemblance to their real-live counterparts. All were dressed in khaki pants and shirts with PRISONER OF WAR stamped in large letters across their backs. Their uniforms contrasted vividly with the high-tech film equipment that surrounded us, making me feel as if we were all wobbling around in a time warp. And in a way, we were. A twenty first-century film was being made on top of the remains of a World War II prison compound, which in turn had been built on top of the remains of an ancient Hohokam Indian village. If ever I needed a reminder that the past never died, this was it.

After a while, Oberle and Warren drifted out of hearing range and I grew bored. It was then that I noticed Lindsey, who had been studying the shooting schedule, staring at me. Curious, I left Harry to Mark Schank's sales spiel about a 1946 Chevrolet coupe and wandered over to her. "Nice day, huh?" When you can't think of anything to say, talk about the weather. Which is why conversations can get so boring in Arizona. We don't have a lot of weather to talk about. Except for summer, when we fry.

Lindsey didn't appreciate my attempt at friendliness. Waving the shooting schedule at me, she snapped, "Can't you see I'm busy here?" Although almost Warren's age, in her early forties, she still looked like a runway model with her impeccable black linen slacks and shirt, flawless makeup, and hair as glossy as a television shampoo commercial. She always made me feel sloppy.

"Just making conversation." I began to walk away, but what she said next stopped me in my tracks.

"Stay away from him."

Him? I glanced back over at the barrier tape, where Mark Schank was handing Harry his business card. Did he think the retired deputy was in the market for a Deusenberg? Beyond the two, standing on a small rise, were Warren and Oberle. "Stay away from who, Lindsey?"

"You know damn well who, you bitch." Lindsey's eyes danced with malice. Then she turned and walked away, until she became hidden behind a large lighting umbrella.

Mark Schank was right. Life throws curve balls.

As I drove toward MaryEllen Bollinger's North Scottsdale condo, I made a mental note to call my therapist. In the meantime, I vowed not to think about my own unhappiness. This lasted until the first afternoon rush hour slow-down on Loop 101, when my frustrations boiled over and I cursed at the witless drivers around me before realizing the true targets of my rage were Jimmy and Kryzinski. One was leaving me for a woman, the other for a city.

How fair was that?

Without her theatrical makeup, MaryEllen looked much younger than she had at The Skin Factory and I envied her peaches-and-cream complexion while deploring the big shiner that marred it. After she settled me on the white sofa and poured me a cup of chamomile tea I started right in. "As I said on the phone, I still have a few questions, but first, I need to ask you something, if only to satisfy my own curiosity. The cops gave you a speeding ticket near Anthem at four a.m. on the night of Ernst's murder. What were you doing up there?" I already knew what she'd told the cops, but I wanted to hear it from her, because a wee hours trip to the far north housing development still made no sense to me. If she'd have kept going, she'd have wound up in Flagstaff.

When she smiled, MaryEllen looked about nineteen. "I was going to visit Clay. My boyfriend."

"The guy who gave you the shiner, right?."

She reached a manicured hand to the bruise. "I didn't have it then. That came later."

In other words, after the cops stopped her she continued on her way, and sometime later that night—or morning, to be exact—her boyfriend hit her. "What did you and Clay fight about?"

"We had a disagreement over where the relationship was headed. But that's been settled now." She sipped slowly at her tea, savoring the delicate flavor.

From the other room, I could hear her roommate moving about. At least I hoped it was her roommate, not the eye-smacking Clay. It had been my experience that women like MaryEllen forgave and forgot too quickly, convinced that they couldn't do any better, anyway. "Okay, let's move on. You've said you confronted Ernst, hoping he'd confess and that it didn't work out, but here's my next question. When he first opened the door and saw you, what did he look like?"

She frowned. "I don't understand."

"Did it look like he just woke up, or did it look like he'd been up for a while?" There was a chance Ernst had entertained an earlier visitor, and the person was still there, hidden out of sight in a back room.

"Oh. Yeah, I got the bastard out of bed. The lights were out when I arrived, but it didn't take him long to get to the door. Less than a minute."

Transferring from bed to the wheelchair would have entailed a certain amount of effort and time, so her answer didn't sound right. I pictured Ernst, lying in bed, waking to the sound of someone banging at the door. He would have to raise himself by his arms, somehow swing off the bed over to the wheelchair, then position himself there. "Was he dressed in street clothes or pajamas?"

"Slacks and a shirt. Because of, um, him not having any legs, the slacks were pinned up."

Another answer that didn't make sense. Not only would Ernst have had to make the bed-to-wheelchair transfer, but also get dressed. Unless he slept in his clothes. But why would he do that? "Exactly what did he say when he opened the door?"

She gave a bitter laugh. "You think he said, 'So glad you could drop by, my dear'? Not hardly. He asked me what the hell I thought I was doing, banging on his door in the middle of the night."

"To which you said…."

"I asked him if he recognized me."

Her answer took me off guard. "How could Ernst recognize you? You told me that every time you went by the set, you made sure he didn't see you, that all you did was call him on the phone." Now that I considered it, her caution made no sense. What difference would it have made if he saw her or not? She would have been just another spectator.

"Because Daddy always said I looked like his little sister."

Ten-year-old Jenny Bollinger, who'd been murdered in 1944 along with the rest of her family. "Did Ernst recognize you?"

"Only after I said who I was. Well, let me rephrase that. He said he didn't but I'm pretty sure he was lying."

MaryEllen was somewhere in her twenties, and the night she'd gone over to Ernst's house, she had been slathered in stage makeup. Considering the sixty years that had passed since the Bollinger murders, it would have surprising if Ernst saw a family resemblance, even if he'd been in the Bollinger farmhouse in the first place. I dropped that line of questioning. "Tell me about Ernst's house, what it looked like."

She gave me a look of disbelief. "You want the *Better Homes and Gardens* tour?"

"Was it neat? Or did it look like someone had been rifling through things?"

"Say, what's this all about? Are you accusing me of theft? Ernst had nothing I wanted, other than the truth!"

That I believed. MaryEllen didn't have the emotional makeup of a thief. In her own topless dancer way, she was much too naive. "When the police searched the house, it looked like someone had been trying to find something. I'm only trying to discover if that happened before you got there or after." And why Ernst answered the door fully dressed.

"Sorry. I guess I'm pretty touchy these days. The answer to your question is no, the house—what I could see of it—looked perfectly normal. But I never went beyond the living room."

If she was telling the truth, Kryzinski was right, and Rada Tesema was probably the person who'd gone through the house in search of his Star of David, leaving a trail of bloody fingerprints. Hiding my disappointment, I said, "Let's see if I have the time line straight. On the night of Ernst's murder, after your shift at The Skin Factory, you drove over to his house and woke him up. His place hadn't been rifled yet. Afterwards, you drove thirty miles north to Anthem and had a fight with your boyfriend. Tell me, did you get into any more arguments that night? Or after your boyfriend gave you the black eye, did you call it a day and go home?"

She actually laughed. "It does sound crazy when you put it that way, doesn't it? Look, I'll admit I was pretty revved up that night. I'd been planning on getting the truth out of Ernst ever since I found out that he was living here in Scottsdale. And as it happens, Clay had stopped by The Skin Factory just before my shift and told me...Well, never mind what he told me. Let's just say I was feeling pretty pissed off when I left the club and decided that the time was right to settle some old scores."

We talked for a little while longer, but she had no more information to give me. Then, just as I was about to leave, she stopped me. "Don't you want to ask my father about Ernst?"

I stopped dead. "Your father's still alive?"

An odd expression settled on her face. "In a manner of speaking. He has Alzheimer's, and isn't all that lucid anymore. Which is just as well."

The excitement I'd started to feel faded. Alzheimer's meant that his memory, or what remained of it, would be spotty. On the off chance that he might be able to help, I took down the address of his nursing home. At the door, I turned and asked her one final question.

"You said you wanted to settle old scores that night. First with Ernst and then with your boyfriend. Did it work out?"

Her beautiful face looked haunted. "No. Nothing ever does."

From MaryEllen's house, I struggled through the height of
the evening rush hour to Shady Rest Care Home, where Chess
Bollinger was living out the last of his days. Once I arrived at Shady
Rest, which was located in Mesa not far from the Ethiopians'
apartment, I realized what she had meant when she'd said it was
just as well that her father was barely lucid. If, for any reason, I
ever needed to spend some time in such a place, I'd want to be
unaware of my surroundings, too. In a flat-out coma if possible.

On the exterior, the immense Shady Rest looked little worse
than other care homes I'd seen before, with a plain, four-story
brick facade uncluttered by too many windows and "landscaping" consisting of nothing more than stained concrete. But it was
worse—much worse—on the inside. When I walked through the
double doors and onto the stained brown carpet, I was enveloped
by a funereal silence. The stench of near-cremated food, overlaid
with a hint of human waste and Pine-Sol, filled the muggy air
but it didn't appear to bother the gum-chewing receptionist, who
was busy painting her nails a silver-sparkled fuchsia.

I approached her desk and cleared my throat. "I'm here to
see Chess Bollinger."

She didn't bother to raise her dirty, black-rooted blond hair,
just kept slathering on the gaudy polish. "Go on back."

"Back where?"

"Where the patients are." Still no meeting of the eyes.

Her rudeness, as well as the funky smells, annoyed me, so I
leaned over her desk and spoke to the top of her head. "Health
Department been by to inspect your kitchen lately?"

Brown eyes finally gazed insolently into mine. "Last month.
We passed." For emphasis, she cracked her gum.

If the Health Department had passed this place, Shady Rest's
management had probably been tipped off ahead of time that
they were coming and so hurriedly cleaned up. Or maybe money
had passed hands. "How wonderful for you. But I haven't been

here before and I have no idea 'where the patients are' is or what Mr. Bollinger looks like, so if you could give me some directions to his room I'd sure appreciate it. And if you don't, I just might dump that ugly nail polish on your ugly, unwashed head."

I had her attention now. "You don't have to get nasty."

"Nice didn't work. Where's Mr. Bollinger?"

With a put-upon sigh, she opened a drawer and took out a chart. "Bollinger, Bollinger, Bollinger. Yeah. Here it is. He's in room 1173A." She put the chart back in the drawer and started polishing her nails again.

"How do I find 1173A?"

Polish, polish. Then, as I reached for the bottle of sparkly goo, she quickly drew it back and vented another sigh. "Take the first left down that hall, then the first right, then another left at the 'T.' Second room down, on the left. Somebody let you out of your cage too early or something?"

I didn't bother to reply, but as I walked down the dimly lit corridor, I wondered if the receptionist's disinterest in the home's residents was echoed by the rest of the staff, if there was any. I hadn't seen a nurse yet, just elderly residents in dirty dressing gowns tottering along behind their walkers, and a few even less lucky souls who sat slumped in tarnished wheelchairs. To my dismay, I saw a puddle of urine under the wheelchair of one elderly woman who was parked along the corridor wall, but when I called out, no one rushed to clean either it or the woman.

By the time I found room 1173A, my mood was as glum as the surroundings. The door was open so I walked in. No paintings or drawings decorated the room's walls, no cards or photographs from loved ones sat on the tiny table separating the beds. It was as anonymous as Motel 6 but much less lush. There were two men in the room, one in a bed near the window, the other—who appeared to be much smaller than his room-mate—in the bed closest to the door. Both lay amid yellowed sheets, hovering somewhere between sleep and insensibility. This didn't seem to bother the stringy, middle-aged woman sitting in a chair next to the smaller of the two men.

"Are you Mrs. Bollinger?"

She gave me a broad, unsettling smile. "Sure am. Judith. Don't like Judy. If you come to see Chess, you're outta luck. He don't know who he is today." She bore no resemblance to her daughter. Unlike MaryEllen's perfect face, this woman's features were so irregular they could have belonged to two different people. One side of her jaw was higher than the other, and her flat, wide nose tilted unevenly to one side, overshadowing a thin, blurry mouth. She'd taken a few hits in her time.

"That's too bad. I'd hoped to talk to him."

"Chess never did much talkin' even before he got sick." Still that unsettling smile.

What was there to smile about? If that had been my husband lying there in this filthy place, I would be howling with grief. Then I reminded myself that family dynamics could be misleading, and maybe Judith-not-Judy Bollinger couldn't afford better than Shady Rest. Anyway, who was I to judge how a wife should act toward a husband who from what I'd heard had been less than ideal.

Keeping my voice as neutral as possible, I introduced myself and gave her my card. "Maybe you could help. I'm working on a case that may involve the murder of Mr. Bollinger's family back in 1944."

Incredibly, she laughed. "I sure don't know nothing about that! And Chess, he ain't gonna be able to tell you anything, either. His brain's nothin' but mush. Like I was telling you, he don't know who he is on a good day and today sure ain't one of those."

Mush. Or, as MaryEllen had more charitably described his condition, Alzheimer's. "That's okay, Judith. I'll visit with you, then." There was no other chair in the room, so I went back into the hall, found one, and carried it back, carefully wiping the seat before I sat down across from her. "Did your husband ever talk to you about his family?"

"Only to say he didn't kill 'em."

While Judith Bollinger appeared to hold little affection for her husband—and considering his many domestic assault arrests, why should she—that didn't mean she would be willing to air the family's dirty laundry. "Do you believe him?"

Her face reflected total disinterest in her husband's past. "Can't say. Who knows what Chess might a done when he was a kid. He sure wasn't no saint."

Remembering Chess Bollinger's long rap sheet, I figured Judith must have known what she was getting into when she married him, but I refrained from pointing that out. What little remained of the original structure of her face made me suspect that she'd never been a pretty woman, so who knew how lonely she'd been at the time or how desperate?

"Judith, did Chess continue to deny his involvement when he got, ah, sick? Sometimes people like to get things off their chest when they're diagnosed with a serious illness."

"Nope. Only the same old same old, that he didn't do it."

We'd been talking about Chess as if he weren't in the room, but a sound from the bed reminded me that he was still very much there. "Ah...ah...Jen...Jen..."

Judith looked over at him, her smile gone. "That's Jenny, his little sister. He's always callin' for her. Don't know why. You'd think he'd say my name. Or MaryEllen's. But no, it's Jen, Jen, nothin' but Jen. Kinda make me wonder, ya know?"

I didn't answer. As far as I was concerned, that particular piece of dirty laundry could stay in the family hamper. In the silence that followed, I studied the ruin that remained of Chess Bollinger. The shrunken old felon had the caved-in look of the near-terminal, with cheekbones jutting out so sharply from his cadaverous face that it was a wonder they didn't pierce his skin. His eyes, milky with cataracts, stared at the ceiling without really seeing it. If it weren't for the rhythmic rise and fall of the sheet covering his chest, anyone passing by might think the old man already dead.

But I was encouraged by his brief words. "Judith, is it all right if I ask your husband a few questions?"

For a moment she looked like she'd say no, but then she gave a little wave of acquiescence. "Ask whatever but don't get your hopes up. He ain't made sense in years."

When I leaned over him, a musty odor, as if he hadn't been bathed in days, rose to meet me. More for his wife's sake than his, I tried not to show my disgust even though I doubted if he could tell whether he was in a nursing home or on Mars. "Mr. Bollinger? Chess? I'm Lena Jones, a private detective who's investigating the murder of a Kapitan Erik Ernst, one of those escaped POWs from old Camp Papago. I'm also looking at the murder of your family because I think the Germans might be connected. Do you know anything you never told the police?"

A hitch in his breathing. A blink, then his eyes seemed to focus on my face. "Jen. Jenny Jenny Jen."

"Yes, Mr. Bollinger. Your sister Jenny died that night, along with your brothers Rob and Scott. And your parents."

His hand, no more substantial than a dried collection of sticks, fluttered toward mine. "Jen."

Judith gave me a frown. "Maybe he can see your hair. Jenny was blond, like you. But in her face she looked like Mary Ellen. I got her picture back at the house. Ain't leavin' it here. People steal things."

I took Chess Bollinger's hand and gave it a slight squeeze. "Yes, Chess, it's Jen. Do you know who hurt me?" In the background, I heard his wife gasp at my lie. Well, private detectives seldom get confused with George Washington.

"Jenny Jen?" His voice was no louder than leaves on pavement. "Daddy hurt."

Was he saying that his daddy was hurt? Or that his own daddy had hurt his family, tied them to the kitchen chairs, beaten them to death, then went outside and blew off his own head with the shotgun? Such personal family massacres had happened many times before, even in Scottsdale, but even allowing for the less sophisticated state of forensics during the Forties, how could such an appalling scenario have passed the detectives by? I squeezed Bollinger's hand again. "Did Daddy kill me?"

When his eyes closed I thought I'd lost him. Then they opened again. "Spilt milk. The gas said it. Mama cried."

The gas said it?

Judith tsked-tsked. "Told ya. That's word salad. The Alzheimer's, it makes them put words together that don't belong, 'specially late in the day like this when they get tired. Sundowning, the doctor calls it, because these Alzheimer's people, their minds is gone by sundown."

I ignored her. "Chess, what exactly did the gas say?"

"Ran ran ran ran ran."

"The gas ran?"

"Me. I ran. After the gas said."

"You ran because the gas said something?"

"It told on me."

"Told *what* on you, Chess?"

He didn't answer. Perhaps it was only my hopeful imagination, but I thought he was trying his best to answer my questions. As with stroke victims, though, there was a big gulf between intent and performance. Gas talking, Chess running. They might have been connected to that bloody day in 1944, but they could also be pieces of disparate memory jumbled together by the ravages of his disease. I decided to start again, from the beginning.

"Chess, it's Jen. Your sister. Who killed me?"

He began to speak but only wet grunts came out, and a thin trail of saliva leaked from his gaping mouth. Using the corner of the bed sheet, I wiped him dry as his wife sat motionless beside me, that discomfiting smile back on her face. Chess remained silent for the next few minutes, then started the word salad all over again. "Gas. Christmas killed me and Mama cried."

Christmas. His family was killed on Christmas Day. Something happened with the gas that upset his mother.

He wasn't through. "Daddy hate hate Daddy hate hate hate the gas hit Mama when she cried."

Judith Bollinger spoke up again. "You ain't getting nothin' more. Once he starts that gas stuff he's over for the day."

Maybe. But I was intrigued by his linking "Daddy" and "hate." Not to mention "hit."

Trying once more, I said in his ear, "You hated Daddy, Chess?"

"Oooooh, hated!" He twisted his head toward me and for a brief moment, less than a second, the eyes that met mine were clear. "Poor Jenny Jen. All my fault."

"What was your fault, Chess? Did you kill Daddy?"

Suddenly his hand gripped mine with the strength of a much younger man. Using me for leverage, he pulled himself up and let loose a banshee wail. "Not me not me not me not meeeeeeeeeeeeee!"

Chapter Twelve

As I drove away from the misery of Shady Rest, I realized I either had to get drunk or see Warren again. Since I didn't drink, Warren won. There was a chance he was still at the set, but the light was fading and already ribbons of purple, pink, and orange streaked the sky. If I didn't catch him there, I could probably find him at the Chinese buffet near the Best Western where the film crew usually ate dinner. But I'd timed my arrival well. Warren was still in Papago Park, standing beside a cameraman, listening to Frank Oberle who sounded pretty rough at this point—describe the aftermath of the POWs' escape. Oberle was sitting next to the reconstructed bathhouse that hid the Germans' tunnel. To his right, a bank of lights glared through a mesquite tree, casting eerie shadows across the ground in front of him. Lit like this, Papago Park looked more like a setting for a Wes Craven horror flick than a World War II documentary.

"We didn't find the tunnel 'til several days after the Germans flew the coop," Oberle croaked, trying hard to ignore the boom mike hovering over his head. "They'd hid the entrance between this here bathhouse and a coal bin, then camouflaged it with dirt and weeds so you couldn't tell it from the rest of the ground. Same with the tunnel's exit over there by the Cross Cut Canal. Smart sonsabitches, they was. Hell. I'm done, Warren. It's been fun and all that, but my voice is shot."

"Cut!" Warren showed no annoyance as the old guard spit on the ground and limped out of camera range. He turned to me with a smile, but it disappeared quickly. "What's wrong?"

I remembered Rada Tesema's desperation, the stench of Shady Rest, and Chess Bollinger's screams. The looming loss of Jimmy and Kryzinski. "Just a hard day at the office."

Oblivious to everyone's stares, he put his arms around me and held me close. It felt so right. "What can I do to make you feel better?"

Now there was a leading question. "I'm fine, really," I said into his chest.

"You always are." When he released me and drew back, his face was filled with concern. "I have an idea. Why don't we take a ride in the Golden Hawk and have dinner in some place far away from all this? How about that place you were telling the cameraman about, the Horny Toad, in Cave Creek? Or was it Carefree?"

Burgers at the Horny Toad sounded great, but even better was the idea of being out on the open road with Warren. The neighboring villages of Cave Creek/Carefree lay about twenty-five miles north of Papago Park, the perfect distance for an evening drive. I looked toward the halogen-lit parking lot and saw the Golden Hawk parked next to Warren's leased Land Rover. "You already bought it?"

He grinned. "Not yet. But watch this." He called over to Mark Schank, who was talking film with Lindsey. "Hey, Mark, you mind if I take the Golden Hawk out for a spin?"

Schank's smile dwarfed his thin face. It was the opposite of Lindsey's glare. "Anywhere you want, but bring it back in one piece or you've bought it."

Warren gave me a squeeze. "Told you. Mark's desperate to sell the thing to someone from the film community. He sees us as his next big market."

Shank gave a dry laugh. "Oh, I've sold to the film community before. And writers. Clive Cussler bought two of my cars."

The idea of going for a spin in the Golden Hawk lightened my mood. Modern cars, which in my opinion all looked alike, bore me, which is why I drive a '45 Jeep. Show me something with a bit of style and I get all gushy. "Are you still thinking about the '57?" The '57, a tail-finned version of the Golden Hawk, was owned by a rival dealer at the same autoplex as Schank Classic Cars. "I think that one's prettier." I preferred the '57's two-tone fawn-and-doeskin color scheme to the '56's gold-and-white.

"Prettier, maybe, but it's an automatic, which I'm not crazy about. I like the '56, a three-speed stick with overdrive, very rare. There were only 786 of them made, so it's more collectible."

More expensive, too, I bet.

As Warren and I climbed into the Golden Hawk (retrofitted with three-point safety harness), Schank asked, "Could you give me a lift back to the autoplex? I've been so caught up in the filming that I'm late, and I'm supposed to call Tokyo in a half-hour."

Although the autoplex was less than a half-mile away in a straight line over Papago Park's rocky ground, Warren happily assented. I offered to sit in the rear seat, but Mark refused. "No problemo. In those days, they made two-doors a lot easier to maneuver in, especially for small-statured people like me, so I'll slip in the back. Getting out won't be a big deal."

The night was warm and soft so Warren kept the windows down. As we cruised along Sixty-Fourth Street toward the autoplex, the scents of sage and gasoline combined in an odd potpourri. A true salesman, Mark chattered the entire way. "I hear your pretty detective friend is working for that Tesema fellow, Ernst's caretaker. That must be something."

Warren uh-huhed.

"I wasn't that surprised to hear that Tesema'd been arrested. He seemed pleasant enough, but you know these immigrants." Sensing that his comment might not be too politic, Mark switched to a safer topic. "My family's lived here since Arizona was a territory. They used to trade with the Pimas."

"Is that so?" From the tone of his voice, I could tell Warren wasn't interested.

"Yeah. Beads for beans. Maybe the Pimas are best known for their cotton, but they raised great beans. The canals around here? Those were originally Pima irrigation canals. For their crops. Great farmers, those Pimas."

"That's what I hear."

I tried to hide my smile, but Warren saw it out of the corner of his eye and gave my knee a squeeze. A warm Arizona night, a beautiful car, a handsome man—what more could a woman want? All we needed now was to get rid of the yakky car salesman.

But Mark was oblivious to my impatience. "Yep, and they made good neighbors, too. Never caused any trouble. Don't know what the family would have done without them. For a while there, we Schanks ran cattle all the way from where we are now clear out to the Superstition Mountains. Course, these days, a lot of that is reservation property. You should have seen the old Schank ranch house, a big adobe built in the 1850s. It was really something. But we tore it down."

Being more than slightly interested in historical preservation, I spoke up. "Are you telling me your family tore down an original Territorial adobe?"

Realizing he'd screwed up again, Mark backtracked. "Uh, it wasn't my decision. I was only a kid when that happened. My father said it was a mess and not worth restoring. But who knows? The old place must've seen plenty of history. Before he died, my great-grandfather said that Wyatt Earp once spent the night there. Geronimo and his band were supposed to have camped nearby, too. Not that I know for sure if any of that's true, you understand. One thing I'm certain of, even though it happened long before I was born. Two of those Germans from Camp Papago surrendered to my grandmother."

Warren's response was as dramatic as mine. Just before the entrance to the autoplex, he pulled over to the curb and looked into the back seat. "Are you serious?"

Mark flushed. "Well, yeah. Maybe I should have mentioned it before, but my grandparents have both been dead for years now, and Dad, who was just a kid when it happened, he's in bad health these days and doesn't want anything to do with the documentary. He'll be pissed if he finds out I told you."

I was thrilled by the possibility of a lone woman bringing the escaped Germans to heel. Shades of Ken Follet's *Eye of the*

Needle, one of my favorite World War II thrillers. "Mark, was your grandmother out hunting when she ran into them?"

He gave us a shame-faced laugh. "Hardly. The story goes that she was hanging out the wash when they walked up to her and surrendered. Dad—who was over by the barn when it happened—said they looked like hell. Cold, wet, in rags and half-starved. Grandma took them into the kitchen, fed them some macaroni and cheese and warmed them up with hot chocolate. Dad recalls those German boys as being meek as lambs, but says that Grandpa was a lot less trusting than Grandma and kept his rifle trained on them."

My mind raced. "Was Ernst one of the men?" Then I remembered he'd been captured by two field hands.

Schank shook his head. "Sorry. They were just two enlisted guys. The newspapers didn't even print their names. Now, let's forget I brought it up, OK?"

Warren ignored Mark's plea for secrecy. "I want to talk to your father. It'd be great to have someone on film who actually saw two of the Germans surrender."

"Sorry." But Mark's face was a study in conflict, and I could see him weighing the chances of selling the Golden Hawk against his reluctance to provoke his father's ire. "It won't work. I wasn't exaggerating when I said that Dad's in bad health. He's suffering from emphysema and has to stay hooked up to an oxygen tank all the time. I run the business more or less by myself these days. Dad lives in Carefree and seldom leaves the house."

Warren was merciless. "Hey, Lena, wasn't that '57 Hawk a sweet-looking car?"

I played along. "Gorgeous. Much sweeter than this ratty old '56. Newer, too."

Another sigh emanated from the back seat. "OK. I'll talk to Dad."

After dropping Mark off at the autoplex, where he promised to call his father before he called Japan, Warren and I headed for

Cave Creek and the Horny Toad. The Hawk was the kind of car you cruised, not pushed, so although it could have easily kept up with high-speed traffic, Warren bypassed the Pima Freeway and its congestion, opting instead for Scottsdale Road. At some point, the Hawk's original radio had been overhauled and while remaining monaural, it brought in the local Golden Oldies station clearly. One saguaro cactus after another swept past us, disappearing into the lavender twilight, while a Fifties doo-wop group harmonized on "Earth Angel." As the sun disappeared below the horizon, emitting a final burst of color, I snuggled close to Warren, breathing in male sweat and Acqua di Gio.

"I like this car."

He squeezed my knee again. "So do I. I've already made up my mind to buy it, but I want Mark to dangle in the wind for a while, maybe get the price down."

I rubbed my hand across the Golden Hawk's silvery dash. "Why don't they design cars like this anymore? It's so simple and sleek."

"Because human beings aren't simple and sleek any more. Life is more complex, and we all have to split ourselves off in dozens of different pieces to deal with it. Our cars reflect that. And I'm no different. Back home, I usually drive the Mercedes because I wouldn't risk one of my classic babies on the L.A. freeways. But when I take one out for a drive along the Coast Highway, I think about the people who once drove it, the simpler time they lived in, their bedrock values. Today everything's so unfocused. There's no cohesive vision of what life is all about and where any of us is headed." He paused, and his voice was uncharacteristically emotional when he continued. "To paraphrase Yeats' poem, 'Things are falling apart, and the center's not holding.'"

To an extent, I agreed with him. Through the rosy lens of Time, the past always looked better, and it was in some ways, discounting a war here and there. As we drove up Scottsdale Road past the upscale strip malls that had replaced cholla and saguaro, I tried to envision what Scottsdale had looked like at the time the Germans escaped. The tiny town was surrounded by ranches and farms then, but the artists that eventually made Scottsdale famous had already started trickling in. The big resorts were going up, too, and both the El Chorro Lodge and the Jokake Inn had begun attracting high-rollers wanting to get away from the big city hustle. Frank Lloyd Wright had just established a rough camp north of town which years later would be known as Taliesin West.

There was a dark side to this rural simplicity, though. Racism of the Old West variety was rampant, and neither the Pima Indians nor the Mexican laborers who were building the city with their sweat and muscle were welcome in most of its establishments. As the war ground on, increasing numbers of Scottsdale High's graduates were being shipped to Europe and the Philippines. The mothers of those who never made it back were given the cold comfort of posting Gold Stars in their windows.

Suddenly the night seemed chilly and I wished I'd brought a jacket. "Maybe things were always falling apart, but without television commentators to sound the alarm, nobody knew."

He looked over at me, an astonished look on his face. "That's a damned deep thought."

"My stock in trade." Snuggling closer to him, I decided to lighten the subject. "Your little plan worked well the other night, by the way. I was impressed that you still get along with your ex-wife. Why'd you get divorced, if you don't mind my asking."

He raised his eyebrows again. "I thought you…Ah, something tells me you don't read *People* magazine. Or watch *Entertainment Tonight*. She left me for one of her co-stars." He named a suspiciously brawny actor known mainly for his work in action movies. "They met on the set of 'Komor the Magnificient.' She was playing Princess A'tali."

"I take it he was Komor."

"Right. At least old Komor is doing his best to be a good step-father. He's even enrolled the girls with his own martial arts instructor. I'll be afraid of them in a few years. Hell, I already am."

"I'll bet you miss them."

"Of course I do." He was silent for a while, and I listened to the sound of the night wind whipping by. After a few minutes, he looked over. "Listen, Lena, I think it's time I told you more about myself, that I…" I never heard what Warren was going to say next about this messed-up world, because ahead of us loomed a sign, THIS WAY TO HAPPY TRAILS DUDE RANCH, and his attention shifted. "Hey, isn't that where your ex-boyfriend works?" There was relief in his voice, as if he was glad to change the subject.

"Dusty? He used to, but he lost his job."

"A drinking problem, I think you told me. Too bad. People grab all kinds of lifelines when they're in trouble, but sometimes those lifelines are worse than the original problem."

"Yeah, I know." But why did he?

We drove on through the night for a little while, until, at my direction, he made a left onto Cave Creek Road. "Hey, aren't we passing through Carefree right now?"

"Yeah. But the Horny Toad's in Cave Creek. Keep on going straight and we'll be there in five minutes."

"Carefree's where Mark said his father lives. Why don't we…?"

"Got ya." I hauled my cell phone out of my carry-all and dialed information. Gilbert Schank had an unlisted phone number, but that meant nothing. I next dialed Jimmy's trailer, where his computer set-up mirrored the one at Desert Investigations. Within minutes he gave me Schank's phone number and address. I thanked him and hung up.

Warren looked impressed. "Wasn't that illegal?"

"Sure was. You going to turn me in?"

"Not while you're still under contract to Living History Productions."

With both of us laughing, he turned the Golden Hawk north off Cave Creek Road into the foothills of Carefree, and after getting briefly lost amid the unlighted, snaky dirt roads, we found ourselves driving up to a sprawling, Territorial-styled house that had more to do with an architect's fantasies than it did with Arizona history. The "adobe" wasn't real adobe, either, just plain old stucco with attitude. For this, the Schank family had torn down the real thing. As they say, there's no accounting for taste.

When we exited the Golden Hawk, a roadrunner hightailed it past us. Warren let out a laugh. "What the hell was that?"

"A roadrunner. Don't you watch cartoons?"

He grinned. "Gotcha. If there's a roadrunner, there must be a coyote."

I laughed. "There's probably a hundred coyotes nearby, but unless they have rabies, they won't bother us."

"Thanks for that little reassurance."

Gilbert Schank's housekeeper, a young Navajo woman, answered the door and told us that he wasn't receiving visitors. "Mr. Schank is unwell."

Before I could say anything, Warren thrust his business card into her hand. "That's unfortunate. I'm Warren Quinn, of Living History Productions. Maybe you know my work? I received an Oscar for *Native Peoples, Foreign Chains.*"

The young woman's eyes lit up. "I saw that documentary, my entire family did! It played the movie house in Window Rock for a whole month. You're really that guy? The one who interviewed Leonard Peltier in prison and told the world he'd been railroaded?"

"That's me. And you are Ms…"

"Evelyn. Evelyn Tsosie. Leonard and the rest of the warriors in the American Indian Movement are my heroes."

Warren's smile gleamed in the light spilling from the doorway. "A great cause. Listen, Ms. Tsosie, I'm working on another historical documentary right now and I think Mr. Schank can help me with it. I promise that if talking to us appears to bother him, we'll leave."

Tsosie looked doubtful, but she was also obviously tempted to help the man who had brought her people's grievances to the big screen. "Wait here." She closed the door softly and was gone for almost five minutes, which is longer than it sounds when you're standing on a doorstep in the dark, until she returned with a smile. "I told him who you are and what your film did for my people. He says to come on in."

Gilbert Schank was no fool. When you lived way out here in God's country, keeping your housekeeper happy was of prime importance.

She ushered us through the foyer and into the living room, which was the size of some barns and decorated in much the same way. Brightly colored stable blankets were tossed over two deep leather sofas, and various farm and ranch implements—possibly from the old Schank spread—were scattered throughout the room. In the corner stood a hoe that had been made into a floor lamp, while separating the two sofas was a battered plowshare underneath a panel of smoked glass that served as a cocktail table. The only reminder that Schank had founded one of the country's largest collectible car businesses was the large Leroy Neiman painting on the back wall depicting a gleaming black Cord.

Warren shrugged off the Cord as if it were a third-hand Chevy Nova. "Impressive, but it's no Golden Hawk."

A deep chuckle drew our attention behind us. "I just got off the phone with Mark...and he told me he was trying to...sell you that '56."

I turned to see Gilbert Schank sitting in a motorized wheelchair, a tube running from an oxygen tank to his nostrils. He no longer resembled the wiry little man who, in his old television commercials, sat astride a large palomino while he extolled the offerings of his vast autoplex. Now his nose was the biggest thing about him. His chest was sunken and his slacks hung loosely over toothpick legs. But although his body appeared as wizened as Chess Bollinger's, his eyes sparkled with total awareness.

"The Hawk's one sweet-running car, even if it is a bit overpriced," Warren said, without missing a beat.

"A steal at...twice the price!" Schank murmured something to Tsosie, and after she gave his oxygen tank a final check, she walked away. Motioning his head toward her as she left the room, Schank said, with halting breath, "Don't get any ideas

that…I'm taking unfair advantage of the…indigenous population. I put Evelyn's mother through college…now I'm doing
the same for her."

"I didn't say…"

Schank's chuckle trailed off into a wheeze as he waved us
toward a sofa. "Now, now, Mr. Quinn. I saw…*Native Peoples,
Foreign Chains*, and I'd be…a fool not to know where you're
coming from. So before…my oxygen tank here runs out…what
can I do for you?"

Warren and I settled ourselves on the sofa, and I let him take
the lead. "I'd like you to tell your story on film, about watching
those two Germans surrender to your mother. You wouldn't have
to come out to the set at Papago Park. We'd bring the equipment
to you and it wouldn't take more than an hour."

In the silence that followed, I could hear the hiss of the oxygen
bottle and the rustle of plastic. Adult diapers? Before Schank
spoke, I knew what his answer would be. "I'm past…caring
about all that," the old man said. "They're all dead, anyway…so
what does it matter?"

Warren wasn't about to give up without a fight. "You're wrong
there. Frank Oberle, one of the camp guards, is still alive and
he's in the documentary. And of course, I'm sure you've read that
Erik Ernst filmed a couple of scenes before he was…"

Schank cut in with a wry smile. "Before he…was murdered.
We get the newspapers…up here." He thought for a moment.
"Sorry. The answer is…no. I can't offer anything…that would
help your film. And I don't want…people to see me like this.
Let them remember me…on my palomino."

Warren took his refusal with grace. "I understand, sir. But if you
change your mind, will you give me a call?" He handed Schank a
different card than the one than he'd given to Tsosie. "That's my
private cell phone number. You can reach me at any time."

He rose to leave but I held him back. As long as we were
here, I had a few questions of my own. "Mr. Schank, since you
grew up in Scottsdale, do you remember anything about the
Bollinger murders? An entire family…"

Schank's crevassed face twitched. "I remember. They were…
slaughtered. Horrible."

"Scottsdale was smaller in those days than Carefree is now
and most people knew each other. Did you know any of the
victims personally?"

He shook his head. "No. Everybody was all…spread out.
There wasn't any…Scottsdale as such. But my dad knew…
Edward…the father. Now, there…was a son of a bitch."

For a moment I didn't know what to say. Gilbert Schank had
skipped Dear Abby's advice to never speak ill of the dead. "Um,
why do you say that, Mr. Scha…?"

"Gilbert, for God's sake. Pretty woman…like you shouldn't
sound…so formal."

"Okay, Gilbert. Why do you call Edward Bollinger a son of
a bitch?"

His chuckle this time was long and dark, but it took away so
much of his breath that in the end, he could only gasp, "Dad
said…mean." Then he closed his eyes and took a few deep hits
of oxygen.

"He beat his kids, is that what you're talking about?"

"That, too." A few more hits. "But I…meant *mean*…in the
other…sense. Dad told me he…was stingy. Counted every…
penny. Wasn't poor but sent his kids…to school in rags." He
fiddled with his tank and the hissing sound increased.

I knew our time with him was running out, so I cut to the
chase. "Mr. Sch…uh, Gilbert, who do you think killed the
Bollinger family?"

The look he gave me was steady but his voice was not. "Like I
said, I was…just a kid. But I always suspected…it was Thomas."
He began to cough.

I waited until he caught his breath, then asked, "Thomas
who?"

As he was about to answer, Tsosie came hurrying into the
room. "I heard him cough." She knelt down beside him, eased
a little more air into the line, then smoothed his perspiring

forehead. He looked at her in gratitude when she said, "You'd better go."

Warren stood up to leave but, fearing this might be my last chance to pump the old man for information, I remained sitting.

"Thomas who, Gilbert?"

Somehow the old man summoned the strength to answer. "Guy who...found...them. Thomas. Edward's...kid brother."

The papers had said that the bodies were found by a family member, but had not named the specific person. When at last I found my voice, I sounded almost as breathless as Gilbert. "Edward's kid brother? But...okay. If Thomas Bollinger didn't get along with his brother, I can see it, maybe. Old grudges ending in a fight, something like that. But why would Thomas kill the whole family?"

"Usual...reason. Money. Edward...had money. Hated Chess and...disinherited him. With rest of...family...dead... Thomas...got it...all."

The last glimmer of light had faded as, with radio blasting, Warren and I headed west along Cave Creek Road toward the Horny Toad. My stomach grumbled, but I was too excited to pay it too much attention. Could Thomas Bollinger possibly still be alive and in decent enough health to do what had been done to Kapitan Ernst? Also, I wondered why MaryEllen hadn't mentioned her uncle. Possibly I could find out tomorrow when I had lunch with Fay Harris. She might have written something about Thomas that didn't make it into her book due to fears of a lawsuit. In the meantime, I turned the car radio down, fished my cell phone out of my carry-all, and punched in Jimmy's number again.

When he answered, he sounded annoyed. "Lena, I have company."

"Who's there? Esther?"

"Yes, Esther and Rebecca. I'm fixing barbeque. The picnic table's all set up and everything."

I could see them now, Jimmy's soon-to-be-family, sitting under the reservation sky, listening to night birds and coyotes. He'd better enjoy that wild ambience now, because when Esther was finished with him, he would be char-broiling burgers for fussy suburbanites. For now, though, he was still my partner. "I don't need this tonight, Jimmy, but I'd appreciate it if first thing in the morning you'd look up Thomas Bollinger, Edward Bollinger's younger brother, and find out whatever you can. I want to know what happened to him after the murders, what kind of money he came into, and most importantly, if he's still alive." A vision of Chess Bollinger flashed into my mind. "And, uh, if he still has all his faculties."

"Tomorrow. Fine." The tension was gone from his voice. "See you then." Without waiting for me to say good-by, he hung up.

Warren gave me a sideways glace. "You're efficient."

I stuffed the phone back into my carry-all. "You have to be in my business."

"Mine, too." He turned the radio back up in the middle of the Del Vikings' "Come Go With Me," one of my Golden Oldies favorites.

I settled back against the Golden Hawk's seat, trying to put Tesema's woes and Jimmy's defection out of my mind. The night was peaceful and I was with the man I loved. What more could I want?

Then an announcer interrupted the Del Viking's harmonies.

"Breaking news from the KGLD newsroom. Popular Scottsdale journalist Fay Harris was found shot to death this evening in her apartment building parking lot. Harris, who has been nominated for a Pulitzer Prize for her coverage of illegal immigrant deaths in the desert, was also the author of *Escape Across the Desert*, now being filmed by Oscar-winning director Warren Quinn. Harris' neighbors say they heard shots…"

Suddenly the night didn't seem so peaceful.

Chapter Thirteen

December 26, 1944

Gunter Hoenig hadn't slept all night. Wrapped in a blanket they had stolen from the farmhouse, he lay huddled against Josef in an arroyo several miles east, fighting the nightmare images that visited every time he closed his eyes. The man by the barn, the woman and children in the farmhouse! Even now the dying woman pleaded with him to help her. Oh, if he only had moved faster and stayed the tire iron before Das Kapitan brought it down on her. But, no, he had remained standing for that one fatal second, unwilling to believe what was about to happen.

He shut his eyes more tightly and turned his face into Josef's warm back, but more memories rushed in. The wounded American sailors gunned down as they swam away from their burning ship, the boatload of peaceful Jews Kapitan had so gleefully torpedoed.

As if roused by Gunter's thoughts, Kapitan stumbled up from his rocky bed on the other side of Josef and moved further down the arroyo. Soon he disappeared into a thicket of weeds, but his nearby presence was heralded by the faint grunts of a man answering Nature's call.

Taking this opportunity—the first since they left the farmhouse—Gunter shook Josef. "Wake up! We must leave this place!" he whispered. He placed his hand across Josef's mouth so that his friend could not cry out.

Josef awoke. After nodding understanding, he pushed Gunter's hand away. "Are the Americans near?"

Gunter shook his head. "We must go back to Camp Papago and tell the authorities what we have seen. Those people in the farmhouse..."

Tears sprang to Josef's eyes and his voice trembled. "Such a tragedy. The children..." He swallowed, swept his tangles of auburn hair out of his face, and began again. "Kapitan was so grieved to find those poor people dead. While you were bundling food into the blankets, we prayed together for their souls. Oh, how his heart broke! But for us to return to Camp Papago now, what good would that do? God has already gathered those poor people to his bosom and our surrender will not change that. We must remain faithful to Kapitan's plan."

Kaptian prayed for their souls? Ach, such hypocrisy! Why had Josef...? Too late Gunter remembered that Josef had been in the other room gathering blankets and not seen Kapitan kill the woman. Three years younger than himself and reassigned to U-237 a mere month before capture, Josef had been spared the killing of the American sailors, the Jews, and the worst of Ernst's violence toward his own crew. In Josef's eyes, Kapitan was the flower of the Fatherland, the savior who would lead them to Mexico.

Gunter forgave his friend's naivete. Josef was only eighteen, too young to be a submariner, too young to be a father to the baby now growing in his even younger wife's belly. Too young to know the world. And too young to be left to the nonexistent mercies of Das Kapitan.

With great sadness, Gunter whispered, "If you will not go with me, Josef, then I will stay with you."

He lay back down beside his friend, hoping that he had made the right decision.

Chapter Fourteen

Fay Harris' body lay propped against the open door of her Nissan, her dead eyes looking into the night. Powder burns stippled the edge of the star-shaped hole in her forehead. Not the ugliest crime scene I'd attended, but ugly enough that I was glad I'd talked Warren into dropping me off at my Jeep and going home to his motel.

With a warning shout, Captain Kryzinski walked toward me. "Lena, get back! This has nothing to do with you."

"Yes, it does. We were supposed to have lunch tomorrow."

"Somebody just canceled your date." Whenever Kryzinski was upset, he attempted to hide it with gallows humor. It never worked. His compassion always leaked out in one way or another. Maybe his relationship with Fay had ended years earlier, but he still cared for her and it showed.

I tried to steady my own voice. Fay and I had known each other for a long time, and her murder hit me hard. "Fay was going to tell me about some of the interviews she didn't use for the book."

"What book?" No wonder he'd been a lousy detective. Every thought he had was always plastered all over his face. He knew damned well what book.

My anger and guilt steadied me. "Quit screwing with me. She was as convinced as I am that the Bollinger murders are tied to Ernst's."

Kryzinski scowled back. "The same perp? That would be something to see, some octogenarian perpetrating a drive-by.

Think he was playing gangsta rap in his Flivver when he popped her one? Leave the murder investigations to the police, Lena. You're way off base here." Then his voice caught. "Oh, Jesus, poor Fay. We...we've had our differences over the years, but she was one of the best. Always played it straight."

Popped her one. The phrase gave him away but he was too upset to notice. Drive-bys were usually sprays, and it looked to me that Harris had only been shot once. "What caliber?"

He flicked a look back at the body, saw what I could see, and gave up the games. "Probably a nine millimeter, but we'll have to wait for the ballistics report. There's some stippling, so the perp was up close and personal."

"You think she knew him?"

He cleared his throat. "We probably shouldn't be so certain it's a 'him.'"

An image of MaryEllen Bollinger flashed through my mind, then back out again. What reason would she have had to kill Fay? She would have been more interested to have the reporter on her side, digging for the truth about the Bollinger family tragedy. Then I recalled something else. "When I talked to Fay earlier, she was on her way to interview the mayor about some sexual harassment claim." It wouldn't be the first time a reporter had been murdered just before breaking a big story.

A pained smile. "We know about that, and the accuser's already recanted. It turned out to be nothing more than an attempted financial shake-down. The mayor's so pissed she filed charges. If you ask me who killed Fay, which you haven't, I'd say it was coyotes."

Coyotes, the two-legged kind, the men who for a fee smuggled Mexican illegals into the U.S. These days, the coyotes' favorite trick was to herd the illegals into small houses and hold them for ransom until their families back in Mexico paid up. If the families didn't, well, dead illegals with execution-style bullet wounds were cropping up all over Arizona these days. Fay had included this nasty turn of events in her Pulitzer-nominated series, and word was out that the coyotes were none too pleased.

Surely she wouldn't have let one of them get close enough to…to do what he did.

When I said so to Kryzinski, he blinked his eyes rapidly for a few seconds, then he made a big show of pretending the tungsten glare of the parking lot lights bothered him. "Maybe her source killed her. That coyote information sure sounded like she'd talked to someone on the inside. Maybe whoever leaked was covering his tracks."

"A coyote Deep Throat? Then why would he wait until *after* the articles were printed?"

"Who knows how coyotes think? Now, you'll have to excuse me but I need to get back to work, to make sure…to make sure she's treated right." He turned and walked away, but not before I saw the tears in his eyes.

I took one final look at Fay's body then returned to my Jeep, which I'd parked down the street from the apartment complex. But I didn't drive away immediately. For a while, I sat frozen in position, worrying about my own culpability. If I hadn't asked Fay to help me with the Ernst case, would she still be alive?

I didn't sleep much that night. Every time I started to drift off, I'd see Fay's face, and guilt jolted me back into wakefulness. By the time morning rolled around, I was exhausted. When I finally made it downstairs to Desert Investigations, I found Jimmy sitting at his desk reading the *Scottsdale Journal*. Once again, Fay had made the front page, over the fold.

"She was a friend of yours, wasn't she? Want to talk about it?"

"No." I've never been big on sharing my sorrows. "Just give me whatever you've managed to dig up on the Ernst or Bollinger cases." Crying wouldn't bring Fay back to life, but at least I could find out who killed her.

"Are you sure you…?"

"Jimmy, just get me the damned information!"

He put the *Journal* down and handed me a big stack of computer printouts. "Here. After I heard about Fay, I came in early and ran this off. You wanted me to find out what I could about Thomas Bollinger? Well, I did, and he's still alive, or at least he was last month when he was ticketed for speeding on SR-60."

The printout was heavy in my hand. "Are you serious? The guy has to be in his eighties."

"Check out the car."

I scanned the first page. Bollinger's ride was a 2006 Lotus Esprit V8 Twin Turbo. No wonder he was speeding. Further examination of the printout showed me that Bollinger was a long way from being as cash-strapped as much of Arizona's elderly population. He enjoyed a credit rating Donald Trump could only dream about. After inheriting his older brother's estate, he formed T-Bol Enterprises, a company which developed golf resorts all around the country. T-Bol's best-known Arizona project was The Greening, an upscale retirement golf community near Gold Canyon Ranch, about thirty miles east of Scottsdale.

Unlike Gilbert Schank, who'd turned his autoplex over to his son, Bollinger appeared still very much in charge of his company. He had also apparently inherited his older brother's propensity for using his fists. In 1955 he'd been arrested for assault outside a Phoenix bar, but the charges had been dropped after it became clear that the other two men attacked him first. The same sort of thing occurred in 1963, but after that case was also resolved in his favor, he managed to stay out of trouble. Unless you counted the impressive array of speeding tickets he'd accumulated over the years. Yet despite his need for speed, Bollinger had only racked up one recorded car accident in his long driving career; and the other driver—a sixteen-year-old girl—was determined to be at fault. In addition to Bollinger's personal information, Jimmy had also downloaded several pages detailing his business dealings, the various charities he was active in, and the community service awards he'd received.

No more bar fights showed up, but it was obvious that the man had a temper. And his inheritance after Edward Bollinger's death bothered me. I told Jimmy so.

Jimmy's face remained impassive. "Skip ahead to page twelve."

Page twelve informed me that in 1943, Corporal Thomas Bollinger was shot in the arm while clearing out a machine gun nest near Salerno, Italy. His wound must have been minor, because three days later, he charged into a bombed-out school, killed a German sniper with his bayonet, and was shot again on the way out while carrying another wounded soldier to safety. He received a Silver Star to go along with his Purple Heart. But not long afterwards, something happened that rendered these courageous acts irrelevant. In early 1944, he was given a dishonorable discharge, stripped of his medals, and shipped back to the U.S.

I flipped through the rest of the printout but could find no details on Bollinger's fall from military grace. Dropping the heavy stack of papers onto my desk, I said, "What did he do? Frag a lieutenant?"

Jimmy looked regretful. "I was lucky to get what I did. Most of that came from some old guy's memoirs on one of those World War II websites. The poster was the man Bollinger rescued at Salerno. His post was dated May 2002, and a month later, someone identifying himself as a son posted a message saying that his father died of a coronary. The site's being kept up as a memorial."

For the next couple of hours I buried myself in paperwork so as not to dwell on Fay Harris' murder and the part I might have played in it. But by noon I couldn't stand it anymore, so I called Captain Kryzinski to see if there had been any developments. God help me, I was hoping her murder *was* a drive-by.

Kryzinski gave me no comfort. "We canvassed the neighborhood and no one saw or heard a thing until the gunshot that brought them all running. And before you ask, no one saw a car driving off, either." He sounded better this morning, although a little hoarse, as if he'd expunged his grief throughout the long night.

"Have you gone through her apartment yet?"

"Yeeeesss." The way he dragged it out intrigued me. "And?"

"Among other items of interest—information we'll be following up on with certain city officials—we found a manila envelope with your name on it. Bunch of notes inside."

Thank you, Fay. "When can I pick it up?"

"Now, Lena. You know better than that. We booked everything into evidence."

"But you made copies for me, right?"

A sigh. "Yeah. I'm busy tonight, but you can drop by my house tomorrow after work and pick them up. I'd rather you do that than let everyone see you at the station again. Not that it matters now. The Chief has always suspected that I've been feeding you information."

Imagine that. After we agreed on a time for my visit, Kryzinski filled me in on Fay's funeral arrangements. Because of the victim's high profile in the community, the autopsy would take place later today. "Barring any unforeseen developments, the medical examiner will probably release the body tomorrow. I've already talked to the family. The service is tentatively scheduled for Saturday afternoon, at Munson's Funeral Home, burial afterwards at Whispering Pines, on Hayden. You going?"

"It's the least I can do."

"No shit. She'd probably still be alive if it weren't for you." With that, he hung up.

I sat there and felt like hell for a while. Then I pulled myself together and called T-Bol Enterprises. Within seconds, I was talking to Thomas Bollinger's secretary. She informed me that she'd give him my message. Then she rang off almost as abruptly as Kryzinski had done.

MaryEllen Bollinger wasn't in, either. Her roommate informed me that she getting a Bindi treatment at Spa du Soleil.

"Bindi?"

"Some kind of Ayurvedic thing."

I decided not to ask what "Ayurvedic" was. "When do you expect her back?"

"In a couple of hours. But she usually takes a nap after her treatment. It really zones her out."

"Ask her to please call me first."

"Sure, but that doesn't mean she will." Click.

The Ernst investigation stalled for the moment, I placed a call to Eddy Joe Hughey in Alabama and asked him when he planned to drive over to Hamilton to see what he could find out about Jack Rinn, AKA Jack Sherwood.

"I got the fax you sent me with his picture and Arizona driver's license," Eddy Joe said in his syrupy drawl. "My, my, he's a good-lookin' boy, ain't he? Bet he's a real heartbreaker with the ladies and all. Anyway, I'm hopin' to hit Hamilton tomorrow. I think I know what's goin' on—I worked me a case like this a while back—but I want to make sure. The fact that he's been tellin' people out there that he hails from Mississippi kinda makes you think he's tryin' to cover his tracks, doesn't it? In the meantime, make sure that client of yours doesn't run off to Vegas with the polecat."

"She's not the type." Beth Osmon was a cool, careful businesswoman. Which is why she hired me.

The drawl vanished. "Every woman's the type when she's in love."

I pictured Eddy Joe leaning his massive bulk back in his office chair, gnawing at the stem of the corncob pipe he never smoked, but always carried to foster his disingenuous good ol' boy image. Then a vision of Warren superimposed itself. Warren, running from his trailer with his shirt askew. But his boisterous daughters had done that, hadn't they? Then I remembered that I had only seen his ex-wife at the trailer door; not his children. Silently cursing my own suspicions, I said to Hughey, "I hope y'all's wrong."

He laughed heartily and, after promising to let me know as soon as he found out anything, hung up.

I was wondering what to do next when the phone rang. Jimmy picked up. "Desert Investigations." He listened for a moment, then called over to me, "It's Bollinger."

"Which one?"

He hit the hold button. "Thomas. He sure doesn't sound eighty."

When I heard Thomas Bollinger's voice, I had to agree with Jimmy's assessment. I could have been talking to a thirty-year-old. His voice had an elastic tenor, much like Frank Oberle's. But unlike Oberle's Everyman twang, Bollinger's voice sounded like money.

"I hear you want to talk to me about the Bollinger murders." Not his brother's murder, his niece's and nephews' and sister-in-law's murders, just "the Bollinger murders." He was distancing himself.

I groveled a little. Rich people like that. "Yes, sir, Mr. Bollinger. If you could spare the time."

"Call me Tommy. Mr. Bollinger makes me sound too old. I can't spare a damned minute, but if you hustle out here to The Greening, you can follow me around while I humiliate my friends."

"Ah…" What the hell was he talking about?

He gave a little laugh. "I'm playing golf with some Army buddies. We're between the third and fourth holes but if you leave now, you can probably catch up to me around the seventh. The old farts can't move very fast."

I knew little about golf, the game being too slow for me, so I had him give me explicit instructions on how to find the seventh hole, then the eighth and ninth, in case I ran into traffic. He expanded my comfort zone by telling me he was wearing a bright orange and green golf shirt, yellow plaid pants, and turquoise visor. Eeeewww.

"If you don't make it here in time, you'll miss me for a week, because then I'm headed down to Mazatlan to check on some property."

"I'm leaving now." Giving him a hasty good-by, I slammed down the phone, grabbed my carry-all, and ran out the door.

Like Sundown Sam's in Apache Junction, The Greening catered to retirees, but there the resemblance ended. Instead of trailers and RVs, half-million-dollar homes cozied up to a spectacular eighteen-hole golf course crowned by a clubhouse that looked like it had been designed by Frank Lloyd Wright on speed. Redwood, stone, glass and salmon-colored steel girders angled sharply up from the desert, all but screaming "Look at me! Look at me!" The cars in the lot weren't battered old pickups, but shiny new Mercedes, Lexuses and Jaguars. These folks might be on the sundown side of sixty, but they still got a kick out of impressing the neighbors.

After parking the Jeep next to a vintage Rolls Silver Shadow, I jogged down the cart track that ran through Golf at The Greening, keeping my eye out for a man dressed like a particularly tawdry rainbow. As I humped over a hill I spotted my quarry in the distance alighting from a golf cart and glowing against the acres of emerald that surrounded him. The men who got out after him were as badly dressed as he. I figured golfers wore such gaudy clothes so the EMTs could find them more easily after their heart attacks.

"Lena Jones, I presume?" Bollinger said, as I jogged up to the group. "I'm Tommy Bollinger. Welcome to the weekly meeting of the Desert Dishonorables. You run all the way from the clubhouse?" He looked like a runner himself, tall, lean, appearing no more than sixty. Only the deep furrows from his nose to his mouth and the snowy hair peeking out from under his visor betrayed his real age.

I agreed that I had hoofed the entire distance, thinking I'd be making points. I was wrong.

"Then stand downwind from us, please." His grin didn't travel to his flinty eyes but allowed me to see that his teeth were his own; slightly crooked, stained by years of coffee.

As I shuffled around so that the wind faced me, his friends, all of them around his own age, snickered. Now that they were upwind from me, I caught an olfactory symphony of Bijan, Armani and Nino Cerruti. Money. Lots of it.

Bollinger's caddy—a young blond hunk which he surely didn't need, given the golf cart—handed him a driver. Everyone stood back while Bollinger ducked his head, gave his fanny a few shakes, and took a big swing. To my amazement, the ball sailed straight and true for almost two hundred yards. I took a closer look at him. Stringbean though he might be, his biceps shamed the caddy's.

"Clean living," he explained. "Nothing but hot sex, red meat and bourbon."

As his companions teed off one by one, the last of them hooking into a stand of cottonwoods to a chorus of catcalls, the look of satisfaction on Bollinger's face was a joy to see. None of his cronies evidenced half his strength.

Bollinger turned to the caddy. "Ned, you drive these old bastards over to the next hole. The girl and I will walk."

Girl. I tried not to take offense as Ned loaded the Desert Dishonorables into the golf cart and drove them away, leaving me hurrying to catch up with Bollinger, who was already striding toward the next hole. "Mr. Boll…ah, Tommy, I wanted to ask you…"

He waved a liver-spotted hand. "I read the papers. I know who you are and why you're here. You want to know if my nephew killed my brother and his family. And if he didn't, did I?"

His bluntness took me aback. "I…"

"Chess and I are both sinners from way back, but neither of us is a killer. Except me. In wartime."

"I'm sure you'd say…"

"Yeah, of course I'd say so. Judging by the intelligence in your eyes, you've already checked me out and think you know all about my past. We'll see about that. Sure, when I was younger I was as hot-headed as Chess, but before you get your female dander up, let me assure you that unlike my nephew, I never hit a woman. Not that some women can't give as good as they get." Over his shoulder he gave me a hard-eyed stare that gave me chills even though the day was warm. "Bet you can kick some serious ass."

"I've kicked a few in my time. Where were you when your brother and his family were murdered?"

He stopped so abruptly that I almost collided with him. "And you're still kicking."

The other Desert Dishonorables had disappeared around a saguaro-stippled knoll, leaving Bollinger and me at the bottom of a shallow valley created by three brush-covered intersecting slopes. From this vantage point, I could see no one. Worse, no one could see me. It was then that I realized Bollinger had failed to return the driver to his golf bag. My chill intensified. That swing of his…

He tapped the head of the driver against his brogan, then flipped it in mid-air, catching it on the way down, one of Tiger Woods' favorite tricks. "I said, 'And you're still kicking.' You don't want to respond?"

"Why respond to the obvious?"

With no expression on his face, he bent down and took a practice swing. The driver came within an inch of my face. When I didn't flinch, he bared his stained teeth at me. "I could have used you at Monte Cassino. You know anything about that?"

I thought hard. "Northern Italy. During World War II the Germans dug in at the monastery above the town. There were heavy Allied fatalities."

He nodded. "Bunch of my buddies were killed there. Brave and stupid. Like you, maybe." He took another practice swing.

I could feel the air split as the driver swept past my face, but at that moment I would rather have died than move. Maybe I *was* stupid.

Bollinger flipped his driver up in the air again, caught it, and for the first time, gave me a smile that traveled all the way to his eyes. It transformed his face, and I could see that when he'd been young, he'd probably been a heartbreaker. "Honey," he said, "if I wasn't queer as a three-dollar bill I could really go for you."

"Things were different back then," Bollinger said, as we headed for the eighth hole, where we could see the other Desert Dishonorables teeing off. "If you were queer, you lost your medals, got a dishonorable discharge, no ifs, ands, or buts. Furthermore, you were lucky if you didn't wind up in the stockade for the duration. It didn't matter how much blood you shed for your country, you were out. No G.I. Bill, no medical, no nothing. That's the dark side of the Greatest Generation no one ever talks about."

I motioned toward the others. "Does that mean...?"

"Hell, yeah. Flaming fruits each and every one, all of us dishonorably discharged from the service, hence our name. This is the only place they can be themselves, talk about what they want to talk about without worrying about the consequences. The silence, that was one of the hardest things about being a fruit in the Army—oops, *gay* is the PC term, pardon my un-PC mouth—being *gay* in the Army. Bullets and bombs flying all around you, but regardless of what was going down, you had to pretend you weren't who you were. When someone you loved was killed...That's how they found out about me, you know. My friend Roger, he...Well, he was hit at Salerno. He was lying there in my arms, his guts over my lap, and I was screaming how much I loved him...The lieutenant, some green fool from Iowa, wrote me up. The rest's history. Bad history.

"Jesus, being over there at that time, under those circumstances, it was the loneliest feeling in the world. Sometimes you believed you were the only person who felt the way you did. Lots of men couldn't take it and ate their guns. But these guys, the Desert Dishonorables, they're the best of the best. They shone through, they survived, but they still have to watch what they say and who they're seen with, for their family's sake. Me, I never married and I'm already richer than shit, so I no longer give a rat's ass. I came out forty years ago, right after I made my first million, and I haven't looked back since."

"Forty years ago, that would be..."

"Long after my brother and his family were dead and buried."

"Did Edward know you were gay?"

"Honey, why do you think I wasn't invited for Christmas dinner?"

I remembered the *Scottsdale Journal* article I'd read, the "family member" who discovered the bodies late Christmas night. That would have been Thomas. "But you went by anyway."

"I'd called Joyce, Edward's wife, and told her I was going to drop off some presents for the kids at eight o'clock."

"I don't understand. He wouldn't let you eat with them, but you were still allowed…"

"No, not allowed. It was a big secret. Joyce was going to meet me behind the barn after her precious husband had drunk himself into a stupor, which he usually had by nine o'clock. That way she could smuggle the presents into the house with Edward being none the wiser. He was a sonofabitch. He didn't just cheat on her, he beat her." He shook his head in puzzlement. "A woman like Joyce, she could have—*should* have—done better. But she loved Edward. Jesus, you should have seen her. Gorgeous, simply gorgeous, with blazing red hair and blue-gray eyes as pale as a lake on a cloudy day. Anyway, I got held up and didn't get out to their place until almost eleven. By then…"

He stopped, looked at me closely, and switched gears. "Come to think of it, Joyce was almost as beautiful as you."

I gave him a cynical smile. "A friend of mine, a Pima Indian, once told me to never trust a man with too many horses. That was his way of saying 'Never trust a rich man.'"

His smile was as cynical as my own. "Not even film-makers?"

Damn. Bollinger *was* good. What else did he know about me?

We had approached the Desert Dishonorables closely enough that I could hear their flirtations—I now realized that's what it was—with the hunky caddy. Far behind them, to the west, I could see a storm front moving in from California and the breeze had already turned cold. I needed to get this interview back on track before the weather changed and sent Tommy Bollinger and his friends back to the comforts of the club house. "You say your sister-in-law was supposed to meet you behind the barn. Did you discover Edward's body first?"

He shook his head. "I didn't see him at all. It was pitch black out there and I probably wouldn't have seen a battleship sitting in the yard. When I realized Joyce hadn't waited around out there for me—no woman in her sane mind would—I headed for the house."

"Knowing how your brother felt about you?"

His eyes clouded with memory. "Hardly. In case he was still sober, I snuck around to the kitchen window and looked in. That's when I saw what had been done to them. Her. The kids. I...I guess she kept them up, waiting for their uncle and their presents. For a while, I thought that Edward had gone nuts and killed them himself. That's the kind of thing you wouldn't put past him, violent as he was. But..." He swallowed hard.

I said what needed to be said. "You inherited from your brother."

"Little more than a pittance, believe me. But I parlayed it into—what did you call it—*really* big money. You think I killed him for that?"

"It's been done."

"Not by me. In my own way, I loved Joyce. I loved my niece and nephews, especially poor lame-brained Chess. The murders destroyed him. He was never the same afterwards, and went on to...Let me put it this way. No one who came in contact with Chess later in his life exactly blossomed, especially not his family. That good-looking daughter of his, God! An I.Q. of one forty-eight, he used to brag, yet all she's doing with it is to shake her tits at some strip club. She refused my help when I told her I'd send her to whatever college would take her. Arizona State, Princeton or even Woo Woo University of Sedona, it was all the same to me just as long as she left the clubs. I'll be honest with you. I could have killed Edward and happily danced on his grave because of the way he treated his family. But I would never have harmed Joyce or those kids." His face fell into sadness.

"Do you have an alibi?"

"The man I was with Christmas Day 1944 died twenty years ago."

"Convenient."

"I didn't think so at the time. As a matter of fact, I almost blew my brains out over it."

I didn't know if he was talking about his lover's death or the death of his family. But I was determined not to let him mislead me again. "Tommy, if you didn't kill your brother and his family, who do you think did?"

He didn't bat an eye. "The Germans, of course."

It was only when I was halfway back to Scottsdale that I realized Bollinger had denied killing his family, but he had never denied killing Kapitan Ernst.

Chapter Fifteen

It always came back to the Germans.

Had they murdered the Bollingers or were they merely serving as a convenient smoke screen for Ernst's real killer? Whatever the answer, I realized I had gone as far on my current investigation as I could without learning more about the Bollinger family tragedy. As soon as I exited the Pima Freeway, I pulled over to the side of the road, fished my cell phone out of my carry-all, and called Warren's cell, expecting to get his voice mail.

Instead, he picked up. "What is it?" He sounded like he wanted to kill someone.

Startled, I said, "I hate to bother you at work, but do you still have your copy of *Escape Across the Desert?*"

"My what?" I heard voices in the background, a man and a woman. Lindsey, fighting with someone.

"Fay's book."

"Oh, God. Fay. I just can't…Yeah, I still have it, but it's all marked up. Why?"

"Because there may be something in there that will get Rada Tesema out of jail." I could hear Lindsey yelling again, two men yelling back.

"Stop that, you people!" Warren's voice was still fierce, but at least now I knew it wasn't directed at me. When he came back on the line, he it sounded like he was trying to control his anger. "Sorry. It's just that what with the weather changing like it is, and Fay's death, things are crazier than usual here. She was pretty popular. Ah, you were asking about the book. It's back at the Best Western, on that card table by the window. I was reading it last night after I dropped you off, trying to get my mind off what had happened. Bad idea. It just made everything worse. Anyway, come by the set and I'll give you the key card so you can pick it up yourself. Listen, back to Fay. Do the cops have any leads yet? Or was it just another drive-by?"

For some reason I didn't want to share my suspicions with him. "That's what the cops say. 'Just another drive-by.'"

"Last time I saw Fay she told me…" He was interrupted by Lindsey shouting again in the background, only to be answered by an entire chorus of obscenities. "Oops. Gotta go. Looks like I'm needed for a little conflict resolution." Without further ceremony, he hung up.

I stuffed the phone back into my carry-all and turned west on McDowell Road, dodging traffic until the red buttes of Papago Park rose before me. The parking lot was packed, not only with trailers and the film crew's cars, but with the cars of the ever-increasing horde of gawkers. I double-parked next to Warren's Land Rover and ran over to the set, to find him pacing back and forth, running his hands through his hair. Backed by a hard wind, a scrap of paper fluttered around his ankles. He ignored it.

"Caro, Lindsey didn't mean it!" The desperation in his voice surprised me, because I'd never seen him anything but cool and controlled on the set.

A heavily tattooed woman waving a mike spewed forth some intriguing suggestions about what Lindsey could do with herself, then finished up with the relatively bland, "Warren, you know she meant every fucking word. Make her apologize, to me and everyone else."

"I'll see you in hell first," Lindsey snarled. Although sleek as usual in black slacks and blouse, her eyes were puffy, as if she had slept badly.

Not wanting to get involved in the altercation, I darted foward, held out my hand to Warren, and said, "Key."

He didn't look at me, just fished out the key card from his pocket and handed it over. Leaving Warren to play referee, I made it back to my Jeep in time to see Mark Schank arrive driving the Golden Hawk. At first I gave him the benefit of the doubt, that his smile was merely companionable, but his next words revealed that his facial muscles were controlled by his salesman's mind. "You interested in selling that '45 Jeep? I like what you've done to it."

His wasn't the first offer I'd had for the Jeep, but it was flattering to hear such complimentary words about my baby from a professional. "Most of the restoration work was done before I bought it from a Jeep tour outfit. They're the ones who put in the Dauntless V-6 engine and T-90 transmission, but I added the '74 Chevy Saginaw power steering. And the Pima petroglyph paint job, of course." Seeing the expression on his face, I said, "Well, I didn't do the work myself, but I…"

He gave me a knowing smile. "Of course not, but you have friends in the business." He patted the Jeep's hood and walked around her slowly. "You made some good choices, especially with those chrome wheels, Remington Mud Brute tires, the leather bucket seats. Talk about adding up-market class to a classic! Yeah, these old Jeeps, they bring back a lot of memories for some folks. By the way, Dad called and told me you and Warren stopped by his house last night. He sounded upset."

"We didn't mean to upset him. We only…"

He waved my apology away. "How much do you want for her?"

"Her?" It took me a moment to figure out what he meant, then I remembered that when men liked a boat or a car, they referred to it as a "her." "Oh, my Jeep. Sorry. It's not for sale."

His saleman's smile returned. "That's what they all say. At first."

Why did I think he wasn't talking about the Jeep? Maybe I should have been offended by the way his eyes were now checking out my own personal transmission, but I wasn't. Sometimes a woman likes to be considered a hot property. "Perhaps. But I'm a woman who means what she says."

"Oh, really?" He lovingly caressed the Jeep's hood and looked deep into my eyes. "Thanks for the warning." Then his eyes shifted to the Golden Hawk and his whole demeanor changed. "Ah, I think Warren's decided to buy her so I'd better get over there."

As he walked off, I suppressed a smile. Mark might like to flirt but not at the expense of screwing a sale. I gave him a wave, jumped into my Jeep, and headed for Warren's room at the Best Western.

By the time Desert Investigations closed its door for the day, I had finished a quick read-through of *Escape Across the Desert* but learned little more than I already knew. Yes, the authorities suspected Ernst of ordering the torture-killing of Werner Dreschler at Camp Papago, but the six other Germans convicted for the crime had never implicated him, not even on the eve of their executions. Why? Did they fear what Das Kapitan might do to their families when he returned to Germany? And yes, two of the escapees—Gunter Hoenig and Josef Braun—were never apprehended, giving rise to various urban myths. According to some, Gunter and Josef reached Nazi sympathizers in Mexico who smuggled them back to Germany. According to others, they went underground with the aid of Phoenix's German-American Bund and were still living in the Phoenix area, plotting the return of their glorious Reich. Myself, I thought it more probable that their bones moldered in the desert.

Nowhere in the book was the Germans' escape connected to the Bollinger murders. In fact, the Bollingers weren't mentioned anywhere. I reviewed the comments Fay tossed off during our last meeting. Regarding Ernst: *"There's a lot I can tell you about the old bastard that didn't make it into the book because of libel law."* About the Bollingers: *"None of what I found out about the Bollingers survived the editing process. My publisher's attorney blue-pencilled everything."*

Now I realized the import of her statements. She had originally written about the Bollinger murders in her book, which meant she *did* believe they were connected. Before she could share her information with me, someone killed her.

A writer's voice can live long after death, however, as I learned early that evening as I sat in the living room of Captain Kryzinski's Scottsdale house. Half-filled shipping cartons lined the bare walls.

"Aren't you jumping the gun a little?" I could hardly stand to think of my life without him. When you're an orphan, your friends become your family.

He proceeded to rub salt in my wounds. "When I make up my mind, Lena, I make up my mind. I'll be gone in a week. My brother's already leased a duplex for me in Brooklyn and I'm going to ship these on ahead." His eyes were sunken, probably in shock from Fay's death. His gray-shot brown hair was as rumpled as his clothes, and his shoes could have used a good shining.

There was no point in begging him not to desert me, so I didn't try. "Better buy some winter clothes. Anyway, the envelope you said Fay left for me. Where is it?"

"In the evidence room, of course." Seeing the expression on my face, he tried a smile but it looked more like a grimace. "Sorry. My attempt at a joke. Like I said, I copied everything for you, right down to the scraps." He reached under the seat cushion he was sitting on and pulled out a thick manila envelope.

Now I'd be up half the night. Then again, remembering the nightmares that so frequently visited me, the prospect didn't look that bad.

I didn't want to grab information and run, so I sat and talked with him for a while, learning more about his decision to leave Arizona. When he was through, I felt like leaving, too. But unlike him, I had nowhere to go.

"Scottsdale isn't the same place it was when I came out from Brooklyn," he said. "The area north of the station used to be dirt roads and horses. Now it's nothing but subdivisions and traffic jams. Course, I'm part of the problem, all of us who've moved out here from points east are. But if I'm going to live in a big city, at least give me one with some energy. Not this collection of suburbs. Place has turned into L.A."

Energy? I'd only been to New York City—and Brooklyn—once, but I didn't remember energy, just a whole lot of concrete. I told him so.

"At least it isn't concrete heated all to hell! Kid, I grew up in Brooklyn, and it's the devil I know. C'mere." He motioned me to the sliding glass doors that led to his patio. "See that?"

Looking over his back yard fence, over the rooftops of the new subdivision that arced around him, I could see the McDowell Mountains to the north, tinted orange and purple by the sun peeking through the storm clouds that had gathered on the horizon. To the east were the Superstitions, wearing a mantel of scarlet. "It's gorgeous. Tell me how you can leave all this."

He thrust a pair of binoculars at me. "Now look again."

I did, and even from this distance could see the tract homes creeping up the base of the mountains, and in several instances, into the very foothills themselves. Gone were the great expanses of wildflowers and cactus; in their place ticky-tacky houses carpeted their former grandeur. It was almost obscene. I tried to put the best face on things. "Oh, well. You can only see them with your binocs."

"I know they're there, and that makes all the difference."

"Yeah." I knew, too. And it did make all the difference.

By the time I arrived at my apartment, the storm, in the way of all bad things, had blown in from California. The wind was frigid and sideways rain hammered my windows. Since Warren had said nothing about getting together tonight—he was probably busy battening down the hatches at Papago Park—I curled up on the sofa and began reading the material Fay had left me, which included notes and several expunged pages of her book's original manuscript. After a quick glance, it was easy to see why her publisher's attorney refused to approve the Bollinger material.

Despite the police investigation that had cleared the Germans, Fay wrote that she believed they killed the family, ordered to do so by Ernst, commenting that Ernst had always been careful about getting his own hands dirty.

One expunged passage read, "After the war, several of Ernst's crew made comments that the U-boat captain asked for volunteers to 'bring justice to a traitor,' and when volunteers were not forthcoming, he drafted them. One crew member, who refused to allow his name to be used, said, 'To be a traitor calls for death, of course, but a swift death. Kapitan Ernst took joy in Werner Dreschler's sufferings and ordered that they continue over several hours. I know. I listened outside as long as I could. By the end of that awful night at Camp Papago, I—along with the other men—was praying for poor Werner to hurry up and die. Then, just before dawn, when it was obvious that Werner could not last much longer, Kapitan had him hanged…but very, very slowly. But nothing ever happened to Kapitan, not even when we made it back to Germany. People were still too afraid of him to bring charges, so while the other Nazis hanged, Kapitan went free."

More than one hundred cigarette burns; countless stab wounds, none of them deep enough to inflict a mortal wound. Then a slow hanging.

The work of a sadist, not a soldier.

Shaking the horrific image out of my mind, I continued leafing through the pages until I came across the clipping from a Connecticut newspaper, dated July 5, 1978, detailing the boating accident that took Ernst's legs.

> BRIDGEPORT—A two-boat collision in Long Island Sound cost a Darien man his legs yesterday. Erik Ernst, a nautical engineer with Sea Solutions, Inc., was taking his dinghy out to his sailboat when a Chris Craft traveling at an excessive rate of speed collided with him. Ernst was rescued by

witnesses on a nearby cabin cruiser who dove into the water and pulled him out.

"It looked like the Chris Craft steered straight for him," said Doris Steinhart, who was celebrating Independence Day with friends aboard the cabin cruiser. A registered nurse at Bridgeport General Hospital, Steinhart attended to the victim's wounds until Air-Evac arrived. "There was plenty of room on either side, and yet the Chris Craft never took evasive action, just kept aiming right at the dinghy."

The powerboat that rammed the victim was later found abandoned near Milford; it had been reported stolen earlier in the day. At press time, police had no leads as to the identity of the person who stole the Chris Craft or the person who rammed Ernst. A police source says the boat was wiped clean of fingerprints.

"We have no suspects, but we are continuing our investigations," said Sgt. Gianni Aliessio, of the Bridgeport police.

Due to the severity of his injuries, both of Ernst's legs had to be amputated above the knee. He is now recovering in a Bridgeport hospital.

An article a month later stated that the police were no further along on their investigation. It added that Ernst was continuing to improve while undergoing rehab. Information at the bottom of the article, however, made me sit up straight.

"There is no basis for the rumors that Mr. Ernst had received several threatening letters just before the incident on Long Island Sound," said Sgt. Gianni Aliessio, of the

```
Bridgeport police. "This appears to
be an unfortunate accident, pure and
simple."
     The accident was doubly tragic for
Ernst. Less than a month before the
accident, Ernst had received national
attention for his award-winning design
of the STL-42, a racing craft now
being manufactured by Sea Solutions.
The New York Times Sunday Magazine ran
a feature article about him, labeling
him, "one of the finest racing design-
ers of the past thirty years."
     "Ernst is a brilliant man and we are
looking forward to having him return
as soon as he is able," said Mace
Grisham, CEO of Sea Solutions.
```

At the bottom of the article, Fay had scribbled GUNTER HOENIG? JOSEF BRAUN? I remembered that they were the two Camp Papago POWs who had never been captured. Did Fay suspect them of attempting to kill their former kapitan? As I mulled over this possibility, two items in the story stood out. In June, Ernst had made the *New York Times*, and shortly afterwards he had began receiving threatening letters. Then he was almost killed. Did the same person who tried to kill Ernst on Long Island Sound in 1978 succeed years later in Scottsdale? Or was the murder a mere coincidence?

Like all decent detectives, I hated coincidences.

With mounting excitement, I leafed through the other material. Many of Fay's notes looked like they'd been made on the run, but with some squinting, I was able to decipher the handwriting, if not necessarily her reporter's vowel-dropping, pseudo-shorthand.

JBol: C li to cops, thre.

Judith Bollinger said Chess lied when he wasn't at the murder scene?

And later on, *MEBol: Hats hm.*

MaryEllen Bollinger hates him—her father? Or MaryEllen Bolinger said Judith Bollinger hates Chess? My bet was on the latter interpretation. Judith's strange smile, that nursing home she'd chosen for her husband…She didn't fit my idea of a loving wife.

One of the more intriguing—and indecipherable—notes had to do with *DepCal*, which I took to be Deputy Harry Caulfield. After DepCal followed the letters *CasNos/ccTrail/C/budSysNK/Van*.

That was no clearer to me than Egyptian hieroglyphics. Neither was *Ols/kdSAuG?CFG*.

CFG. A person's name?

Another series of letters stumped me. *Gemuetlichkeit*. Next to it was a phone number with a west valley exchange.

But all wasn't lost. I also found a few names thankfully spelled out, phone numbers, many local, some in Connecticut, and a few long numerical sequences I recognized as an international exchange. Germany? Two of the local numbers, both west Phoenix exchanges, drew my attention: GEMUETLICHKEIT, (623) 555-7241, and *Ian MANTZ. S*, (623) 555-3820. The note after the Mantz number said, *INTV RE HOENIG*. Interview Ian Mantz regarding Gunter Hoenig, one of the escaped POWs? More German names followed, scribbled hastily, with phone numbers for each. But the only name circled in red was that of Ian Mantz.

I flipped a few more pages, mostly photocopies of the same newspaper stories I had read about the Bollinger murders and the Camp Papago escapes. Nothing new there. I was about to put everything away when an envelope fell out from between the pages. It was addressed in block printing to Fay Harris at the *Journal*, and bore no return address.

After reading the letter inside, I looked at the envelope more carefully. A Phoenix post mark, dated a year earlier, right after *Escape Across the Desert* had been released.

Then I read the letter again.

> MISS HARRIS—ERIK ERNST MURDERED THE BOL-
> LINGER FAMILY. DO NOT LET HIM GET AWAY WITH IT.

There was no signature.

I was drifting off to sleep to the sound of rain when the phone rang. The clock face told me it was 2:56 a.m.

As woozy as I was, I recognized the voice immediately and realized that the call had been forwarded from Desert Investigations.

"He's after me and I can't reach anyone. You've got to help!"

"Who's after you, MaryEllen?"

"Clay! He's going to kill me!"

Clay, he of the fast fists. "Call 911. That's what they're there for."

"They'll never find me. I'm in my car."

Through the phone, I could hear traffic noises. "Where?"

"On Scottsdale Road, headed south from Camelback. I was going home from work and when I realized he was following me, I turned back toward the club. But they're all locked up! Then I remembered that you're close by."

Lucky me. Phone still pressed to my ear, I hauled myself out of bed. "Drive to my office immediately. I'll meet you out front." Fortunately, I still had my T-shirt on, so all I had to do was struggle into my jeans and Reeboks. Now hold on." I swtiched to the other line, dialed 911, told them what was happening, said to send a car. When I switched back to MaryEllen, I was already halfway down the stairs, my snub-nosed .38 held barrel-up. This whole thing was probably a false alarm, but it always paid to be safe.

Her car rounded the corner through a sheet of rain as I, huddled under a waterproof jacket, reached the street. Sure enough, a late model Corvette painted Darth Vader black turned with her. If the Vette had been any closer, it would have been in her trunk. MaryEllen swerved to a halt in front of Desert Investigations and I ran around to the driver's side, rain half-blinding me. "Keep your window rolled up," I yelled through the glass, then turned to face the Corvette, which was now silhouetted by a lightning strike so close I could smell the ozone.

Undeterred, a tall man with the over-muscled physique of a body-builder climbed out of the Corvette and splashed toward us. He had something in his hand, but in the rain I couldn't see what it was. Where were the cops? "Stop there!" I yelled, my voice almost drowned out by a thunderclap.

Clay's baritone carried well. "Fuck off, bitch. This doesn't concern you."

If I couldn't see what was in his hand, he couldn't see what was in mine. "Step back, Clay. I've got a gun and it's aimed right at you."

He laughed. "As if, you stupid broad. Now clear out of my way. I need to teach that woman of mine a lesson."

With a great show, I cocked the .38's hammer.

"The fuck?" Wiping the rain out of his face, he took another step forward, although slower this time.

"Want a bullet in the balls, stud?"

That stopped him. Now I was close enough to see what he had in his hand: a knife so wickedly thin it could have been a scalpel. Was the lesson he had in mind for MaryEllen a disfigured face? I didn't get a chance to ask him because a patrol car came around the corner and pulled up beside the Corvette. Two uniforms exited, both friends of mine.

"Got some action going, Lena?" Vic Gonzales, Yaqui Indian/Hispanic, single, easy-going.

"A man with a knife making threats."

"Ooooh. Big bad man with big bad knife," Stan Jessup, two ex-wives, six kids, short temper.

Clay gestured toward me with the knife. A new lightning strike nearby illuminated the blade, making it look twice as big. "Listen, officers, that cunt…"

Then he was on the ground, but damned if I could see how it happened. Maybe the rain had made the street too slippery. Behind me, I could hear the muffled sounds of MaryEllen's sobs. She still hadn't rolled down the window. Smart girl.

A crack—not lightning this time. A scream. I closed my eyes. What you can't see you can't testify to in court. Another scream. When I opened them again, Clay was on his knees holding his right wrist. It looked crooked. The knife was on the ground. It looked okay.

"You gonna press charges, right, Lena?" Stan Jessup, giving Vic Gonzales an amazed glance. Rain dribbled down his chin.

I smiled. "Sounds like a plan. Think of something nice, six-months-off-the-street nice."

MaryEllen exited the car. Before anyone could stop her, she ran through the storm to Clay, knelt down and put her arms around him, shielding him from the downpour. "You hurt him! But it was all my fault!" Then, to Clay, in a crooning voice, "Oh, baby, I'll be good from now on, I promise."

Disgusted sounds from both cops.

I wasn't disgusted, just sad. MaryEllen had been trained from birth to love abusers, so the only sound I made was when I clicked the hammer home on my .38.

Chapter Sixteen

I spent the next morning working through Fay's notes again, placing calls to the phone numbers she'd jotted down. Ian Mantz, the name circled in red and somehow connected with POW Gunter Hoenig, turned out to be a dentist in Glendale, a growing city on the west side of Phoenix. His receptionist told me he was busy with a patient, but that she'd have him return my call. Several other men on Fay's list were now deceased, and the persons who answered their phones had no idea what she had talked to them about, if she'd talked to them at all. One had died ten years earlier.

I struck paydirt when I tried the number next to Gemuetlichkeit. A chipper female voice with a slight German accent answered "Gemuetlichkeit."

"Ah, my name is Lena Jones and I'd like to speak to Mr. Gem...Gemal...lickit?"

A giggle. "I should have answered in English, but you know how it is. I have been speaking German to everyone all morning. I am Helga, and there is no Mr. Gemuetlichkeit here, but you have reached Gemuetlichkeit, the Phoenix German-American Club. How may I help you?"

Of course. A German-American club. Before she wrote her book, Fay would certainly have contacted them. Trying not to get too optimistic, I explained who I was and why I was calling.

"Hmmm. Fay Harris, Fay Harris. Why does this name sound so familiar?"

"She's the journalist for the *Scottsdale Journal* who was killed the other day."

"Mein Gott!" Oh, but that is terrible! Yes, yes, I remember Miss Harris now. She called here hoping to speak to some of our older members, men who might be able to help with a book she was writing about that POW camp in Papago Park. I said to her that I was not comfortable giving out that kind of information but that she could visit us in person. Besides hosting dances for our younger members, Gemuetlichkeit also functions as a senior center for German-Americans, and for them we have little weekly luncheons, free for those who need it. But anyone may come, German or not, old or young. All we request is that non-seniors or non-members donate to our Meals On Wheels program."

In other words, bring your checkbook. "Did Fay attend any of those luncheons?"

"Several. She made many friends. Our older gentlemen grew quite fond of her."

I smiled, picturing Fay flirting with a roomful of elderly men. Then my eyes began to sting and I forced the picture away. "Anyone in particular?"

"I am so sorry, but I must say again that I do not give out personal information about our members. But if you come visit us, there are several gentlemen I will introduce you to. Older, gallant gentlemen whose lives might be brightened by a new face."

Dreading the drive, I agreed to attend the next luncheon. "Tell me when and where."

"Noon today."

My plans to have lunch somewhere with Warren—although the rain had stopped, it was still too wet out to film—died. I said I'd be right over. Before I hung up, I asked her, "Helga, what does Gem…Gemlicket or whatever mean?"

That infectious giggle again. "I forget that everyone who calls here does not understand. They think I am excusing them for sneezing. Gemuetlichkeit means, hmm, how would it translate? Ah. Cozy. Or coziness. That is what we offer here at Gemuetlichkeit. A cozy place for old friends to meet."

As I was leaving my office, my phone rang. It was Warren. "Lena, something's come up. I'm sure you realize we're not shooting today…"

"I know. Too wet."

"Right. I'm going to take advantage of the down day by flying back to L.A. to attend a meeting with some investors. I'm at the airport now, but if all goes well, I should be back Sunday."

"You'll miss Fay's funeral." Kryzinski had called. It was on for Saturday morning and a big crowd was expected.

"That can't be helped, but at least I can send flowers."

I gave him the funeral home information, then added, "Say hi to Angel and the twins."

"Will do. Anything you need before I leave?"

I couldn't think of anything which didn't entail heated massage oil and a Muddy Waters album played low in the background, so I simply told him to have a nice trip.

As I sped along Loop 101 north of Phoenix, I passed mile after mile of strip malls and housing developments where not long ago golden desert stretched as far as the eye could see. Phoenix and all its surrounding suburbs was becoming Los Angeles, but without the ocean breeze to cool increasing tempers. As the Jeep raced through Deer Valley—which hadn't seen deer in decades—I spied the dark Hedgpeth Hills to the north, surrounded by an old lava field. Madeline, one of my foster mothers, used to drive us out there for hikes. An artist, she would take her sketchpad along and sit drawing under the shade of a mesquite while I collected rocks near the wash. Those had been some of the happiest days of my life. But then she got sick.

I averted my eyes from the Hedgpeths and focused on the rushing traffic. One thing I'd learned from my days in foster care was to keep my vision narrow. If you look at the broad picture, it'll damn near kill you.

Gemuetlichkeit, the German-American Club, was located near Glendale's arts district, an old area of town where brick-fronted antique shops and art galleries stood side-by-side with taco stands and check-cashing businesses. In a cultural blend that was almost schizophrenic in its extremes, Hispanic laborers looking for work brushed shoulders on the narrow streets with yuppies looking for fumed-oak Victorian armoires.

I found Gemuetlichkeit sharing quarters in a refurbished warehouse with an antique store specializing in Fifties memorabilia. On one side of the center corridor, Roy Rogers and Trigger stared at me from a lunch pail, while on the other side, I heard the raucous din of a polka band going flat out behind the club's closed door. My heart sank. I was prepared to be charming, but not to dance.

As it turned out, I didn't have to worry. The music was merely a recording and most of the people sitting at the long wooden tables were long past the polka. Or any other dance, for that matter, since many were in wheelchairs. The average age of the lunchtime crowd appeared to be seventy, with a sprinkling of young whippersnappers in their sixties. I looked around for Helga, who'd had a young voice, and found a likely prospect in a matronly brunette chatting with an elderly woman who had to be ninety, at least.

I walked over. "Helga?"

When she turned to me with a broad smile, I caught a whiff of White Shoulders cologne that sweetened the tobacco-scented air. Her bright pink lipstick was the exact color of her dress. "Ah, you must be Lena! We are pleased to have you visit Gemuetlichkeit. Come, there are several gentlemen I would like you to meet." Without further ado, she led me to a card table in the corner where four elderly men, finished with their lunch, were conversing in German. She introduced me, then left to attend to a woman who was having trouble maneuvering her walker between two tables.

The men weren't too old to appreciate a young blonde, but unlike their younger counterparts, their appreciation was relatively discreet. When they had finished checking out the fit of my black turtleneck, they each gave me a polite handshake. One bird-thin man, dressed formally in a dark blue suit, held my hand longer than the others. Even at his advanced age, he was heartbreakingly handsome, his hazel eyes flickering back and forth from green to brown. His accent was thick, but I had no trouble understanding him. "Our lovely Helga tells us you are a detective and that you are looking into the death of our dearly departed Kapitan Ernst."

His companions laughed. One, who introduced himself as Klaus Brautigan, said, "Ha! *Dearly departed.* That is rich, Stefan."

I acknowledged my role in the case, adding that I believed the wrong man had been arrested for his murder.

Stefan nodded. "The Ethiopian. Yes, it is an easy thing to blame immigrants."

Murmurs of assent from the rest of the table. I was certain they all had their own stories to tell about this issue, but I didn't want to go down that path now. "I don't believe Rada Tesema killed Ernst."

"Are you certain of that? To know our Ernst was to wish to kill him. I, myself, toyed with the idea many times."

More dark chuckles, but it took me a moment to overcome my shock. "You knew him?"

A smile. "Yes I did. We were in Camp Papago together."

I looked at him more closely, mentally erasing the map of wrinkles across his face, and realized that I had seen his face peering out at me from one of the old *Scottsdale Journal* articles. U-boat Captain Stefan Schauer had been in his twenties when the picture was taken. Schauer hadn't escaped with the others, but had stayed behind leading the Christmas Eve sing-along that covered the noise the escapees made. For his pains, he'd been transferred to another camp.

"You immigrated to Arizona after the war!"

Another nod. "During my time at Camp Papago I developed an affinity for cactus."

Several snorts from around the table. "And American women!"

"Those, too, Klaus. They have given me great joy through the years."

His friend Klaus nudged me with a bony elbow. "He's been married four times, the dog. And he is looking for number five. So be careful, pretty girl!"

One thing puzzled me. Before coming to Arizona to film, Warren had instituted a world-wide search for former inmates of Camp Papago, yet I had never heard him mention Stefan Schauer. When I said this to the former U-boat captain, he gave me a sly smile.

"The famous director found me, all right, but why would I wish to appear in a film that would record my wrinkles for all posterity? It is much better to leave my old loves with the memory of my young and handsome face."

Klaus cackled. "That is not the way it was at all. Stefan is writing a book about his adventures, and he did not want movie viewers to know how little he really has to say."

Schauer gave him a cutting look. "I have much to say, my friend. But the money was not right. Warren Quinn made me an offer I could very easily refuse."

Vanity, thy name is Man. I was reminded yet again that however often we want to lump the elderly into one big, homogenous mass, they remain individuals. Just like the rest of us.

As if to prove my thesis, Schauer continued, "My exploits during the war, especially while on leave, are the stuff of legend. There was sweet..."

I listened for a few minutes to Schauer's recitation of his conquests—some of them surprisingly recent—until finally, not having hours to spend at Gemuetlichkeit, I steered the conversation back to Ernst. "Did you see Ernst after he moved to Arizona?"

Now a frown. "Unfortunately, yes. He came here once, several years ago, but in spite of our club's name, he found little coziness and he did not return."

"Why did he not find, ah, coziness? Did he offend someone?"

Schauer's nose twitched. "Kapitan Ernst's presence offended everyone."

"Who, in particular?"

The twitch again. "You desire that I give you names of others who might have killed him? Ah, that I will never do. Other than to offer up myself, of course. I would cheerfully have shot him, and taken pleasure in his dying gasps. However, I have an alibi, an excellent one."

Shot. Did Schauer not know how Ernst had died? Or was he merely being clever? As for his so-called alibi, he'd probably been with a woman, for what such an alibi was worth. But I asked anyway. "What's her name?"

"Dr. Alicia Feldman. The morning before Das Kapitan's murder, she repaired my hernia at Humana General Hospital. As Ernst lay dying—slowly, I hope—I was lying in my hospital bed, savoring the delights of morphine. Today, you see, is my first day back at Gemuetlichkeit since my operation. I am still, as you say, woozy, which is why my friend Klaus drove me here."

His story would be easy enough to check, but it held the ring of truth. I decided to ask him something else that had been bothering me. "Did you know Gunter Hoenig or Josef Braun? They were both among the escapees from Camp Papago."

A chuckle. "Ah, yes. The only two who were never found. Good for them, I say. In my dreams, I see them in Mexico, drinking tequila with dark-eyed senoritas. Sometimes I see them in Munich, drinking schnapps with voluptuous frauleins."

Why had I bothered to ask? Of course the old wolf's fantasies would involve women.

I looked at the other men. "Did anyone else know Ernst? Or Gunter and Josef, or anyone else who was at Camp Papago?"

Head shakes all around. Disappointed, I made ready to leave.

But then Schauer's friend Klaus added something that rekindled my hopes. "Oh. I forgot. I myself was not at Gemuetlichkeit the day Erik Ernst visited, but I hear that Gerhardt Mantz met him. And that Gerhardt…"

"Klaus!" For an old man, Stefan Schauer's voice was surprisingly firm and still carried the don't-talk-back authority of a U-boat captain. "Our friend Gerhardt is dead now, so these things no longer matter."

Klaus fell silent and the other men averted their glances.

Schauer pasted a smile on his face, one much less genuine than before. "Klaus gets confused, as do we all at this age. Do you not, Klaus?"

Klaus' smile was as false as Schauer's. "Oh, yes, yes. Very confused. You must forgive me for being such a foolish man."

But my smile was genuine.

As soon as I left Gemuetlichkeit I drove around the corner, parked the Jeep in the shade of a low-hanging olive tree, and called Jimmy. "Run a check on some guy named Gerhardt Mantz. See if he's any relation to Ian Mantz, a Glendale dentist. Looks like Gerhardt used to attend the German-American club in Glendale and once met Kapitan Ernst. When it was brought up, everyone turned paranoid. While you're at it, check out former U-boat captain Stefan Schauer. He was at Camp Papago and knew Ernst, too."

"Small world, eh? Listen, do you need this right now, or can you wait? I'm still running knee-deep in work. You want me to finish everything before I leave, don't you?"

Did he mean finish for the day, or forever? Because he wanted to take some time off between jobs, he had little more than a week left at Desert Investigations. After that, he would become my competitor. Glancing at my watch, I saw that it was only a few minutes past two. If Ian Mantz practiced in Glendale, I hated the idea of driving all the way back to Scottsdale, then driving all the way back to the west side again. "Do it now, please." So what if I ticked Jimmy off? He was going to leave me anyway.

His voice sounded as irritated as I felt. "All right, all right. It shouldn't take more than a few minutes. I'll call you back." Without waiting for my reply, he hung up.

I spent the next half hour trolling Antique Row, purchasing at one store a chartreuse Fifties bedside lamp shaped like a horse's head. From another store I bought a Lone Ranger and Tonto bedspread, also from the Fifties, then was gratified to see the beginning of a trend. Without even thinking, I was purchasing items for my bare apartment. One of the things I'd learned during my anger management sessions was that turning an apartment into a home was a sign of hope, not futility. I was no longer that lonely foster child who'd been shifted from home to home several times yearly with her belongings in a sack. I was now a grown woman, free to put down roots.

Free to decorate.

I was pondering the wisdom of purchasing a complete Fifties living room suite crafted from bleached saguaro cactus skeletons, made comfy by cushions covered with bright Navajo designs, when my cell phone rang. It was Jimmy, telling me that Kapitan Stefan Schauer had immigrated to the U.S. in 1953, and worked at an aircraft design firm in Seattle until his retirement. In 1998, following a particularly nasty divorce—there had been joint accusations of infidelity—he had moved to Phoenix. No wants, no warrants.

Gerhardt Mantz was born in Bonn, Germany, in 1922, immigrated to the U.S. in 1940, became a successful farmer, but eventually sold his farm to a developer and started a small construction firm. He retired in 1987, and died in a car crash with his wife Eva in 1999, leaving behind a son, four grandchildren, and six great-grandchildren. That was the bad news. The good news was that the Ian Mantz of Fay's notes was Gerhardt's son. Born in 1946 at Phoenix's St. Joseph's Hospital, Ian received his DDS at University of Southern California, and after filling a few thousand teeth in the U.S. Army during the waning days of the Vietnam War, he returned to the Phoenix area. He was a member of the Lion's Club, Rotary, and the Glendale Chamber of Commerce. Neither he, his wife Huong, nor any of his children had ever been arrested. He owned his house free and clear, enjoyed a Triple A credit rating, and had never been sued.

Ian Mantz was such a sterling character, in fact, that he immediately aroused my suspicion. But what could possibly be his connection to Ernst? They lived on opposite sides of Phoenix, and from what I'd heard at Gemuetlichkeit, Ernst had only attended the club once before he'd been frozen out. But that one time he had met Mantz's father. Could Ernst have delivered an insult which his son had avenged years after his father's death? No, the idea was ridiculous. I had to stop reading mystery novels.

Since I'd left Fay's notes back at the office, Jimmy gave me Ian Mantz's business and home addresses. I decided some boot-licking was in store. "I appreciate it, partner, I do."

He sighed. "I know you do. It's just that…Oh, never mind." He hung up, but gently, this time.

Satisfied with the afternoon's work, I bought the cactus living room set and arranged to have it delivered the next day.

Ian Mantz's office wasn't all that far from the German-American club, and I was soon standing in his waiting room, telling his receptionist that I didn't mind waiting, since that was what the room was for.

"But Dr. Mantz has a full schedule!" She couldn't have been older than twenty, and was apparently inexperienced with some-one who actually wanted to see a dentist.

"That's fine. I'll be here when he comes up for air." I took a seat between a glum young woman with a swollen jaw, and a teenager with a mouth full of braces and acne so acute it looked like strawber-ries were erupting from his skin. Neither acknowledged my presence. Both appeared to be listening to the sound of a faraway drill.

The only reading material in the waiting room was *Sports Illustrated, Better Homes & Gardens,* and a two-year-old copy of *Phoenix Magazine.* Ordinarily I would have passed by the *Better Homes & Gardens,* but now that a truck load of furniture was on its way to my place, I decided to give the ladies' mag a try. Maybe I'd find out what color walls would compliment my new cactus-and-Navajo blanket living room furniture. Navajo White seemed too obvious.

Shortly before five, with all patients gone and the receptionist herself packing up to leave, a balding middle-aged man with the trim build of a runner stuck his head out the door. He didn't look happy. "You're still here?"

I winced, as I tried to work a cramp out of my leg. My muscles weren't used to such inactivity. "I sure am, Dr. Mantz. Do you have a few minutes now? Or do I have to come back tomorrow?"

"Oh, come on in. We might as well get this over with. And as long as I'm not working on your teeth, you can call me Ian."

I dropped the *Sports Illustrated (Better Home & Gardens* had been no help), and limped after him to a back office thankfully free of dental equipment. The office was more or less generic, with a book case, an oak desk, matching leather chairs, a couple of brass lamps, and a full wall of photographs showing Ian Mantz receiving awards, playing golf, target shooting, and posing in a speed boat at Lake Pleasant with an older man who resembled him. Gerhardt Mantz, his father? But what drew my eye was the glass-fronted cabinet displaying a collection of antique daggers and knives, the long blades on some almost qualifying them as swords. Among the weapons I could identify were a Muela boar knife, a Hebben Claw II, and several skeleton throwing knives. The centerpiece was a short Japanese Katana sword, which contrasted oddly with its neighbor: a wooden-handled paring knife no different from those used in kitchens everywhere.

Ian Mantz closed the door behind me and gestured me into a deep leather chair across from his desk. With a happy sigh, he took off his lab coat, hung it on the back of his own chair, and stretched for a moment before sitting down. I couldn't help but notice that his short-sleeved blue shirt not only matched his eyes, but showed off his gym-toned biceps. Daggers and muscles. An unusual combination for a dentist.

"Speak, Miss Jones. I've booked some time this evening at the Glendale Collectibles Club and I don't want to miss it." His voice was as brusque as his manner.

I decided to be blunt. "What was your late father's connection with Erik Ernst?"

"Erik who?" His face showed no emotion at all, but his right hand began a tappity-tappity on his desk blotter.

"Erik Ernst. A former U-boat captain, one of the German POWs who escaped from Camp Papago in 1944. Somebody beat him to death the other day."

He displayed no emotion, but looked away briefly. There was more tappity-tappity as he looked over to the wall of photographs, even more as he glanced at the display case with its alarming array of knives. When he looked back at me, his eyes remained determinedly steady, yet his fingers continued their dance. "What makes you think my father had a connection with him?"

When I recounted the conversation I'd had at Gemuetlichkeit, he surprised me. Instead of offering a flurry of denials, he threw back his head and laughed heartily. "Oh, God, I'll bet you talked to Klaus Brautigan! That old fart's memory is connected directly to his mouth with no censor in between to stem the tide. So he told you about Dad running into Ernst at Gemuetlichkeit? Did he also tell you what happened in the parking lot afterwards?"

Stefan Schauer had stopped Klaus before he could tell me anything more, but I wasn't going to let Mantz know that. "Some. But I'd like to hear your version."

Mantz's keen look proved he wasn't fooled. "Some, huh? Well, it's nice to see that the loose-lips-sink-ships creed is still in effect with those old boys, but I guess none of it matters any more, Dad being dead and all. Plus the fact that there were about twenty witnesses to the brouhaha, not all of them Gemuetlichkeit members. So yeah, I'll give you my 'version.' I was walking from my office to join Dad for lunch. I saw the whole thing. What happened is that my father attacked Erik Ernst. He knocked him right out of his wheelchair, and then after punching him half unconscious—although Ernst gave almost as good as he got—kicked him in the balls. If I hadn't grabbed my dad and hauled him away, he probably would have killed the old bastard."

I tried to picture two elderly men—one of them legless—wrestling on the ground in the parking lot, screaming at each other in German. Nasty. "What could your father have against Ernst?"

His smile vanished as his fingers grew still. "As much as an honorable man can have against a dishonorable one. You see, Miss Jones, my father's real name was Gunter Hoenig."

Chapter Seventeen

March 23, 1945

As soon as Das Kapitan left the cave, Gunter took Josef aside and tried once more to talk his friend into leaving with him. "We will hike out of these mountains the way we came in and give ourselves up. This idea of Kapitan's, that we will wait out the end of the war here, it is madness!" He no longer brought up the deaths in the farmhouse. His friend had not seen Kapitan kill the woman, and would never believe.

When Josef shook his head, wisps of auburn hair fell across his forehead. "We must obey Das Kapitan. We are Germans! To turn on him now, when he has led us through that barren desert to this miraculous refuge, would be the utmost treason. And Gunter, you know well what Kapitan does to traitors."

Oh, yes, Gunter did know. How could he ever forget Werner Dreschler's agony that seemingly endless night? But Dreschler's treachery toward the Fatherland had earned him few sympathizers, whereas he and Josef had remained been loyal Germans throughout all the questioning, telling the Allies nothing. "To abandon Kapitan is not treachery, Josef." Outside of their cave, birds sang and water skipped merrily over the rocks, but here in the stone chamber, Gunter thought his words rang with a graveyard echo.

"Kapitan would see it as treachery." Then Josef lowered his voice, as if afraid Erik Ernst lurked around the corner. "You know the

rumors, that Kapitan has friends in the Gestapo. If either of us displeases him, our families would pay. I would not see Marlena again! Never see our baby! I will never know if I have a son or a daughter!" Filled with an emotion he couldn't control, his voice rose to a near shout, and Gunter had to reach out a calming hand.

The conversation had always ended in this stalemate. Josef had too much to lose. Gunter was unmarried and his own parents were dead, so the only power the Gestapo had over him would be to take away his own life. So what if they did? After the war's horrors he had seen these past few years, death might be a comfort. Josef was in a far more vulnerable position, with his entire family, including his pregnant wife, remaining in the same Bavarian village where the Hoenigs and Brauns had lived for centuries. To take them away would be a simple thing. All across Germany, hundreds of people—perhaps even thousands—had vanished. Evil had taken up residence in the Fatherland and Gunter was not certain, if he lived through these dangerous times, that he could bear to return.

"I understand, Josef." Sadly, he reached over and tousled his friend's auburn hair. "We will not speak of this again."

To ease his disappointment, Gunter gathered up the pencils and thick notebook he had taken from a nearby ranch house, along with the small paring knife he used for sharpening. For weeks he had written down his feelings about the war, his captivity and escape, but now perhaps it was time to put aside angry words and focus on the beauty around him. As a child, he had loved to draw, but time and duty had stilled his hand. Not that the world lost anything by being denied his artistic endeavors, but the attempt to capture on paper a singing bird or high-stepping deer never failed to lift his heart. Already smiling in anticipation, he moved toward the mouth of the cave, pausing only once to call back to Josef, "I think today I will hike closer to that odd mountain in the distance and draw whatever I find there."

Josef's answering voice was light with relief and hope. "Bring me back a masterpiece, Gunter. Something with birds and fairies and beautiful girls."

Gunter would do that, if only to make his friend happy.

❦

After what seemed like hours, Gunter heard footsteps. It was probably Das Kapitan, on his way back to the cave after his morning's search for food. To be on the safe side, he put his little knife into his pocket, tucked his journal inside his shirt, and hid himself in a small copse of yellow-bloomed bushes. A few moments later, Kapitan emerged from the brush, two bled and gutted rabbits dangling next to the long butcher knife on his belt. Thanks to Kapitan's hunting skills, they would eat meat tonight, a welcome respite from the stolen sack of beans that made up their usual diet. When this war was over, he would never eat another bean. His diet would consist of nothing but steak and ice cream.

He stepped out of the yellow bush and raised his hand in greeting. "Heil, Kapitan! I see you have once again been successful!"

The smile Kapitan gave him was fierce, like a wolf's. "The rabbits in this place are as stupid as the Americans and it takes little skill to snare them. But I have an idea. We have become too thin eating only the rabbits, beans, and the berries we glean from this valley. We big Germans must have our fat so that we will be strong enough to play our part when this lax country submits to the iron boot of the Reich. Therefore, tomorrow we will return to that farm at the mouth of the valley where we found such largess in the root cellar. We will wait until the tall man leaves for the fields, then we will overpower the two women we saw earlier and take what we will. Butter. Eggs. Perhaps even a chicken or two. And for dessert, we will explore the delights of the young fraulein with the long, yellow hair."

The golden girl, Gunter had called the young fraulein in his dreams. Before heading into this valley, they had all watched her from behind the ridge as she, dressed in her Sunday finery, joined her mother and father in the old pickup truck and drove away.

He had to keep Ernst away from her. "Kapitan, if we wait for Sunday they will be gone and the entire contents of their larder will be ours for the picking."

Kapitan's smile grew more wolfish. "I hunger for dessert, Gunter. It has been too long. Much too long."

Gunter knew that when Kapitan had finished sampling his "dessert," he would do to the girl what he had done to the woman in that other farm house. The memory of that woman's ruined beauty, her pleading eyes, rose up again. No, Gunter could not allow it! Almost without thinking, he withdrew the small paring knife from his pocket and charged Ernst.

But Kapitan was faster. He sprang aside, allowing the momentum of Gunter's unplanned charge to dissipate into empty air. Then Kapitan made a charge of his own and knocked the off-balance Gunter to his knees. Before Gunter could stumble to his feet, Kapitan unhooked his butcher knife from his belt.

"You will pay for your treachery, farm boy," Kapitan snarled.

With despair, Gunter watched his death approach.

Chapter Eighteen

I stared at Ian Mantz in shock. His father was Gunter Hoenig? One of the two German POWs who had never been caught? "That's impossible!"

He shrugged away my disbelief. "Improbable but not impossible. Dad never talked much about the old days in Germany and Mom never talked about their early lives together, either. It should have tipped me off that something was out of whack in ye olde Mantz household, but I told myself that they belonged to a generation which didn't talk much about themselves. But the day before I went to Vietnam, he told me I had a right to know the truth about who he was, so he sat me down and told me everything. He said that his real name was Gunter Hoenig, that after a few days on the run from Camp Papago, he, Ernst and his old friend Josef Braun finally found shelter in a cave somewhere in the Superstition Mountains. There was a lot of tension between him and Ernst. Josef, who I guess had the weakest character of the three, was content to follow orders, but after…well, I'll get to that in a minute. Anyway, after living rough for a couple of months, Dad was having second thoughts about Ernst and the whole situation. It all came to a head when Ernst wanted to raid a farm house they'd passed on the way up. Dad refused, said he wouldn't be a party to another murder."

Somehow I managed to keep from jumping out of my chair. *"Another* murder?"

Ian sighed and leaned back against his chair. "The murder of Werner Dreschler, for a start, the German who was tortured to death at Camp Papago. Ernst set that up, but coward that he was, he let the other men take the fall. Literally, since they were all hanged."

He paused again, as if gathering emotional strength for what he was about to say. "And the murder of the Bollingers. Ernst killed them, too, but this time, he did it all by himself. Dad told me that sometime Christmas night, Ernst found their farmhouse. Maybe Edward Bollinger caught him raiding the chicken coop or something and...and Ernst did what he did. By the time Ernst brought Dad and Josef up to the place to collect food and other survival supplies, the Bollingers were all dead, except for the woman. Dad was going to call for a doctor, but Ernst finished her off right in front of him."

I had always suspected that Erik Ernst had murdered the Bollingers, but now that my suspicions were confirmed, I felt no triumph, only a great sadness.

Ian wasn't finished. "Dad wanted to leave Ernst right then, but Josef refused because he was afraid Ernst's contacts in the Gestapo would kill his family if he deserted their Kapitan. Since Dad was the older of the two I guess he felt responsible for Josef, so he went with them into the Superstitions. In a few days they found a cave—the place is riddled with them, you know. Everything was fine for a while. They pilfered food from various places and managed to catch small game. But then Ernst got the bright idea to raid another farm house, and to, uh..." Here he lowered his eyes. "...maybe rape one of the women. Dad not only refused, but he attacked Ernst. Unfortunately Ernst wasn't about to take that kind of insubordination, so he went after Dad with a butcher knife."

Since Ernst was still alive and more or less well until someone bashed his brains in sixty years later, I figured Gunter wasn't much of a street fighter. Ian's next words proved me right.

"He managed to cut Dad up pretty badly. In fact, Dad probably would have died on the spot, but he had a notebook stashed in his shirt which deflected the worst of it."

I could almost see the two men fighting: Gunter Hoenig for his life, Erik Ernst for the right to go on killing. Ernst was the stronger, and he had the bigger knife. But somehow Gunter survived. I looked up at the photograph of Ian sitting in a speedboat with another man: his father. "How did your dad get away?"

The smile came back to Ian's face, but this time there was no trace of sadness in it. "He was lucky. Very, very lucky. I guess Ernst believed he'd killed him, because he covered Dad with some brush and rocks and left. But Dad wasn't dead. He regained consciousness, managed to dig himself out from under, and took off. He told me he'd decided to go all the way back to Camp Papago, but he only made it as far as the farm Ernst wanted to raid." His smile turned dreamy, like a child listening to a far-off fairy tale. "His knife wound wasn't deep, but it was bad enough, and it got infected. By the time my mother found him hiding in the hayloft, he was only half-conscious." He went on to describe how his mother, sneaking out sulfa drugs left over from treating a sick cow, helped him recover.

This part made no sense. "Why didn't they contact the authorities? Or at least a doctor, for God's sake!"

"*They?* For a couple of weeks, there was no *they*, just my mother helping him back there in the barn. She was, what, only sixteen, seventeen? Nothing more than a kid who'd heard about the Camp Papago escape and imagined it to be as romantic and adventurous as a dime store novel, so she made him a bed up there, brought him food and water, and took care of him all by herself. By the time her parents discovered what was going on, it was too late to contact the authorities."

"What do you mean, too late?"

He gave me a sharp look. "Ms. Jones, you have to understand the way it was then, during wartime. My grandparents were simple people, but they knew the U.S. authorities had rounded up Japanese-Americans and put them into camps. They also knew there'd been talk about doing the same thing to the Germans. Did I forget to tell you that my grandparents were Germans?" Duly noting my reaction, he continued. "They immigrated to the U.S. from a small villiage outside Frankfurt shortly before the war and weren't citizens yet. My grandfather still wanted to alert the authorities, but my grandmother was terrified that when it was discovered that an escaped German POW had been living on their ranch for the past two weeks, they'd wind up in camps like the Japanese. Grandmother, helped along by my mother's tears, won the argument and so Gunter stayed."

"For the duration of the war?"

He shrugged. "It wasn't that long. Gunter left Ernst and Josef at the end of March, and Hitler committed suicide in April. The Germans surrendered a few days later."

I thought for a moment. In those days before holographic drivers licenses and data base background checks, assuming a new identity would have been relatively easy. Especially in the confusion after the war. "So Gunter Hoenig became Gerhardt Mantz."

"Correct. And that August, Eva Schmidt, my mother, became Mrs. Gerhardt Mantz. He remained on the farm, working with my mother's parents until they died, and then sold it and bought another one over here, where there's a decent-sized German community."

I pointed to the degrees on Mantz's wall. "I take it he did well in his new life."

Mantz nodded. "Very well. After a few years, he sold the new farm to a developer and started a construction company. It paid my way through college and dentistry school." He smiled. "And everyone lived happily ever after."

"Except for the Bollingers."

"My father never harmed those people!"

Knowing that Mantz had a vested interest in guarding his father's reputation, I allowed skepticism to show on my face. "And you believe that because...?"

He rose to the bait. "I believe it because of what he did when he saw Ernst at Gemuetlichkeit. My God, he tried to kill the man with his bare hands! He would have, too, if I hadn't come along and stopped it. I told you that my father was an honorable man. The Bollinger murders weighed heavily on him through the years."

Not heavily enough. I remembered Chess Bollinger, lying in a filthy nursing home bed, crying, *"Not me, not me, not me,"* like a litany, like a prayer. I remembered Chess' ruined life, his wife's and daughter's ruined lives—all because a weak, troubled boy had carried around a burden that should never have been his in the first place.

"You say your father was an honorable man. Then why, if he knew Ernst killed the Bollingers, did he stand by and let Chess, *a kid*, stand trial for their murders?"

Ian shook his head. "He didn't know anything about it. Like I told you, his stab wound was infected by the time Mom found him. His condition was pretty iffy for a couple of months, and Mom's family kept him away from any kind of bad news. By the time he was well enough to read the Sunday newspapers my grandfather always picked up on the way back from church, the trial was over and done with. Chess Bollinger had been found innocent. But before that, in April, Edward R. Murrow broadcast from Buchenwald about the horrors he'd seen there, and the paranoia among German-Americans increased to near-panic levels. Then in November, the Nuremberg trials began and the whole world learned what had happened at places like Auschwitz and Buchenwald."

Granted, German-Americans—and especially Gunter Hoenig AKA Gerhardt Mantz—were probably frightened, but the way I saw it, fear was no excuse for keeping his mouth shut about murder. I told Ian so.

His answer took me aback. "As soon as Dad found out about the Bollinger trial, he did notify the authorities."

"What do you mean? You just told me…Listen, I read up on everything that was written about the case. There was no mention anywhere that someone fingered Ernst for the murders."

"I know, I know. But Dad was an enemy combatant living in enemy territory under a false name. Technically, that made him a spy, and the penalty for spying was death by hanging. Still, Dad did everything he could to bring out the truth without endangering himself and my mother's family. Remember, they were afraid they'd go to prison for harboring a fugitive. So Dad wrote several anonymous letters to the sheriff *and* the judge in the case naming the real killer. But no one followed up."

Of course not. Unsigned letters telling the authorities they'd been dumb enough to accuse the wrong man—or boy, in this case—would have been summarily dismissed. I made a mental note to call Harry Caulfield. He'd been a mere deputy at the time and new to the job, but perhaps rumors of Hoenig's letters had reached him. Then I remembered the unsigned letter I'd found among Fay's notes. It bore an August 2002 post mark—the month after *Escape Across the Desert* hit the shelves. Yet according to Jimmy's research, Gunter Hoenig had already been dead three years.

I narrowed my eyes at Ian. "They say the apple never falls far from the tree. After your father died, did you continue your father's letter-writing campaign?"

He wouldn't meet my eyes. "Don't be silly." But he flicked his eyes to the photograph of himself and his father out on Lake Pleasant in their speedboat. Liars always give themselves away.

"You father liked boating, right?"

He looked puzzled. "Sure. The whole family does. We have a Chris Craft and a twenty-six-foot Columbia, not that a sailboat's much good on Lake Pleasant."

"Did your father ever go boating in Connecticut? Say, around the time Erik Ernst lost his legs in that boating accident?"

"Don't be ridiculous." He rose from his desk and started walking toward the cabinet that housed the daggers, but stopped when he saw my hand slide into my carry-all. With a cold smile, he veered away from the cabinet and opened the office door instead.

"Time for you to leave, Miss Jones."

Since I was already on the west side, I decided to drop by the jail and visit Rada Tesema. He deserved to be filled in on my progress, or lack thereof. But when two corrections officers—one black, one white—led him into the visiting room, my planned conversation went south. He limped, but that was the least of his injuries. One eye was swollen shut, and his upper lip was split, probably because his broken front tooth had exited through it.

"What happened to this man?" I demanded of the guards.

The black guard eased Tesema gently into the chair. "Aryan brothers got him in the lunchroom. Told him to go back to where he came from, that America already has more niggers than it needs."

"Has the doctor seen him?"

"Yeah," the white guard said. "Nothing's broken, except for the tooth. He should be all right in a couple of days, as long as they don't get to him again. We're going to do what we can to make sure that doesn't happen." He gave Tesema a comforting pat on the shoulder, then he and the other guard exited the room, leaving me to speak privately with my client.

"Oh, Rada, I'm so sorry."

His smile looked like it hurt. "I am sorry too, Miss Jones, that I am such a poor fighter. But is okay. The people from synagogue, they are here yesterday. One nice woman, she has son who is dentist. Says he will fix tooth for nothing when I get out. Put on crown. Put one on back tooth, too. They also taking up collection to fly family over. But is a lot of money."

No kidding. The wife and all those children. "That sounds good. I'm sure you'll be out of here in no time." I tried to sound upbeat, but I could hardly convince myself, let alone Rada.

He gave up trying to smile. "Miss Jones, will I see family again?"

"Of course you will. I've almost solved the case." If liars go to Hell, I'd better get myself fitted for a fire-retardant suit.

It was six o'clock and almost dark when I arrived back at Desert Investigations to discover that Jimmy was still running background checks. When I told him to go home, he said that he wanted to have everything finished before he left Desert Investigations for Southwest MicroSystems. Which was just days away, I realized. God, what was I going to do?

"No dinner with Esther tonight?"

He shook his head. "She's picking out furniture."

Funny. So was I. "Why aren't you helping?"

I couldn't tell if the twist his mouth made was meant to be a grin or a grimace. "Esther has very specific tastes." After a moment's silence, he added, "But she says I can decorate the den any way I want to as long as it's that new color in all the magazines. Persian Pink."

Since Jimmy didn't seem like a Persian Pink kind of guy, I said nothing. Then I remembered that my own "new" furniture was due to arrive tomorrow morning. A sofa, two chairs, an end table and a cocktail table. What should I buy next? A kitchen table? Since I always ate my ramen noodles while watching CNN, I'd never owned a table. What kind of table would go with cactus skeleton living-room furniture? Oak? Pecan? Pine? Or maybe I should continue the Fifties theme and get one of those chrome and vinyl sets I'd seen, the kind with pictures of horseshoes and lariats on the plastic seat cushions. And maybe even a Roy Rogers cookie jar to put in the center of it.

Plates, too. I needed crockery! Did they make dishes with spur-and-lariat designs? Excited by the realization that my formerly cold apartment was developing a Fifties Western theme—however childish—I began jotting down everything I would need to build a new Lena nest. Pots and pans (I'd learn to cook), salt and pepper shakers (cactus shapes would be nice), maybe a few rugs (Navajo, of course), and a…

My phone rang and when I picked it up, I heard the Alabama drawl of Eddy Joe Hughey. "My, my, y'all cowboys sure do work late out there."

He always made me smile. "Not as late as y'all, since y'all have two hours on us. But something tells me you didn't call to congratulate me on my work ethic."

"Why, sweetie, I called just to hear your sexy voice." The drawl lightened as he got down to business. "And to tell you that I found some disturbin' info on our Mr. Jack Sherwood, AKA Jack Rinn. That Beth Osmon of yours is in for some cryin' time."

So I was right. Jack Sherwood *had* been too good to be true. "Let's have it."

"I drove over to Hamilton this morning and talked to the woman who calls herself Mrs. Rinn, a pretty little gal named Alea. Looks somethin' like my second cousin, once removed. Anyway, after I told her some cock 'n' bull story about me lookin' into an inheritance issue on her husband's side, she was thrilled to tell me all about him. Oh, and there's no doubt we're talkin' 'bout the same ol' boy. The pictures of Mr. Rinn, musta been a dozen all over her livin' room, look just like the pictures you faxed me of Mr. Sherwood. So do the kids."

"The kids?"

"Yeah. Four. The skunk."

Poor Beth. "Go on. Tell me the rest."

"I'm not sure Alea's in on her husband's little scam. In fact, I tend to think she isn't, but it looks like Mr. Sherwood/Rinn brings home the bacon by romancin' rich women all across the country, then, while they're pickin' out their trousseaus, he talks them into investin' in some get-rich-quick scheme of his."

"Such as shopping centers, right?"

"Oh, yeah. He's used that one several times. Anyway, once he has his mark's 'investment' money, which can run into the hundreds of thousands, he flies out of town 'on business' and is never seen again."

The way Eddy Joe talked, it sounded like Sherwood/Rinn had been running his scam for some time. "Do you have any idea how many women he's done this to?"

"Hard to say 'cause he prolly uses a different name each time. Now, I don't mean any disrespect toward y'all Scottsdalians, but guys like him tend to work transient cities like yours. You know, places where nobody knows nobody else's daddy and the past is a big, blank slate. Sherwood/Rinn blows into these places with nothin' but a good suit and a smile, hangs out where the money hangs out, and cozies up to lonely divorcees and widows. He's slick, I'll say that for him. I could use some of that charm my own self."

I didn't think Eddy Joe was lacking in the charm department, but that was neither here nor there. "Were charges ever filed?"

"Not that I've been able to dig up. The boy's a genius when it comes to knowin' what woman to pick. It's always someone who'd rather be dead than let anyone know she's been played for a sucker."

Eddy was right when he said that the Sherwood/Rinns of this world were drawn to places like Scottsdale, small but wealthy cities where roots ran shallow. Almost nobody was born here; their birth certificates were on file in places like Minnesota, North Dakota, New Hampshire and Ohio. I'd once read a report which said that the majority of Scottsdale's citizens had moved here from out of state, and that percentage seemed to be increasing all the time. The city's physical beauty and mild (except for summer) climate attracted not only people who'd earned the lush life, but also people on the run from old ghosts and failures. Hot on *their* heels came jackals like Sherwood/Rinn, ready to take advantage of everyone's vulnerabilities.

"Beth might be different," I said to Eddy Joe. "She comes from tough pioneer stock, so maybe she'll be mad enough to file charges."

"He ask her for money yet?"

I winced. "No." There was the rub. A man could call himself any damned thing he wanted to as long as there was no fraud involved. And since Sherwood/Rinn hadn't put the touch on Beth yet—accent on *yet*—he was in the clear.

"Listen, baby cakes, I'm gonna fax you the newspaper article that ran when Mr. Sherwood/Rinn married Alea. Got a big picture of the happy couple. If that's not enough for Mrs. Osmon, I can scramble around and get some pictures of him with other women, too. I'm figuring he's made the society pages in various cities."

I doubted it. In this jet-friendly age, where the rich all tended to hang out at the same watering holes, Sherwood/Rinn would probably prove camera-shy. "Let's go with what we have. I'll call Beth in the morning."

Eddy Joe sighed. "Yeah, you do that. Too bad I always have to be the bearer of bad tidings. In the meantime, don't you go thinkin' all men are skunks just because we've trapped one stinker in the barn. Most of us are OK fellas."

"Thanks for those reassuring words."

"Keep the faith, Lena. Even a PIs gotta believe in love sometime."

"I guess." I hung up, wondering if he'd given me good advice or bad.

As I was getting ready to leave for the day, the phone rang again. This time it was Warren, calling from L.A. People were talking in the background. None of them sounded happy, especially not Warren. "I could use you over here in L.A. Maybe you could shoot me a couple of people and resolve this mess."

"That bad, huh?"

He groaned. "And how. Anyway, I called just to hear a friendly voice and to tell you how much I miss you."

Miss you? We'd seen each other mere hours earlier.

Before I could formulate an appropriate answer, he said, "The usual formula is for the responding party to answer, 'I miss you, too.'"

I was going to have to start studying how normal people behaved. "OK. Me, too."

He laughed. "Lena Jones, you are the most self-contained woman I've ever met, which is why I'm so crazy about you. You're such a change from what I'm used to! But you're also a terrible liar. Tell you what. As soon as I get things ironed out here I'll fly back and we'll have dinner someplace romantic. Then I'll show you why you should miss me when I'm gone."

When I laughed, Jimmy made a disgusted noise. I ignored him. "Uh, me too." Warren and I laughed some more, until Jimmy turned around with an expression his ancestors must have worn when they were hiding behind mesas, waiting for the wagon trains to come by.

That silenced me. "Call when you get back." With as much dignity as I could muster, I said good-by and hung up.

"You white people are disgusting." But Jimmy smiled when he said it.

"Yeah, and I'm sure you never are."

A blush darkened his already dark face. "Touché." He turned back to his computer.

I checked my watch again. It was still only six-thirty. Figuring that a man his age would be home in the evenings, I called Harry Caulfield, only to be told by his answering machine that he wasn't in. I left a brief message about my interview with Ian Mantz, and asked if there had ever been any scuttlebutt around the sheriff's office about anonymous letters accusing Ernst of the Bollinger murders. As I hung up, I noticed Jimmy shutting down his computer.

For once, dinner alone looked bleak. "Say, since Esther's all tied up, what are you going to do for dinner tonight?"

"Maybe heat up the barbeque leftovers and watch some TV. One of Warren's old docs is on PBS tonight."

I raised my eyebrows. "Which one?"

"*Native Blood, Foreign Chains.* I saw it once and wouldn't mind seeing it again."

Maybe I should do the same, leaving out the barbeque. But watching one of Warren's films tonight would only remind me of his absence. That's when I realized I was lonely. Maybe my therapist was right, relationships were habit-forming.

Jimmy already had his hand on the door so I stopped him with a shout. "Jimmy! Why don't we have dinner together? We could walk over to Malee's on Main for some Chicken Pad Thai. I'll even pick up the check."

He paused. "That sounds better than leftovers."

"And we can talk. Really talk."

He looked less optimistic about this. "There's no agenda here, is there? I'm still taking the new job."

Life always has an agenda, but there was no point in telling the truth. "Of course not. We've we've both been so busy lately, you with Esther, me with my cases, that we haven't had time to just be friends again."

His face relaxed. "Chicken Pad Thai it is."

Malee's was less crowded than usual because most of the snowbirds had departed for Minnesota and other points north. The aroma of mysterious Asian spices filled the air, untainted by tobacco smoke, and the low murmur of conversation served as a counterpoint to the Thai music that emanated from the restaurant's sound system. The hostess seated us at a table in back, where a Thai waitress arrived almost immediately to take our orders. As we waited for our food, we sipped creamy Thai tea. Lit only by candlelight, the tribal tattoo on Jimmy's face looked blacker than ever, and I tried to envision him with it removed. He'd look like a stranger. "So, Jimmy. Other than looking for furniture and houses, how's Esther doing?"

"Fine."

"How's Rebecca?"

"She's fine, too."

"Great."

Now it was his turn. "How's Warren?"

"In L.A."

"How's Dusty?"

"God only knows."

"How's Kryzinski?"

"Packing."

"How's Rama Tesema?"

"Miserable."

Before I grew more depressed, the waitress arrived with our Chicken Pad Thai. We busied ourselves eating for the next few minutes, then attempted a more promising line of chatter.

"Does Esther get a good furniture discount from Neiman Marcus?"

"Sure, but the prices are still a little high for us, so we're getting the bulk of our things at Ethan Allen."

"What are you taking along from your trailer?" I pictured the paintings of Pima petroglyphs which adorned his kitchen cabinet doors. Perhaps he could hang them in his den, alongside the photographs of both his biological and adoptive parents. Then the new house would still feel like home. I told him this.

He looked down at what was left of his Chicken Pad Thai. "They're not Persian Pink."

Time to switch to a safer topic. "Ah, I never filled you in on what I discovered when I interviewed that dentist. Did you know that one of those two Germans who escaped from Camp Papago and were never caught actually survived?"

"Are you talking about Erik Ernst? He didn't exactly give himself up, you know. A couple of farmhands nabbed him when he stole food from a shed. And as for survived, better ask the Maricopa County medical examiner how lively he is these days." He gave me a wicked smile.

This is what happens when you don't take the trouble to update your partner, even when your partner is leaving you in a matter of days. "No, no. I'm not talking about Das Kapitan. I'm talking about Gunter Hoenig, one of Ernst's U-boat crew members." As we finished up our Chicken Pad Thai, I relayed everything Ian Mantz told me.

Jimmy frowned. "That's an interesting story, but what about the other guy?"

"What other guy?"

The waitress came by and removed our plates. We ordered home-made coconut ice cream for dessert, which she brought almost immediately. Someone in the back put a cool jazz station on the music system, and the soprano sax of Kenny G drifted out. Relaxing, maybe, but I missed the Asian music.

After the waitress had gone away again, Jimmy said, "Gunter's friend Josef Braun. He was on the same U-boat, remember? We know that Ernst was eventually captured and was transferred to a prison camp with stronger security until the end of the war, and now you tell me that Gunter Hoenig melted into the local German-American community. But where'd Josef end up?"

My spoon stopped halfway to my mouth. "You know, partner, that's a good question."

What *had* happened to Gunter's friend Josef Braun? If he was alive and living somewhere in Arizona, was he still strong enough to beat a man to death?

After dinner, Jimmy climbed into his Toyota truck and headed back to the reservation while I climbed the stairs to my apartment above Desert Investigations. Out of habit, I turned on CNN but quickly grew tired of the non-stop violence in the Middle East. Seeking a more soothing brand of mind candy, I flipped through the channels until I arrived at TVLand, and sat happily through *Leave It to Beaver* and *Here Come the Nelsons*. On neither show did anyone decapitate anyone else or announce that he had AIDS. The most serious problem either program dealt with was the Beav not being invited to a friend's sleep-over. Had life really been that easy in the Fifties? Or were both programs lies designed to take that generation's mind off its own woes?

Whatever, the past sure looked rosy in retrospect.

After the Beav solved his sleep-over problem (Mom called the neighbor and discovered it had all been a misunderstanding), I switched the channel to PBS. Although I'd told Jimmy I hadn't planned to watch *Native Peoples, Foreign Chains* I watched anyway, marveling at Warren's delicacy when asking indelicate questions No wonder he and Lindsey fought all the time. In fact, they battled so often that I was amazed he kept her on the payroll.

When the credits rolled on *Native Peoples, Foreign Chains*, I read them carefully and discovered that Lindsey worked as assistant director on that film, too. Then I remembered that Warren told me that she'd been with him ever since he started Living History Productions more than ten years earlier. Why didn't she move off on her own? By now, she should have been able to get a job as a director, not merely continue along in the same rut, playing second fiddle to a very big fiddle. Perhaps, they had once been romantically involved, but so what? Where was the drive Hollywood was so famous for, the ambition? Maybe Lindsey couldn't bear to leave. While Warren no longer appeared romantically interested in her, Lindsey's "stay away from him" comment hinted that she still carried a torch for him.

As I readied myself for bed, it occurred to me that it was time to do something to repair my own fractured life. Therapy had broken it apart but so far hadn't bothered to put it back together again. So many people I loved were leaving me. Warren would go back to L.A., too, once he finished *Escape Across the Desert*, and I would be left alone, drifting, with my usual defenses stripped away. Where was the hard Lena, the old Lena who never lay awake staring at the ceiling? The Lena who was never lonely because she knew better than to care about anyone in the first place?

Now I had opened my heart only to find everyone vacating it.

And all the new furniture in the world couldn't change that.

Chapter Nineteen

Bad news should always be delivered in person. After calling Beth Osmon the first thing in the morning to make sure she was in, I drove to the northern limits of Scottsdale as fast as rush hour traffic would let me. I found her near the horse barn on her forty-acre spread, still tidying up her property after the storm we'd had Wednesday night. The expression on her face told me she'd prepared herself for the worst.

"He's a phony, isn't he?"

Without a word, I handed her the folder that contained, among other things, the faxed copy of Alea and Jack Sherwood/Rinn's wedding announcement. She took it with gloved hands and glanced at the first page. Then she looked up. "The shithead."

"The Alabama PI who collected this called him a skunk."

She snorted. "They're more polite down there." For all Beth's bravado, I could see lines of pain around her eyes. She wasn't a bad-looking woman. Although in her mid-forties, she'd managed to keep the damage of years of sun and trail-riding to a minimum, and her lean, hard figure would shame many a twenty-year-old. The gray streak that contrasted with her shoulder-length brunette hair only added to its beauty. Why couldn't a woman like this find an honest man?

"If you want, Beth, I can take care of this myself."

"You'll shoot him for me?" A smile broke through the sadness.

Relieved, I smiled in return. She would be fine. "Sorry, shooting shitheads is against the law. What I meant was that I can confront Mr. Rinn myself, show him what we've discovered, then tell him to hop a plane back to Alabama. There's no point in having you do the dirty work. You've been through enough."

She didn't answer right away, merely swallowed a couple of times while she looked toward the corral where three Appaloosa yearlings were playing. Two had the standard white-blanketed rumps, but one was a dark bay with snowflake spots. When she saw me looking at them, she said, "The first Native American horse breed. And regardless of those little Morgans back east, probably the finest breed this country has ever developed."

I let her continue on, knowing that she was merely putting off the moment of heartbreak. As she talked, the musky scent of horse drifted to us—a scent I had always found preferable to that of gasoline. The yearlings capered in the paddock, while in the barn, several other horses called to them. Only a few feet away, a coyote with engorged mammaries loped home to her den, oblivious to the family of Gambrel's quail that scurried to safety in a cholla patch. If you didn't look at the subdivision surrounding Beth's ranch, you'd think this was Paradise.

"The Nez Percé Indians bred them, you know." Her voice was still firm.

"The Appaloosas?"

When I looked back at her, I saw that her eyes were still dry. "They're some of the fastest, toughest horses ever bred. The only reason the U.S. Cavalry was able to catch the Nez Percé during the Indian Wars was because Chief Joseph thought his people had already crossed the border into Canada. Their horses had always been able to outrun the Cavalry's remounts."

I knew the story but let her tell it. She needed to.

"Chief Joseph was wrong. His people were still in the U.S. After killing most of the Nez Percé, the Cavalry slaughtered their Appaloosas, too, hoping to make the breed extinct so no Indian would ever be able to escape the Cavalry again. But a few got away." She stretched her arm in a wide gesture, taking in the corral and barns. "These are their direct descendants. And they're as tough as their ancestors."

So was Beth. Like the Appaloosas, she'd be all right.

Finally Beth spoke again. "Let's go up to the house. I want to read the rest of this and think for a while. Jack hasn't asked me for money, so no crime's been committed. Yet." Her voice was clear, her eyes dry. "I may want to let this play out."

A thrill of alarm crept up my spine. I was no fan of letting amateurs play detective. "Uh, Beth, that may not be a good…"

As we walked up the steep drive to her hilltop home, she waved my protest away. "I'm not talking about going after the shi…the skunk with my grandpa's long-barreled Colt or anything foolish like that. Writing my memoirs from prison doesn't appeal to me. But if I simply drop him, what will have been gained? No, I'm going to mull over my options."

Judging from Beth's house alone, you'd never know she had enough money to buy the Arizona Diamondbacks during a pennant-winning season. In contrast to the glitzy, over-designed houses dotting the hills around her ranch, Beth's old Territorial adobe was the real thing. Built in the late eighteen hundreds by her copper-mining great-grandfather, the place could have used some patch-up, and the dry-rotted window sills probably all needed replacing. But the rambling wreck blended into the desert landscape with an easy integrity newer homes such as Gilbert Schank's phony adobe never would. It would stay here, too. Beth had no children. When we talked previously, she had told me that after her death, the ranch house, the surrounding land, and the Appaloosas would be passed intact to an organization that provided therapy for handicapped children.

When Beth opened the scarred wooden door to the house, the expression on her face told me that my news was beginning to hit her. But she refused to give in to it. She led me into a living room that looked like it had been furnished by her great-grandmother's hand-me-downs. Faded chintz sofas, unraveling Navajo rugs, scarred Victorian oak tables, and dozens of fading family photographs in tarnished silver frames created a motley but friendly clutter. Unlike Scottsdale's nouveau riche, Beth wasn't into appearances.

She took off her gloves and sat down on one of the ratty sofas to read. I sat across from her in another one, biding my time. When she finished, she closed the folder with a snap.

"Okay. How much do I owe you?"

When I told her, she walked over to her desk, making out the check on the spot. As she handed it to me, she said, "I might get back to you in a couple of days. Will you be in town?"

This startled me. Because of Desert Investigations, I almost never went anywhere and she knew it. "Of course. Where would I go?"

She smiled. "I thought you might be planning a trip to L.A."

The blood rushed to my face. "What makes you think that?"

"One of the extras working on *Escape Across the Desert* is my maid's nephew. He's playing one of the Camp Papago guards."

Then, when I turned to go, she added something that mystified me. "They say the cobbler's children have no shoes. Is the same thing true of private detectives?"

I was halfway to my Jeep before I figured out what she meant.

As soon as I walked through the door at Desert Investigations, I told Jimmy what I wanted him to do.

He looked appalled. "Run a check on Warren? For God's sake, Lena, why?"

"Let's say I want to play it safe." He continued staring at me until I snapped, "If you don't want to do it, I'll hire someone who can!"

He let out his breath with a great sigh. "All right. All right. But I probably won't be able to do it today. I'm backed up here, what with the end of the week and all."

"Monday's fine. Thanks, partner." Jimmy would do what I wanted, so why did I feel depressed?

Not being in a reflective mood—I didn't want to think about anything, especially Fay Harris' death and my own possible culpability—I turned my attention to some paperwork I'd been putting off too long. I was only a tenth of the way through it when the phone rang. It was Ian Mantz, son of Gerhardt Mantz/ Gunter Hoenig. "Ms. Jones, I'd like to apologize. I don't think we parted on a very good note yesterday."

I'd as good as accused Mantz's dead father of driving the boat that amputated Ernst's legs, and to top it off, hinted that the son carried on the father's legacy by writing anonymous letters to the press. Yet he was the one who called to apologize. Something wasn't right. I shoved aside the billing and focused my attention on his voice. Words didn't always give liars away, but their tone usually did. "Don't worry about it, Dr. Mantz. I probably wasn't as delicate in my questioning as I could have been."

"I want to make it up." Ah, here it came, the hidden agenda, the real reason for his phone call. "I'd, uh, like to share something with you."

Like what, Ebola?

He spoke into my silence. "Let's have lunch today. Then we can talk some more."

"Sorry. I'm having some furniture delivered."

"Then how about dinner? At my house. You could meet the family. All of us. We live within blocks of each other."

While I was intrigued by the prospect of meeting Gunter Hoenig's grandchildren, I couldn't help but remember the dagger display cabinet in Ian's office. Maybe there were more at his house. Firearms, too. "How about someplace public?" I tried to make it sound like a joke.

A dry chuckle. "I assure you that Huong, my wife, won't poison the sauerbraten, and my four daughters are very peaceable. Like their grandfather before them, they're volunteers at Hospice of the Valley. But to prove that my intentions are honorable, you can bring a friend if you wish."

Gunter Hoenig, a U-boat gunnery mechanic, had been a Hospice volunteer? Life never ceases to amaze. "Just a second." I covered the mouthpiece with my hand and glanced over at Jimmy. For the first time that morning I noticed his appearance.

His purple Hawaiian shirt clashed with his olive chinos, and his black socks didn't look all that great with his scuffed white Nikes. While never exactly a fashion plate, my partner usually chose his outfits with care. I guess house-hunting could be rough on a person.

"You seeing Esther tonight?"

He shook his head, then turned away from me to fiddle with his keyboard.

"Then how about dinner?" I said to his back.

"Again?"

Before he could say no, I added, "With Gunter Hoenig's son and granddaughters."

He turned around. "The German POW? One of the two who was never caught?"

"That's the one."

His eyes, which had looked a little bleary, brightened. "Count me in." Then he went back to his keyboard.

I uncovered the mouthpiece, told Ian that my partner would be coming with me, then took down directions to the Mantz house. Feeling more intrigued than ever on several fronts, I then hung up and went back to my billing.

My "new" fifty-year-old cactus furniture arrived shortly before noon, and for the next hour I fussed around, trying to figure out what should go where. In the end, I put one of the chairs next to the rack that held my collection of Delta blues vinyls, and the other chair across from the sofa so that I could look at the big oil painting I'd bought a year earlier from an Apache artist. Living room thus arrranged, I then straightened up the bedroom, pleased by the way the horse-head lamp looked next to my Lone Ranger and Tonto bedspread. Some people might think that the entire Fifties Southwestern theme veered into overkill, but the way I saw it, the furniture created the innocent childhood nest I'd never had. While I was still positioning the pillows (one sham had a picture of Silver, the other of Scout), and trying to decide whether I needed a Navajo blanket to hang over the blond wood headboard, I heard a knock at the door. Not being in the habit of inviting guests into my lair, I immediately stiffened. The last person who'd arrived at my apartment unannounced had tried to shoot me. Hoping it was just the Jehovah's Witnesses, I snatched up my .38 and called through the door, "Who is it?"

"Jimmy. I wanted to see your new furniture, but if you're busy…"

I put the .38 down on an end table and let him in.

He toured the apartment, his face so expressionless I couldn't tell if he liked it or not. Unaccountably nervous, I explained the effect I was trying for, then finished up with a lame, "Well, you know, sort of a kid's version of the Wild West. Kind of camp, I guess, but I like it."

That brought a smile. "So do I. It's different." The smile disappeared as quickly as it had arrived. "I'd better get back downstairs. By the way, Harry Caulfield returned your call. He said he was on the way out and won't be back until late tonight, but that you can reach him tomorrow morning."

I felt a stab of disappointment, but guessed my questions about anonymous letters could keep until tomorrow. My decorating jones sated for the day, I locked up and walked back downstairs with Jimmy.

Ian Mantz lived in Arrowhead Ranch, which wasn't an actual ranch at all, merely an upscale subdivision on the west side of Phoenix. It was an easy commute to his Glendale office, although a colorless one, with strip malls and subdivisions lining the entire route. In the dusk, though, with a gaudy Arizona sunset spreading its rosy light over the valley, the faux Mediterranean buildings almost fit the landscape. After getting lost in a maze of curved streets, we found Ian's house at the end of a cul de sac, framed by identical twin palms almost dwarfing the two-story stucco-and-glass structure.

"Nice." But there was no enthusiasm in Jimmy's voice. I'd been around him long enough to know that he much preferred his reservation trailer to the nicest suburban dwelling. Then I remembered he'd spent weeks house-hunting in subdivisions even more banal than this. Why does love make people crazy?

"I guess." I preferred my little walk-up apartment, too. "Well, let's do it." We exited my Jeep (Jimmy had left his truck back at Desert Investigations) and walked up to a massive mahogany door that looked like it had been built for giants. Before returning to the office, Jimmy had driven back to the rez to change into something more appropriate—clothes that matched—and I'd donned the caramel-colored pants suit I'd bought at a designer's resale shop. But I still felt shabby compared to the elegant woman who opened the door.

"*Willkommen!*" A brunette with almond eyes and honey-colored skin, Huong Mantz's accent was more Vietnamese than German. A wartime marriage? While the lines around her eyes and mouth proved that she was no longer young, her svelte model's figure only added to the elegance of her white linen dress.

Ian stood behind her, smiling proudly. He was flanked by four young women, three of them so alike in their dark-eyed brunette beauty that they could have been triplets, offset by one slightly older blond who had inherited her father's blue eyes. Racing along the entryway, a Schnauzer yapping at their heels, were several of Ian Mantz's grandchildren, ranging from brunettes to redheads to blonds: the American pot was melting nicely in the Mantz household. The din was such that I wanted to turn around and flee. Only my duty to Rada Tesema, as well as the delicious aromas wafting from the kitchen, kept me there.

As Huong led Jimmy and me into their elegant two-story living room, I admired the Mantz's good taste, a mixture of East and West. The oyster-colored silk sofas and chairs were subtle enough not to detract from the vivid rugs or the tall red laquer curio cabinet decorated with brilliant dragons highlighted by ivory insets and gold leaf. Contrasting with all this Asian splendor were some of the worst oil paintings I had ever seen: a gaudy rendering of the Grand Canyon looking like a Sherwin-Williams factory had exploded in it, and several hapless portraits of desert wildlife that displayed an abysmal lack of anatomical accuracy.

Ian didn't notice my astonishment. "First we'll have dinner, then some friendly conversation. And then..." Ian smiled at his wife and daughters. They smiled back. "And then we have something to give you."

Dinner was as good as it smelled, a mixture of East and West, with a choice of sauerbraten or lemon grass chicken as main dishes, and everyone including the children ate with gusto. By the time we were finished, there wasn't enough left on the plates to give to the Schnauzer. After a dessert of Sachertorte, Huong herded her grandchildren into the family room to watch sit-coms while the rest of us filed back to the living room.

"You probably wonder why the girls didn't bring their husbands," Ian said, as we settled ourselves.

The four "girls," who ranged somewhere between twenty and thirty, smiled in unison. "*Grosvati*, which is what we called Granddad, was the big family secret—even from us—for the first years of our lives," explained Ilsa, the blonde. "Dad didn't tell us the truth about him until we were old enough to keep our mouths shut. When we married, we didn't even tell our husbands. Especially Silke. Her husband's a cop. Really old school, too."

Silke pulled a sour face. "I'm nuts about the guy, but his legalistic ass is as tight as a crab's."

"Silke!" Huong's hands fluttered to her face.

"Sorry for the language, Mom, but Bill would have turned us all in for harboring a fugitive and you know it."

Whoever thought women couldn't keep a secret had never met the Mantz women. With a conspiratorial smile toward Ilsa, Silke resumed her story. "After Grosvati's funeral a few years back, Dad called a family conference and told the guys everything. They were pissed—sorry again, Mom—but since it no longer mattered, they decided not to let the cat out of the bag. I guess they decided it was preferable to live with a big bunch of liars than see us dragged off to jail. Still, they wanted to be left out of this little gathering, so they're all over at Ilsa's house, drinking beer and playing cards."

Ian waved his daughter into silence. "So now you know the big family secret, Ms. Jones. Are you going to turn us in? Or repeat anything we've told you?"

I imagined my smile was as wry as his as I answered his question with another of my own. "You're not hiding any more illegal aliens, are you?"

He raised his hand in the Boy Scout's salute. "No Islamic terrorists, no IRA thugs, no undocumented yard workers from south of the border."

"Then your secret's safe with me." But I'd learned little more than I already knew when I left Ian's office, so why had he invited me to dinner? To illustrate what a nicely blended American family Gunter Hoenig had established? If dinner hadn't been so delicious I would have felt downright crabby.

As Jimmy and I stood up to leave, a look passed between them all. Then, after receiving a silent chorus of nods, Ian gestured for us to wait and left the room. When he returned, he carried three fat cardboard boxes from Kinko's. "This is for you. It'll tell you everything you need to know about my father. But promise me you won't turn it over to the press or the police."

I considered his request and answered with a half-truth. "O.K. I promise." If there was anything in the box that would help free Rada Tesema, I'd break my word in a heartbeat. But the Mantzes weren't dumb. Anything more incriminating than the information they had already given me would probably be long gone.

Ian placed the Kinko's boxes in my hands. "For you, then. The journals of Gunter Hoenig."

Chapter Twenty

Another late night. Before Jimmy and I left the Mantz household, Ian explained that Silke, the only fluent German-speaker in the family, had years earlier translated Gunter's journals into English and given each daughter a copy. Mine were copies of copies, blurred and faded, but as complete as those that would one day be handed down to his grandchildren. Still, I planned to keep a sharp eye out for any interruptions in the narrative flow that might indicate a page had been removed.

Back home in my apartment, I propped myself up in my Lone Ranger bed and began reading. Like many journalers, Gunter turned out to be a pack rat, saving any printed snippet that captured his attention, so the first box I picked up not only contained journal entries dating from the Sixties, but a host of newspaper clippings ranging from comic strips to news items. Overwhelmed, I put that box aside and picked up another, and was happy to see on top an entry dated August 28, 1945, soon after Gunter Hoenig's marriage to Eva Schmidt, the girl who saved his life. As I read, I realized that by then, the escaped POW had already assumed the identity of Gerhardt Mantz, a cousin of the Schmidt family who had immigrated from Germany before America entered the war. The real Gerhardt Mantz had moved to Alaska to look for gold in the bush, then disappeared. Despite a search by officials and a few relatives, he was never found and was given up for dead. It was Eva's father who told Gunter to take this long-lost cousin's name.

To my disappointment, the journal said little about Camp Papago or Gunter's few months on the run. However, it did detail his fear of being discovered and hanged as a spy. After the Reich surrendered and the war with Germany ended, his tone lightened and for a few entries he wrote hopefully about emerging from hiding. But with the beginning of the Nuremberg Trials and the revelations of Nazi atrocities in the concentration camps, he changed his mind. A one-line entry dated December 4, 1945, said:

I am ashamed to be German.

A few pages later, next to Gunter's own handwriting, he had saved a clipping of an Associated Press article dated Dec. 17, 1945. It detailed some of the items entered into evidence at the Nuremberg Trials. One of them was a lampshade made of tattooed human skin.

Gunter's note, scratched in the margin, said, *Germany has become a land of ghosts.*

He never mentioned his homeland again.

The next few years contained entries about work, making new friends, his happiness at becoming a naturalized American citizen—albeit under an assumed name—and his sorrow that he and Eva could not seem to have children. Then I came across an entry dated, July 14, 1946.

> *Today Gerhardt Mantz is a father! This morning, my beloved Eva gave me a beautiful son. We have named him Ian. The doctors say Eva will have no more babies, so we will wrap our Ian in a blanket of love large enough to cover ten. If only my good friend Josef, along with his wife and child, were all here to toast the future with schnapps. We would sing until dawn.*
>
> *But I guess I will never see Josef again. Like me, he probably abandoned Das Kapitan. I pray he made it back to Germany to be with his own true love. But wherever he is, may the good God be with him.*

Ernst did not appear again in Gunter's journal until June 12, 1978. In an entry at the bottom of the page, he wrote:

Kapitan still lives. This can not be allowed. I remember
Joyce Bollinger's eyes pleading with me, my failure...

I flipped to the next page only to find out that the sentence
remained incomplete. Had someone removed the page? The next
few pages were not only out of order, but were interspersed with
more newspaper clippings that didn't seem to have anything to do
with anything, other than to display Gunter's own wide interests.
I leafed through them in increasing frustration until I struck pay
dirt about three-quarters of the way through, where—stuck to the
back of a recipe for Sachertorte—I found a Darien, Connecticut,
newspaper clipping dated May 12, 1978. It had a photograph of
Erik Ernst receiving an award for his design of the STL-42 racing
sloop. Did someone send this to Gunter, or did he discover it on
his own?

If memory served, Ernst had his boating accident in June of
1978. I resolved to check my case notes the next morning. Just a
few pages away from the newspaper clipping was another journal
entry. This one had me shaking my head in amazement.

> **September 5, 1988**
> *Too late I have learned you can not save someone from*
> *himself. I have tried to help Joyce Bollinger's one surviving*
> *child. I believed that since there have been miracles in my*
> *own life—my beloved Eva is the greatest among them—so*
> *why could there not be miracles in his?*
>
> *But my efforts have been in vain. The troubled boy I tried*
> *so hard to help has grown into a bad man. He was cruel to*
> *his first wife, and now he is cruel to his second, and even his*
> *little girl.*
>
> *It is time for me to turn away from him.*
>
> *Joyce Bollinger, I have failed to save your son, just as I*
> *failed to save you. May you and the good God forgive me.*

A few more entries, all out of chronological order, showed
that for almost three decades, whenever Chess Bollinger screwed
up, Gunter had picked up the pieces. Hiding behind fictitious

names, Gunter bailed Chess out of jail again and again and in some cases even paid his fines.

Then the journals ran out of steam. From the drama of Chess' messed-up life, they shifted to family matters. One entry bragged about Gunter's new son (no date, but I figured it had to be in the Sixties), one rhapsodized about his wife (*She grows more beautiful each day!*), and one mentioned Ian's new wife: *Huong is amost as beautiful as my Eva, but in a different way!* Bored nearly to tears, I read about Gunter's granddaughters (*God has blessed me!*), and the advent of two great-grandchildren who—according to Gunter—were the most beautiful and brilliant children to ever grace the earth. Tolstoy said that happy families were all alike, but he left out the part about them also being boring. Now Gunter's familial happiness was putting me to sleep.

Disappointed, I tried the last box and, to my delight, saw that these pages were more organized. Going straight to the last entry, I found one dated September 14, 1999, a brief paragraph about a trip he and Eva planned to take to Edmonton, Canada, to visit her sister, who was in failing health.

A man may pass, but his family endures, Gunter wrote in that last entry. His words proved prophetic.

The next page—obviously added as a eulogy by someone other than Gunter—was a copy of a short clipping from the *Calgary Sun,* dated September 26, 1999.

> RED DEER, ALBERTA—Thirty-two cars were involved in a chain reaction accident late last night just south of Didsbury when a truck carrying farm equipment jackknifed trying to avoid a disabled vehicle. As of press time, eight people were confirmed dead, including an elderly couple from Phoenix, Arizona. The names of the victims are being withheld pending notification of their families.

"Huh!" I sat back on my pillows and began to think. Why would a man of such advanced age as Gunter Hoenig—who must have easily been in his eighties—drive all the way to Canada? If his sister-in-law was ailing, why not simply fly? Then I remembered that earlier the same year, Gunter ran into Ernst at the German-American club. Had Ernst, seeing that his old crew member was alive and well, suspected Gunter had driven the boat that crashed into him and threatened to go to the police? Perhaps the visit to Canada wasn't meant to be a mere visit. Perhaps it was a final hiding place, and as such, Gunter had wanted to haul along family mementos that he didn't dare leave to the mercy of the U.S. Postal Service.

It made sense. But a jackknifed truck destroyed all of Gunter Hoenig's carefully laid plans.

As I continued to search through the box, I found several loose items: a copy of the couple's obit from the *Arizona Republic* and some "Humor in Uniform" columns from *Reader's Digest*. Smiling, I leafed through Gunter's amateurish drawings: submarines that looked more like Bratwurst than U-boats, improbably structured horses, cats, dogs, birds and even children—or maybe they were Christmas elves; it was hard to tell. Indeed, Gunter's drawings were rough enough to verge on the abstract, and at times I could hardly tell if their subjects were animal, vegetable or mineral. Now I understood the reason for the clumsy oil paintings in Ian Mantz's house; filial love was blind. I studied the drawings, wincing at Gunter's attempt to capture nature with a less-than-talented eye. For a few minutes I tried to decipher one particularly wobbly piece, then finally gave up and looked at my clock. Two forty-six a.m. I was in for another red-eye morning.

My prediction proved to be accurate, but Gunter Hoenig's journal wasn't the reason.

Saturday dawned clear and crisp, but halfway through Fay Harris' funeral, the skies clouded over again. Kryzinski stood stoically through the graveside service, even though his eyes grew more alarmingly hollow with every word the minister spoke. Fay's co-workers at the *Journal* provided a chorus of sobs. Many of the journalists looked not only sorrowful but frightened, as if they were worried about the enemies they might make covering their own beats. Warren, who'd returned from L.A. on the red-eye, stood beside me. From the way his hands were shaking, I wondered briefly about his own relationship with Fay, then dismissed the thought. He'd liked and respected her, that was all. As for me, I was so overwhelmed by grief and guilt that I could only nod when Warren asked me to lunch with him on the set.

When the service ended and I finally made it back to Desert Investigations, I tried to work, more convinced than ever that the Bollinger, Ernst and Fay Harris killings were all connected. Outside the office, the usual hordes of tourists strolled Main Street, but this time I'd taken the precaution of keeping the lights off. There was still enough light coming through the picture window to work in, but depressed, I just sat there for a while staring off into space. Instead of trying to work, I should probably have taken Warren's advice and followed him over to the set.

Finally rousing myself from my guilt-induced stupor, I called Information and got the phone number for the Bridgeport, Connecticut, Police Department. Knowing that police forces everywhere were open on Saturday—a popular day for mayhem— I called and asked for Sgt. Carmine Aliessio. The receptionist informed me that *Captain* Aliessio had retired the previous year, but she helpfully put me through to his replacement. Captain Homer Swayze listened to my story, told me the files on the Ernst case were probably in storage somewhere "across town," but that he'd call his pal Carmine to see if he was interested in talking to me. Figuring I'd reached a dead end, I gave him my phone number, said that Aliessio could call me collect, and hung up.

To my surprise, Aliessio called me mere minutes later. He was as forthright as retired cops can be, no longer having to worry about bureaucratic red tape or manipulative defense attorneys. "So somebody finally nailed the bastard? Ha! Second time's a charm." His voice was hoarse but chipper, as if he'd been wait-ing a long time for someone to talk to. Through a connection so bad that it hissed, I thought I heard a TV in the background, tuned to a game show.

"I take it you didn't think the incident in 1983 was an accident."

A laugh. "You think right. The witnesses said the Chris Craft headed straight for him and never once tried to turn."

"I'm surprised you remember it so well after all these years."

"It's hard to forget a double amputation on the water. Ever worked one?"

I informed him that while some areas in Arizona had man-made lakes big enough for power boats, Scottsdale didn't. "Messiest thing I ever worked on the job was a seven car pile-up with a loaded cattle truck."

He laughed. "Maybe I should come out to Arizona, see the sights."

When I told him we didn't have many cattle truck pile-ups anymore, what with the widened freeways and all, he sounded almost disappointed. "Oh, well. Guess I'll have to keep watching *Jeopardy* for my fun. Anyway, back when Ernst had his 'accident,' we were all pretty sure it was an attempted homicide, but we couldn't put a case together. When we interviewed his neighbors and co-workers, we found out the guy wasn't exactly the King of the Prom, especially among the Jewish engineers, you dig?"

I told him I dug.

At that point, my office door opened and Jimmy walked in. I was surprised to see him, thinking he'd be out looking for houses or furniture on a Saturday, but he waved away my questioning glance and settled himself in front of the computer. I turned my attention back to Captain Aliessio.

"Beats me how Ernst made it over here after the war, but I guess the Navy figured it could use his expertise, which they did," he was saying. "You know, like the rocket people used Von Braun. Nice, huh? All those Nazis getting fat off the American dime? Anyhoo, during our investigation, we turned up a few interesting items in Ernst's apartment."

Aliessio was enjoying this, stretching out the conversation as long as possible. I decided to hurry him along. "Anonymous letters, perhaps?"

He whistled. "As a matter of fact, yes. Six. All singing the same song. Whoever wrote them was convinced Ernst killed some Arizona family named Bollinger back in the Forties. We checked and found out that the surviving Bollinger son went to trial for the killings. Correct me if I'm wrong, but when the jury let him off, the prevailing belief was still that he'd done it. How'm I doing so far?"

"You're doing fine, Captain."

"Your guys get letters, too?"

"After the trial, the sheriff's office received quite a few. I've placed a call to one of the deputies who worked on the case to see if he heard about anything else."

We were both silent for a moment, listening to the crackle of the telephone connection between Connecticut and Arizona. The sound of fate following Ernst across the continent?

Aliessio broke the silence. "Regardless of what we let the press think, we never believed it was some stoner kid taking a joyride in a stolen boat. When we asked around the marinas, we did get a couple of leads, but they never went anywhere. One woman said she saw a stranger eyeing a nearby Cigarette Top Gun, but when he saw her watching him, he walked away."

"Did she give a description?"

"Only that he was thin, looked sun-burned, and was on the up side of fifty."

The up side of fifty. I caught myself holding my breath and forced myself to exhale slowly. "You said you had a couple of leads. What was the other one?"

"Some rich kid sunning herself on the deck of her daddy's big old Hatteras-T-DD. Rough life for the privileged, eh? Anyway, she said some guy walking past asked her where the head was. Only he called it 'the gentleman's room,' which she found pretty funny."

He was going to make me ask. "Description?"

"Old and skinny. And..."

Lord deliver me from bored, retired cops. Maybe Aliessio should move to Harry Caulfield's Apache Junction trailer park for a little action. "And?"

The satisfaction in his voice oozed through the hissy line. "She said he spoke with a German accent."

I slammed my hand down on the desk so hard Jimmy looked around to see what was happening. "You okay?" he mouthed.

I waved him back to his computer. "She was sure the accent was German, not Swiss or something else?"

"Oh, yeah, she was sure. Seems Daddy had business interests in Berlin and sometimes took his family along with."

Life having a finite chance for coincidence, I guessed that whoever had written the sheriff's office after the Bollinger trial had to be the same person who'd written the Bridgeport police. I told Aliessio so.

He agreed. "Sure makes you think, doesn't it?"

"Sure does."

He cleared his throat. "That kid, the one they put on trial out there. What happened to him?"

When I told him, Aliessio grunted. "Before I let something like that happen to me, I'll eat my gun."

I remembered Chess Bollinger's vacant eyes, his wife's malignant smile, the dingy nursing home where Lysol couldn't quite disguise the smell of decomposing flesh. If I kept going the way I was going, who would be around to care for me?

"I'm with you there," I said.

On that note, we ended the call, and after asking Jimmy why he wasn't out house-hunting and receiving a none-of-your-business look, I went back to work. Harry Caulfield still wasn't answering his phone, so I left another message. But as soon as I hung up, the phone rang again. I looked at the caller I.D. and was pleased to see that Harry Caulfield had returned my call. He'd probably been in the shower.

But I was wrong. The man on the phone identified himself as Detective Manuel Villapando with the Apache Junction Police Department. His voice was cool, with absolutely no inflection.

A bad sign. "You just left a message on Harry Caulfield's answering machine. Would you mind telling me what you were calling him about?"

I'd been around long enough to recognize a police investigation in progress. "Why do you want to know? Has something happened to Harry?"

"Were you close?"

Were. All my happiness at having Warren back in town dissipated. "Mr. Caulfield is helping me with an investigation."

"And that was?"

"Please. Tell me what's happened."

"Mr. Caulfield was found dead in his residence this morning. He appears to have died some time last night."

If Harry was dead, why could I still see him with his eyepatch and pirate smile, his trailer with its life-affirming sign, IF THE DOUBLE-WIDE'S A-ROCKIN', DON'T COME A-KNOCKIN'? Now two people involved in the Ernst investigation were dead—first Fay, now Harry. Reminding myself that professionals don't cry, I cleared my throat. "I take it his death wasn't natural." Cops didn't sound as cautious as Villapando when someone keeled over from a heart attack.

Villapando side-stepped my question. "Ms. Jones, are you going to be at your office for the next few hours? I'd like to send someone over to..."

Forget that. I owed Harry. "Detective Villapando, are you at Harry's trailer now?"

His voice turned cautious. "Yes."

"I'm on my way." I slammed the phone down, and after a brief explanation to Jimmy, ran out the door.

I arrived at the mobile home park at the same time as Harry's friend, Frank Oberle. The trailer was taped off, but that hadn't kept a large crowd from forming.

"Jesus, Jesus," Oberle muttered as he hauled himself stiffly from his battered Ford Contour. The grocery sacks sitting in the passenger's seat were testament that he'd been out shopping. When he saw me, his face flushed with rage. "You! This is all your fault!"

He teetered forward, his knobby finger stabbing toward me. "Why'd you have to get him involved in all this shit again? You see what's happened, huh, don't you?"

I shielded my face from that accusatory finger. "Mr. Oberle, I didn't mean…"

To my relief, the door to Harry's trailer opened and a dark face peered out. "I take it you're Ms. Jones." The man spotted Oberle, who was about to wrench open the Jeep's door to get at me. "Don't get physical with her, Frank, or I'll have to take you in."

I noticed that I was "Ms. Jones," but Oberle was "Frank." They knew each other. Well, Apache Junction was still a relatively small town. "Are you Detective Villapando?"

"The same. You can come in for a minute as long as you don't touch anything." Then, to Oberle, "You wait outside. You don't need to see this. I'll come out and explain things as soon as I've finished with Ms. Jones here. In the meantime, why don't you go put your groceries away before they spoil. I'll catch up with you later."

Fortunately, Oberle did as Villapando suggested, so I hopped out of the Jeep and followed the detective into the trailer. The sea of crime scene techs parted, leaving me an unobstructed view of the mess on the floor. At first, the scene before me made no sense. Harry lay on his stomach, surrounded by what appeared to be blood-spattered snow. After a closer look, I realized the "snow" was feathers, probably the remnants of a ghetto silencer, which was nothing more than a pillow draped over a gun to baffle sound. Gang-bangers and mobsters sometimes used this method because it was cheap and more or less effective.

Villapando's voice brought me back. "What kind of weapon do you carry, Ms. Jones?"

When I opened my carry-all and showed him the .38, he didn't ask me to take it out. No surprise there. Judging by the amount of blood and feathers in the room, the murder weapon was probably something more along the lines of a 9-mm, like the gun that took Fay down.

Villapando gave me a severe look. "I checked you out."

"Of course you did."

He gestured around the room with a brown hand. "You have any ideas on this?"

I told him everything, with the exception of my visit to Ian Mantz/Hoenig and the existence of Gunter Hoenig's journals. Maybe I would part with that information later, maybe not. For now, there was no point in dragging the Mantz family secret into this. "There were a couple of things I needed to get more information on from Harry, that's why I kept calling," I finished up.

"Such as?" Villapando stared at me like a scorpion eyeing a centipede.

"Such as the anonymous notes accusing Ernst of murder, which supposedly turned up not long after Chess Bollinger's trial. I wanted to ask Harry if the notes were still around, and if so, could he arrange for me to take a look at them."

"To compare them to the notes in Connecticut? We can help you with that."

I doubted it. Villapando would probably keep any information he discovered to himself. Unlike Captain Kryzinski, he owed me nothing. Then again, I didn't owe Villapando anything, either.

Which he knew. "So you think whoever killed the reporter is the same person who killed Caulfield?"

"Probably. Your ballistics people can confirm it."

He gave me a wry smile. "Probably."

Time to lay my cards on the table, although I knew it would net me nothing. "Detective Villapando, I've shared with you. Now share with me."

He didn't answer right away, and when he did, he confirmed my suspicions about the lack of cooperation I was likely to receive from the sheriff's office. "There's not much I can tell you at this point. Pending autopsy, I'd say Mr. Caulfield was killed sometime late last night, but no one heard anything other than a couple of backfires, which they're now certain were gunshots. No one saw anyone arrive or leave. No one knows if Mr. Caulfield had enemies."

Or maybe the residents of the trailer court didn't feel like talking to the police. One thing this case had taught me was that for all their seeming frailty, the elderly can be as wicked as the rest of us.

Since I had nothing more to add, Villapando dismissed me. As I turned to go, he added, "You're not planning to leave town, are you?"

"I seldom do." Especially now that I would soon be the only employee at Desert Investigations.

As I reached my Jeep, Frank Oberle came back, this time on foot. "You!" The finger came up again.

Not wanting to get my eye poked out, I peeled out of there as fast as I could.

"Did you forget something?" Warren, crackling over a bad cell phone connection.

I've always hated people who talk on their cell phones while speeding along the freeway, but I was so eager to blot the scene at Harry's trailer out of my mind that when mine rang, I'd answered immediately. Something else to feel guilty about.

"Forget what?"

"It's one-forty-five. You were supposed to meet me at the set for lunch at one." He sounded furious.

The semi next to me blared its air horn at a dogging Infiniti, nearly making me jump out of my skin. "Sorry. I…I got caught up in something." Phone pressed to ear, I edged over to the exit ramp, Warren nagging at me all the while. The light was with me, and after hanging a right, I pulled to a stop in a Dairy Queen parking lot. The aroma of overcooked chili dogs wafted from the building, merging with the odor of automobile emissions. As it usually did when I was upset, my stomach rumbled.

Warren continued to rant. "Where are you? I hear traffic."

"I'm at a Dairy Queen outside of Apache Junction, off I-60." I flashed back on what I'd seen in Harry's trailer. So much for putting it out of my mind. "For your information, Harry Caulfield's been murdered. I was at the crime scene, talking to the cops."

"Caulfield? Isn't that the guy...?"

"Frank Oberle's friend. The guy with the eyepatch. You met him the day he came out to the set to keep Frank company."

A silence. Then, "Lena, I don't think you should be involved in that case any more. In fact, I want you to pull out."

"Excuse me?"

"You heard what I said. Quit the Ernst case. Now." He sounded less like a prospective lover than a Hollywood director used to being obeyed. The tiger showing its true stripes?

I spoke carefully, not wanting to provide a spectacle for the gaggle of teenagers lined up at the Dairy Queen window. "Did you just give me an order?"

"Of course I did. You either give up that case or I'll..."

"Or you'll what?" I could hear my teeth grind as cars rushed past. No one tells Lena Jones what to do. No one.

"Or...or..." He paused, as if aware of what was about to happen. "Baby, I..."

Baby? The guilt and stress of the past few days rose up, and I snapped, "Cut the Hollywood crap, Warren. My name's Lena, not Baby. And if you want to continue this ridiculous conversation, you'll have to call me later." Like in twenty years.

Ending the call, I stashed the cell back in my carry-all. Then I shut the Jeep off and joined the teenagers in line. Maybe a chili dog would erase the memory of Harry Caulfield's bloody trailer.

Later that afternoon I was sitting on my cactus wood sofa, nursing my guilt and flipping back and forth in Gunter's journals when a phone call rolled over from Desert Investigations. Jimmy had obviously left for the day. I picked it up and heard Beth Osmon's voice.

"Jack came by this morning and told me he has to fly back to Mississippi on business." She sounded pretty cheery for a woman suffering from a broken heart. "He offered me the opportunity to invest in a Tupelo shopping mall, so of course I wrote him a check."

Of course? Jack Sherwood/Rinn was a scam artist who specialized in lonely rich women. I'd given her proof of that only the day before. "Beth, um, you'll probably not see your money again. Remember what I told…"

"It was just a couple hundred thou. Here's the deal, Lena. Since he's given me a phony name and asked for money for a phony project, he's now committed a crime and can be prosecuted. Right?"

The situation was more complicated than that. Since she'd given him the check in Arizona, prosecution should begin here, but since he was on his way back to Alabama, jurisdiction could turn into a snake's nest. Not to mention the fact that the courts were backlogged already. However, I told her to go ahead and file a complaint with Scottsdale PD.

"That's not enough. I want to confront him."

Even though she couldn't see me, I shook my head. "That's never a good idea. We don't know how violent he is. Remember, he's probably been using false names all over the place, and simply because no one has lodged an official complaint against him doesn't mean he hasn't physically assaulted someone."

"Which is why I want you to be with me."

I stifled a groan. Did she think Sherwood/Rinn would be stupid enough to return to Arizona now that he had her money? "He won't be coming back, Beth. He's probably…"

She cut me off. "Of course he won't. That's why I went down to Scottsdale North yesterday afternoon and swore out a complaint. The police chief's a friend of mine, so he's expediting it. But I don't want to see Jack merely prosecuted, I want satisfaction! Let's fly out to Alabama and confront him there. In his home, in front of his wife. If she knows what he's been doing, I want to prosecute her, too. For conspiracy. I want to see them all rot in prison."

This woman scorned had enough fury for a bushel of them, and while I admired her spunk, I was less thrilled by the scenario she'd laid out. From what Eddy Joe had told me, Hamilton, Alabama, was a small town located more than ninety miles northwest of citified Birmingham, and as usual in small towns, Sherwood/Rinn would have deep roots there and a wide circle of friends. What good could such a confrontation do, other than give Beth a chance to vent? Remembering that the couple also had four children, I also wasn't crazy about bringing Mrs. Sherwood/Rinn into the mix. What would happen to them if Mommy and Daddy both went to prison? If no relatives were available to take them in, they would wind up in foster homes. Given what I knew about some foster homes, I would rather see Alea Sherwood/Rinn go free, even if she was her husband's partner in crime. Of course, I wasn't about to tell Beth that.

"It's really not…"

"I'll triple what I'm paying you. Plus pay all expenses."

I sat up straight. With Jimmy soon leaving for Southwest MicroSystems, Desert Investigations would be strapped for cash. "Uh…"

"Make that quadruple."

If I held out a little longer, would she go quintuple? I decided not to chance it. "When do you want to fly out?"

"Tomorrow."

Sunday? Oh, what the hell. There was little more I could do on the Ernst investigation until Monday, and Southern towns were supposed to be quiet on Sundays, what with everyone either in church or barbequing. Besides, it would do me good to get out of town and help me through the increasing load of guilt I was carrying over Fay's—and now Harry's—deaths. "Sounds good to me," I told her. "I'll make the airline reservations and notify Eddy Joe Hughey in case he's free and wants to drive to Hamilton with us."

As it turned out, Eddy Joe was not only free, but was happy for the chance to meet up again, so little more than twenty-four hours later, he was chauffeuring Beth and me across the forested hills of northern Alabama in his pearl Eldorado. There was something about the almost over-lush landscape that attracted and repelled at the same time, as if I'd seen it all before in a movie I couldn't quite remember but that had somehow been unsettling.

Loquacious as ever, Eddy Joe chattered as he drove, about politics (he was against them), movies (he harbored a grand passion for Julianne Moore) and Alabama weather (too humid). To my amusement, Beth seemed enchanted with both Eddy Joe's bulk and his just-as-massive charm, which I hoped meant that she was on her way toward recovery. I had to admit that Eddy Joe was cute, in a big, sloppy sort of way. With his swoony brown eyes and light brown hair greying at the sides, he looked—and acted—like an oversized, over-friendly golden retriever.

"I did me a little more pokin' around in our Mr. Sherwood/ Rinn's life, and I've found us several more women he suckered," Eddy Joe said, as he made a hard right off SR-78 and onto SR-43 into Hamilton. "Turns out one of them, a great ol' gal livin' down in Mobile, is the third cousin four times removed of the county sheriff up here, so I contacted him and he's demandin' to go along with us to arrest our boy's thievin' ass."

The confrontation was turning into quite a party, and I didn't know how I felt about that. "Are we supposed to meet him at the police station?"

"Nah, nobody steals nuthin' on Sundays around here, so he's meeting us over at the Elks Lodge with a couple deputies. He got the faxed warrant from Scottsdale this morning, which makes me think our lovely Miss Beth musta pulled a few strings. We'll all drive over to the Rinn house together."

Oh, whee. "I thought the whole idea was for Beth to confront Mr. Rinn herself."

Eddy Joe nodded his big, shaggy head. "Sheriff Corliss is a patient feller. He and his boys will lay back in the woods until Miss Beth gives the skunk a piece of her mind." Here there was a delighted titter from the back seat. "Then he'll move in and y'all can start worrying about extradition."

"The sheriff doesn't expect any violence?"

Sandy curls bobbed again. "Nah. He says he always suspected Jacky Rinn was a weasel, but doubts he'd hurt a fly."

I've heard serial killers described in much the same way, so I didn't feel any better about our mission than I had when Beth first proposed it. Since I'd left my .38 at home, I also felt naked. "Um, Eddy Joe, are you, um…"

"Packin'? Sure am. I never go any place without Sweet Melissa." He patted the slight bulge on the left side of his chest. "But rest assured, ladies, Mr. Rinn's a lover, not a fighter."

Which was exactly the problem.

After meeting up with the sheriff, we caravanned through Hamilton, a tidy little town that appeared to have no bars at all but a church on every corner. We continued north on SR-43 until we reached a gravel road that cut through a thick stand of oaks, and as their branches closed in overhead, I began to feel claustrophobic. As pretty as Alabama was, with its emerald fields and nearly rain forest lushness, I missed the wide-open spaces of the Southwest. Shortly before we emerged from the oaks, the sheriff's Jeep Cherokee pulled to the side and let us continue on alone. I didn't like the setup and told Eddy Joe so.

He laughed. "This ain't Phoenix, Lena. Last time someone was shot dead out here was eight years ago, in a hunting accident."

My suspicious mind wondered if it was really a hunting accident or someone settling a score, but I kept such dark ruminations to myself as the trees cleared and Jack Rinn's place came into view. Contrary to popular opinion, crime frequently did pay. The house, a rambling tri-level of dark red brick offset by green shutters, sat at on a rise at the end of a lane bordered by acres and acres of rolling pastureland. A few well cared-for horses stared at us from the pasture on our right, while on our left, a herd of black fat Angus were too busy grazing in knee-deep grass to give us more than a passing glance.

"He owns a better spread than I do!" Beth sounded outraged.

Eddy Joe demurred. "Property values aren't the same here as in Scottsdale. But those sure are some fine horses, ain't they? Did ya see the big sorrel over by the pond?"

"You like horses?" For a moment, Beth forgot her ire. Horse people are like that.

Eddy Joe noticed, too, and used it. "Oh, yeah. I have me a Tennessee Walker named Eloise in back of my place, eatin' me out of house and home. Now, Miss Beth, I want you to wait in the car and appreciate the equines for a while so Lena and I can go up to the house and make sure everything's copacetic."

Thus soothed, Beth agreed.

Happy that he was showing some common sense after all, I remained quiet until the Eldorado pulled up to the front door and the door opened to reveal a tiny, dark-haired woman in her mid-twenties. Wearing a pink maternity dress with matching pumps, she looked like she'd just arrived home from church. Ignorant of our purpose, she expressed delight at seeing us, and I had to remind myself that the biggest crooks often sported the widest smiles. As Eddy Joe and I exited the car, she said, "You here to see Jacky about that inheritance, Mr. Hughey?"

Eddy Joe gave her a big smile. "Sure am."

Alea Rinn seemed even happier. "Oh, he's been waitin' for y'all. Say, you folks want somethin' to eat? I cooked up some fried chicken for lunch and there's plenty left over." Oh, the South. She was already offering us food.

"We already ate," Eddy Joe lied. "Just lead us to that ol' boy of yours so we can get our business out of the way."

After trying to tempt us with pecan pie for dessert, Alea led us through a living room packed with Sunday-best-dressed children into the den where a more casually dressed Jack Rinn sat hunkered over a computer. I figured he was probably trolling for more victims because the second we entered, he hit his screen saver. Or was that to keep his wife from seeing what he was doing? I hoped so. I'd really hate for Beth to send a pregnant woman to prison. Almost as tall as Eddy Joe, Rinn had such Elvis-black hair and Elvis-blue eyes that it reminded me

Hamilton was only an hour's drive away from Tupelo, where The King had been born. A distant relative, perhaps?

Unaware of what was about to go down, Alea gave her husband a peck on the cheek. "These are the folks about that inheritance thing."

"Mr. Rinn!" Eddy Joe stuck out his beefy hand in a great show of bonhomie. "I'm Eddy Joe Hughey and this here's Lena Jones, one of my business associates. We got somebody outside who's dyin' to talk with ya!"

Rinn looked puzzled but not particularly suspicious as he ambled after us through the house, Alea following. "I figured you'd call first."

Neither Eddy Joe nor I answered. We both kept smiling and smiling until Rinn was out of the house. Then Eddy Joe waved at the Eldorado and Beth Osmon stepped out.

Sherwood/Rinn paled and almost went down. "Beth! I...I..."

By then, Alea knew something was wrong. "Jacky, who is...?"

Beth didn't give her time to finish. In a split second she closed the distance between her and her faux fiancé and slapped him hard across the face. "The only reason I don't shoot you, you sonofabitch, is because I couldn't get my gun on the plane!" Then she drew back her hand, as if to smack him again.

Before she could, Alea jumped in front of her cringing husband. "You! Stop hittin' my Jacky this minute, or I'll...!"

My cue. I inserted myself between Beth and Alea. "That's it. No one's hitting anyone any more."

Eddy Joe made a sour face. "Ah, Lena, you're no fun."

At that moment the sheriff's Cherokee rolled out of the oak stand, up the drive, and came to a stop beside us. Sheriff Corliss quickly exited with his two deputies. He produced a pair of handcuffs and before his quarry could move, had Jack Rinn shackled, nose down, on the SUV's hood. He drawled Rinn his rights, then shoved him in the back seat with a deputy on either side. Before the door closed, we could hear Jack Rinn bawling, "I did it for us, Alea! For our family!"

Sheriff Corliss ignored him. "Now that's what I call a nice day's work. We can get him booked in time to go back to the lodge for some pok...Um, for that church fund-raiser we're havin'." Turning to Alea, he said, "Ma'am, I'm sorry for your trouble, but it looks like Mr. Rinn here ain't been a good Christian. Course, his attorney, who I do suggest you call sooner than later, might beg to differ." To Eddy Joe and me, he said, "Y'all get along now. We don't need any more excitement here." With that, he climbed into the Cherokee and backed down the gravel drive.

Beth looked gratified but my heart went out to Alea, who stood frozen in place as the Cherokee disappeared into the oaks. Maybe I was wrong, but I didn't think she knew anything about her husband's out-of-state "business dealings." "Mrs. Rinn, Alea, you deserve an explanation."

For the first time, Beth looked at her, really looked at her, at the pregnant belly, at the dark-haired children peeking through the front door of the house. "You didn't know, did you?" she asked.

Shock glazed Alea's eyes. "Know *what*? Why'd Sheriff Corliss take Jacky away? Will somebody please tell me what's goin' on?"

Before I could stop her, Beth stepped around me and put her arm around Alea. "Let's go back into the house, honey. We need to talk."

On the plane back to Phoenix late that night, Beth fell asleep, leaving me wide awake to reflect alone on love, men, and family.

After the grief I'd just observed, I wasn't sure I had the nerve for any one of the three.

Chapter Twenty-One

I'm not a good traveler. Jet-lagged and exhausted both emotionally and physically, I vowed to spend the entire day hunkered down in the office and to leave by five to catch up on my sleep. Until then, the phone and I would be good friends. After telling Jimmy all about the Alabama trip, I finished my fourth cup of coffee and placed a call to Sea Solutions in Connecticut, where Erik Ernst had worked before moving to Arizona. I danced around with Human Resources for a few minutes, then was transferred around to various departments until I found myself speaking to someone who had actually known him.

"Oh, yeah, Erik," said nautical engineer Geraldine Howe, whose voice made her sound ready for either rehab or retirement. "You say someone murdered him? Gee, why am I not surprised. That man was a pig if ever there was one, but sad to say, I made the mistake of going out with him."

"You *dated* Erik Ernst?" The very idea of Ernst having a love life took my breath away.

A chuckle. "Just that one time. I'm not proud of it, but in my defense I was new on the job and knew nothing about him or his reputation other than the fact that his manners were courtly, very Old-World. That sort of thing can be attractive to a young woman, especially one like me who was raised in a house full of roughneck, foul-mouthed brothers who believed the highest form of entertainment was putting a whoopee cushion on their sister's dining room chair. Anyway, Erik asked me out my third day at Sea Solutions and dumbass that I was, I said yes."

I had to smile. A little roughneck had rubbed off on her, too. "I take it things didn't go well."

"Hoo, boy, you take it right! But I'll say this for the smarmy sonofabitch. He didn't stint on the expense. He took me out to a nice dine-and-dance place and plied me with champagne. The good stuff, too. For an hour or so I thought I'd found the love of my life, even if he was old enough to be my father. You know how it is, age can be a plus for some girls. I've never minded a man with a few miles on him, especially if he owns a nice boat. Which Erik did."

I tried to envision Erik Ernst as a ladies' man but failed: the vision of his caved-in head kept intruding. "Okay, so he swept you off your feet for an hour or two. Then what happened?"

"Drunk is what happened. Sloppy drunk. Like a smart little girl, I only sipped at my champagne, but Erik ordered schnapps for himself and downed it like there was no tomorrow. After a while, things started to get ugly. Real ugly. Turns out Mr. Manners was one mean drunk."

I'd met a few of those in my life, and knew that extricating one's self from the situation wasn't always easy. "Did he get abusive?"

"Not toward me, he didn't, but…Look, the whole thing started off kind of easy, so I wasn't prepared when it all went south. You know how some guys are. Once they have a few drinks, they want to take a stroll down Memory Lane and revel in their triumphs, usually something about running a few yards with some stupid football. But that's not what Erik treated me to." Now she sounded angry.

"Such as?"

I could almost feel the heat from the phone as she continued. "Such as his adventures during World War II. I tried to head him off by telling him I'd lost two uncles on an aircraft carrier in the Pacific, but by then he was too drunk and full of himself and his so-called triumphs to listen. He went on and on about being some big deal U-boat commander, about how many American ships he blew out of the water, as if that was going to make points with *me*. Then to top it all off, he started crowing about some POW camp in Arizona where he oversaw some kind of hush-hush trial by the inmates where a traitor wound up getting tortured to death. It was all so disgusting that I told him I was going to the ladies' room. Instead, I snuck over to the bar, called a cab, and went home. The next day at the office I avoided him, and since by then he was sober, he got the message."

"That POW. Did Ernst give a name?"

"Sorry, it's been a while and I can't remember. But I think it was Vernon somebody."

"Does Werner sound familiar? Werner Drechsler?"

"My God, that's it! Werner! So…you're telling me that it really happened, Erik wasn't just running his mouth?"

I remembered the newspaper articles about the event, their description of Werner Drechsler's wounds—more than one hundred shallow stab wounds and cigarette burns, before he had died by hanging. "Yeah, it really happened. Out here, at a place called Camp Papago."

A long silence. Then, "War is one thing, but torture is another."

My feelings exactly. "Can you remembering anything else about that night?"

"Only more of the same. You know how drunks are. Once Erik started in on the 'traitor' thing, he just kept going on and on about it while I tuned out."

We talked a little while longer and she corroborated other stories I'd been told about Ernst. From the very start, he'd been a problem employee for Sea Solutions, so much so that after his "accident" the company had urged him to "retire" before he got fired.

"He was in danger of being fired? Even after the accident?"

"Oh, yeah. Mr. P.C. he wasn't," Geraldine said, laughing. "After Erik's accident, everyone felt sorry for him, sure, but a pig's a pig. Then one day in the lunchroom, he spouted off too much about certain minorities, using the usual ignoramus terms, and claimed that the company's affirmative action policy was a crime against nature. That in a just society, the genetically lacking—which was everyone not German, apparently—would make way for the genetically superior. After that little spiel, he was called into Human Resources. Except we called it Personnel back then. He was told it was time to weigh anchor, to sail off into the sunset, somewhere as far away as possible. Otherwise, Sea Solutions might be in for a nasty lawsuit by one of our many minority employees. When Erik decided to accept the severance package and move to Arizona, we were all so thrilled we actually gave him a going-away party. Which, I might add, he capped off with an off-key rendition of "*Deutschland, Deutschland über Alles.*" May the pig *not* rest in peace."

"One final question. Do you have any idea what kind of severance package Ernst received?"

Geraldine laughed again. "Since I am now married to the director of Human Resources—one of those minorities Erik so hated—I know exactly what kind of severance package he received."

The amount she gave me wasn't as high as I'd been led to believe from my short tour around Ernst's house. "That brings up another question."

"Fire away."

"Did Ernst own a house or other property in Connecticut? A yacht of some sort?" The newspaper article about his accident had stated that he'd been taking his dinghy out to his boat when the accident occurred. He might have been able to get big bucks when he sold it. And if he owned a house, the property values in those seaside villages back east could be sky high. If Ernst had cashed out before moving to buyer-friendly Arizona, he could still have accumulated a nice little nest egg.

She snorted. "Yacht? Not hardly! Just that little twenty-eight-foot Catalina he kept moored outside the marina to save money on slip fees. And no property at all that I know of. Erik lived in an apartment. It was a nice one, from what I hear, but still an apartment. I don't think he had any money, only what he made at Sea Solutions. And what he made, he spent, just like the proverbial drunken sailor. I wasn't the only girl he wined and dined big time."

I had one final question before I ended the conversation. "In all the time that you knew him, did Ernst ever hint about a big secret that he was privy to, something that was 'like gold'?"

"No, nothing like that."

After promising I'd keep her up to date on the investigation, I hung up, cursing myself for not having Jimmy investigate Ernst's finances earlier. Perhaps they were irrelevant, perhaps not. But I needed to know more. I glanced over to Jimmy's side of the office.

"I need to ask a favor." It would be one of my last. Friday was his last day at Desert Investigations, and I had no illusions that Esther would be eager to have him continue any kind of relationship with me. I wasn't just losing a partner: I was losing my best friend.

Oblivious to my gloomy thoughts, he smiled. "Happy to do it, if I can."

"An acquaintance of Erik Ernst led me to believe that he might have been having money troubles. I'd like you to find out the truth."

"If Ernst left Germany owing two Deutschmarks from a crap game, I'll find the paper trail. When do you need the info?"

I looked up at the clock. It was almost time for lunch. If I'd made it this far, there was a good chance I could make it through the entire day. "Think you can have it by five? I doubt if I got as much as two hours sleep last night, so I'm leaving early."

He shook his head. "Sorry. I'm so backed up I haven't even been able to run that check on Warren yet."

Appalled that I had requested such a thing, I looked down at my desk so he wouldn't see my guilty expression. Then I remembered the dismay on Alea Rinn's face when she learned how her husband had been supporting the family. I looked back up. "Run both checks as soon as you can. But first, why don't we drive over to Honey Bear's for barbequed pork? It's supposed to be good for jet-lag."

"Sorry again. I'll be lucky if I have time to order out for a pizza. The house deal fell through. They received an offer from another buyer who was willing to pay more, so now we have to start all over again. Esther's found a condo she's interested in, and I'm supposed to meet her there at two."

First he was ready to leave the wide open reservation for a small house, and now for a condo. His world was narrowing by the minute. "Where's the condo?"

"Right in back of Scottsdale Fashion Square."

The mall was in the middle of Scottsdale, at the intersection of the city's two busiest streets. "But the traffic will drive you nuts!"

He shrugged. "Can't do anything about that. Esther likes the idea because she could walk to her job at Neiman Marcus. And the condo's not that far from here, either, so I could walk to work, too. See? An eco-friendly solution to the whole thing."

Here. "Jimmy, haven't you forgotten something?"

"What?"

"Friday's your last day here. You'll be working at Southwest MicroSystems, and they're located on the northwest side of Phoenix. Several freeway interchanges and twenty-five bumper-to-bumper miles are hardly walking distance."

Now it was his turn to look shame-faced. "Oh. You're right. I forgot. Eco-friendly for Esther, maybe, not so much for me." He dismissed the apparent inequity. "Relationships sure require compromise, don't they?"

All the compromise seemed to be on Jimmy's part, but I wasn't about to say so. I wanted our last few days together to be as peaceful as possible.

Before deciding what to do about lunch, I placed a call to the Maricopa County Sheriff's office, hoping to find someone who might have access to the old Bollinger murder records. After being passed from one civilian to another, I reached a deputy who promised he'd try to hunt down the files as soon as he found the time. Which would be, of course, when pigs received their pilot's license. After that, I called Reverend Giblin to find out how close his church and Tesema's synagogue were to raising enough money for seven airline tickets.

"Not close enough," the Rev said. "Checked on the cost of airfare from Ethiopia to Arizona lately?" The figure he gave me raised my eyebrows.

"That much?"

"His wife refuses to leave without all six children, so it's everyone or no one."

"What did Tesema say about that?"

The Rev cleared his throat. "He told us he'd expect no less from her, that she was a good mother."

Feeling more tired and depressed than ever, I hung up. Being an orphan is no fun, but if you have a big family, you have big trouble. Just look at Alea Rinn. Once the legal system finished with her husband, she and her own children might wind up relying on the kindness of strangers. As I sat there musing on other people's miseries, thinking I should call it a day and get some sleep, the phone rang. It was Warren, full of apologies.

"Lena, I don't know what I thought I was doing the other day, trying to order you around. Call it an attack of director-itis. Can you forgive me?" He sounded more emotional than I'd ever heard him.

There's nothing sweeter than hearing a man beg for forgiveness, so I said yes, but I made a mental note to have a serious talk with him about relationship parameters. Not that it mattered, since he'd be going back to L.A. soon. But then he threw a wrench into the entire conversation. "Listen, apologizing for my behavior wasn't the only reason I called. I heard from Angel last night. The producers of *Desert Eagle* love the notes you made on the script and they want to hire you as a consultant."

When he told me how much his ex-wife's producers were willing to pay, my jaw dropped. "Are they serious?"

"When it comes to money, Hollywood's always serious."

I didn't immediately turn down the offer because I was intrigued by the idea of consulting for a television show. No real tragedy, no real blood, just a mere sixty minutes—closer to forty, if you counted the commercials—of safe make-believe. And I wouldn't have to move, because as I'd once told Warren, Southwest Airlines flew to L.A. every hour. Desert Investigations could stay in business. *If,* and it was a big *if,* I could find someone as good as Jimmy at running the computer side of things. Still, it was best not to make any hasty decisions. "I'll think about it."

"Great. Hey, if you don't have any lunch plans, why don't you stop by the set?" He paused for a moment, then added softly, "Please, honey. I've missed you."

I remembered the love-struck, unhappy women I'd met in the past few days. Beth Osmon. Alea Rinn. MaryEllen Bollinger. Disgusted by my own paranoia, I pushed my fears aside. "I'll be right over, uh, honey."

When I hung up, I found Jimmy staring at me as if I'd lost my mind.

The set had dried after last week's downpour. The rain had coaxed even more wildflowers into bloom, and masses of desert goldeneye waved their buttery petals in the freshening wind. But not everything was beautiful. The food off the caterer's truck—the caterer I myself had hired for the film crew—was terrible. The bun on my meatball hero turned out to be rubbery enough to bounce, and the meatballs themselves were crammed with as much soy "texturizing" as beef. "Told you to get the turkey club," Warren said. "Want to trade?"

Feeling guilty that I'd inflicted this food on my now-friends, I shook my head. "I don't trust turkey off a cart. Especially when the bread has green spots."

"I tore them off."

"Thanks, but I prefer the feel of rubber to the taste of penicillin."

The temperature was a little cool for April, and the wind had picked up. Nearby, several "German" extras loafed around in a sunny spot, waiting for the order to climb into the shallow pit dug by the film crew. I told Warren the pit didn't remotely resemble pictures I'd seen of the POWs' escape tunnel to the Cross Cut Canal, but he assured me the final product would look realistic enough. "Camera magic and digital imaging. Plus a little judicious editing."

"Nothing's real about Hollywood, is it?"

He took another bite of his turkey club. "Nope. Not Hollywood or the people who live there. Or people anywhere, as far as that goes."

I looked at him. With the wind ruffling his streaked blond hair, and his sharp blue eyes squinted against the dazzling sun, he looked closer to thirty than forty. "Warren, that's a strange comment."

"You think?"

"Yes, I do think. What did you mean by it—that *no one's* real?"

He shrugged. "Nothing deep, only that most of us are careful to present to the world the face we want others to see. Usually that face is the opposite of what's going on inside. Like Lindsey, for instance."

Lindsey was sitting on a rock at the edge of the set all by herself, making notes on the script. Even with the wind, she'd managed to keep her hair under control and her chic black outfit dust free. "What about her?"

"She seems like a self-contained woman, doesn't she?"

Self-centered would be a more accurate description. I let it pass. "Yeah. But?"

"But why do you think she has to put up such a tough front?"

The look he threw my way made me squirm, so I decided to turn the tables. "If what you say is true, what kind of false image are you careful to present?"

He grinned. "Me? Oh, I'm the King of the World and always have been."

His eyes, I noticed, didn't match his grin.

Somehow I managed to make it through the rest of the day but by five I was ready to sleep the clock around. After locking up—Jimmy was away talking condos to the real estate folks with Esther—I went upstairs to my apartment and nuked a carton of Michelina's Chili-Mac. I gobbled it down while listening to an old vinyl recording of Lowell Fulson performing "Reconsider Baby." Once I'd eaten, I tossed the empty Michelina's container into the trash, said goodnight to Lowell, and crawled into bed, surrounded by Gunter Hoenig's journals.

Talk about a surfeit of riches. Gunter didn't seem to think any topic was too small to write about, so I spent another few hours reading through entries about vacation trips to Yosemite, his grandchildren's birthday parties, and various pet dogs and cats. He was also a great fan of the Phoenix Zoo, and had purchased family memberships for the entire Mantz clan. Apparently he always took a sketch pad along when he visited, too, because the third box was filled with scores of poorly executed sketches of giraffes and zebras. Or at least I thought they were giraffes and zebras. Who knows? Given his lack of talent, they might have been long-necked deer and nervous donkeys. Mercifully, I finally drifted off to sleep.

Even more mercifully, I didn't dream.

Just after sunrise the next day, I drove over to the set, curious to see how Warren would film the "Germans" emerging from their escape tunnel by the Cross Cut Canal. I eased the Jeep into the vacant space next to the Studebaker Golden Hawk, inwardly congratulating Mark Schank on his sales tactics. To know the Hawk was to love it, so he was making sure Warren saw it every day. I walked over to the canal, where I found the set swarming with activity, with crew members adding finishing touches to their equipment and extras slapping dirt on their clothing, faces and hair to make it seem that they'd been crawling through yards of tunnel. Once again I marveled at how hard film people worked.

To help ward off the early morning chill, Warren handed me a Styrofoam cup from the caterer's truck. Coffee the way I liked it. Black, no sugar, hot enough to blister my tongue. The man knew my tastes. Some of them, anyway.

The Cross Cut Canal was a couple hundred yards east of the present-day boundary of Papago Park. Sixty years ago the canal had been nothing more than a shallow ditch, but since then it had been enlarged and paved into a deep concrete chasm able to swallow entire semi trucks. Like the other Arizona canals, it looked deceptively smooth on the surface. But I knew the Cross Cut contained an undertow so wicked that most unfortunates who fell in either immediately drowned or were battered to death against the concrete supports of the roadways overhead. Today it was swollen by the rains of a couple days earlier, and was even more dangerous than usual. If it had been this full when the Germans escaped, they'd either have been killed or made it all the way to Mexico on their raft.

You couldn't tell the Cross Cut's danger by the faces of the merry crowd that stood along its banks. Housing tracts lined both sides of the canal, and now early-rising suburbanites eager to watch the morning's filming stood shoulder to shoulder with the film crew, milling around three deep as the security people I'd hired pushed them behind the yellow-taped line. If any of them fell into the shallow hole the film crew had dug to simulate the end of the POWs' escape tunnel, they'd probably break a leg. And we certainly didn't want any of them going into the canal.

"Amazing how cool the desert is in the morning." Warren slyly used his comment as an excuse for a warming hug.

"Mornings aren't cool in August." Since I didn't pull away from him, I decided I was making progress. While crew members scurried around us, we huddled closer, and I was forced to admit that I liked being with him, touching him. Maybe it was time we advanced to the next stage of our relationship.

In a casual tone which I could tell wasn't really casual, he said, "I hope you've given some thought to our discussion yesterday. The *Desert Eagle* offer."

I looked down into the canal's dark water. "It sounds tempting, that's for sure."

He gave me another hug. "A little money never hurt anyone."

Remembering Beth Osmon, I wasn't so sure. But not ready to get into a major conversation on the subject, I simply said, "I guess."

"Another reason I'd like you in L.A. is because, well, I think we might have a future together."

I dropped my coffee. "Jesus, Warren!"

He bent down and picked up my now-empty Styrofoam cup. "Sorry. But we Hollywood types tend to move fast."

Which helped explain L.A.'s high divorce rate. While Warren fetched me another cup of coffee, I stood by the edge of the canal, trying to calm my nerves. I had only known him for a few weeks, yet here he was, talking about the future. I was tempted to get back in my Jeep and head for the hills. And yet...

As I stood there stewing about this new wrinkle in my life, someone bumped against me. Hard. I attempted to balance myself, but whoever it was bumped me again.

And knocked me right into the canal.

My initial reaction was one of shock, not fear. The water from Northern Arizona's melting snowpack remained so cold, even this far south, that it made my teeth chatter. I fought back the fear that threatened to paralyze me and tried to remember how long the human body could withstand hypothermia. An hour? Five minutes?

At this point, the answer was irrelevant. Although I've always been a strong swimmer, drowning was the more immediate danger. Kicking desperately against the current, I managed to stay on the water's surface for what felt like hours but was probably only seconds, listening to the screams of observers along the bank. I could see Warren struggle through the crowd to the very edge of the canal, start to take off his shoes as if about to dive in but stagger back as several men—probably locals who knew the canal's immense power—grabbed him and pulled him back. Then the current began to sweep me downstream.

I fought to swim back to the side of the canal where hands reached down to grab me, but my waterlogged clothes and shoes made that impossible. Pausing in my struggles to strip them off was out of the question; the undertow was so strong, so eager to suck me under, that only my unceasing strokes and kicks kept me on the surface. Yet with all that, the current pushed me past everyone who could help and carried me alongside the autoplex and toward the tunnel under McDowell Road. As I flailed to remain on the surface, the undertow began to win, to suck me down. I managed one long, deep breath before I went under and as the frigid water closed over my head, despaired that it might be my last.

But I wasn't ready to give up. While the current rushed me through the muddy, debris-filled waters, tumbling me end over end, I spread my arms, attempting to right myself. For a moment, it worked. How far away was the tunnel now? If the current slammed my head against its concrete supports, I might lose consciousness, and with consciousness, my life.

Strengthened by desperation, I turned myself around underwater so that my feet pointed in the direction of the current. Just in time. My feet—thankfully still clad in those thick Reeboks—slammed against the tunnel walls with such savagery that I almost screamed. But realizing the fate that lay in store for me if I did, I clamped my jaws tighter. Then I allowed the current to carry me along underwater until my already inky surroundings turned even darker. Now I was in the tunnel itself. Above me, six lanes of morning traffic rushed by, oblivious to my predicament. For a moment, I thought I could hear tires on asphalt. Or was the roaring in my ears caused by oxygen starvation?

I had been underwater so long that my lungs felt as if they were ready to explode through my chest. My eyes were fading, too. White spots danced in front of them, while in back of the white spots, the water started to glow a deep red. Mercifully, the water didn't seem to be all that cold any more. In fact, it was almost comforting. All I had to do was relax and let the water…

No! Such defeatism was nothing more than my oxygen-starved brain attempting to make its peace with death. For the first time I felt panic, brought on by this forewarning of what would surely happen if gave in. I had to rage and fight and keep on fighting or I would lose control of my body. Out of pure instinct, my mouth would open, eager to suck in anything—air, mud, water.

I had to reach the surface or die.

As soon as the McDowell tunnel swept over me and the water grew lighter, I thrashed toward the surface again. I had almost made it when something hit me hard on the shoulder, a log, possibly, carried along on the current. Whatever it was hit me again, spinning me around in the water to confront the corpse of a large dog. In my horror, I lost my sense of direction again, but then the dog twirled past, headed downstream. I looked up again to see the pale sky beckon and realized that it didn't matter if I faced north or south, as long as I was headed upward, toward that wonderful pale blue.

The second I broke the surface, I took a deep, gasping breath. Then the undertow pulled me under again.

But not before I had seen the canal curve to the west, and at the point of the curve, what looked like an old maintenance ladder embedded in the concrete. If I could only reach it…

I somersaulted so that my head faced downstream again, then—resisting the undertow's attempt to drive me back to the bottom of the canal and certain death—began to fight my way back to the surface.

Something hit me again, but I ignored it—I didn't want to see more death—just drove upward toward the blue, kicking, pulling against and with the water. Whatever worked.

My head pushed into the sunlight again and as soon as I took another deep, life-giving breath, I started stroking downstream at an angle across the current, toward the outside of the canal's curve. And, yes! That *was* a maintenance ladder I'd seen earlier. Nothing fancy, just rusty metal bars sunk in concrete, but I'd never seen anything so beautiful in my life.

Now the current worked with me, carrying me toward the ladder. I stroked harder.

Reached out.

Took hold of a rung.

Pulled myself up.

But I was too exhausted, too cold, too waterlogged to climb all the way to the top. All I could do was lock my hands around the ladder and hang there shivering, half in and half out of the water, until the Scottsdale Fire Department arrived and fished me out.

Despite my protestations, the EMTs hauled me off to Scottsdale General, explaining that since canal water was grossly contaminated, I needed to be checked out. I was at risk for serious complications, including pneumonia.

The doctor was still working on me when Warren arrived, cutting a noisy swatch through the Emergency Room. "Didn't you hear me? I said I'll pay, so give her everything she needs!" he shouted to the startled clerk who had followed him in from the reception area and was attempting to hold him back.

"Sir, you can't…"

From the opening in the cubicle where they'd stashed me, I could see him throw a handful of credit cards at her. "Fuck your insurance forms! Now get out of my way!"

Not waiting to see if the clerk picked the cards up from the floor, he sidestepped her and rushed to my cubicle. I was naked, only partially covered by a sheet, the emergency room techs having cut off my soaked clothes. "Oh, Lena, I thought I'd…" He couldn't finish, so he pushed his way through the clutch of nurses that surrounded me, grabbed my hand and began kissing it. Then he saw the skin, torn from my death's grip on the ladder, and began yelling all over again. "Bastards! If they let anything happen to you I'll…"

"You won't do anything," the doctor snapped, pulling the stethoscope away from my chest. His name, which I hadn't quite caught due to the continued ringing in my ears, sounded vaguely Slavic. "Now be quiet or I'll call Security and have them remove you from the hospital." Actually, the doctor looked like he could do that all by himself. He was almost six inches taller than Warren, with the bulk of a weight-lifter. While Warren might be in good shape in his sleek Hollywood way, he wasn't in the doctor's league.

Only partially to distract Warren from his escalating emotionality, I asked, "When you were coming back with the coffee, who did you see standing near me?"

It took him a moment to focus, and when he did, he looked puzzled. "Why do you ask? It was an accident, wasn't it?"

"Someone shoved me once, and then, when I didn't go into the canal right away, they shoved me again before I could regain my balance."

Fear fought with rage across his face. "When I find out who did this to you I'll…"

Now I knew why family members weren't always welcome in emergency rooms. "Hush. The doctor needs to listen to my lungs."

With a dry smile, the doctor bent over me again. I'd not only swallowed plenty of water but had breathed in some, too. Remembering the dead dog that had floated past me while I flailed in the water, I shuddered. God knew what kind of bacteria was swimming around in my body.

Lung inspection finished, the doctor straightened up. "Not too bad, considering. But we're going to play it safe."

By the time the nurse finished shooting me full of antibiotics, my arm was sorer than before. So was my rump. And I was still naked.

Using Warren's cell phone, I called Jimmy and explained the situation. After he calmed down, I asked him to get my spare apartment key out of my desk and fetch me some clothes. "Underwear, jeans, shirt, shoes, the works."

Although Jimmy didn't sound too thrilled about searching through my underwear drawer, he agreed and soon arrived, clutching a grocery bag to his chest. A tube sock with a hole in the toe peeked over the edge. "I'm not much into style," he explained, "and I didn't know what went with what, so I brought a couple of everything."

I wasn't much into style either, so as soon as I'd shooed everyone out of the cubicle, I simply put on what came out of the bag first; lavender panties, cocoa-colored bra, black jeans, and a red tee shirt I'd picked up at a Chamber of Commerce mixer that said SCOTTSDALE—THE WEST'S MOST WESTERN TOWN. White socks and pink sneakers completed my ensemble, and I didn't care. All I wanted to do was get back to my apartment and wash the canal crud off. Once dressed, I joined Warren and Jimmy in the reception area, where Warren had made peace with the clerk he'd been so rude to earlier. I refused to let him cover my brief hospitalization and instead handed the clerk my own insurance card. Lena Jones always pays her own way. Once outside, with a prescription for yet more antibiotics clutched in my hand, I listened tiredly as Jimmy and Warren sparred over who was going to take me home.

"Look, Warren, I'm headed back there anyway," Jimmy said, sounding cross. "Besides, don't you have a movie to make?"

Somehow it had escaped my notice that Jimmy didn't like Warren. I filed the realization away for later examination.

"Forget it. I'm taking her." More rough than gentle, Warren grabbed my sore arm and hustled me toward his Range Rover, which was parked in the red zone outside the Emergency entrance. A ticket already decorated its windshield and I figured a tow truck wasn't far behind.

I was too spent to argue so I let myself be pulled along. Jimmy frowned, started to say something, then stopped. After a second, he began again, but I knew it wasn't what he'd originally planned to say. "Whatever you want, Lena. I'll follow right behind and meet you back at the apartment." With a wave, he headed at a run across the hospital parking lot to his legally parked pickup truck.

On the way back to my apartment, Warren kept up a constant stream of chatter, trying, I guess, to relax me. I tuned out, trying to remember who'd been near the canal right after Warren left me to fetch another cup of coffee. Faces flickered by like stills from an old movie. The sound man. A couple of camera guys.

The usual neighborhood looky-loos. And Lindsey, arguing with the crew.

Then I remembered that only a few seconds before someone shoved me into the canal, I saw Warren moving toward me.

His hands were empty.

Chapter Twenty-Two

I spent the night shivering, even though I wore winter workout sweats. Warren had refused to leave and lay next to me, fully dressed except for his shoes. We slept spoon-shaped, separated by the bed-clothes, and throughout the long night, he never put a hand where it shouldn't be. Once, though, when I awoke in the middle of the night, I found him sound asleep, but his soft mouth was giving the nape of my neck little butterfly kisses. For a moment I lay there, halfway tempted to turn around and kiss him awake, but decided against it. I was too sore. When I finally fell back asleep, I dreamt that Warren was in the canal with me, yet every time I reached out for him, he pushed me under.

It was preferable to my usual dream.

My alarm rang at five, waking me with a start. The minute I began to move, I knew I was in for a bad day. Every muscle, every bone, sang with pain.

"What...?" Warren reached out and touched my hair. "Lena. Did we..." He fell silent, the condition of our clothing answering the not-yet-formed question. "How do you feel, baby?"

"Like hell." I threw the covers off, and ran into the bathroom, where I promptly threw up. To my horror, he followed, and as I heaved canal water into the toilet, he held my head, then handed me a towel.

I wiped my mouth. "I told you I don't like being called baby." The second the words were out, I realized how churlish they sounded. But I couldn't help it. I was too miserable for courtesy.

He didn't seem to mind. "Now gargle." He handed me my Scope.

I gargled, then spit the detritus into the toilet bowl. As I kneeled in front of the bowl, Warren rubbed my back. "May I say something to you?"

"Not if you're going to nag me about my abhorrence for pet names."

"Hardly. It's just that, well, I think it might be a good idea if you stayed away from mirrors today."

I wiped my mouth again and stood up. Ignoring Warren's suggestion, I stared straight into the bathroom mirror. At some point in the canal, I'd acquired a black eye and a split lip. When I hustled him out of the bathroom and began my shower, I found more injuries. Bruises and scratches along both sides of my body, and a reddened area the size of a man's fist on one breast. I looked like the loser of a prize fight. After showering under the hottest water I could stand, I finally dried myself off and approached the mirror again. Using some old bits and pieces of disused makeup I found in the cabinet, I patched the damage on my face as best as I could, but not having MaryEllen Bollinger's expertise, I was still a mess.

When I finally emerged from the bathroom wrapped in a faded terrycloth robe, Warren was still there. He was going through my kitchen cabinets.

"Where's the cereal?"

"I don't have any."

He crossed to the small refrigerator and began opening up various compartments. "Eggs?"

"None of those, either." I leaned my sore back against the wall, watching him.

He stared at me. "Lena, what do you eat?"

"Um, usually I have a Danish or one of those microwave egg thingys."

"You don't cook. At all."

"Microwaving is cooking."

For a minute it looked like he was about to laugh, then his face changed and I thought he would cry. But he didn't do that, either. He just grabbed me—carefully—by the arm and said, "I'm taking you out for a decent breakfast. Eggs. Steak. Lots of protein. After what you've been through, you need it." He began herding me toward the door.

"Warren, haven't you forgotten something?"

"What?"

"I need to dress. And quite frankly, I think you need a shower yourself. From the smell of things, I think I threw up on you."

Once we arrived at U.S. Egg, I fended off his continued concern by bringing up work. "Shouldn't you be at the set?" When you're not used to having someone take care of you, it's difficult to know how to respond.

He patted my hand once again, as if trying to reassure himself it was still there. "While you were in the shower, I called Lindsey and told her to get started without me. She's probably already at work."

I groaned. "Oh, Warren! She'll have everyone up in arms by the time you make it over there. In fact, I'm betting you'll have to spend the rest of the day calming everyone down."

He pooh-poohed my concerns. "She'll do fine. Most of the shots are location only, showing the various places where the German POWs were either captured or turned themselves in. She has a nice feel for atmosphere. By the way, I like your new furniture."

I felt so pleased I didn't care that he'd abruptly changed the subject. "You don't think it's too much?"

"It's perfect."

"I'm thinking about getting plates with spurs and lariats on them."

"Even more perfect. And how about one of those chrome and vinyl breakfast sets? We had one of those when I was a kid. I think they used to make them with Western prints."

I smiled so broadly my face hurt. "Yeah, I was thinking the same thing."

As we talked, I noticed people staring at my black eye, cut lip, and scratched arms. Oblivious to the frowns Warren was receiving from our waitress and several restaurant patrons, he simply shook more Tabasco on his chorizo omelet.

I brought the conversation back to where I wanted it. "Warren, are you sure about leaving Lindsey to work alone this morning?"

He nodded, but it wasn't convincing. "Lindsey's exterior work is some of the best I've seen. It's only where people are concerned that she has trouble."

I ducked my head against the other customers' stares and forked in another mouthful of hash browns. "She sounds perfect for the National Geographic Channel. Nothing but monkeys and mountains."

He laughed, added even more Tabasco to his plate, then scooped up the beans with a warm tortilla. "Hot damn!"

Sharing breakfast with Warren after a night of non-sexual closeness, I had to fight the urge to flee. The only thing that kept me seated at the table was the memory of my therapist telling me it was time to stop running away from emotional intimacy. Sex I had no problem with.

Still, it was time to confront what had been bothering me all night. But I'd start slow. "Lindsey was near me when I went into the canal."

He looked away. "So were a lot of other people. The whole damned film crew."

"You were there, too."

He looked back, his blue eyes cold. "What is all this about? Of course I was there. I needed to direct the extras as they crawled out of the tunnel."

"But where was the coffee you supposedly went after? I didn't see it."

"Supposedly?" All the expression stripped away from his face and he appeared to choose his words carefully. "Before I reached you, someone knocked the cup out of my hands. If you hadn't…if you hadn't gone into the canal when you did, you would have seen spilled coffee all over my leg." With that, he pushed his chair away from the table, stood up, and to the astonishment of the other customers, rolled up his chinos. "You see?" Red splotches covered his calf, and angry blisters blossomed above the knee. He gave me a wry smile. "Maybe like that woman at MacDonald's, I should sue our caterer for making the coffee so hot."

For a moment, I wondered if he'd splashed hot coffee on himself *after* I'd survived the canal. Then I looked down at my hash browns. Jesus, what was wrong with me? "I'm sorry."

"So am I."

He'd leave me now, no doubt about it. If I could, *I* would leave me. "I don't know what else to say, Warren."

"You don't have to say anything." He rolled his pants leg back down, walked around the table, and kissed me on the cheek. "When I first met you, I could tell you were a complicated woman, but I was born and raised in the neurosis capital of the world, so nothing you do, nothing you say, can shock me. Hurt me, maybe, but that goes with the territory when you love someone, doesn't it?"

There it was. The "L" word. I just kept staring at my hash browns. "I guess."

When he sat back down, the mood in the restaurant had changed. The other men now looked at him with pity. "Yes, Lena, it does. Now stop looking at those damn potatoes and either eat them or give them to me."

Unusually for Jimmy, he wasn't in when I opened up Desert Investigations at nine, but I wasn't worried. The day before, he'd followed Warren and me from the hospital all the way up to my apartment, making a big show out of checking around to make certain no boogie men were hiding anywhere. Then he'd gone downstairs to the office. I thought I'd heard his pickup truck leaving the parking lot around ten last night, so I figured he was spending some comp time with Esther and would be in later. I forgot about my absent partner and went straight to work, happy to be away from the sympathizing stares of the public.

After calling Captain Kryzinski at Scottsdale PD and reassuring him that I was fine, just fine, after the previous day's adventure, I asked him if there were any new developments in the Erik Ernst case. His answer was depressing.

"You're wasting your time, kid," he said. "Tesema's as guilty as they come."

I then placed a call to Dectective Manuel Villapando at the Apache Junction Police Department, where I struck out again. Villapando confided to me that his superiors believed Harry Caulfield's murder was nothing more than a burglary gone bad.

"Like you, Miss Jones, I'm convinced Harry's murder is tied to the Ernst case, but so far we've found no concrete evidence to that effect. And Ballistics is backed up, as usual, so there's still no proof it's the same gun which killed Harry and the *Scottsdale Journal* reporter. Just to make things even worse, there's been a spate of break-ins at a couple of the more upscale senior communities around here, with some of the old folks getting roughed up pretty bad, and I'm sure you know how short-handed we are, so..." He trailed off. In other words, his superiors were steering him in the opposite direction. Well, nothing new there. My own experience in Scottsdale PD had taught me that more and more police departments, swamped by the rising tide of crime, were focusing on crimes they had a good chance of solving, not those they probably wouldn't.

"I understand, Detective." I wished him well and rang off.

His mention of upscale senior communities sparked my memory, so I placed a call to Tommy Bollinger. At first, his secretary told me he was in a meeting and tried to foist me onto his voice mail, but when I told her it concerned the Bollinger family murders, she put me right through.

"Have I ever received anonymous letters?" Tommy asked, in response to my question. "Of course I have. A gay multimillionaire's bound to receive his share of hate mail."

"I'm talking about letters that accused Erik Ernst of your family's murder."

A long silence. Then, "Ah, there were plenty of crackpots around, even back then."

"In other words, you did."

"Yeeeess." His voice slowed to a crawl, as if he was more interested in listening than talking.

My cue. In great detail, I told him about the anonymous letters Harry Caulfield and Fay Harris had received. All he said at the end of my spiel was, "Interesting."

"It doesn't intrigue you that someone else claimed to have definite knowledge that Ernst killed your family?"

A bitter laugh. "Ms. Jones, I never believed Chess did it. If only Edward had been murdered, that would be different. But the whole family? That little girl? No way. As to the anonymous letters, I handed them over to the Maricopa County Sheriff's Office years ago, but to my knowledge, they never followed up. Now if you'll excuse me, I really am in a meeting. My secretary wasn't lying."

Before I could ask another question, he hung up, leaving me frowning at the phone. I sat there for a while, trying to figure out why he no longer seemed interested in the solution to his family's murders, and reached one possible conclusion. He was growing worried over what I might find out. Remembering his biceps and his strong golf swing, I couldn't help but wonder where he'd been when someone pushed me into the canal. But he'd never given me the chance to ask.

I was still going through my notes on the Ernst case when the office door opened and Jimmy came in, looking as red-eyed as I did. Instead of sitting down, he placed a fat file folder on my desk, and said, "We need to talk."

"You and Esther make an offer on the Scottsdale Fashion Square condo?"

"It's not about the condo." He frowned so deeply that even the tribal tattoo on his forehead pulled down.

A frisson of alarm crept down my back. "Jimmy, there's nothing wrong with Esther or Rebecca, is there?"

He reassured me. For a moment. "They're fine. This is about the check you wanted me to run on Warren. I was too busy to get right to it when you asked, and I'm sorrier about that than you'll ever know. But after what happened to you yesterday, I ran him through every data base I could. It's not like the information about him was buried deep. In fact, if we lived in L.A. or were more entertainment-oriented, we'd both probably know what I'm about to tell you."

Annoyed, I pushed the folder away. "A Tinseltown scandal. Big deal."

The folder came sliding back. "Considering that you were almost killed, I think it is."

It was time to say what I'd lately begun to suspect. "Jimmy, are you jealous of me and Warren?"

He snorted with disgust. "I won't dignify that question with an answer. Go ahead and read those printouts. Or are you afraid to find out the nasty truth behind your precious golden boy?"

Okay, so there was some little secret Warren had kept from me; he had already hinted as much. But who didn't have secrets, these days? Granted, Hollywood lives didn't exactly reflect the Middle American experience, but neither did mine. Deciding that I might as well pacify my partner and make our last few days together at Desert Investigations as peaceful as possible, I picked up the folder and shoved it into my carry-all. "It's pretty thick, so I'll go over it tonight. I don't have time now."

He snorted with disgust. "You think it's thick, that's nothing. To give you the full flavor of what your Mr. Warren Quinn's been up to, I would have had to download twenty years of the *Los Angeles Times*, not to mention the *Hollywood Inquirer*. But in case you don't find the time to go over that file tonight, I'll sum up the essentials right here and now. What do you want me to start with? The porno movies he made or his girlfriend's unsolved murder?"

For a moment I was speechless, but with great effort, I managed to recover. "Which came first?" The chicken or the egg? I attempted a laugh but failed. I did well to keep my voice steady.

Jimmy was merciless. "Porno first, then I'll get to the girl-friend, Crystal Chandler, although they kind of run together since she was in a couple of his movies. You'll love the titles. Stuff like *Here Comes Crystal.* And *Crystal's...* Well, you get the idea. He made something like thirty of the damned things, about half of them starring her, using tricks he learned from his dear old dad. I'll tell you more about Daddy in a minute. All was going great for Warren-the-Pornographer until one night fifteen years ago, when Crystal was found strangled in one of the bedrooms during a party at his house. LAPD took him in for questioning but they didn't have enough to make a case."

I felt sick. "What's this about Warren's father? You said he learned his 'tricks' from him?"

"Tony DiMeola, known as the..."

"The Porn King." Even I had heard of him. DiMeola fre-quently appeared on cable talk shows, rhapsodizing self-righ-teously about the First Amendment. Thomas Jefferson, were he still alive, would puke. "Oh, my God."

"I don't think He has anything to do with this."

"But...but Warren's last name is Quinn!"

"Now it is. You'll read in the printouts I gave you that after his girlfriend died, Warren went into detox—he had a big time heroin habit—and when he came out, he took his mother's maiden name. They're big on that out there in Tinsel Town, the name-changing stuff. Remember Barbara Hershey? In the seventies, she changed her name to Barbara Seagull. Anyway, everybody in Hollywood knows who Warren started out as, but here in the hinterlands all we know is 'Oscar-winning-Warren Quinn.' The porno issue, or that poor girl's death, never comes up."

There was no point in listening to any more. For now. "Jimmy, print out everything. I don't care if it's as long as the frigging unabridged Encyclopedia Britannica. I'll read it all tonight." Instead of having dinner with Warren.

He walked over to his computer and hit a few keys. For the next half-hour, the laser printer hummed and clicked as page after page hissed along the rollers. To kill time, I drank a Tab, then another, and another. By the time the printout was finished, caffeine jangled through my bloodstream. I snatched the papers up and announced I was leaving.

Jimmy looked up at the clock. It was only two, but I was too sore at heart—and in body—to put in a full day. "Lena, don't you want to talk first? That information I gave..."

I headed him off at the pass. "I need to take a couple of aspirin and lie down." Then read the rest of the printout and cry myself to sleep.

He started to say something else, then thought better of it. "You do that. I'll be here if you need me."

Yeah, for a couple more days. Then you're leaving and taking half the company with you. I swore never to allow myself to need someone again. Or if I did, to make certain I had an attorney draw up an iron-clad non-competition contract.

After calling Warren and putting off our dinner date until the next evening, I left for the day. As I climbed the stairs to my apartment, Jimmy's printout felt like it weighed a ton. My idea of getting to bed early never panned out, and by the time midnight rolled around, I was still reading. But I'd also begun to feel less alarmed by Warren's past. The Warren I knew was a far cry from the Warren who had joined his father in the porno industry, dated the help, and threw one party too many. As for the murder, Jimmy's summation may have been colored by personal animosity. LAPD appeared to believe Warren's story that he was in a different bedroom with a different porn actress when Crystal Chandler was strangled. They had set their sights on Rock Steady, the dead woman's ex-boyfriend and sometime co-star. For lack of concrete proof, the case against Rock had stalled, and so the Crystal Chandler murder was eventually consigned to the Open-Unsolved Files, right along with the Black Dahlia case.

From one point of view, the murder investigation had been good for Warren. As an article in the *Hollywood Tattler* phrased it on the eve of last year's Oscar ceremony, "After Ms. Chandler's murder, Warren Quinn—nee Warren DiMeola—took a sobering look at his life in more ways than one. He didn't like what he saw so he checked himself into the Betty Ford Clinic for a six-week run. When he finally emerged, he dropped his father's name—they are still estranged—and began making movies that mattered, such as *Native Peoples, Foreign Chains*. Vegas has given even odds that the ex-porn director will walk away from tomorrow night's ceremony a winner."

In other words, all's well that ends well and everything's right with the world.

Except for Crystal Chandler.

The morning sun shone cheerily into the windows of Desert Investigations, but it did little to lighten my mood. What little sleep I had managed to get was haunted with dreams of death. I hadn't decided yet what to do about my new knowledge: give Warren the benefit of the doubt, as I wanted to do, or break it off. We were supposed to have dinner tonight, but I was tempted to call and cancel again, saying that I was still too bruised from my ride down the Cross Cut Canal. It wouldn't even be a lie. If anything, I was sorer today than yesterday.

As I picked up the phone to call Warren, Jimmy cleared his throat to catch my attention. I put the phone down.

"Lena, did you, ah…?"

"Yes. I read the printout. Every last word."

"I'm worried about you."

"I'm worried about you, too." Truth be told, Jimmy looked almost as rough this morning as I had yesterday. His hair was disheveled, he wore a clean but badly wrinkled Metallica T-shirt, faded khakis, and scuffed Nikes without socks.

I jumped at the chance to move the spotlight away from my own troubles. "Hey, big guy? Did you dress in the dark or something?"

"Or something."

In other words, his condition wasn't up for discussion. Fine. I sipped my third cup of coffee in silence as his fingers flew along his keyboard. I had almost drained the cup when he said, "There!" The printer began spitting out pages.

I put up my hands in a cease and desist gesture. "Please. No more about Warren, Jimmy. I have all the information I need. And then some."

Jimmy ignored my plea and grabbed the printout from the printer. "Erik Ernst's finances. That's the other thing you wanted me to look into before I..." He lowered his eyes.

He'd started to say, "...before I leave Desert Investigations for Southwest MicroSystems." Then he'd thought better of it. I pretended I hadn't noticed and gave him a bright smile. "Just sum up the info for me, okay? I've done all the reading I care to for a while."

He cleared his throat again. "Ernst was flat broke. No savings, no IRAs, no investments of any kind. The insurance policy he carried at Sea Solutions lapsed years ago, so he didn't even have that. His house is paid off, but he had a big property tax bill looming and no money to pay it. Frankly, the only thing keeping the guy afloat was his monthly Social Security and a piddly little pension from Sea Solutions. No stocks, no bonds, which isn't that unusual with that generation. He was really in rough shape, Lena. I'm telling you, I sure wouldn't want to be ninety and try to live on his income, especially if I had to keep shelling out a couple of thou per month to have a practical nurse to get me from my bed to my wheelchair."

I frowned. Although the woman I'd talked to in Connecticut said that Ernst had been a big spender with little put aside, what Jimmy described sounded just this side of penury. "Why did he have to pay for home care? I thought the state paid when you have a disability."

"The state helps if you're *indigent*, not driving a big, fat Mercedes. Yeah, the state lets you keep your house if it's your primary residence, but your income has to be even lower than Ernst's to qualify for state aid. As little as he had, the combination of Ernst's pension and his Social Security check put him over the limit, so he had to pay for home care all on his own. That's another thing that drove his bank account into the basement."

I thought about that for a minute. "As broke as you say he was, he obviously had the means. And if things got really bad, he could sell the house."

"But he wouldn't be in his home, then, remember. And as soon as he cashed out, the state would snatch their property taxes, and it's a pretty hefty bill. He'd also have to pay taxes on the net he realized from the sale unless he bought another house that cost even more than his old one—which he wouldn't and couldn't. It's my guess, if things continued on the way they were with him, he'd probably have lost his house over the tax bill anyway and then wound up in some low-rent, state-sponsored nursing home. Have you seen those places?"

As a matter of fact, I had. Shady Rest, where Chess Bollinger was babbling out the end of his days. Try as I might, I couldn't envision the vain Das Kapitan allowing himself to be moved to a place like that.

"How about reverse mortgages? Anything like that in his files?" Reverse mortgages had become increasingly popular with elderly home owners. The bank drew up a contract, advanced them a sizeable amount every month toward their home—which they then lived on while remaining in their homes—and when they died, the bank took the house.

Jimmy shrugged. "He could have taken one out, I guess, and it might have been a good solution for him. But I found nothing like that in his records."

Then I remembered something else. "Wait a minute. You say Ernst was paying Loving Care almost two thousand a month for Rada Tesema's services. If he was so broke, where'd he get *that* money?"

"He didn't start out broke, Lena."

With that, Jimmy handed me a thick print-out of Ernst's savings and checking account activities. Ernst had arrived in Arizona with a fairly healthy balance in his savings account, but over the years it had slowly dwindled. His checking account actually showed a negative balance. A couple of months ago, he had written several NSF checks, two of them to Loving Care. As

I studied the bank records more closely, I saw something odd. Maybe Ernst had started off paying two thousand a month to Loving Care, but later the bill had dropped by half. Then I remembered that Tesema told me he'd begun visiting Ernst only three times a week, compared to his earlier everyday schedule.

And I remembered something else: MaryEllen Bollinger telling me that Ernst had answered, the door right away during her wee hours visit. Since it was impossible for a legless elderly man to transfer himself from bed to wheelchair that quickly, it meant he'd been sleeping in his wheelchair.

Pitiful.

"Jimmy, didn't you just say that Ernst wrote a couple of bad checks to Loving Care?"

He nodded.

"And they just kept sending Tesema over?"

"Doesn't seem likely, does it?"

No, it didn't. The next call I placed was to Loving Care. Myra, the young woman who answered, sounded young and inexperienced, so I took a chance. "Maybe you can help me. I'm, um, Lena Ernst, Mr. Erik Ernst's niece, and I'm trying to clear up his estate. I see that he owes you some money?"

Myra asked me to excuse her while she checked the records and put me on hold. By the time she came back on the line, I was listening to the third Neil Diamond song in a row and was ready to tear my hair out. "Oh, yes. Our records indicate that Mr. Ernst wrote…ah, that he owes us for two months' services. And as you know, we did, ah, have to terminate his contract last month. For, ah, late payment and all."

Because he kept writing bad checks. I pretended outrage. "You mean you just cut my poor old uncle loose to fend for himself? A ninety-year-old double amputee?"

Now Myra sounded frightened, but instead of calling her supervisor as a more experienced employee would do, she attempted to explain. "No, no, we didn't do that. I'd just started here when we had to cut him, and I remember his service representative telling him what his options were, how he could start getting aid from the state."

"Is this a phone conversation you're describing?"

"Don't I wish. Dial-A-Ride brought him in. He threw a big tantrum right here in the office. Everyone heard it. He called Mrs. Griffith—that's his service representative—all kinds of names, and screamed at her that he was captain of something and captains don't take charity, that they pay their own way."

"So he didn't want the state to help."

"No. Mrs. Griffith was really upset, and after he left, I heard her talking to another rep about maybe calling Adult Protective Services to have them go see if he was in the first stages of dementia and no longer mentally able to see to his own welfare. In the end, they decided not to."

"Why was that?"

She lowered her voice. "You won't tell anybody I said this, will you?"

"My lips are sealed."

"Mrs. Griffith decided that Mr. Ernst was just stubborn and mean, not senile."

Which anyone who knew Ernst could have told her. "One more question, Myra, and then I'll let you go. If Loving Care terminated its service contract with Mr. Er..., er, with my uncle, how come his home care worker was still going out there?"

"No he wasn't."

"He wasn't?"

"His care provider was, let's see, oh, yes. Mr. Tesema. A nice man, a really nice man. Our clients just love him. Anyway, Mrs. Griffith had Mr. Tesema terminate his visits back in early March. And then she gave him another client."

March. Yet in mid-April Tesema was still regularly showing up at Ernst's house. I thanked Myra and ended the call.

I hung up to find Jimmy watching me. "I heard most of that. Tesema was going over there out of the goodness of his heart, wasn't he?"

"That's what it looks like." Which brought another interesting wrinkle into the case. Loving Care would have fired Tesema if they'd known he continued to visit Ernst off the clock. Like all businesses, the home care agency needed to make a buck, and you can't do that by giving your services away. But what if...? As soon as the thought entered my head, I shook it out. No matter how angry Ernst got at Tesema, he wouldn't rat him out to Loving Care, which would be cutting off his nose to spite his face. Then I realized that Ernst had a track record of doing exactly that. The night of the murder he and Tesema had fought over the Star of David necklace, and he'd hurled racial insults at the very man upon whose good graces he was dependent. And there was this: Ernst's "secret," a "secret like gold." Maybe he had been holding Tesema's kindness over his head, threatening to tell Loving Care all about their situation if the already-exhausted Ethiopian didn't increase his number of visits. Maybe Ernst even threatened to tell the U.S. Immigration and Naturalization Service that Tesema had been cheating his employer.

Another visit to the Fourth Avenue Jail was in order.

As an afterthought, I asked Jimmy one more question. "Did Ernst leave a will?"

"Not that I could find. Looks like he died intestate."

Regardless of Ernst's lack of liquid assets, his estate would probably realize some money from the sale of his house. With no family or friends, he could have left the residue to a battered women's shelter, a crisis nursery, an animal rescue organization, or even to Gemuetlichkeit. But he hadn't, so the government would get it all. The self-centered man died as he lived, with no thought for anyone other than himself. While I was still thinking about Ernst's financial mess, the phone rang. When I picked it up, I heard the voice I didn't want to hear. Warren.

"Dinner's off, Lena. Lindsey's on her way to Scottsdale General Hospital and I'm headed there now."

I tightened my grip on the handset. First Ernst, then Harry Caulfield, then Fay Harris. Then, almost, me. Now Lindsey. Oh, and Crystal Chandler. Standing right in the middle of this unlucky group was Warren. I took a deep breath to settle my thoughts, then asked what happened.

"Accidental overdose, probably. She's done it before. I stopped by her room this morning to plan today's location shots and found her on the floor. The EMTs just took her away. I…I think she's going to be all right, but I need to be there for her."

Like he'd been there for Crystal Chandler? "What kind of overdose?"

"We don't know yet."

The other day, before things had gone to hell in a handbasket, Warren had said something about Lindsey being fragile. Is this what he'd meant?

"Did you see a note?"

A long pause. Then, "No."

He was lying. Lindsey had left a note, but he didn't want me to know, so maybe it *was* a suicide attempt. But while Lindsey hadn't been thrilled over my developing relationship with Warren, I would never have pegged her as the suicidal type. Given her hard-edged manner, I was more inclined to see Lindsey as a woman who might cause harm to others, never herself. Then again, what the hell did I know? "Do you want me to meet you at the hospital?"

"Thanks for asking, but considering everything, it's probably not a good idea. I'll call you when I find out more." He hung up without so much as a good-by.

Suddenly exhausted, I leaned my head back against my chair and closed my eyes. Just when I believed I'd figured people out—Ernst, Warren, and even Lindsey—they pulled an about face on me.

Chapter Twenty-Three

When the corrections officers escorted Tesema into the visiting area, I could see that his bruises were healing nicely, but now that I wasn't distracted by them, I realized he'd also dropped a lot of weight. From worry, no doubt. I didn't blame him. His situation was no better than before. At least he could help me fill in a few blanks.

"Mr. Tesema, I found out that Kapitan Ernst was no longer on Loving Care's client roster. Was he giving you money under the table? And if so, did he threaten to let the company know about it? Is that what the big fight was about, not your Star of David?" There was no point in being delicate. I had to start finding out the truth about everyone connected with the case. There had been too many lies, too many deaths.

He looked alarmed. "No, no! I would not accept such money. That is against the rules."

Although I probably shouldn't have, I believed him. "Then why did you continue working for him without getting paid?"

A flush spread over his dark skin. "I feel sorry for Das Kapitan."

Sorry for that old Nazi? Then I remembered my own jumbled emotions when I'd discovered the extent of Ernst's financial woes. You didn't have to like someone to pity them. "How long did you work for him without getting paid?"

He squirmed in his seat, looked at the floor, the walls. Then he sighed. "Since Loving Care tell me to stop. Six, seven weeks.

In beginning I argue with them, say he was helpless, sick. They tell me State of Arizona would help, gave me some forms to take to him on my last day. I show forms to Das Kapitan, but he just begin yelling. Say he go down to Loving Care and tell them what he think. But then he…"

Tesema hung his head.

"He what?"

"He cry."

Oh, Jesus.

Tesema looked up. "When Das Kapitan stopped cry…When he could talk again, he told me he only needed me free for short time, that he would make big money soon, then he sign back up with Loving Care and everything go back the way it was."

It sounded like castles in the air to me, because how could a jobless, legless ninety-year-old make "big money"? I knew that Warren paid Ernst a small amount for his participation in the documentary, as he had Fay Harris and Frank Oberle. But not enough to keep Ernst living in the manner in which he'd been accustomed. Besides, Living History Production's checks would only continue as long as filming continued—two months. Not enough to make any real difference to Ernst's dire situation. Since Das Kapitan wasn't stupid, he must have been talking about another source.

"Did Ernst tell you where the money would come from?"

"He said someone owed him."

"Someone owed him money?"

He squirmed in his chair again, looking even more uncomfortable than he had before. "No. He said he knew secret. That the secret was like gold."

There the phrase was again, a "secret like gold." A crazy idea entered my head. After the escape, Ernst and the other two German submariners—crew mates Gunter Hoenig and Josef Braun—hid for several weeks in the Superstition Mountains, the supposed site of the Lost Dutchman Gold Mine. Could knowledge of the mine possibly have been what Ernst was hinting at? After some hard thinking, I discarded the theory. If Ernst had somehow found the mine, he wouldn't have waited decades to claim his riches. His "secret like gold"—if it truly existed—had to be something else.

In every investigation, there comes a time when you realize that, because of your original lack of knowledge about the case, you didn't ask the right questions. So you have to start all over again from the beginning. Re-interview the same witnesses and re-think the same material.

I hadn't talked to Frank Oberle since Harry Caulfield's murder, so as soon as I left the Fourth Street Jail, I fished my cell out of my carry-all and punched in his number. When he answered, the weakness in his voice shocked me. He no longer sounded like the vigorous man who had so enjoyed recounting his Camp Papago experiences for Warren's camera. At first he refused to see me, but finally gave way and made an appointment to meet for dinner at a popular Apache Junction eatery.

"They got a nice senior discount there," he explained.

Eager to mend fences, I said, "Oh, don't worry about that. Dinner is on me."

He snorted. "I'm not taking a damn thing from you, missy."

Missy. Dinner promised to be an uncomfortable affair.

It was. When I arrived at the restaurant, I found Oberle waiting near the entrance for me, a chip the size of Arizona on his shoulder. "Don't know why I'm doin' this, missy. My friend Harry would still be alive if it wasn't for you. By the way, what the hell happened to you?"

"Fell into the Cross Cut Canal."

He smiled as if the prospect of my near-death experience delighted him.

The restaurant was crowded with seniors taking advantage of the discount. As the waitress led us, at Oberle's request, toward a corner booth in the smoking section, I checked out the plates. "Senior" apparently meant microscopic portions; a few teaspoons of entree, a daub of mashed potatoes, a couple of broccoli florets, a tiny roll. It would have taken two orders to fill me up, not that I was eligible for the senior discount anyway. I was at least thirty years away from that happy day.

After we were seated and I'd coughed a few times as cigarette smoke swirled around me, I again recounted my reasons for wanting to meet with Oberle, ending with, "Perhaps Harry said something to you that might lead to whoever killed him. I'm almost certain his death had something to do with the Bollinger killings."

Scowling, Oberle took a menu from the waitress. "Harry told ya everything ya need to know."

"If you don't mind, I'd like you to go over it again. Such as…" I stopped as the waitress wrote down our orders—for Oberle the senior pot roast, for me a chef's salad, *not* senior-size—then I continued. "Such as Harry's theories on the Bollinger murders. From what I can remember, he was pretty certain Chess didn't kill his family, that someone else did."

"Yeah, Harry was always makin' excuses for the little shit."

"Why do you think he did?"

Oberle shrugged. "Who knows why anyone does anything? I'd bet my double-wide on Chess being the killer, regardless of what those idiots on the jury decided. That boy was never any good. Matter of fact, I wouldn't put it past him to still be killin' people. They say once murder gets in your blood it's hard to let go, like that Bundy guy. He developed a real taste for it."

"Ted Bundy was a serial killer, and that's a whole different thing. Most murders are one-offs, like the Bollingers'."

"One-offs, my ass. Total up the body count, missy. We got the Bollingers, we got that reporter girl, we got Harry. Do the math." The dark gleam in his eye made me suspect he would dearly have loved to add me to the list.

"You left out Ernst."

"Yeah, old Ernst. Who cares who killed that sonofabitch? I sure don't. Talk about a creep. Ha! He coulda gave Chess lessons. Back at the camp Das Kapitan High and Mighty was always tellin' everyone to go here, go there, actin' like he was the guard and we was the prisoners. Whoever chopped his legs off with that boat did everybody a favor. I'm just sorry they didn't get his friggin' head."

"They eventually did," I said, remembering the mess in the wheelchair.

"Boo-hoo." He flashed another smile.

Then I looked behind me and saw that his smile wasn't to celebrate Ernst's death. It was for the waitress, bearing our food.

As I'd hoped, Oberle loosened up as we ate. He restated everything Harry told me about the Bollinger investigation, every now and then adding a few new nuggets. Such as the fact that Harry told him Joyce Bollinger had been about to divorce her husband, an action rare in the Forties. "He said a family friend stated that Joyce knew Edward was cheatin' on her, that he gave her, uh, that she got...this...this disease." He dropped his voice and leaned over the table. "You understand what I'm talkin' about?"

My mouth being full of iceberg lettuce, I simply nodded. Sexually transmitted diseases weren't new, although they were more freely discussed in these free-wheeling times. It occurred to me that if Edward Bollinger played around on his wife enough to contract an STD, he had also widened the field of possible murder suspects. A jealous husband, or perhaps an infected and discarded girlfriend, providing she'd been strong enough to smash in his head. Then I reminded myself that Edward hadn't been beaten to death; he'd died via shotgun. With the muscle man of the family out of the way and the rest of them tied up, a woman could have killed the others, although it wasn't likely.

I washed the lettuce down with some tea and waved away the cigarette smoke that kept drifting toward me from the smoking seniors surrounding us. "Who was this family friend who told Harry about that?"

"Damned if I know."

"He never said?"

"Nah. Person's probably dead now, anyway." He took another bite of his pot roast.

So much for the jealous revenge theory. The chances of finding out the identities of Edward Bollinger's paramours more than fifty years after the fact were nil, so I tried again. "Did Harry have any more theories on the case? Maybe something so vague he wasn't comfortable sharing it with me?"

A sad smile. "Oh, Harry had a buncha theories. He said that after them bodies was removed, he took Chess for a look-around and the kid told him there was a lot of stuff missing. Food, knives, pots, a coupla sleeping bags, plus some tools his dad kept out in the shed. And the car, of course, Edward's fancy-dancy Olds convertible, the one that made him so popular with broads. You know, show a woman a shiny car and half the time she don't bother to check out what kinda creep's drivin' it."

Remembering the Golden Hawk Warren was thinking about buying and how much I'd been impressed by it, I felt my face redden.

Fortunately, Oberle didn't notice my discomfiture. "That missing car's what made people first think it mighta been the Nazis. Hell, they coulda drove that car all the way to Mexico."

I corrected him without thinking. "You mean the Germans." Gunter Hoenig certainly hadn't been a Nazi. And from what I'd read in Gunter's journals, Josef Braun hadn't been a Nazi, either, just some scared, confused draftee trying to stay alive until the war ended.

Oberle responded to my attempt at political correctness with a sneer. "Whatever." Then his face relaxed. "Oh, hell, you're right. Gunter and Josef, they was good boys. Always polite, always did their work. You know about them Iron Crosses they made for extra money?"

I told him I'd read about the crosses in Fay Harris' book.

"Well, Gunter, he was the artistic type and made lots of stuff. Besides them Iron Crosses, he was always cranking out necklaces with little birds on them—roadrunners, I think—dangling from some fishing line he'd traded for a few cigarettes. He even made one for my daughter. She's still got it. It's real pretty."

Remembering the crude drawings in Gunter's journals, I doubted it. Then again, "pretty" was in the eye of the beholder. Before Oberle could continue with more jewelry descriptions, as he seemed ready to do, I nudged him back to the subject at hand. "Harry told me he was convinced the Germans had nothing to do with the murders themselves. The thefts of a few household objects, maybe, but not the murders. You said he had lots of theories. Do you remember some of the others?"

"Hell, there was so many!" He used his dinner roll to mop up the rest of the pot roast sauce. After wiping his plate clean, he lit a cigarette, and added a few smoke rings to the miasma around us while I tried to stifle a cough. "Let's see. Oh, yeah, the Olds. Harry thought someone mighta killed them for it. Chess sure could have. Somebody said they saw the little shit driving the car around town the day of the murder, but he got alibied out. Crazy, if you ask me, because how many beige 1939 Oldsmobile convertibles coulda been tooling around Scottsdale in those days, especially with the gas rationing? Wasn't nobody driving anywhere they didn't have to."

Gas rationing was something an adult would worry about, not a teenager. "The boy who alibied Chess at the trial, who said Chess was hiding in his room when the family was being murdered, how believable was he?"

"Believable enough for the jury. But you know what I thought of them. Twelve Grade A idiots. That neighbor farmer who saw them alive earlier Christmas Day *after* Chess supposedly took off for his buddy's house, he was old and half-blind. Couldn't see across the road."

According to Oberle, Chess had been acquitted due to the testimony of his best friend and a half-blind farmer. The farmer was undoubtedly dead, but I wondered if Chess' friend was still alive and kicking. "Do you remember Chess' friend's name?"

He grinned and blew another smoke ring. "Matter of fact, I do, 'cause it's the same as my wife's brother. Maurice."

I wondered how many Maurices there were in Arizona. "How about the last name?"

Oberle fairly crowed. "That *is* his last name! Maurice. Sammy Maurice. The little bastard had two first names! That's enough right there to drive you to a life of crime, which just between you and me and the gatepost, Sammy Maurice led. He turned out almost as bad as his buddy Chess."

A shiver ran up my spine. "What exactly did he do, this Sammy Maurice?"

"What *didn't* he do, more like. Sammy started off his illustrious career with a few shoplifts, graduated to outright burglaries, then finished up with grand theft auto. Back when the murders went down, he and Chess was so tight they'd lie for each other without turning a hair, which is why as far as I was concerned, Chess' alibi didn't hold water."

"You say 'When the murders went down.' What about afterwards? Did they keep up their friendship?"

He stabbed his cigarette out in the ashtray. "You catch on quick, don't ya, missy? No, they didn't. Harry told me that after Chess' trial, they never talked to each other again. Ashamed, maybe."

The shiver came back for another round. Had Chess and his friend *both* killed the Bollingers, but only one had been careless enough to leave bloody footprints? It occurred to me that the famous alibi served a double function. Not only did it help acquit Chess of the murder of his family, but it provided cover for Sammy Maurice as well. "Is Maurice still alive?"

"Only the good die young. Last I heard, Sammy was livin' the high life out in Sun City."

The next day was Friday, supposedly Jimmy's last day at Desert Investigations, but instead, he gave me a reprieve, citing his extra workload and asking if he could stay on for a few more days to finish up. Somehow I managed to keep from jumping up and clapping my hands, and confined myself to a simple "By all means, if you don't mind it eating into that R&R time you'd planned before starting at Southwest MicroSystems."

He pulled a face. "I've been thinking about it, and there's no chance I can enjoy the time off knowing that I left you with unfinished work."

After placing a call to Sammy Maurice and making sure he'd be home later that morning, I left the office with a song in my heart.

The song lasted until I reached the film set on the edge of the Cross Cut Canal. After everything that had happened, Warren was finally getting around to shooting the scene where the Germans exited their escape tunnel, prepared to float to Mexico. Although I wasn't yet ready to talk to Warren about his past and get his version of Crystal Chandler's murder, I did want to find out how Lindsey was doing after her overdose. As I made my way through the crowd of extras, I could tell that Warren hadn't been sleeping well. His blond hair looked dull and the deep shadows around his eyes almost mimicked my own bruises.

When I asked about Lindsey, he sounded abrupt. "The doctor's probably going to release her tomorrow, as soon as she gets a psych eval and referral."

Psych eval. Then the doctor suspected the overdose was a suicide attempt, too. "They can't force her to stay if she doesn't want to, can they?"

"No, but I can. I told her she can come back to work as soon as she sees a therapist, not before. I also told her that the therapy had better be long-term, too, if she wants to remain with Living History Productions."

His coldness unsettled me. While I was no fan of Lindsey's, the prospect that he might fire her troubled me and I said so.

He looked back at the canal, where the water was now running slower than it had been a few days earlier. "It's for her own good. She's had, well, issues for a long time now, and I can't allow them to halt production."

Of course. Ultimately, everything in Hollywood was all about money, and nothing—not fires, floods, earthquakes or suicide attempts—would be allowed to interfere with the bottom line. From what little reading I'd done on documentaries, their budgets were even more strained than on the larger, star-studded productions. I wondered if the same held true for pornography. Probably not. A few people, a few sex toys, a bed, and some low-grade camera equipment were all any director needed, making the profit margin on sleaze sky high.

I decided to ask the question that had been bugging me for weeks. "She was in love with you, wasn't she?"

He looked away from the canal to me, then back to the canal again. "What does that have to do with anything?"

That coldness again. "It could have everything to do with her suicide attempt. If she felt she was being thrown over for me…"

"My thing with Lindsey ended years ago, even before I married Angel. Now I'm sorry, Lena, but I have a scene to direct."

With that none too subtle brush-off, he began rounding up the extras and placing them around the pseudo tunnel exit. I watched for a while longer, hoping the action would stop long enough for me to ask a few more questions, but after an hour passed I went back to my Jeep. As I started to leave, I saw Mark Schank drive up in the Studebaker Golden Hawk.

Schank leaned out the window and waved me down. "Heard you had some trouble down here the other day."

"Just an accident." Uncomfortable, I changed the subject. "I see you're still driving the Hawk. Warren hasn't made up his mind, yet?"

He smiled his phony salesman's smile. "We're getting there. But I don't have any appointments this afternoon, and I thought I'd watch the action. I'm really into film, especially work like Warren's. He's such a genius." But his eyes remained calculating as they caressed my Jeep.

Not wanting to hear another sales pitch, I made my farewells and headed for Sun City, a famous retirement community which existed economically between proletarian Sundown Sam's RV Park and Tommy Bollinger's snooty The Greening. Sun City was located on the far northwest side of Phoenix, about twenty crow-fly miles from Scottsdale. Easy-care houses and condos sat amid "lawns" of gravel dyed the color of grass, and the nearby shops stocked everything the active retiree could want: overpriced sports wear and large-print books.

The community was also much more comprehensive than either Sundown Sam's or The Greening. Anyone who lived here never had to leave. For entertainment, its SunDome hosted a variety of touring shows, ranging from the Bolshoi Ballet to Wayne Newton. The various clinics and hospitals which ringed the development specialized in the ailments of the aging, but if their expertise wasn't enough, an abundance of funeral parlors, crematoria, and cemeteries waited to welcome you with open arms. All in all, if you had to get old before you died, Sun City was the place to do it.

As I pulled the Jeep up in front of Sammy Maurice's house, the front door opened and a stooped prune of a man tottered out.

"How much you want for that Jeep?" he bawled across his green-dyed gravel. The old car thief still had an eye for mechanical beauty.

I climbed out of the Jeep and walked up the drive. "She's not for sale, Mr. Maurice."

His rheumy eyes looked wistful behind his thick horn rims. "Too bad. I'd love to flash that little beauty around town. And call me Reverend Sammy, like my friends do. Only my enemies call me Mr. Maurice."

"*Reverend*, did you say?"

His smile revealed a mouth full of dentures. "For the past thirty years. Retired now, if a pastor can ever be said to be retired. I can still deliver the odd sermon when called upon." He opened the door and led me into a dark living room so overstuffed with chairs it was almost impossible to maneuver. "Take a seat, any seat, plenty of choices, right?"

Cautiously I inched my way into a pink floral chair, which turned out not to be as comfortable as it looked. It was so hard it could have been embalmed.

He plopped down across from me on a gold-and-brown plaid sofa and put his feet up on a red leather ottoman. As my eyes became accustomed to the dim light, I realized that none of the furniture in the room matched, neither in color nor style. Like so many other pack rats, he had probably collected the various pieces over the years and it had never once occurred to him to discard the old in favor of the new. I also figured he had to be single, or at least widowed. No woman would put up with this gaudy mess.

"Like I said on the phone, I wanted to talk to you about your involvement in the Chess Bollinger trial."

He still smiled, the very picture of a man with nothing to hide, but I knew from previous experience that most murderers looked that way. "I'll admit I was intrigued when you called earlier. But before we get started on the Bollingers, how about some iced tea? Or Diet Coke? Nelda can get you some orange juice, if that's what you prefer."

Nelda? Maybe I'd been wrong about his marital state. "Tea will be fine."

He turned his head and bawled again. "Yo, Nelda! Make that two teas!"

A thin voice called back, "Yeah, yeah. Keep your pants on."

Sammy grinned at me. "No respect, no respect at all. But what can you expect from an old con like her?"

Before I could ask what he meant, a tiny woman carrying a loaded tray emerged from the kitchen. Her clothing was as mismatched as her house. Bright red stretch pants clashed with a lavender print blouse, and far too many rhinestones adorned her wrinkled hands and neck. Her makeup would have looked more appropriate on a Vegas showgirl. "Raspberry tea with a dash of mint," she announced. "Fresh made, none of that powdered chemical crap."

"Language, Nelda," Reverend Sammy chided.

"Up yours, sweetie." Nelda put the tray down on the coffee table and sank down on the sofa beside her husband. Then she snuggled up to him like they were both teenagers. I had the feeling that if I weren't in the room, she'd nibble his ear.

I took a sip. Delicious. Like Nelda said, none of that chemical crap. After complementing the brewer, I said, "Reverend Sammy, wouldn't you prefer this conversation to take place in private?"

He waved his hand. "My wife knows all about my past, as I know about hers. We met in a halfway house in the Sixties."

Nelda twinkled at me. "Yeah. He was on parole for car theft, me for bank robbery."

So he hadn't been kidding when he'd called her an "old con." "I, uh, take it you're both, ah, reformed?"

He smiled. "Now we steal souls for Jesus."

The state of my own soul being somewhat iffy at the moment, I stayed on message. "How much do you remember about the Bollinger case?"

"Everything. It was the second most defining moment of my life."

"Second?"

"Setting up my prison ministry was the first."

Nelda elbowed him. "That means I come in third, you old bastard." She didn't seem all that upset at not winning the race. If life was a race.

He kissed her hand. "A very close third." Then to me, "What exactly do you want to know?"

"I want to know if your testimony in court was truthful, if Chess Bollinger really was with you when his family was murdered."

He nodded. "I've told a lot of lies in my life, but none about the Bollinger murders. Chess was with me all that day and all that night. And, no, he didn't kill his family."

"Uh, all that night?"

Nelda giggled. "She thinks you're queer, Sammy."

I experienced my second blush of the week. What was it about old people that made me feel like such a kid? "No, no, not at all. But...but what *were* you guys doing all night? That was never made clear in the newspaper articles I read, and I still haven't been able to get my hands on the court transcripts. I doubt if you two were up all night playing cards or Monopoly."

Reverend Sammy's smile matched his wife's. Dentures gleamed. "No, we weren't. We were doing what we so frequently did those days. Vandalizing public property."

Vandalizing. Where had I run across a mention of vandalism lately? Then I remembered. Harry Caulfield had told me there'd been some instances of vandalism on Christmas Day, 1944.

"Do you mean to tell me that you and Chess were the kids who wrecked Scottsdale High School?"

All these years later, he still managed a guilty look. "I'm afraid so. After spending the day getting drunk on some liquor that I sneaked out of my parents' house, we walked to the school at around, oh, six in the evening—it was already pretty dark—and spent a while going through the classrooms, tearing up books, writing on walls, that kind of thing. Then we set fire to a couple of trash cans and split. But we still weren't done. From the school, we moved on to a barber shop and trashed that. Neither of us had any idea that while we were acting like fools, Chess' whole family was being murdered."

He gave a trembling sigh. "Look, I was a dumb kid. In my confused mind, I believed things would be worse for Chess if the cops found out what we'd done that night, so I helped him hide up in our attic and I kept my mouth shut. Chess believed the same thing, too, and begged me not to tell, not even after the cops caught him and charged him with murder. But when the trial started up, I realized I had to tell the truth or they might hang him! It took me a week or two to get my nerve up, and that's when I stepped forward. But I'd waited too late. Nobody, other than that blessed jury, ever believed me. They brought in a not guilty verdict, but Chess was still branded for life as a murderer who'd escaped justice."

I thought back over Chess' deeply troubled life, the run-ins with the law, the prison sentences, the violence against women. I tried to imagine what it must feel like to be fifteen years old, to learn that your family was dead and that you were the suspect. You didn't have time to grieve, just time to hide. Then, after days in your friend's attic, you feel the handcuffs snap around your wrists. The only way to bear it would be to go numb, to refuse to allow any emotion to take hold. The problem was, such a solution came at a stiff price. If you continue to deny your own feelings, you'll wind up always denying the feelings of others.

Such as your wife's. Your child's.

Or the feelings of any other poor wretch you come across.

Chapter Twenty-Four

As soon as I left Reverend Sammy's house, I checked the messages on my cell and heard Warren apologizing for being so curt that morning. Then he added, "Let's have dinner tonight. Call me or just come by. On second thought, come by. I want to see your beautiful face."

I needed to do something first, so on my way back to Scottsdale, I stopped in at Schank Classic Cars, figuring that Mark Schank would probably have made it to work by now. My guess was right. He was in the showroom polishing a chrome strip on an elderly Rolls Royce Silver Shadow when I walked in. I got straight to the point. "Say, Mark. Maybe you can help me with something. I'm looking for a picture of a '39 Oldsmobile convertible."

His salesman's smile, which he'd plastered in place when he first saw me advancing across the showroom floor, broadened and his eyes narrowed in calculation. "I see Warren's love of the classics is contagious. Well, the '39 Olds is a superb model, truly superb, and you'll look wonderful driving it up Scottsdale Road with that blond hair of yours blowing in the wind. Although I don't have that model here on the lot at this very moment, with my contacts, I can have one here next week. It's…"

My next words erased his smile. "I don't want to buy one, Mark, just see what one looks like."

I'll give him this. The smile returned almost immediately, although a little stiff around the edges. "I have pictures of several in a catalog in my office. But I can assure you that the moment you lay eyes on that little sweetheart, you'll fall in love like Warren did with the Golden Hawk. As I'm certain you already know, the '39 Olds came in a convertible model, which is perfect for Arizona's beautiful climate. And if you wish, we can retrofit it with air conditioning."

Which the car would need when "Arizona's beautiful climate" heated up to a hundred and twenty degrees and the sun turned into a blowtorch. "I'll bear that in mind. Now can I see that picture, please?"

Still extolling the charms of classic cars and the '39 Olds in particular, Mark Schank led me down a hallway filled with photographs of antique cars into an office, where to my surprise, I saw Gilbert Schank ensconced behind a massive desk. Still in his wheelchair, still sucking oxygen through a tube. And still the car salesman, because his phony smile mirrored his son's. Although Gilbert had shrunk alarmingly since his vigorous years on television, I could still see the strong physical resemblance between him and Mark. Both were little taller than jockeys and both had the same thin faces and beaky noses. "Miss Jones. How nice to…see you…again."

"And you, too, Mr. Schank. How are you feeling?" Mark had told me his father almost never left the house, but here he was, as big as life. Or what was left of it.

A grimace. "I'll live…unfortunately. Just came down…to keep my…hand in. Always try to…at least once…a month. You here…to buy a car? By the way…you look…like hell. What…happened?"

I forced a laugh. "I fell into the canal."

"Dumb thing…to do."

"So I noticed."

Perhaps sensing that I was growing uncomfortable discussing my messy physical condition, Mark explained the purpose of my visit. His father frowned in concentration. "A '39 Olds? How…strange. Someone had…where did I hear…?" He scratched his head with a trembly hand.

"Edward Bollinger had a cream-colored '39 Olds," I volunteered. "It disappeared the night of the murders."

His frown went away. "Yes, now I…remember. The authorities…looked all over…for it. Such a…shame, a beautiful…car like that."

"Yes, a shame." But not as big a shame as the smashed-in heads of the Bollinger family.

As I struggled over what to say next, Mark plopped a heavy three-ring binder down on the desk and leafed through it. "Here it is. This one's owned by…" He stopped, not wanting to give up the seller's name. "Well, it's owned by a businessman back east. He's eager to sell, and at a bargain price, too." The figure he quoted didn't sound like a bargain to me.

When I studied the picture, I couldn't understand the car's expense. Yes, the Oldsmobile was sexy in a homely, Humphrey Bogart sort of way. It was a gleaming deep purple, and had a long hood and a deeply sloping trunk, but the headlights looked like a myopic bugs' eyes, and the grill was as tall and pinched as an Edsel's. I was willing to bet that the car's narrow, split windshield had caused many an accident, too. I closed the binder. "Nice, I guess."

For a brief moment Mark's genial manner slipped. "Nice?! You guess?!" Then he recovered himself. "Ah, well, *chacun à son gout*, to each his own taste, and all that. Tell you what. You don't really look like an Olds person, but I have a nice little Camaro out on the lot, a '72 painted exactly the same deep green as your eyes. And it has airbrushed red flames shooting along the body! That one's a convertible, too. You'd be surprised at the price."

I doubted I'd be surprised at all. "Thanks, but I'm not in the market."

His face grew sly. "Oh, a beautiful woman's always in the market for a new car. Let me tell you about the Camaro. It's…"

"Mark, the lady…says she's…not in…the market." Oxygen hissed.

At his father's admonition, Mark halted the sales pitch and returned the binder to its shelf. "Right. Well, I hope I've been of help, Miss Jones."

I had one more question. "Is the Olds rare?"

Despite his frail physical condition, Gilbert Schank managed to offer a joke. "It certainly…is now."

"I mean, was it rare in 1944, when the Bollingers were murdered."

He shook his head. "Oh, no. Not…rare. But…snazzy."

As his son had pointed out, *chacun à son gout.* With nothing else to ask, I said good-by to Mark's father and received a shaky hand-wave in return. I watched as the old man picked up a paper from the desk and held it so close to his face that it almost touched his beaky nose. He squinted at it for a moment, then a spasm of pain crossed his features. He grunted, closed his eyes and let the paper drop.

Leaving Mark to tend to his father, I headed for the exit.

But not before wondering how I would age.

By the time I made it to the Papago Park set, filming was finished on the canal bank and the crew had reassembled near the reconstructed prison camp. But for all Warren's apologies on my cell, he was still cranky. While I watched from the shade of a mesquite, he snapped at a cameraman, telling the man to get a move on before the sun got too high in the sky. "I need shadows! So see if you can get that Ariflex in position sometime before noon!"

Putting off our discussion yet again, I backed away and drove to Desert Investigations, where I found Jimmy so intent on work that he barely grunted a greeting when I came in. By now, my earlier good mood had vanished, so I called Warren's cell and left a message that something had come up and I couldn't have dinner tonight. I promised to call him first thing in the morning, then hung up. Jimmy and I worked in silence for the rest of the day.

When five o'clock came, Jimmy headed toward his truck and I went upstairs to see if a *Leave It to Beaver* marathon might improve my mood. At least the characters on the TVLand reruns were happy.

On Saturday, I was still in a funk, so I decided not to go down to the office just to watch Jimmy type. Instead, I nuked a Sausage 'N Egg Hot Pocket, turned on CNN, and sat back to see who else in the world was having a bad day. The Midwest, apparently. A serial killer was working his way through Kansas and Nebraska, and in Minnesota, two state senators were arrested after throwing punches at a Wal-Mart opening. I then switched to the FOX news channel, only to find the talking head du jour extolling the virtues of the latest Hollywood water diet. I tried TVLand again, but the Beav wasn't on, just some rerun of a '50s Western. Since I wasn't in the mood for singing cowboys, I switched the TV off and roamed the apartment aimlessly for a few minutes, trying to figure out what to do with myself.

I needed to relax, but had no idea how to accomplish that. I could read more of Gunter Hoenig's journals, but they would probably just stress me further. Or I could read a book. After glancing through my bookshelves, I realized I had read them all, some of them twice. For a few minutes I thought about going over to the Scottsdale Library, this time just for fun, but decided against it. I'd just wind up gravitating to the Criminal Justice section like I usually did, and that definitely wouldn't be relaxing.

Maybe I should call someone, just to chat. Warren, perhaps. But thinking about the conversation I needed to have with him made me more tense than ever, so I dismissed that possibility. I could always call my foster father and find out if enough money had been raised yet to bring Rada Tesema's family to the U.S., but I figured I already knew the answer. If the Rev had been successful, he would have informed me. Besides, on Saturdays he always switched off his phone to work on his sermons, and only made call-backs in case of emergencies. Frustrated, I opened up my address book and went through the list of girlfriends I'd accumulated over the years, but soon realized that all were living lives almost as complicated as mine. Finally realizing that I didn't know anyone who could provide me with mindless conversation, I broke down and hit Captain Kryzinski's number on my speed dial.

"Yeah?" He sounded much the same as always. Gruff, abrupt. It meant nothing.

"How goes the packing?"

After an uncomfortable silence, he said, "Lena, I shipped everything out three days ago. Don't you remember me telling you I leave for New York tomorrow?"

Hearts, being attached to a human being's upper left quadrant by a network of tendons and muscle, aren't supposed to fall, but I'd swear mine did. "Tomorrow?" I barely recognized my own voice.

A sigh. "Yeah, tomorrow. My plane leaves at 8:30 a.m."

There was so much I wanted to say, but all I could do was ask, "Do you have a ride?"

"Cab's gonna be here at seven sharp."

"Cancel it. I'll take you to the airport. It's the least I can do."

"You sure? You weren't all that, ah, *supportive* about my decision the last time we talked."

"I'm sure."

"See ya then, kid. But if you don't show..." With that undefined threat hanging in the air, he hung up.

I sat there, thinking about how much I'd miss him, both personally and professionally. Then I shrugged, went into the bedroom, picked up Gunter Hoenig's journals, and carried them back into the living room. Who needed to relax?

For the next few hours, I sat on the sofa reading and re-reading various journal entries, still puzzled by Gunter's ongoing guilt over Joyce Bollinger's death. If his writings were accurate, he had tried to save her, so how could he consider her death his fault? His constant references to her pale blue eyes made me almost believe that he had half-fallen in love with her, which was a ridiculous theory, given the condition she would have been in at the time. But Gunter had been a young man. He had spent most of his war years stuffed into the hull of a submarine with nothing but other men for company, only to eventually wind up in a prison camp surrounded yet again by nothing but men. Joyce Bollinger was quite possibly the first woman he'd seen in years, and from what I'd heard, she had been extraordinarily beautiful, maybe even beautiful enough to impress a young man so deeply that he never forgot her or her children.

Ah, how different men must have been in those days.

As I went through the journals this time, instead of trying to keep them in some semblance of order I set aside the entries relating directly to the Ernst case, making a series of neat piles on my new cactus wood coffee table.

> 1945: *I will always remember those pale eyes, their pleas to me.*
> 1950: *But I guess I will never see Josef again. Like me, he probably abandoned Das Kapitan.*
> 1978: *Kapitan still lives. This can not be allowed.*

I stared at the pages, thinking. Then I got up and paced for a while. Something…

When I sat back down and went through the pages I'd selected again, an idea that had only been half-formed finally coalesced.

Could Gunter Hoenig still be alive?

Was it possible that he hadn't, after all, died in that Canadian car crash?

I snatched up the phone again and called Jimmy's direct line. "Look, I know you're trying to finish up loose ends, but could you please do me a favor?"

A sigh. "What is it now?"

"I want you to follow up on that Canadian car crash which supposedly killed Gunter and his wife."

"*Supposedly?*"

"Trust me. Something's not copacetic there." As soon as he agreed, I hung up before he could change his mind.

Things were becoming clearer. If Gunter Hoenig was still alive, he would be in his eighties, but as I had already seen with Tommy Bollinger, old didn't necessarily mean helpless. Still, if Gunter had killed Ernst, why would he feel the need to kill Fay Harris? And Harry Caulfield? I thought about it for a while, then came up with an answer. Fay, who had hoarded all her unused notes from *Escape*

Across the Desert, might have reached the same conclusion I'd just reached—that Gunter was alive and living in the Phoenix area. If so, she would have recognized that she was sitting on a story which might rival the Pulitzer-nominated piece she'd written on human trafficking. As for Harry, even into his eighties he maintained a cop's mind and heart. If he had begun to suspect that Gunter was still around and might have murdered Das Kapitan, he would contact the authorities. Unless someone stopped him.

Granted, in his journals Gunter came across as a gentle man, especially given his romantic writings about his golden-haired wife, his joy in his son and grandchildren, and his cute-but-awful drawings of animals. But when driven to extremes, even gentle men could do cruel things. If Gunter had driven the speed boat which almost killed Erik Ernst, what else might he have done?

I looked at the journal pages some more, shifting them from one pile to another. As I was transferring all of Gunter's drawings to the same stack, my attention was caught by one in particular—the clumsy line drawing I'd puzzled over days earlier without success. Deciding to solve this one mystery, at least, I studied it carefully. On the top left of the page were two animals of indeterminate species, possibly a jackrabbit and a frog. Below the frog were two stick figures. To their right was some spindly object which I was almost certain was a tree.

The amateurism of these figures was nothing compared to the big mess in the center of the page, a series of wobbly but concentric circles. A nest of snakes? I started to laugh at such an outrageous guess, then remembered that in breeding season, some snakes do slither into a dark lair together and form a tightly packed lump called a "snake ball." But if Gunter had drawn such a thing, why hadn't he bothered to give them little dots for eyes like he had for all his other animals? I turned the drawing upside down, then sideways. Deciding the lines probably weren't snakes after all and that I was wasting my time, I went ahead and placed the drawing on top of the others.

By now, I'd been sitting in one position too long, and my canal-bruised muscles were stiff. To get my circulation going,

I decided to rearrange my new furniture. I moved the cactus wood sofa to a spot underneath the living room window, but when I sat down on it again, I could no longer see out. Duh. So I shoved the sofa against the opposite wall, where it merely looked stupid. Frustrated, I tried angling it kitty-corner so that it faced the window *and* my television, but that looked even dumber. After an hour of furniture pushing and dragging, I gave up and returned everything to its original position.

All that furniture hauling wasn't exercise enough to relax my muscles, so I went out for a slow, careful run. After logging only five miles, I limped back home and moved the furniture around some more. Is this what owning furniture does to you? Turns you into an idiot?

Disgusted with myself, I took a quick shower, dressed in a less grungy T-shirt and jeans, and drove over to the nearby multiplex to see the latest Clint Eastwood movie. It turned out to be a poor choice, with a body count almost as high as that in the Erik Ernst case.

I should have opted for the Disney.

But on the way home, an idea occurred to me, and I sped up, almost catching the attention of a bored motorcycle cop lurking in the parking lot of the Olive Garden Restaurant. I slowed down, but only until I was out of his sight. Then I put pedal to the metal and raced all the way to my apartment.

Reeking of popcorn and JuJu Beans, I ran up the stairs, unlocked the locks, and rushed to the coffee table, where I'd left Gunter's journals separated into various stacks.

I stared at the top drawing again.

Not snakes.

A topographical map.

Chapter Twenty-Five

On my way to take Captain Kryzinski to Sky Harbor the next morning, I left a note on Jimmy's desk reiterating how important it was that he follow up on Gunter's supposed death in the Canadian car crash. Then, secure in the knowledge that Warren was an early riser, I called him, but when he picked up, he sounded every bit as snappish as yesterday. Our phone connection was foul, too.

"I'm in a hurry here, Lena, so be quick." Hiss, hiss. Was that his phone, or mine?

"Are you on set?" A hollow background noise that made its way through the hissing didn't sound right for either his motel room or Papago Park.

"No, I'm...Damn! Gotta go." A click and he was gone.

I stood by my desk staring at the phone, tempted to call him back and give him a piece of my mind. But when I checked my watch, I saw that only by exceeding the speed limit could I drive over to Captain Kryzinski's place, pick him up, and get him to the airport in time for the slow slog through Sky Harbor's long security lines. Pushing Warren's rudeness to the back of my mind, I grabbed the file folder containing the Erik Ernst case notes and ran out the office door, pausing only to lock it behind me.

When I reached Kryzinski's house he was waiting at the curb, wearing a tacky brown suit and an ugly bolo tie. He had a frown on his face and his cell phone was in his hand. "I was about to call a cab."

"Sorry. I had some last minute business to take care of."

"At seven on Sunday morning?"

I didn't want to go into it. "You have everything you need?" Only a carry-on bag little larger than a woman's purse sat by his feet. Not much to show for twenty years in Scottsdale.

He picked it up and climbed into the Jeep. "I told you I already shipped everything."

"Even your clothes? Maybe you'd better go back into the house and…"

"Lena, let's get started or I will call that cab."

Feeling more miserable than ever, I let the clutch out and aimed the Jeep toward Sky Harbor. The traffic was heavy for a Sunday and Kryzinski back-seat drove all the way, but we arrived at the airport with forty-five minutes to spare. Kryzinski wanted me to let him off at the curb, but I refused and found a spot in the Terminal Four parking garage. Despite his protests, I followed him into the terminal itself.

All the while, his cranky expression became crankier. "This is silly. They won't let you past security. Why don't you go back to the office, since you're so determined to work on Sunday?"

"Humor me." How could I tell him how much I'd miss him, that when he left he'd be taking with him some of the happiest years of my life, and that I wanted to put off our inevitable parting until the very last moment? So I didn't tell him. But as soon as he reached the first security check-point, I found myself hugging him, pressing my face against his chest.

"Please don't go," I whispered to his bolo tie.

He pushed me away gently and patted my cheek. "Sweetie, it's time for you to start living your life."

Before I could tell him not to call me Sweetie, he turned and was gone.

I spent the next few minutes in the nearby ladies' room, drying my eyes. You'd think that a childhood spent saying good-by to one foster parent after another would inure me to this sort of thing—and it had, for a while—but therapy had begun to dissolve the scar tissue around my heart. Silently I cursed my short-sighted therapist, who'd grown up in a large, loving Hispanic family. What the hell did she know about serial good-byes?

Face repaired, I emerged from the ladies' room only to suffer another shock. Standing where I'd last seen Kryzinski were Warren and Lindsey, she leaning against him in the same way I'd leaned against my boss. After the security guard handed back her ID, Lindsey turned, threw her arms around Warren's neck, and gave him a long, hard kiss. But unlike Kryzinski did me, Warren didn't push her away.

My mood must have shown on my face because when I arrived back at Desert Investigations to find Jimmy still hard at work, he asked, "What's wrong?"

"Everything's peachy. How about you?"

"The same." He gave me a smile that held little humor. I noticed that although he'd dressed with more care than the other day, he still looked rough. Especially in his eyes.

"Poor Jimmy. The house-hunting must be doing you in."

He sighed. "No more hunting. Yesterday we made an offer on the condo."

It was probably the size of a mouse trap. "Well, that's good, isn't it? You two can finally get settled?" As if he wasn't already settled in his reservation trailer with the prayer lodge in back.

"Sure, after we buy all new furniture. We're supposed to hit the stores again today. Esther's picking me up around noon."

"Gonna buy some Persian Pink stuff, eh? Wonderful. I'm sure your new condo will look, ah, interesting." Since I had nothing to say to Esther because of the changes she was putting both me and my partner through, I'd make certain to be somewhere else at noon. Refusing to meet his eyes, I sat down at my desk and started going through the Erik Ernst case files. With increasing puzzlement, I reread my notes on the interviews with everyone involved: Rada Tesema, Tommy Bollinger, Fay Harris, Harry Caulfield, Frank Oberle, and Ian Mantz. Slowly, I began comparing them to the old newspaper articles I'd printed out at the library and the information I'd gleaned from Gunter Hoenig's journals. When I was through, I sat there frowning. Someone was lying.

As I re-examined the Harry Caulfield notes for the umpteenth time, I paid no attention to the hum of the printer until Jimmy called over, "Lena, I have something for you."

I looked up. "Such as?"

"That note you left me, asking me to come up with more information on that Canadian car crash? The one which supposedly killed Gunter Hoenig?"

"What do you mean, *supposedly?*" But I could guess what he was about to tell me.

He didn't disappoint. "There was no death certificate issued for him, either in Canada or here."

"But the *Calgary Sun* article said, 'an elderly couple from Phoenix.'"

"Newspapers say lots of things, then they run the truth on the corrections page next day." He handed me a printout from the *Calgary Sun* dated September 27, 1999.

> In an article yesterday about a thirty-two car collision on a highway near Didsbury, the Sun misidentified the home town of two of the victims. Killed in the crash were a couple from Phenix City, Alabama, not Phoenix, Arizona, as our article previously stated. The victims' names are being withheld pending notification of their relatives.

"Want to see the next day's article? It identifies the dead couple as Nathan and Emma Lassen. Of Phenix City, Alabama."

"Thanks, but that's not necessary." Someone—probably Gunter's son—had inserted the original misleading article into the journals in order to convince me that Gunter Hoenig was dead. To disguise his manipulation of truth, he'd also stuffed in all those loose recipes and drawings.

But had he, in his rush to cover his father's tracks, realized what one of those drawings portrayed?

It didn't matter. Since Ian Mantz had taken so many pains to make me believe that his father was dead, it meant Gunter was still alive. There was also a good chance that Gunter had finally succeeded where he had once failed—at the murder of Erik Ernst. I felt a brief stab of disappointment. I had liked the Gunter I'd met in his journals, the gentle man who loved animals and children. I could allow him his viciousness toward Erik Ernst—a killer himself—but not toward Fay and Harry.

Those deaths were inexcusable.

When I next looked at my watch, I discovered it was past ten. On the chance that Ian Mantz and family weren't in church, I gave him a call. His wife told me he was busy and would have to call me back, but I insisted he come to the phone. "Tell him I want to talk to him about the death of an elderly couple named Nathan and Emma Lassen in Didsbury, Alberta."

"Didsbury? What...?" Her voice rose in alarm.

"Yeah, Didsbury. Tell your husband that he either talks to me or to the INS." And after that, the Apache Junction Police Department, but I figured raising the spectre of the INS with the Mantz family would be scary enough. For all I knew about immigration law, the entire family was living in the U.S. illegally.

Within seconds, Gunter Hoenig's son came to the phone. To his credit, he didn't bother pretending ignorance. "Okay, so you figured out Dad wasn't killed in Canada. Big fucking deal. What'll it take to make you go away?"

"The truth."

I could almost hear him shrug. "Which truth are you interested in? That Dad lived in the U.S. illegally since 1944? Or that he was afraid old Das Kapitan would frame him for the Bollinger murders?"

Either. Both. "Where is he?"

A pause. "At Stately Pines Cemetery. He died last summer."

"And your mother?"

"She's dead, too. Died of a broken heart right after Dad."

Before he could lie to me again, I said, "Then your father's death certificate will be on file with the state under his assumed name of Gerhardt Mantz. But why don't you spare me the trip downtown?" Actually, I wouldn't have to make the trip. If Gunter Hoenig had been issued a death certificate anywhere in Arizona, either under his real name or his alias of Gerhardt Mantz, Jimmy would download a copy for me before the day was out.

"I'm not about to 'spare' you anything, Miss Jones."

I decided to try one more question on him. "Did your father ever talk about some sort of secret, a secret that was 'like gold'?"

"Gold? I don't know what the hell you're talking about."

"If you would just try…"

He cut me off. In a voice dripping venom, he said, "Try, my ass. You know what you can do with yourself?"

"I doubt that you'll give me any suggestions I haven't heard before. Why don't you just tell me the truth for a change?"

"You wish." After barking some obscenities divided equally between German and English, he slammed down the phone.

I had hit a dead end as far as Gunter's son was concerned, but if Gunter himself was still alive and living under yet another false identity, Jimmy would find him. But what of the other German POW, Gunter's friend Josef Braun? Had he, like Gunter, blended into the American scene? And if so, who had helped him? Then I remembered the numerous Japanese soldiers found hiding out in Philippine caves decades after the end of World War II. They had been astounded when told that the war was over and they could go home.

Could I have been too hasty in fingering Gunter as Erik Ernst's killer?

An hour later I was walking through the musty corridors of Shady Rest Care Home, on my way to see Chess Bollinger. One more scenario for the Bollinger/Ernst murders had occurred to me and if anyone had the answer, it would be Chess. I just hoped I could get some sense out of him for a change. My hopes were high, because Alzheimer's patients were usually at their best early in the day, before the "sundowning" effect kicked in.

To my disappointment, both Chess' wife and daughter were in his room. Judith Bollinger, still wearing her unsettling smile, sat in a corner chair, knitting something ugly. MaryEllen sat on the edge of her father's bed, holding his hand and weeping. Her black eye had almost faded away, but I wondered how long it would be before her boyfriend freshened it up with another one.

Chess' eyes were closed. He could have either been sleeping or dead. "How is he?" I asked MaryEllen.

She smiled. "Better."

A small laugh from the corner. "You call taking a dump in your pants *better?*"

Hitting Judith would have landed me back in anger management therapy, so I forced myself to remain calm. "Mrs. Bollinger, I'd like to talk to him again if I may."

Judith had no objections, not that I expected any. She probably wouldn't mind if I attached electrodes to her husband's testicles.

MaryEllen was another matter. "I don't want him bothered. He's been so peaceful this morning." She lifted his hand to her lips, kissed it, and watched with delight as his eyelids fluttered open.

"Baby." Chess' voice was whispery but clear.

"Oh, Daddy!" She leaned over him and gave him a kiss on his forehead. "You recognize me!"

Chess frowned. "Why wouldn't I?"

Before MaryEllen could answer, Judith piped up, "Because you have Alzheimer's. Can't recognize nobody half the time."

When he flicked his eyes toward her, I saw anger. Then he looked at his daughter again and his expression softened. "Your eye. Did I...?"

MaryEllen shook her head. "No, Daddy. I, um, I ran into a door."

Judith laughed again. "A door named Clay. You'd like him, Chess. He's cut from the same cloth as you."

MaryEllen stood up, and for a moment, I believed she'd do what I wanted to do. Instead, she burst into tears and ran from the room.

Judith sniffed. "Girls these days."

I ignored her and stepped closer to the bed. "Mr. Bollinger, my name's Lena Jones and I'm a private investigator. I'd like to ask you a few questions." From the hallway, I could hear MaryEllen's sobs.

Chess' eyes clouded. "Private invest...? What'd I do now?"

Plenty, I wanted to tell him. Take a look at your life's legacies. One takes glee in your suffering, while the other cries in the hall. Out of a pity he didn't deserve, I didn't say it. "Mr. Bollinger, I want to prove that you didn't kill your family."

"Not me! Not meeeee!" His voice began to rise, then stopped in mid-howl as he closed his eyes and began to drift off. I was losing him.

Maybe I could bring him back. From what little I knew about Alzheimer's, most patients could remember what happened a half-century ago better than they could remember what they had for breakfast, so I gave his shoulder a shake. "Chess, wake up! I want to talk about your father's car! Did you ever go joyriding in it?"

When he opened his eyes again they were clear. A mischievous smile played at the corner of his mouth. "Joyriding? Oh, yeah. But I always get caught and Daddy beats me." His voice sounded high, adolescent, and I noticed that he spoke in the present tense, as if he were still fifteen years old. In his mind, I guess he still was.

So Chess had gone joyriding in Edward Bollinger's car. That didn't surprise me. At the time, he'd been a more-or-less normal teenaged boy, and teenagers have always been fascinated by cars. "Chess, did you..." I stopped, remembering to keep my questions in the present tense. "Do you have anyone with you when you take the car?"

A smile. "You betcha. I got a lot of friends, all wanting rides in Daddy's snazzy car."

I nodded in encouragement. "What are your friends' names?"

"Tommy. He's really my uncle but he's more like my friend. And Sammy. Oh, lotsa guys. I was always real popular, not just 'cause Daddy had that Olds."

We were getting where I wanted to go. Chess had been a lonely boy, and lonely boys were always vulnerable to overtures of friendship. "How can you be popular, Chess? You live way out of town on that farm." Near where three escaped German POWs had been hiding in an arroyo.

He stuck out his lower lip like a thwarted child. "I go to school, don't I? I take that big school bus like everybody else on our road, like all my friends."

"You never had a friend in your life." Judith again, throwing her poison into the mix.

Chess raised himself up on a scrawny elbow and stared at her. His eyes were clearer than I'd yet seen them, and I realized our sweet trip down Memory Lane had ended. "Wait 'til I get my hands on you, bitch. I'll make you sorry you ever drew breath." The vicious expression on his face told me all I needed to know about the kind of man he had once been.

But Judith knew he wasn't that man any longer, that she was now perfectly safe. "You ain't gettin' your hands on me ever again."

I tried to deflect the coming brawl between a grudge-carrying woman and her bedridden batterer. "Chess, try to remember. Did you have any friends with German accents?"

But I no longer existed for him. His focus was now on his wife. "I'll kill you, bitch, I will! I'll ."

Judith laughed and laughed, until her high cackles finally drove me from the room.

Once in the hallway, I looked for MaryEllen, but she was gone, the ongoing war between her parents proving too much for her. Frustrated, I headed for my Jeep, determined to return the next day in hopes that I would find Chess by himself and that he would be semi-rational again. When I entered the parking lot, I found MaryEllen sitting on the curb, too distraught to drive. A young couple emerging from a pickup truck ignored her; I guessed they were used to seeing tears at the Shady Rest Care Home. In fact, they didn't look any too cheery themselves. Which family member they were visiting? A grandmother? A mother? Or even worse, a child?

As the couple disappeared inside, I went over to MaryEllen and sat down on the curb beside her. "I'm sorry. That must have been hard on you."

Her face was a tragic mask. "Daddy and I always got along great until she started in on him."

Right. Chess was a saint whose only problem was his wife. I'd heard such rationalizations before from the families of batterers, as well as the batterers themselves. "MaryEllen, as unpleasant as your mother is, have you ever considered that she might have a point?"

"Are you crazy?" I heard an echo of Chess' rage in her voice. "You heard her, didn't you? My God! She was always pushing his buttons. It's all her fault! Without her, Daddy would be…"

"Without her, your Daddy wouldn't be one bit different. Don't forget that he beat his first wife. And that he beat you."

She wouldn't meet my eyes. "No, he didn't."

I decided to go for it. "Stop covering up for your father. He's not worth it. I've seen his arrest record, and I read the report of the time he put you in the hospital. You were, what, nine years old? What in the world could a nine-year-old do to push a grown man's buttons, to make him break two of her ribs? I know you love your father, and that's admirable. But it's not admirable to blame your mother for the kind of man your father allowed himself to become. He was a violent felon long before he met her." I took a shot in the dark. "Just like your boyfriend was a violent felon before you met him."

She ducked her head, but not before I could see admission in her eyes. I hoped she was beginning to get it. Striving to make my point, I continued. "I had a rough childhood, too, MaryEllen, and I…" How much should I tell her when the details didn't matter? "I shared a lot of your experiences and they left their marks on me. But I eventually learned not to let the pain of my past determine the course of my future. Sure, I have my scars, but you know what they say about scar tissue."

She looked up at me, then, her pale eyes challenging. "No, I don't know. What do they say?"

"That scar tissue is stronger than the tissue around it." We weren't talking about physical scars.

Her smile wasn't pretty. "My pain can make me strong, huh?"

"Only if you learn from it. If you don't, you'll turn into your mother."

Chapter Twenty-Six

I didn't want to go back to Desert Investigations just yet, because there was a chance I might run into Esther bringing Jimmy back from their furniture-shopping expedition. True, I could have gone straight upstairs to my apartment and looked through Gunter's journals again, but I decided that since I was already on an ugly roll of unpleasantness, I might as well continue. After leaving Shady Rest, I drove to Papago Park to confront Warren about all manner of sordid things. Bad movies. Airport kisses. Dead girlfriends.

The Studebaker Golden Hawk was in the parking lot, but I didn't see Mark Schank anywhere. Did that mean Warren had purchased the car yesterday? I felt a brief pang. When he went back to L.A., I'd never see it again. I walked past the crowd of onlookers and slipped under the tape barrier. When I finally found Warren, deep in conference with some techs, his expensive aftershave was mingling with sweat and sage. They say scent is the strongest of the senses, possessing the capability to even reach out to the dying with its evocation of pleasurable past experiences. Which was probably true, because as angry as I was after observing the scene with Lindsey at the airport, smelling Warren made me want to touch him.

But I refrained. "I saw you at Sky Harbor with Lindsey."

He gave me a puzzled look, not a guilty one. "What were you doing there?"

"Saying good-bye to a friend."

"Oh. So was I." After a long silence, he ordered an adjustment on a lighting umbrella, then told everyone else to take a break.

"Twenty minutes after we started?" one of the techs asked.

"You having trouble with your hearing, Gene? Take a break or get off the set."

The tech stared at him with his mouth open for a second, then wandered over to the caterer's truck for more coffee, but not before I heard him mumble, "Same old shit, different shitter."

Warren, who must have heard the comment, ignored it. "I guess we need to talk."

He had no idea how much we needed to talk. I still hadn't broached the subject of his messy early life, nor the subject of Crystal Chandler's murder. Compared to that, the clinch with Lindsey at the airport was minor indeed. I followed him away from the crew and to the small clearing where several folding chairs had been set up. If Warren wanted privacy, he'd made a bad choice, because the morning breeze was blowing in from the west, which meant that our conversation could quite possibly be heard by the usual crowd of onlookers downwind. Not that it mattered. If Warren had been foolish enough to kiss Lindsey at the airport in front of God and everybody, I didn't care if he made a further fool of himself in public.

However, once we'd sat down, he kept his voice low. "Since you were at the airport, you probably saw everything that happened. With Lindsey."

"Of course I did. That's one of the reasons I'm here, to get..." I started to say, "...to get everything straight, especially about you and your dead girlfriend."

But he raised his hand, stopping me in mid-sentence. "May I explain?"

"Go right ahead." The breeze ruffled his hair and it was all I do to keep from reaching out and smoothing it back down.

"Lena, Lindsey kissed *me*. I didn't kiss her."

Okay. So we would talk about Lindsey first. Then we'd get to Crystal Chandler and his possible involvement in her death. "She kissed *you*? Some distinction."

"It's a big distinction. After what happened the other day, I told her to pack her bags and go back to L.A. That if she didn't, I would…" He didn't finish.

"Would what?" Strangle her?

A sharp sound nearby made me jump, but then I realized it was only the backfire of a semi on the road between the Papago Buttes. The breeze made it sound as if a gun had gone off right next to me. "Would what, Warren?"

"Nothing." He examined his shoes. They looked fine to me. Reeboks, like my own, and every bit as dirty. "What Lindsey did has nothing to do with us."

"What she did? Such as the big fat kiss?"

"I wasn't talking about the kiss. But as for the scene at the airport, like I told you, she grabbed me before I could do anything about it. Then, well, there was no point in making a difficult situation even worse. What could I have done, anyway? Slap her? Scream for help? The woman's gone through enough without having to experience that kind of public humiliation."

It's hard to talk while you're gritting your teeth, but I somehow managed. "Why all this concern about Lindsey?"

I could tell that Warren wanted to yell at me like he'd been doing all day to his crew, but somehow he managed to control himself. "Once I care for a woman, no matter what happens I always feel a certain amount of loyalty toward her, even after the relationship ends. You saw how well Angel and I still get along, and it's not only for the kids' sake. You also know that Lindsey and I were involved for a while, but that's ancient history. I guess maybe I should have gone into more detail. I started to, once, but chickened out."

Who knows? Maybe he had tried. But it made no difference now. I'd already found out everything I needed to know. "You have a lot of loyalties. Are you certain you have room for another one?"

He nodded. "I sent Lindsey away for your sake, but I can't say any more than that."

"Then this conversation's over." I stood up and turned toward the parking lot, but before I could take a step, he'd jumped out of his chair and cut me off. I stepped back, increasing the distance between us.

He moved forward and put a hand on my arm. Not with unnecessary roughness, but firmly enough for me to know I wasn't going anywhere. "I'm not going to let you walk off like this. Not until you've heard the truth."

I don't like it when someone says they're not going to let me do something, but since I was curious, I sat down again. "All of the truth, Warren? Or just some of it."

He looked around quickly, and seeing that no one was near, lowered his voice almost to a whisper. His next words came as a surprise. "Lindsey's the one who pushed you into the canal."

For a moment I didn't think I'd heard him right. "What!?"

He placed his hand softly across my mouth. "Don't tell the world, for God's sake. Getting her out of town accomplished two things. It protected you and it kept her away from the police."

I pushed his hand away. "She almost killed me, so why are you trying to protect her?" I wanted the bitch stewing in an Arizona jail, not soaking up rays in Malibu.

"You have to believe me when I tell you that Lindsey had no idea the canal was so dangerous. None of us did. And anyway, that morning she wasn't quite herself. She'd noticed the way I look at you, and that night she stayed up crying, taking one too many Triazolams— that's her drug of choice these days. After she pushed...after what happened to you, she went back to the motel and finished off the whole damn bottle. If the maid hadn't gone in to clean the room, she'd be dead now."

And if I hadn't managed to grab the bottom rung of that rusted ladder, I'd be dead, too. I wondered who Warren would have mourned for most, me or Lindsey. Not being known for my tact, I said so.

He paled. "How can you say that? You know how I feel about you. Damn it, Lena, I fell in love with you the second you strode into that conference room and started telling me how you could make my film set more secure. You were so self-sufficient, so in control, so beautiful. That's a combination no man in his right mind could ignore." He tried for a smile. "And then I saw your 1945 Jeep."

I'd been impressed by him, too, but to paraphrase a popular Hollywood movie, handsome is as handsome does. "I'm not a big believer in love at first sight. Lust, maybe, but not love."

He surprised me again. He leaned forward and caressed my cheek. "Poor Lena. To live with so little trust."

Since the explanation for that would have taken several hours, I remained silent.

He tried a smile. "I'm not saying I don't feel lust for you, because you know I do. And it's about time we did something about that instead of just drooling at each other like we have been. But lust is the very least of it. I want you to come back to Los Angeles with me, to…"

It was my turn to stop him. "Before you go any further with this, Warren, you need to know that I ran a check on you. I know all about *Here Comes Crystal* and the rest of the porno crap. And I know that for a while, you were the lead suspect in the murderer of your girlfriend Crystal Chandler."

His mouth dropped. "You ran a check on *me*? When?"

"I asked Jimmy to do it the day after I almost drowned in the canal."

"But the next morning, when we were having breakfast, I explained…"

"Yeah, you said you dropped the coffee."

He stared at me, more than a hint of outrage in his eyes. "You saw the burns on my leg."

"Easy enough to fake. Remember, I saw them the next day, when you would have had time to dump any cup of coffee on yourself. Warren, I'm a detective. An ex-cop. You can't expect me to not to be suspicious."

"Of *everyone*?"

"Yes."

"What would be my motive for killing you?"

"I haven't figured that out yet."

Any self-respecting man would have gotten up and walked away then, but he didn't. He just sat there studying me as the breeze chased a tumbleweed across the set. I would have felt better if he'd gotten angry again, but he only looked hurt. Finally he sighed and spread his hands in defeat. "I don't know what else I can say. Just that I..." He closed his eyes for a second, then opened them again. They were the exact same color as the sky. "Just that I love you."

There was the "L" word again. He sure knew how to get to me. But I kept the conversation on track. "Tell me about Crystal Chandler." I knew I was tempting him to walk away, but I didn't care. If he did, I wouldn't have to make a decision about him or worry about moving to L.A. to work on some television show. I could just stay here in Scottsdale and watch Desert Investigations go bankrupt.

"You already know what there is to know. Crystal was strangled to death at my house, and her killer was never caught."

"That's right. And you had an air-tight alibi."

He looked off at one of the buttes, where a dust devil was swirling up the slope. A hiker was trying to scurry out of its way. "You could say so, since I was in bed with three other women at the time."

"*Three?*"

When his eyes met mine again, they showed no emotion. "Yeah, it's an old story. Young man makes good, young man goes bad in the adult film industry, young man gets clean and sober and repents of his evil ways. You weren't raised in Hollywood so you don't know how it is. There's so much pressure to succeed, but no rule book on how to do it. So I did what a lot of Hollywood brats do and took the easy route by following in my father's footsteps. He'd done well, so why couldn't I? Hell, Dad even helped me get started in the business. He got the finances together for my first project and loaned me a couple of his actors. Crystal was one of them. When the movie was a hit, he was *proud* of me, Lena! I can't stress enough how different it is out there. So different that it didn't occur to me—to him—that there was a huge price to be paid. Anyway, I was incapable of thinking anything through to its logical conclusion in those days. Too many chemicals. What his excuse is, I'll never know. But I've turned away from all that. I've paid the price and made peace with myself and the things I've done. I hope you can accept that."

I noticed he didn't come right out and deny killing Crystal Chandler, so I asked. "Did you murder her?"

A bitter laugh. "The women I was with that night—one of them was Lindsey—say I didn't. The cops say the same thing."

Now it was my turn to study the dust devil. It had caught up with the hiker, who with cries of disgust was batting sand away from his face. I knew just how he felt. "You know, Warren, I read a big batch of material about that night, and no one named Lindsey Reynolds was ever mentioned."

"Her name was May Morning then."

"That…that's an odd name. Even for an actress."

"Not for an adult film actress."

After that revelation, all I could say was, "Oh."

Life is so damned complicated. We all want to do the right thing and love the right people, but it never seems to work out for some of us. Instead, we wobble along like drunken monkeys, bouncing from one mistake to the other. After a childhood filled with beatings and rapes, I'd struggled to make a decent life for myself and had—I thought—succeeded. But I couldn't seem to shake my attraction to troubled men. Now I'd found the great-granddaddy of them all. As I looked at Warren, sitting there looking so irresistible in the Arizona sunlight, I realized that he still hadn't answered my question.

"Warren, did you kill Crystal Chandler?"

He was silent for a moment, watching the dust devil as it dissipated into little more than a dirty wind. Just as I was about to ask my question again, he faced me. There were lines of pain around his mouth but what looked to be truth in his eyes.

"Did I kill Crystal? Honey, I've been asking myself that question for years. You see, I can't remember."

When I pulled the Jeep into the parking lot at Desert Investigations, I could see Esther's car and the ruffled edge of some Persian Pink thing peeking out of a Neiman Marcus bag in the back seat, so I bypassed the office and went straight upstairs to my apartment. I didn't feel like talking to anyone anyway.

Warren and I had left things unfinished. After he'd aired what seemed like enough dirty laundry for a hundred Hollywood bios, I'd told him I needed time to think. He said he understood. But he was wrong. The real reason I couldn't make a commitment to him or anyone was that I wasn't ready to share my nightmares.

Hoping to ease my skittery mind, I put on an old vinyl of Tampa Red and listened to his bottleneck guitar while I nuked some ramen for lunch. But the scratchy sound of the vinyl got on my nerves after a while, so I turned the stereo off, lay down on the floor, and started doing crunches. After working myself into cramps, I took a long shower, then sprawled naked across my non-Persian Pink Lone Ranger and Tonto bedspread and tried not to think about Warren.

Nature abhors a vacuum, so within minutes I was thinking about another troublesome subject: the Erik Ernst case. After trying unsuccessfully to block that from my mind, I gave up and started reviewing what I knew. Out of sheer mental exhaustion, I decided to skip the details and just list the major events in chronological order.

On Christmas Eve, 1944, Erik Ernst, Gunter Hoenig, Josef Braun, and twenty-five other Germans POWs escape from Camp Papago. Christmas night, the Bollinger family is murdered. Some forty years later, someone rams Erik Ernst's dinghy with a speedboat. He loses both legs and his attacker is never caught. More than two decades after that, he is murdered. Days later, a reporter who wrote the book about the Camp Papago escape is found shot to death. Next to die is a deputy who worked the Bollinger case.

Could it be any more obvious that the Ernst murder was tied to the Bollingers?

Yet despite my efforts, Scottsdale PD still believed that the Ernst killing was unconnected to the Bollingers' deaths. It was possible they might change their minds after ballistics tests on the bullets harvested from Fay Harris and Harry Caulfield were completed, but I didn't think so. Even if the bullets matched, and I was certain they would, the prosecuting attorney would be able to dream up a scenario—however unlikely—that separated these two murders from the bludgeoning death of Erik Ernst.

One thing I knew for certain: Rada Tesema was no murderer. While he might be desperate to bring his wife and children to America, I refused to believe he was foolish enough to jeopardize his precious green card in order to steal a few pawnable trinkets, let alone evil enough to kill a helpless old man. The very fact that Tesema continued to care for Ernst after the money ran out was proof that he was driven more by compassion than malice.

But if not Tesema, who? Gunter Hoenig, wherever he might be?

I was tempted to go through Gunter's journals yet again, but stopped myself, deciding that I needed to strike out in an entirely new direction. It might be worthwhile to compare Fay Harris' notes on the Bollinger murders to Chess Bollinger's ramblings, so I peeled myself off the bedspread, smoothed the wrinkles out of the Lone Ranger's face, and found the fat manila envelope Fay had prepared for me before she died. Since her notes were more organized than Gunter's journals, it didn't take me long to find the pages I was looking for.

While I was able to decipher Fay's puzzling shorthand on most of the pages, two notes still challenged me.

CasNos/ccTrail/C/budSysNK/Van.

I pulled out a notepad and began working on a possible translation. *CasNos.* Casa Nostra? Had Fay found hints of organized crime in both murders? Or had she meant *Case Notes?* Then there was a slash, followed by *ccTrail*, possibly a hasty misspelling meaning *copies of Chess' trial transcript.* Or if no misspelling, how about...*copies in trailer?* The trailer in question might be

Harry Caulfield's, who had once worked on the Bollinger case. *C/budSysNK/Van*. On other pages, I'd noticed that Fay used *C* for various words; sometimes *copy*, sometimes *Chess*. And *Sys*? Could that be *system*? Or *says*? After squinting my eyes at the line for a while, I wrote down *Case notes. Copies in trailer. Chess' buddy says...* meaning Chess' buddy, Sammy Maurice.

I was almost there.

NK/Van. If my reasoning was correct, that would be *Not Kill, Vandalizing*. Sammy Maurice confirmed that he and Chess were out Christmas night laying waste to Scottsdale High School, not to Chess' family. Somehow Fay had found that out, possibly from a conversation with Harry Caulfield, who might have kept case notes on the Bollinger case in his trailer. Tomorrow I'd call Reverend Sammy and ask him if he'd ever talked to Fay, but I was pretty sure I now knew what the answer would be: a definite yes. With a thrill of satisfaction, I realized that the deciphered sentence now read *Case notes. Copies in trailer. Chess' buddy says not kill. Vandalizing.*

Tomorrow I'd call Detective Villapando again and find out if the search of Harry Caulfield's trailer turned up any material related to the Bollinger killings. Maybe the murderer hadn't found them.

Confidence rising, I tackled the next line. *Ols/kdSAuG?CFG.* *Ols.* The only thing that leapt immediately to mind was *Olds*, as in '39 Oldsmobile. Edward Bollinger's had disappeared forever the night of the killings. *KdSAuG.* I wondered if the first part in this series meant *kid*. Possibly. In 1944, two kids were involved in the case, Chess and Sammy. *SauG. Sig Sauer*, as in the popular firearm? At the time Fay made her notes, no firearm of any kind had been involved in the crimes. Oops. Wrong. Edward, the first of the Bollingers to die, had been killed by his own shotgun. But not a Sig Sauer.

After studying the rest of the series for almost an hour and trying out various combinations, I gave up. Tomorrow I'd get on the phone and find myself a code-breaker. For now, I put aside Fay's notes and picked up the case folder I retrieved from my office early this morning. As I leafed through my own notes, I came across yet another puzzle.

Spilt milk. The gas said it. Those were the worlds Chess had mumbled during my first visit with him. At the time, I'd dismissed them as word salad ramblings of the typical Alzheimer's patient, but what if I'd been wrong? As my later visit proved, Chess sometimes had moments of lucidity. What if he'd been describing something that actually happened? During the same conversation—if you could call an interview with Chess an actual conversation—he also claimed that his Daddy had killed him. Since Chess was still alive, in a manner of speaking, that part was obviously wrong. But what about the rest?

The gas said it. Gas: sometimes inert, sometimes active. Gas: to talk, to yak, to gab. Gas: without it, cars won't run. Spilt milk? Spilt gas? During WWII, spilling gas would be a major infraction, and Chess' abusive father might think it worth a beating. Still, gas couldn't talk, so how was it possible that "the gas said it"?

Suppressing a scream of frustration, I tossed the case folder aside and sat there staring at the walls, trying to empty my overloaded mind so that sane thoughts could make their way in. But my brain wouldn't cooperate and threw nothing more than scrambled words and initials back at me. Hoping that another shower might help—I'd been known to solve crimes while standing under a shower—I went back into the bathroom, but a half hour later emerged from the shower stall feeling more confused than ever. Something was blocking me.

Halfway through dressing, I figured out what the block was.

Unfinished business.

And it had nothing to do with the Erik Ernst case.

The sun had dipped behind the Papago Buttes and the film crew was gone, leaving only a solitary guard patrolling the perimeter, so I headed for the Best Western. As I had hoped, the Golden Hawk was parked outside Warren's motel room. It only took me seconds to get up enough nerve to knock on his door.

"Lena, what...what brings you here?" Like me, Warren smelled of soap and freshly laundered clothes. "I thought you needed time to think."

"I think fast. May I come in?"

He stood aside, then closed the motel door behind me. "I wasn't sure I'd ever see you again. When I discussed my past with you, you backed off so fast I can still feel the burn." His voice was wary, but mine would have been, too, given the circumstances.

I took a seat in one of the club chairs by the window, putting my carry-all on the heavy oak card table next to the film's shooting script. "I've been unfair to you."

Looking a little more hopeful, he sat down across from me. "Not necessarily. Merely careful. You've been through a lot in your life, and I don't blame you for not being anxious to get involved with someone who carries around the kind of baggage I do."

"We all carry baggage. The only thing that matters is how well we distribute the weight." I reached my hand across the table.

He didn't take it. Instead, he got up, came around the table, and drew me into his arms.

"So. Did you buy the Golden Hawk?" The motel room smelled like sweaty sheets, and my head was nestled in that concave place between Warren's shoulder and chest. We'd said so many heavy things to each other already that now it was time to simply relax and chat.

He kissed me again, then drew away and smiled. "Sure did. Yesterday. When I walked into the showroom with my checkbook, Mark almost pissed himself. Now he's tempting me with a '48 Hudson. Sometimes I suspect he isn't as interested in film as he says he is, that he just keeps showing up on the set to sell me cars."

I nuzzled his ear. "Oh, I don't know about that. You're pretty easy to tempt."

"Only by the right woman."

We sweated up the sheets some more until I fell asleep in his arms...

...and was four years old again, riding through the night on a white bus, mere seconds before a bullet put an end to my memories.

I heard singing, but the only thing I cared about was my ,mother's promise. "Yes, I'll shoot her! You just watch. I'll shoot her right now!" She held me on her lap, and to my four-year-old eyes, the gun she pressed against my forehead looked like a cannon.

"No, Mommy!" I cried. "Please don't!"

No one tried to stop her. They just sang louder, as if attempting to overwhelm her anguish with their voices. The tunes I recognized as hymns from that peaceful, far-off life lived among tall trees and green fields. But the words were different.

> *Abraham loves me, this I know.*
> *All his writings tell me so.*
> *Little ones to him belong.*
> *We are weak, Abraham is strong.*

Mommy wasn't singing and I couldn't hear Daddy sing, either. He usually accompanied these strange hymns on his guitar, but for some reason he wasn't with us. Then I remembered. A few days before, we'd left Daddy in the forest glade, along with a group of crying children.

Now I was the only child left.

"See, I'll kill her now!" Mommy screamed.

But she kicked me in the stomach first. I fell through the open door of the bus at the same time I heard the shot and pain stabbed my head. The concrete rushed up to meet me and my...

...my own screams blended with my mother's. Although one part of me lay bleeding on the Phoenix pavement, the other part of me remained wrapped in my mother's protective arms.

"Mommy!" I screamed.

"My poor baby!"

But it was a man's voice, not my mother's. I opened my eyes to find Warren holding me close, rocking me back and forth, just as my mother had oh so long ago. "My poor baby."

Still shivering, I buried my face in his chest. "Don't call me baby. Please don't."

The next time I awoke, daylight filtered through the closed curtains. I heard Warren's rhythmic breathing, but as I started to sit up, it changed. When I looked over at him, his eyes were open, staring at me.

"Do you always dream like that?"

"Yes."

"Do you want to talk about it?"

"No."

He pulled me to him.

After we made love, we showered together. Then he ordered breakfast brought to the room from the restaurant next door. He didn't bring up last night's memory-nightmare again, just tilted me back against the pillow and fed me as if I really were a baby. His hair was damp and dark from the shower, and the contrast made his blue eyes even bluer.

"You need someone to take care of you."

I opened my mouth to receive another bite of toast. "No, I don't."

"Yes, you do."

"Like hell."

"Like real."

I started to get up. "Warren, I told you..."

Gently, he pushed me back down and fed me another piece of toast. "Okay, okay. But here's what I want to say. There aren't that many scenes left to shoot, the one today with Frank Oberle standing around as the gaffers dismantle one of the barracks—I've decided to actually put that in the documentary—then the helicopter shot of the Germans running across the desert. Two more after that, but both are interiors I'll shoot on the sound stage in North Scottsdale. My guestimate is that we'll finish this week, then close up shop and go back to L.A."

My mouth was empty again but since no more toast was forthcoming, I knew that he was ready to say what he really wanted to say.

I was right. "Now that I've found you, I can't leave you behind. I want you to come with me."

Wanting and getting are two different things. The memory-nightmare had left me feeling vulnerable, and vulnerability was just too threatening. This time I didn't let him push me back down. I sat up and put my hand against his chest, keeping him at a forearm's distance. "It's too early." He knew I wasn't talking about the time of day. "Don't look at me like that, Warren. I didn't say that something more permanent isn't possible between us, but it's too much too soon."

"Honey, I…"

"And don't call me honey, either. Just let me finish. My feelings for you, they're…they're strong. But I have a business to run, too. I can keep Desert Investigations open and commute to L.A. and work on *Desert Eagle* with Angel. It would give you and me time to…" I stopped. Time to what? Count the skeletons in our mutual closets?

Just because Jimmy was leaving in a couple of days—he'd already warned me no other extension would be forthcoming—that was no reason to close down an agency which meant so much to me. And oddly, my tumultuous night with Warren had brought forth a possible solution. Just before falling into my memory-nightmare, I'd remembered my trip to Hamilton and the drawling chatter of Eddy Joe Hughey as we drove up from Birmingham. He was sick of Alabama's humidity, he'd said. Well, maybe he would jump at the chance to exchange it for some Arizona aridity. Although his computer skills would never be as brilliant as Jimmy's, they were far better than mine. More importantly, I knew we'd work well together. But that didn't mean Warren couldn't be an important part of my life.

"If I stay here, it would give you and me time to get to know more about each other before we make a major decision," I continued. "For now, I have too many open cases. Do you expect me to desert people like Rada Tesema?"

He shook his head. "You're not the type to walk away from anything."

How little he knew me. For years I'd been an expert at walking away from love. But I simply added, "Besides, we need to make sure what we feel for each other is love, not lust."

Warren was silent for so long that I thought I'd lost him. Finally, he gave me a rueful smile. "You're way too pragmatic. But if that's what you want, I guess I'll have to live with it."

I didn't realize I'd been holding my breath until I let it out in a sigh. "There's an up side to taking things slow, you know."

"Oh, really?"

"It'll give you time to hire a PI to check *me* out."

He laughed, then gave me another kiss. I could smell toast on his breath. "Honey, I already know everything about you that matters."

"Don't call me..."

"Yeah, I know. Don't call you honey."

I couldn't say any more because he'd covered my mouth with his own.

Later, I followed Warren over to the set and watched as Frank Oberle stood by the barracks while the gaffers tore them down. A boom mike dangled above his head just out of camera range. The breeze, still blowing in from California, scuttled mesquite leaves around his feet.

"Today's there's nothin' left in Papago Park to show what went on here sixty years back," Oberle said, raising his voice so that he could be heard over the shrieks of hammers ripping out nails, the clatter of falling boards. "The Germans is gone, the stockade towers is gone, and the only buildings left have been drug off to an empty lot on Scottsdale Road behind the McDonald's. In the restaurant, people are just sittin' there, chewin' on their Big Macs, not even knowin' what those raggedy-ass buildings are.

But I'll tell you what they are. They're American history, plain and simple."

When Warren yelled, "Cut!" everyone on the set, and even the crowd behind us, cheered. So did I, amazed to discover that the old man could speak with such poetry.

Overwhelmed by the response, Frank wiped his eyes. "Wish Harry was here."

So did I. And Fay, too.

I wished that Warren had been able to entice more of the former POWs into taking part in the production, men like Kapitan Stefan Schauer from the German-American Club. The greatest coup of all, of course, would have been an interview with Gunter Hoenig, who—despite what his son insisted—was probably still alive.

Thinking of Gunter made me remember his friend, Josef Braun, a man lost to history all these years.

Or was he?

I looked toward the crumbling barracks, then the parking lot. I closed my eyes and listened to the set coming down, people talking, the traffic going by on nearby McDowell Road, heard the rush of water in the Cross Cut Canal.

That was when I put it all together.

After telling Warren where I was going so that he wouldn't worry if I was late for the dinner we'd planned that evening, I stopped by my apartment to pick up the equipment I needed. Then I hit the freeway. Little more than an hour after leaving the Papago Park set, I took the Peralta Trailhead turnoff of SR-60 toward the Superstition Wilderness, a massive preserve protected by the sheer walls of the sharp-toothed Superstition Mountains—the same mountains that supposedly hid the Lost Dutchman Gold Mine.

And, perhaps, a lone German holdout from World War II.

Regardless of their beauty, getting into the Superstitions could be depressing. New ticky-tacky housing tracts had begun their inexorable march toward the mountains, but after a mile they thinned and the gravel road began, cutting through ranch land thick with grazing cattle. The scenery never failed to charm, because due to our damp winters, the Wilderness bloomed gaudy with wildflowers: yellow brittlebush, white phlox, magenta hedgehog cactus blossoms, orange mariposa, lavender Arizona lupine. The only blots on this wild beauty were the plastic Circle K bags hanging on the spines of saguaro cacti and the profusion of beer cans littering the side of the road.

When nature met man, nature usually lost.

After seven miles on gravel, I arrived at the Peralta Trailhead parking lot and stashed my Jeep in the shade of a palo verde tree. I signed in with the park rangers, assuring them that I had a fully charged cell phone as well as enough water to get me through the one or two days I might have to spend in the Wilderness. Having seen enough injuries and even deaths in this untamed place, they disapproved of solitary campers such as myself, but didn't have the authority to ban them.

I had trekked the Peralta Trail many times in the past. A loop more than eighteen miles long, it followed a stream bed for a great part of the way, and was well-maintained even though it climbed from an elevation of approximately twenty-five hundred feet to thirty-seven hundred feet in less than three miles. Still, it was an easy enough hike for someone as fit and well-prepared as myself, although it could prove risky for anyone out of shape. You wouldn't know that, though, by the number of people funneling through the trail's narrow entrance. The different languages drifting to me on the sharp morning air showed that the Wilderness continued to attract a sprinkling of foreign rock climbers: Australians, Germans, even some Japanese. These pros all carried the proper hiking and climbing gear.

The locals were another story. While a few dressed appropriately, many wore sandals and some went bare-headed, as if unaware of how merciless the Arizona sun could be. Even more shocking, a few carried no water. I took some comfort in the fact that these innocents would never make it the two miles to the Fremont Saddle, the top of the trail's first major climb. When they hurt themselves, more experienced passers-by would give them the assistance they needed to limp back to the parking lot. If badly injured, they could be lifted out by helicopter.

As expected, the crowd on the trail thinned dramatically by the time I crested the thirty-seven-hundred-foot-high saddle, but three more hikers, their heads wisely hidden by large sun hats, still struggled up the long slope behind me. Judging from the great distance between them, they were solos like myself, taking advantage of the still-cool weather to get in some sight-seeing before summer's hell-heat arrived.

Curve-billed thrashers flew above and Gambel's quail scuttled down the trail in front of me as I stood on the crest of the saddle and looked northwest toward Weaver's Needle, the famous Superstitions landmark Gunter Hoenig had drawn so poorly. I looked at his map again and smiled. The concentric circles he'd sketched in his amateurish attempt at topography did resemble a nest of snakes, but now I knew why he felt the scribbles necessary. He wanted the map's reader, probably his son, to know exactly how high to climb to find the cave where he, Ernst, and Josef had hidden during the long winter and spring of 1944-1945.

They hadn't hidden in the Needle itself, but underneath an outcropping on the calcite cliff across from it.

The Needle, a more than four thousand-foot high spire of alternating layers of basalt and ash, was the centerpiece of the Wilderness, a destination for treasure hunters and rock climbers alike. Supposedly veined with silver and gold, the Needle was rumored to be the site of the Lost Dutchman Gold Mine. After more than one hundred and fifty years of intensive yet fruitless exploration, it remained a popular destination for everyone entering the Superstition Mountains. Without realizing it, the Germans had taken refuge in perhaps the only place that would be totally ignored by a later generation: the seemingly bland cliff southeast of the Needle. Why would a rock climber or treasure hunter bother with that nondescript rock wall when the glorious Needle, with its magnificent views and possible riches, rose nearby?

Sitting down on a boulder, I took a short break, carefully sipping water from my large canteen. After I rubbed more sun block on my face and dabbed my lips with the tube of mint-flavored ChapStick I always carried in my jeans pocket, I began the descent down the saddle into East Boulder Canyon, which wound its way south of the Needle.

I've always loved this section of trail. Hoodoos, oddly shaped rock formations, towered high above me. Some seemed benign and almost humorous, resembling scampering mice or rabbits with exceptionally long ears. But others looked like Indians holding upthrust spears, which must have been an unsettling sight for the old prospectors who streamed into the Wilderness in search of gold. One of those treasure hunters was Maria Jones, a no-nonsense woman who led a band of adventurers into the Superstitions in the late 1950s, and whose Pinon Camp remained near the southern base of the Needle. Most signs of human habitation had long since returned to the earth, but the camp's sheltering pinon pines made it a popular overnight camping spot, even though the water in the nearby stream was considered unpalatable—when it was flowing, which it never did in summer. Already the water had slowed to a mere trickle.

I rested in the shade of Maria's old camp for a few minutes, admiring the colorful scatterings of Mexican gold poppy and sparkling white anemone that added brilliance to the soft sage of the brush-covered valley. Here, the air was even more perfumed than back at the saddle, with the green sharpness of juniper softened by a trace of sweet wild hyacinth. As I sat on a boulder, a solitary hiker walked by, her smile as wide as her hat brim. She waved a brief hello, but intent upon her destination, she continued toward Weaver's Needle without saying a word. I looked back toward the saddle and saw no other hikers, but the day was so pleasant more were certain to arrive. Fine by me. Like that solo woman hiker, they would make a beeline for the Needle without even glancing at the cliff opposite.

Taking full advantage of the break, I called Warren on my cell, but the rock walls around me filled our conversation with ear-piercing static, so I kept the conversation brief. After reassuring him I was fine but that it might be necessary to spend the night at Pinon Camp, I hung up. I didn't want to stay in the Wilderness overnight, but just in case, I carried food, water, sun block, waterproofing, a sleeping bag, and my loaded .38. Unless I was foolish enough to come between a nursing javelina and her piglets, Pinon was probably as safe as most Scottsdale hotels.

Rest over and still no other hikers in sight, I left Pinon and pushed north up the creek bed, hardly sparing a glance at the Needle. By now I had trekked more than six miles over rough terrain, climbed to the top of saddlebacks, descended into canyons, and walked through temperatures ranging in the sixties during the early morning to somewhere in the eighties at—I checked my watch—ten o'clock, and still rising. The day promised to be a scorcher, but there was still a chance I could finish my business by noon. If Gunter's map was correct, the cave was little more than a few yards ahead, up the rocky southern slope that led to yet another hoodoo-crowned cliff. I was under no illusion the cave would be easy to find. Back at Camp Papago, the Germans' escape tunnel had been so well disguised with brush and rock that the guards couldn't find either its entrance or exit for days. But I hoped that while Gunter might have been a clumsy artist, he might be a better map-maker.

Half a mile northwest of Pinon Camp I stationed myself next to a dead mesquite, faced south with Weaver's Needle at my back, and with my binoculars began searching the cliff face underneath a jackrabbit-shaped hoodoo. At first, all I saw were rocks and brush.

Once I found the high outcropping—as indicated on the map, it looked like a frog—I lowered the binocs straight down to where two ancient saguaros framed a small forest of catclaw and jojoba. Living bushes co-existed with dead ones, and from a distance the jumbled mass appeared impenetrable. But the thirty-foot slope up to them appeared gentle, not at all impossible for even an unequipped hiker to climb.

I took a quick look around to make certain no other hikers had crested the Fremont Saddle behind me, then fished my flashlight from my backpack and strapped on my cell phone, canteen, and holster. After slipping my hands into climbing gloves, I tucked the pack underneath a creosote bush and started up.

The footing was rough, with loose shale and rounded rocks threatening every moment to roll under the soles of the hiking boots I had changed into at the Peralta Trailhead parking lot, so I picked my way along carefully. After stumbling up the slope for a few yards, I finally found the remains of a disused trail, so narrow and faint it looked like little more than a goat track. Hidden by brush from the more heavily traveled Peralta Trail below, it wound around a rock fall, then disappeared. Adrenaline rising, I looked up to find the trail hadn't ended, but had metamorphosed into a sort of rock ladder that climbed straight up toward the twin saguaros now little more than fifteen feet above me. It was all I could do to refrain from venting a victory yell. I started up again and within minutes found myself standing on the narrow trail outside Das Kapitan's cave.

The Germans' hideout, less than three feet above the trail, was a true cave; a natural formation, not a lost gold mine. I knew I would find no Dutchman's gold here, and that was fine. I wasn't looking for riches.

Just one missing German.

I believed that when Ernst had been captured raiding the farmworkers' storage shed in that dry summer of 1945, he'd left Josef Braun behind. After Ernst never returned, Josef had continued to plug up the opening with rocks and fill the spaces between them with carefully transplanted shrubs. Unless a person knew in advance that the cave was there, it remained invisible to the naked eye. Was Josef in there now, dozing in the warm afternoon? Or had he moved on to a new life decades ago?

"Josef! Josef Braun!" I shouted, after stepping away from the cave's entrance.

No answer. Either he was gone or was still barricaded in there and was now arming himself with whatever weapon he'd managed to scavenge.

"Josef, my name is Lena Jones. You're in no danger from me." Which, if he'd killed Erik Ernst, was a lie. But the chances were good that an Old World German wouldn't see a woman as a threat.

Still no answer or sounds of movement of any kind, so I spent the next few minutes perched on the narrow trail, pulling away rocks while carefully avoiding slipping over the edge and rolling down the slope to the valley floor thirty feet below. The difficulty in removing the debris filling the cave's mouth made me realize that it must have been sealed for years. Josef was long gone. Disappointed, but determined to finish what I had started, I kept going. Just as my shoulders were about to give out, the opening revealed itself and I shone my flashlight into the darkness beyond. While the opening was little more than two feet in diameter, the cave was much larger inside. In case there was another opening into the cave and something other than an escaped POW had taken up residence, I picked up a rock and threw it in. No mountain lions snarled and no rattlesnakes threatened. Satisfied, I took my flashlight out of my pocket, stood on my tiptoes, and pushed myself inside.

Once through the mouth of the cave, I gazed around a chamber so high that a tall man could easily stand without hunching over, and three men could stand together, arms outstretched, without touching the walls. The chamber narrowed toward the back, where my flashlight beam revealed yet another chamber beyond, reachable through a low passage only slightly smaller than the one I'd used to enter this room. The passageway had once been blocked by rocks, but at some point they had tumbled down and now lay scattered on the cave's dirt and rock floor. I would explore that chamber as soon as I finished sifting the trash heaps in this one.

And trash heaps they were. Ernst—and then, probably, Josef—had been too canny to toss garbage outside the cave, which would have piqued the curiosity of local prospectors. Instead, the men had created more-or-less neat piles of refuse, which made the cave redolent with the stench of rotted food unexposed for decades to the cleansing air outside. I wrinkled my nose against the smell, then remembered my ChapStick, which was not only mint-flavored, but mint-scented. I fished it out of my pocket and rubbed it around my nostrils. To my relief, I now smelled mint, not decades.

Stench no longer permeating my nostrils, I knelt and began going through the litter on the cavern floor. Small geckos scurried out of my way and up the walls, their tails twitching in agitation. I ignored them. Within a short time I found the remnants of enough food to convince me there was more than enough to enable the Germans to survive for months, especially if their diet had been supplemented by game kills. Toward the back of the chamber, the bright beam of my flashlight revealed the bones of several small animals, probably rabbits and ground squirrels. So why had Ernst ventured out of this protected valley and into more populated territory, only to be recaptured? From what I could see, there had been no reason for it yet. Nearby, I also found several rusted kitchen implements: a couple of can openers, some pots, knives, and even a dust-covered bucket which the Germans probably used to haul water from the stream below. Back then the water had been purer than it was today, so I doubted if they suffered from the effects of contamination. Gunter made no mention of dysentery in his journals.

Ah. The water. When Ernst had been captured, it was early summer, when the stream below would have begun drying up. So it wasn't hunger that had driven him away from this perfect sanctuary. It was thirst. And that was why Josef eventually left, too.

I poked around in the cave's front chamber for a little while longer, uncovering more and more foodstuffs: dried beans, rice, even a few cans. To give the devil his due, Ernst had taken good care of his men. In one of the trash heaps, I did find a rather incongruous item: a tattered copy of *Look* magazine. Although the magazine had been ripped in half and the ink was so faded that I couldn't quite read the date, several faded photographs portrayed women's suits with big shoulder pads, and men wearing snappy fedoras. Forties styles. Which one of the trio had picked the magazine up and why? Did the men take turns reading it simply for pleasure during the day, while the light was still good? Or had they used the magazine to widen their prison-camp English vocabulary? I guessed now that I would never know. Josef Braun wasn't here, and neither were the answers to my questions.

Deeply disappointed, I dropped to my knees and scrambled my way past fallen rocks to enter the second chamber.

And that's when I found him.

Josef's skeleton lay huddled in the far corner of the cave's second chamber, only partially hidden by the rocks and empty cans Das Kapitan had covered him with. He had been murdered, of that there was no doubt. When I beamed the flashlight on the body, I could see his shattered skull, where a few deep auburn hairs still clung. One of the rocks in the cave would probably prove to be the murder weapon, but I'd leave that to the crime scene techs. Or maybe even the FBI.

No dog tags were wrapped around what was left of the neck to announce the skeleton's identity, which didn't come as a surprise, because I'd read that before escaping, the Germans disposed of the U.S.-issued tags that revealed their nationality and POW status. Even if they had escaped in their POW-stenciled uniforms, time would have erased those identifiers, too, for only rags remained of Josef's clothing. Yet even rags can tell a story. Near the skeleton's pelvis, in a tumble of fragile cloth which had once been a pocket, I saw the glimmer of metal. Carefully, so as not to disturb the decades-old crime scene more than necessary, I lifted the crumbling fabric away to reveal an Iron Cross dangling from the end of something that looked like fishing line. Sixty years ago, Gunter had made necklaces like these to sell for cigarette money. I brushed the dust away from the cross, then cleaned it with saliva and the tail end of my T-shirt. When I turned it over, I saw writing on the back. Holding the necklace with my left hand and the flashlight with my right, I squinted at the tiny letters Gunter had inscribed.

Zu meinem guten Freund Josef.

To my good friend Josef.

I held the cross against my heart for a moment, then without planning to, reached out and gently touched Josef Braun's battered skull. "Poor boy. You never made it back to your wife, did you?"

Josef didn't answer. His empty eye sockets just stared into eternity.

But I could envision Josef's final moments.

Summer, 1945. Probably sometime in late May or early June, when the stream Ernst and Josef had been relying on dried up, rendering continued survival in the Wilderness impossible. For all his extremism, Ernst was no kamikaze. Unlike those death-embracing Japanese pilots at the end of World War II, the submarine captain wasn't ready to die for his Nazi beliefs, at least not if he could help it. So he'd made another raid, probably not for food but for water, and been caught. From all accounts, he'd surrendered peacefully enough when confronted. Maybe he believed he could escape again, this time into Mexico.

If so, history had intervened in his plans. After being hidden away in the Superstition Wilderness for almost six months, Ernst had no way of knowing what was happening in Europe, that on April 30, a defeated Hitler committed suicide and that one week later, Germany surrendered. But even if Ernst had known what was going on in Europe, the end for Josef Braun would probably have been the same. Maybe he decided that his friend Gunter had told him the truth about seeing Ernst kill Joyce Bollinger and confronted him. Or maybe Josef had become increasingly dissatisfied with cave-dwelling and had wanted to surrender. Whatever the truth, I would never know for sure.

But it was easy enough to imagine Ernst going into the back of the cave where the bulk of the men's refuse had been piled, and calling Josef in on some sort of pretext. As Josef leaned over, Ernst delivered the first, stunning blow with a specially chosen rock. Judging from the state of Josef's skull, it had taken more than one blow to finish him off, which shouldn't have been surprising since Josef was a strong Bavarian farm boy, not a barely breathing, wounded woman. Once Ernst's dirty work was finished, he covered the body with rocks and garbage, blocked up the entrance to the second chamber, and left the cave, perfectly disguising the entrance with rocks and brush. Not even the coyotes had been able to claw their way inside to get at Josef's body. Ernst had hidden the scene of his crime so well that it had remained undiscovered for more than sixty years, and it would have remained undiscovered forever if Gunter hadn't drawn his map.

Did Gunter ever suspect what had happened to his friend? I couldn't help but believe that as the years went by and nothing was heard of Josef again, he began to wonder. Maybe he drew his map as a precursor to packing into the Wilderness himself to find out the truth, but then, as it so often does, life got in the way. But there was also the possibility that Gunter didn't want to know, that he preferred to believe his friend was back in Germany, working in the green fields of Bavaria with his wife and the child she had been carrying when he was called to war.

I gave the skull a final soft touch, then began to back out of the chamber. As I did so, I heard scrambling from the rock face below the cave. Had one of the hikers I'd seen earlier back on the Peralta Trail noticed me climbing up the rock face and decided to see what I'd found?

The Lost Dutchman Gold Mine, perhaps?

Then again, the climber could be someone more sinister than a casual gold-seeker. I'd told Warren where I was going, but doubted if I was in any danger from him. Something else occurred to me then. When I reviewed my early morning conversation with Warren on the set, I remembered the breeze blowing in from the west. It might conceivably have carried our words to the crowd of by-standers. Careless, yes, but that kind of thing happened when you let your personal drama get in the way of your job.

No matter. The person—and I knew who it had to be—nearing the mouth of the cave was in more danger from me than I from him. When he looked in the cave's first chamber, he would see nothing but darkness, yet he himself would be illuminated by the daylight behind him. Not good planning on his part. I didn't even consider myself trapped, not back here in the second chamber, well-protected from whatever firepower the killer might throw at me. Of course, there was always the problem of ricochets, but all I had to do was hunker down behind some rocks. He, however...

"Lena? Lena Jones? Hey, it's great running into you like this!"

I didn't answer the killer, just let him continue to call out to me. Then, with no response forthcoming, he foolishly stuck his head into the cave opening. I was already prepared, with my flashlight in my left hand and my .38 in my right. Before he could enter the cave, I shone the strong beam straight into his face, momentarily blinding him.

"Why if it isn't Mark Schank," I called. "Don't tell me you made the hike all the way out here just to sell me that Camaro."

Chapter Twenty-Seven

Having followed me all the way from the Peralta Trailhead, Mark must have been hiding behind some creosote bushes when I'd looked back up at the Fremont Saddle. He could easily have blended in with the other hikers, and when the crowd thinned after the steep ascent began, he stayed far enough behind that I couldn't recognize him.

At first Mark pretended that yes, he only wanted to talk cars, but when he saw his first pitch wasn't working, he tried another. "There's been a big misunderstanding, Lena. Come on out so we can talk." He forced an insincere salesman's laugh. "This trail I'm standing on is pretty damn narrow and I'm not great at heights."

"Don't be such a baby, Mark. It's thirty feet at the most, and not that steep." My voice echoed around the rocks, almost loud enough to wake the dead, although Josef showed no signs of stirring. But Mark was active. I could hear him walking back and forth on the narrow trail, muttering to himself. He was probably armed, what little good that did him. Both Fay and Harry had been shot at close range, which probably meant he wasn't confident of his ability as a marksman. By contrast, I could shoot a mosquito off a fly's ass at twenty paces.

To let him stew, I turned off the flashlight. At that, he stopped pacing and leaned forward, staring blindly into the cave's inky interior. I wondered if he would try shooting me in the dark.

I didn't have to guess long. Fool that he was, Mark did shoot. Twice. As I had suspected, the bullets, probably full metal jackets, ricocheted around the cave's rock walls, throwing up splinters of rock and the stench of cordite. The noise almost deafened me but I knew I was safe in my natural fortress. Mark didn't know about the cave's second chamber and when I remained silent, he fired twice again, obviously unaware that in this situation he could shoot himself more easily than he could shoot me.

When he heard no screams of pain or pleas for mercy, he began firing again. The second round bounced around and around the first chamber, then back out the cave's opening. I remained cautious. Before he snapped off his first shots, I'd managed to get a fleeting look at his weapon, a 9-mm semiautomatic, probably a Beretta. In all, I'd counted six shots, which meant he would have nine rounds left. My .38 only held six, so I was loathe to risk an out-and-out gunfight. Even fools got lucky. Edging my head carefully around a rock, I peeked out.

What was this? Mark still couldn't see me, but I could see him. He leaned against the edge of the cave opening, one hand grasping desperately at a protruding rock, almost as if he feared he was about to slip off the trail and roll down the slope. His head shook back and forth in a stuttery tremor, and he made odd, gulping sounds. Then I saw the seep of blood high on the shoulder of his white business shirt. The idiot *had* shot himself.

"Throw down your gun, Mark!" I shouted. "I'm armed, too, and I have a better sight line than you. No ricochet problems, either."

Low curses answered me at first but they faded into whines. "I need help, Lena. I'm bleeding to death."

A plaintive whine, but I knew better than to trust it. Monsters like Mark could act pathetic whenever it suited them. Besides, from what I could see, the placement of his wound wasn't serious, but I didn't want to take a chance. "If you throw down the gun, I'll come out and stop the bleeding." For good measure, I added, "I'm trained in CPR, too. Just in case. And I still have a lot of water left in my canteen."

I heard only pained breathing for a few moments, then a loud clatter, as if he'd tossed something onto the rocks below. It sounded nothing like metal hitting calcite. "Nice try with the rock, Mark. Now how about tossing the gun for real?"

The cursing rose again, fell again. Still, he refused to give up. In his untrained opinion, he was the pursuer, I was the prey. And he was oh, so wrong. He couldn't perch out there forever on the narrow trail. No matter how minor his wound, blood loss and the afternoon heat would eventually weaken him enough that he would get dizzy and lose his balance. But I had all the time in the world, a cool, safe place out of the sun, plenty of water, and even the company of Josef Braun. I could easily last days in the snug cave whereas Mark probably wouldn't make it through the night. However, there was an alternative scenario, this one much less palatable. Another hiker might come along, attempt to help him, and get shot for his pains. Mark might not have enough ammunition for every hiker who came down the saddle, but how many innocent people would be hurt before he figured that out?

Once more I tried to talk him into surrendering. "You're finished, Mark! How long do you think it's going to be before someone calls the park rangers?"

He summoned up enough strength for a defiant answer. "I'll take care of them just like I'm going to take care of you, bitch."

Which was exactly what I feared. Since reason wasn't working, I tried psychological warfare. I uncapped my canteen and took a noisy drink of water, making the process loud enough for him to hear my satisfied gurgles. The cave's echo amplified the sound even further. "Boy, you must be getting thirsty out there, Mark. How hot is it now? Eighty-five? Ninety? This might even be the first day of the year where we get up to a hundred! It's always hotter against rock, too, and there you are, having to hold on to it. Come to think of it, how are your hands? Getting cut up? I thought ahead and brought along some climbing gloves, but when you followed me out from the set, you didn't have that luxury, did you? You had to come as you were to our little surprise party, white shirt, wingtips and all. I'd like to help you, guy, I really would."

I waited for an answer. Nothing. As miserable as he had to be, Mark remained panting and scrabbling at the mouth of the cave, refusing to either leave or surrender. Yet could anyone blame him? I might have done the same thing if I had murdered three people in a state where the death penalty was still in effect.

In the unlikely event I could raise a signal on my cell phone, I switched it on, but couldn't even raise static. Mark used the noise of the dial beeps to attempt to home in on my position. He fired another couple of rounds, but was careful this time to keep his torso sheltered against the cliff face. Naturally, he missed again, and I could hear his furious cursing as he realized it. For a moment, I was tempted to end the standoff by simply shooting him, then decided against it. There had already been too many deaths in this long string of sorrows. The first to die had been Werner Drechsler, the POW who had been tortured and hanged at Erik Ernst's instigation. Then came the five Bollingers, then Josef Braun, and sixty years later, Erik Ernst himself. Finally, Fay and Harry. If Mark had his way, my name would be added to the list. But I've always been the oppositional type; want me dead and I fight to live.

In the end, what had all those killings been for? As I had finally figured out, there were three different killers and three different motives. The Ernst murder was the most understandable, because blackmailers are so frequently killed.

The Bollingers' killer...In his own perverse way, he had killed for love.

Ols/kdSAuG?CFG. Fay's notes proved she had guessed, but out of fear of a libel suit her publisher's attorneys hadn't let her print the solution to the crimes in *Escape Across the Desert.* If they had, Ernst, Fay and Harry would probably be alive today.

And Gilbert Schank would be in prison where he belonged.

Ols/kdSAuG?CFG. Oldsmobile. Kids. Auction guy. Chess' friend Gilbert.

Classic car dealer Gilbert Schank, who in those days rode the schoolbus with Chess, probably shared joyrides in the Olds with his friend. In a prescient echo of his future profession, he had fallen in love with Edward Bollinger's '39 Oldsmobile. Sixty years later Gilbert still described the Olds to me as "one smooth, snazzy ride," but at the time, I didn't realize what I was actually hearing. Nor did I understand the import of Chess' statement: *the gas said it.*

But that was clear now, too.

With gas rationing the rule of the day, Edward Bollinger kept a close measure of the gas in his precious 1939 Oldsmobile, and at some point, realized someone had been sneaking rides. The obvious suspect would be his own delinquent son. On Christmas evening, the half-drunk Edward was probably infuriated when Chess didn't return home in time for Christmas dinner and decided to confront his son and beat him within an inch of his life. What Edward didn't know was that someone else had also been sneaking rides.

Gilbert Shank.

I shouted out to Mark. "Tell me if I'm wrong, Mark, but here's how I think the Bollinger killings went down. After he'd had his own Christmas dinner, your dad made his way down to the Bollinger place for a little *àpres*-meal joyride. He'd always been successful before, so why not now? But this time, something was different. Edward Bollinger was waiting by the car with his shotgun, mean as only a drunk can be."

Silence from the cave mouth. He was listening. It was so quiet, I could hear birds calling outside, the tiny scurryings of a gecko on the rock wall near me.

Encouraged, I continued with my tale. "I remember seeing Gilbert, your dad, on those stupid television commercials you hated so much, and although he wasn't a big man, I imagine he was pretty spry as a teenager. Stronger than Edward, too, since Edward had worn himself out physically by heavy smoking and drinking. So it wasn't too hard for your father to wrestle the gun away from Edward. I doubt if he meant to blow Edward's head off, though. That part of it was an accident. Right, Mark?"

"You don't know what you're talking about!" But his protest rang hollow, convincing me that my theory was right. Time passes away, but truth never does.

Enough light filtered from the outside to the second chamber that I could see Josef lying beside me, mute witness to this end story. Reassured by his presence, I touched the cracked leather of his boot. Mark was alone out there with his rage and fear, but I had the company of someone Frank Oberle had described as "a good boy." A gentle boy. The kind of boy who had trained the rabbits around Camp Papago to eat from his hand. Had he been comforted in his lonely tomb when the geckos made nests in his bones?

Suddenly I heard a noise outside and lifted my gun, concerned that Mark might try to rush me. But he was merely shifting position. Good. Maybe he was getting a cramp.

I gave Josef's boot a final pat and like a modern-day Scheherazade, continued spinning my tale. "Meanwhile, back at the ranch, right, Mark? Edward Bollinger is dead, and by now, Gilbert's adrenaline is making him crazy. He wants nothing more than to get away without being seen, because he knows if he's caught, he'll be shipped off to whatever hellhole passed for a juvenile detention center in those days. But shotguns make a lot of noise, enough that Joyce Bollinger hears it all the way back in the house. Maybe she thinks her drunken oaf of a husband had fallen and accidently shot himself, so she goes out to investigate. Good mother that she is, she keeps the children inside. Maybe she takes a flashlight because the countryside's pretty dark. At first she doesn't see her murdered husband, just a friend of her son's holding a shotgun. Too bad for her and too bad for the Bollinger children that she recognizes little jockey-sized Gilbert with his beaky nose."

I'd created the scene so well that I could smell Joyce Bollinger's fear. Or was it Mark's? Rank. Acid. The stench overpowered the musk of the cave, the scent of wildflowers outside, the mint of my ChapStick.

"Joyce has no way of knowing that the shotgun is now empty, so when Gilbert orders her into the kitchen, she complies. Maybe she thinks she can calm him down—mothers can be good at that—and maybe she almost does. From everything I've heard about her, Mark, she was an extraordinary woman. She certainly made an impression on..." No, best not to mix Gunter up in this. Except for that botched murder attempt against Ernst back in Connecticut, Gunter had harmed no one.

"It doesn't work out that way, though. Gilbert is too far gone. Yet this is where his smarts kick into play. With what would eventually become his silver-tongued salesman's pitch, the same one he'd use to sell thousands of cars, he convinces Joyce that all he wants is to get away, but to do that, he needs to tie the family up so they can't get to the phone before he's put miles between him and the farmhouse. How am I doing, Mark?"

Nothing. But I knew he was listening.

"Gilbert finds some rope, farms are lousy with them, and ties up Joyce first. He probably wonders briefly where Chess is, but then again, kids always tell each other the damnedest things. Maybe he knows Chess is out with Sammy, terrorizing the town. Anyway, after tying up Joyce, he ties up the children: twelve-year-old Jenny, ten-year-old Robbie, eight-year-old Scotty. Maybe he thinks about not killing them. Maybe, for a minute, he thinks about hopping in the car and driving like hell for Mexico before they untie themselves and call the authorities. Or he could just give himself up. Killing that family really wasn't necessary, was it? Your father was only fifteen at the time, and if he'd confined the killing to Edward alone, there was a fifty-fifty chance he'd draw a lenient judge, someone soft-hearted enough to put him away for only a few years. When he was released, his life would still be in front of him. Too bad for everyone involved that your father turned out to be as murderous as he was hot-headed."

Mark called me names that would make a sailor blush. Good. Anger causes people to make mistakes.

"For a while I wondered why Gilbert didn't give himself up at that point, until I remembered how he felt about cars. Even back then he was obsessed with them. If he gave himself up, he'd have to return the car, and he refused to do that. After all, he'd killed a man over it. By the way, Mark, where is the damned thing?"

Mark didn't answer, but remembering Gilbert Schank's protective Navajo housekeeper, the long shared history between the Schanks and the Tsosies, I could guess. "I'll bet Edward Bollinger's Oldsmobile is hidden somewhere up on the Navajo Reservation. Did your dad ever take you up there for a spin?"

Bull's eye! He let fly a few more curses, then subsided to groans, the better to lull me into sympathy.

"Hey, Mark. I'll bet that shoulder hurts. Why don't you throw the gun down the slope and let me out of here so I can call Air-Evac for you? I wouldn't want to see you get an infection. Or get dizzy and fall off the trail. You could bang yourself up pretty bad on that slope."

Recognizing that his pity-ploy had failed, he began cursing again. The man was nothing if not consistent.

The longer I talked, the more blood he would lose, so I soldiered on. "After Gilbert finishes tying up Joyce Bollinger and her children, he runs out to the car and gets the tire iron. Then he comes back to the kitchen and...Well, we both know what he did." I paused and took a deep breath to steady myself. "Afterwards, he's so upset he forgets to be careful, so he leaves his bloody footprints all over the kitchen, footprints so small that they eventually clear those big German POWs of the murder.

"But there *is* a German in at the death, isn't there? Kapitan Erik Ernst is hiding outside in the bushes and he gets a good look at your dad, probably when your dad opens the kitchen door and the light shines across his face. I'll come back to Ernst in a minute, because he's what started this whole thing up again. That night, after killing the Bollingers, your dad realizes he's in a world of trouble. In a panic, he drives off. He doesn't go straight home but drives around and around until he can clear his mind. Somebody sees him, but it's so dark out that they just take it for granted that it's Chess joyriding in his father's car again. Eventually, Gilbert decides to go home and tell his father what he's done. Is that the way it worked, Mark?"

"You tell me, Miss Know It All."

At least he'd cleaned up his language. "I don't know how strong the relationship was between Gilbert and his own father, but from what happened afterwards it's clear that your grandfather did everything necessary to cover your father's tracks. He burned your dad's bloody clothing, didn't he?"

Mark was so quiet I could hear a hawk call in the sky outside, hear the wind rushing through the valley. Wherever Josef Braun now was, could he hear it too?

Before I continued, I touched Josef's boot again. I hoped he had sailed on the wind, all the way across the Atlantic to Germany and that little Bavarian farm where he'd left his pregnant wife. I hoped he'd seen his baby before drifting away to that place where we all eventually end up.

I shifted my position to make myself more comfortable. How much longer would this take? Just as I began to resettle myself, Mark used the slight rustlings I made to fire off another round, but he came no closer than before. At this rate, he would empty his clip before he fainted from loss of blood.

Cheered by this thought, I continued. "Your grandfather did more than just burn your dad's clothing, didn't he? He talked one of his Navajo farm hands into driving the Olds along back roads all the way up to the Navajo Reservation. Later, when Chess was fingered for the murders, I'll bet your family breathed a sigh of relief. It never crossed their minds to tell the truth just to keep an innocent kid out of prison."

Mark finally spoke. "You're so smart." From his tone, it wasn't a compliment.

"Smarter than you, since I'm not the one out there bleeding in the hot sun. Attract any bees, yet? I hear the Africanized variety has been spotted out here in the Wilderness."

I let that scary image hang in the air for a moment, then continued. "Anyway, I promised I'd get back to Erik Ernst and his role in the Schank family saga. Sixty years have passed, your father has made a bundle from selling classic cars, and you're not doing badly, either. Your life is about to get even better, because your father is in failing health, and you're about to inherit everything. Ah, life is good. But then Warren Quinn decides to make a documentary about the German escape from Camp Papago, and guess who he decides to use as his chief talking head? Eric Ernst, the one man alive who can place your father at the scene of the Bollinger killings. That sure came as a nasty shock to your dad, didn't it, Mark?"

"What the fuck do you think?" His bitterness told me my solution to both the Bollinger and Ernst murders was right on the money.

"You're not really interested in film, are you? You only pretended to be a film buff so you'd have another excuse to keep turning up on Warren's set to keep an eye on things. The Golden Hawk just gave you another excuse, an even better one, because it enabled you to talk to Warren on a regular basis."

"The sonofabitch doesn't know shit about cars. He just thinks he does."

Maybe. But Warren knew a hell of a lot about people. Which brought me to my next question. "How long have you known about your father's crimes?"

Silence.

"Then I'll guess. When I saw you and your father together at your office, I noticed the strong resemblance between the two of you. Give or take forty years, you two could be twins. I'm betting that the first day of shooting, you didn't know a thing about the Bollinger killings, that you just ambled over to the set thinking you could sell something nice to the rich Hollywood director. That's when Ernst saw you, saw the stunning resemblance between you and the blood-spattered boy he'd seen sneaking away from the Bollinger farmhouse sixty years earlier. He'd probably seen you two together on your commercials, but since you were always filmed head-on, he couldn't see your profiles. And you were both always mounted on horses…"

"I was on that damned jackass!" Mark howled.

"Yeah, that must have been humiliating. Anyway, since you were both always on some sort of equine, he couldn't see your heights. Or lack thereof. But after Ernst saw you in the flesh, three-dimensional, as it were, he put two and two together and came up with blackmail. That would have been, what, six or seven weeks ago?" When Ernst realized he had to do something about his financial situation or wind up in a state-run nursing home. "Say, Mark, when Ernst showed up that first time at Schank's Classic Cars, how did your father take it?"

He controlled his pain and rage long enough to answer. "Better than you'd think. He just told Ernst to get out of his office, that he had nothing to lose anymore, that he'd probably be dead from emphysema in a few months anyway."

I started to nod, then remembered he couldn't see me, hidden as I was behind my sheltering rock wall. "But you had plenty to lose, didn't you?"

"Damn straight! Ernst said he'd go to the cops if Dad didn't pay up, and that meant a pack of high-priced attorneys bleeding us dry while they angled for continuance after continuance. By the time the system was through with Dad, there'd be nothing left for me to inherit. I've worked too damn hard to let that happen!"

And co-starred in too many bad commercials. "Tragic, all that lovely money, going, going, gone. Um, before you killed Ernst, did you at least try to reason with him?"

"I never meant to kill him. I went over to his house late that night when I knew his caretaker would be gone, and tried to make him see things our way. I even offered him some money, although not as much as he wanted. I talked myself blue in the face, but the old sonofabitch refused to listen."

Just as I thought. But there was something else I'd never been able to figure out about that night's scenario. "You're relatively young and strong, so why did you duct tape Ernst to his wheelchair? Or did you think that would make him more *reasonable?*"

"Give me a break. I only did it because the mean bastard kept ramming me with it! He even bloodied my shins! So, yeah, I found some duct tape in one of the kitchen drawers and taped him down so he couldn't do me any more damage. But once I got him all taped up, he just went crazy on me. You wouldn't believe the mouth on that old Nazi."

Oh, yes I would. Everyone who'd known Ernst remarked on it. Still, for a moment I felt a brief twinge of compassion for Das Kapitan. Old, sick, broke and alone, dying the same kind of death he'd dealt to Joyce Bollinger so many years back. Then, remembering her dying agony, my compassion faded. "So you bashed his brains in like your father did the Bollingers. And like Gilbert, you let someone else take the blame. Only this time, the patsy wasn't a delinquent teenage boy, but a hard-working Ethiopian immigrant."

"I didn't *plan* to kill Ernst!"

Sure, it was just one of those unfortunate accidents. "What'd you kill him with? The cops never found the murder weapon."

A mumble.

"I can't hear you."

"A hammer, that's what. It was in the same drawer as the duct tape."

"Where is it now?"

"In the Cross Cut Canal."

I'd probably floated right past the murder weapon when Lindsey shoved me in. "Okay, I'll concede that you didn't plan to kill Ernst. But you *did* plan the killings of Fay. And Harry."

"You can probably guess why." Every moment he sounded more and more like a sulky child.

"Sure I can, but I'd rather hear you tell it." And I'd rather keep him bleeding in the hot sun. Once he fainted, this mess would be over. I could crawl out of the cave, phone for help, and start the wheels of justice turning. I would also do something for Josef, whose presence had given me so much comfort. I reached out and touched his boot again. "It won't be long, Josef," I said quietly. "Soon we'll both be out of here."

Mark's voice drifted into the cave. "That damned reporter was going to include a chapter on the Bollinger killings in that book of hers, the one Warren's using as the basis for his stupid documentary. I guess she fancied herself some sort of detective, because she came up with a plat map that showed who was living where back then. And there were the Schanks, less than a mile from the Bollinger farm. Hell, Dad even rode the same school bus as that worthless Chess! Anyway, she found all this out and showed up at the dealership when Dad was there, demanding to talk to him. He took her into the office, she told him she was writing a book on the escape and was going to include a chapter on the Bollingers, and that she knew he…" He stopped for a moment to catch his breath. Good. He was weakening. Or pretending again.

"Any minute now, Josef," I whispered.

A gust of wind came up, almost carrying away Mark's next words. "Dad told the reporter that if she attempted to tie him to the Bollinger murders, he'd sue her and her publisher until they were all piss-poor penniless. It didn't scare her, but it sure as hell scared her editor, and he made her drop that chapter from the book. At the time, I knew nothing about any of it. I didn't find out until Ernst showed up at the dealership. Then, after Ernst, uh, died, the reporter started nosing around again, so I protected my father."

And protected your inheritance at the same time. "How about Harry Caulfield? Why did he have to die?"

"Same…same reason." This time the wind didn't carry away his words. With a grunt, he leaned his chin on one of the rocks at the cave mouth, and his voice echoed around both rooms like a ghost's. "The Ernst thing got Harry so stirred up that one day he called my dad and asked if his old house had been close to the Bollinger farm."

Mark rightly took my silence for a sign to continue. "Harry told Dad he was going to get the Bollinger case reopened. Jesus, once a detective, always a detective."

And this detective's patience was running thin. "Oh, for God's sake, Mark. You make it sound like none of this was your or your dad's fault, that if people had minded their own business, everything would be fine."

I'd had it with him. I was tired of his self-righteousness, tired of his tenacity. He was like a spider glued to his web. He wasn't going to fall off the trail, not even if he bled out. If anything, he'd probably slump unconscious into the cave opening, and I'd have to kick his body away before I could get out.

I decided to bring the standoff to a close. But not before I gave Mark a piece of my mind, the better to help empty his firearm. "It would never have been fine because you're a conscienceless jackass. And so is your kid-killing father!"

The slur so incensed him that he fired off another few rounds, but not enough to empty his semiautomatic. Regardless, it was time to take the offensive.

No problem there. "Hey, Mark! Bullet coming through."

I inched my head around the rock and snapped off a round, taking care to aim slightly above his head. He responded exactly as I wished, by panicking. In his haste to back away from the cave's entrance, he dropped his semiautomatic in panic and collapsed onto the narrow trail with a shriek. Before he had time to recover, I dove through the second chamber's opening and exploded out of the cave. I found him on his hands and knees, cringing against the cliff wall.

Now I aimed my revolver at the center of his torso. Chest shot or gut shot, either would suffice, although I hoped it wouldn't come to that. "Clasp your hands behind your head and stand up slowly." I stepped back to give him room.

He looked at me, his face a mask of hate. "Go fuck yourself."

With a grunt, he launched himself forward in an attempt to drive me off the trail. It didn't work. Ready for this last-minute effort, I merely pressed myself to the cliff wall and watched as he lost his footing and began the long roll down to the valley floor below.

Chapter Twenty-Eight

When I finally reached Mark, I found him crumpled against a spine-studded prickly pear cactus on the valley floor. A white bone poked through a tear in his pants, revealing a compound fracture. Compared to that, the rest of the cuts and scrapes he'd sustained while rolling down the slope were relatively minor. As he lay on the ground moaning, I unclipped my cell phone and called 911. Although my conversation with the dispatcher was interrupted several times by static, I managed to convey my message: hiker down on the Peralta Trail approximately a half-mile southeast of Weaver's Needle.

Send AirEvac.

And cops. The hiker was a suspect in the killing of Erik Ernst, Fay Harris and former Maricopa County Deputy Harry Caulfield.

Help summoned, I left Mark's side to search for the Beretta and found it ten feet up the slope, nestled underneath the magenta blossoms of a barrel cactus. I couldn't leave it for hikers to find, so I hauled it out with a stick, trying my best not to superimpose my fingerprints over Mark's, and clicked the safety on. Prepared for a possible overnight in the Wilderness, I'd carried a large Baggie full of trail mix in my backpack, so I dumped out the mixture for the field mice, turned the Baggie inside out, and slipped the Beretta into the clean side of the Baggie. It wasn't flawless crime scene technology, but it was the best I could do under the circumstances. When I returned to Mark, his eyes were still closed, but the tautness of his body hinted that he'd regained consciousness.

I gave him a poke with the same stick I'd used to retrieve the Beretta. "How's it going, guy?"

"Bitch."

I smiled. "How unoriginal."

There was no point in letting the man suffer more than necessary, so I gave him a sip of water from my canteen, then slid the sheet of waterproofing from my backpack and erected a rough lean-to over his face to keep off the sun. Good deeds thus accomplished, I sat back a few feet away and waited for help.

I had just begun to hear the whupa-whupa-whupa of helicopter rotors over Weaver's Needle when two young men came around a bend in the trail, headed back down the Peralta Trail from their trip to Weaver's Needle. Loaded with climbing gear, they were dirty-faced but smiling. When they saw Mark, the smiles faded and they rushed over to help.

"*Was geschah hier?*" one said. "Ah, sorry! What happened here?"

Germans, about the same age as Gunter and Josef when they followed Das Kapitan into the Wilderness.

I flicked a look at the cave above us, where another German lay awaiting rescue.

"What happened? Oh, it's a long story. A long, sad story."

Chapter Twenty-Nine

As soon as the medics loaded Mark into the helicopter, I hiked back to my Jeep and zipped back to Desert Investigations. When I'd copied the Erik Ernst file, I drove up to Scottsdale North and turned it over to Captain Jocelyn Alcos, Kryzinski's replacement. She was a hard-eyed woman whose abrupt demeanor boded ill for my future relations with the Scottsdale Police Department.

"Don't think we're not going to look carefully at your involvement in this," she snapped, staring at the business card I'd attached to the file. "I don't approve of private detectives acting like one-woman police departments."

The words were out of my mouth before I could stop them. "They wouldn't have to if you guys would do your jobs."

Her eyes narrowed further. "Keep yourself available for further questioning."

"You know where to find me." Fighting the urge to genuflect, I walked out of Kryzinski's old office for the last time.

Then I went home and showered the Wilderness away.

Warren had a fit when I met up with him on the set later and told him what had happened. His sharp voice turned everyone's attention toward us, but I didn't care. I was too tired, both physically and emotionally.

"Jesus, Lena! When you said you were going out for a hike I never thought…What did you think you were doing, going into those mountains alone?"

"My job," I answered quietly.

That shut him up for a moment. Then, "Some day you're going to get killed!"

"Goes with the territory, Warren. If you want a relationship with a private detective, you'd better get used to being scared."

He took a deep breath and sat down on a boulder with his head in his hands. I said nothing, just let him struggle through his emotions. This was my life, and however dangerous, it was the only thing I knew.

When he looked up, the expression on his face told me he loved me enough to accept that.

After leaving Warren's motel room the next morning, I battled my way through rush hour traffic to Shady Rest Care Home. With the morning newspaper tucked under my arm, I walked the dank halls to Chess Bollinger's room, praying that his wife wasn't there. My prayers weren't answered. There Judith sat, malicious as an adder, in the corner.

"Well, if it's not the famous detective. Think you're a big deal, don't ya?"

I ignored her. Lifting Chess' untouched breakfast away, I leaned over the bed. "Chess, can you hear me? It's Lena Jones."

His eyes were open but I couldn't tell if there was anybody home. Maybe he was hiding in the only way he now could from his victim-turned-persecutor, but maybe he had slid back into the twilight world of lost memories Alzheimer's patients inhabit until their hearts forget to beat.

I held the newspaper open so that if he was awake and aware, he could see the front page.

OLD MURDERS SOLVED! the headline screamed, over pictures of the Bollinger family, both Schanks, and the 1939 Oldsmobile as several Navajo law officers and FBI agents pushed it out of a shed on the Navajo reservation where it had been hidden away for more than sixty years. It still gleamed.

I read every word of the two-page article aloud to Chess, my voice rising to cover the sounds of his wife's sulky departure when I reached the part about the arrests of Gilbert and Mark Schank and the part where it said that Chester Bollinger was now officially cleared of involvement in his family's murders. Mark was now residing in Rada Tesema's old digs at the Fourth Avenue Jail, but Gilbert had been sent straight to the jail's medical clinic, a smart judge deciding that the combination of piles of money and a current passport made him a flight risk. However, I doubted he would live to stand trial for the Bollinger killings.

Once I was through reading, I folded the newspaper, headline out, and laid it next to Chess on the bed. "Now everyone knows you didn't do it, Chess. Everyone."

No awareness crossed his features. He lay there staring at the ceiling, his eyes blank.

On my way out, MaryEllen almost ran me down in the hall. She had a newspaper in her hands, and was in such a rush to get to her father's room that the presence of another human being in her path barely registered. I almost called to tell her that her father was out of it again, but stopped myself in time. Perhaps the sound of his daughter's voice would temporarily lift the descending curtain of Alzheimer's.

I wished her luck, in more ways than one.

After being released from the Fourth Avenue Jail, Rada Tesema spent only enough time at his apartment to pack his meager belongings and tender his resignation at Loving Care. He'd received permission to use the money raised by his synagogue and Reverend Giblin's church for a one-way ticket back to Ethiopia.

"America not for everyone," Tesema said, as we sped along the Hohokam Freeway to Sky Harbor Airport two days later. I'd volunteered to take him to the airport, since I couldn't bear the thought of going to Desert Investigations and seeing

Jimmy's empty desk. Today was Jimmy's first day at Southwest MicroSystems.

I pulled my attention away from my own sorrows and focused on Tesema's. "I'm so sorry, Mr. Tesema. Maybe if you gave it another chance?"

He shook his head. "I miss family. This place, it not for me."

He was right, of course. America wasn't for everyone. Despite the myths, our streets were not paved with gold, hard work did not always guarantee success, and perfect justice remained more of a dream than a reality. Those of us born here accepted these truths. For immigrants, they came as a shock. As my Jeep barreled along the freeway and the exhaust from other cars almost choked us, I fleetingly wondered if no dreams at all are preferable to dreams denied. Then I pushed that heresy away. For good or ill, we Americans are defined by our dreams.

When I let Tesema off at curbside Delta check-in, he gave me a smile that just about finished breaking my heart. "You a good woman, Miss Jones. My family, we will offer up prayers for you."

Considering the way things were going, I'd need them.

But maybe not, because as soon as I drove back to Desert Investigations, I found Jimmy at his desk. Working.

"What are you doing here?" I asked. "I thought…"

He gave me a sad-eyed smile. "Esther and I broke up yesterday. Right in the middle of Ethan Allen. She was determined to go Early American and I made the mistake of saying, '*Whose* Early American, mine or yours?' Then we were off and running. It soon became pretty clear we were operating from totally different philosophies. Esther has this idea in her mind of what life should *look* like, and I have this idea of what life should *be* like. There's a big difference, you know."

Yeah, I knew. All of my foster parents had taken great care to *look* loving on those rare occasions when the social workers came to call. What went on after the social workers left was the real deal, and it wasn't half as pretty as the picture my foster parents painted.

Almost afraid to ask Jimmy what he planned to do now, I stared down at the mail on my desk. One letter was from

Beth Osmon, and it bore a Birmingham, Alabama, postmark. Intrigued, I opened it to find a short note.

> *Dear Lena,*
>
> *I'm writing you from Birmingham, where I'm spending some time with Eddy Joe. Oh, he's so cute! I just can't get enough of that accent.*
>
> *Tomorrow, we're going to drive up to Hamilton to meet with Alea Rinn and do something about her situation. The poor girl has been devastated by all this.*
>
> *Maybe you're surprised by my actions, but the more I thought about it, the more I realized that I couldn't let Jack's pretty babies starve.*

No, she couldn't. Beth wasn't that kind of woman.

Warmed by the reminder of another woman's courage, I summoned the nerve to ask Jimmy what I needed to know. "Now that Esther's no longer in the picture, what do you plan to do?" Unasked was the question: *Are you still leaving me?*

He smiled. "The same thing as before. Live in my trailer on the Rez. Work with you."

Somehow I refrained from letting out a whoop. "You're not going to take the job at Southwest MicroSystems?"

"Nah. Me and big corporations don't mesh all that well. I'd have to cut my hair, buy new clothes, maybe even get rid of my tatts. Who needs that? Besides, I was only taking the job to please Esther."

"Maybe she'll be back." In my selfishness, I hoped not.

He shook his head. "It's over, Lena. I'm running toward something, and she's running away."

Running away. I had already come to that conclusion about myself. If I moved to California to be with Warren, I'd be running away, too. And Lena Jones doesn't run. In the meantime, however, thank God for Southwest Airlines and Angel's offer to consult on *Desert Eagle.* I could stand to make some real money for a change. Maybe I'd even make enough to buy some snazzy classic car to tool around Hollywood in. But not a '39 Olds.

For now, I had to get busy. Putting my chrome dreams aside, I called out to Jimmy, "Hey, partner! What's the next case on the table?"

Filming is seldom done in sequence. The final day of filming on *Escape Across the Desert* included a scene from the beginning of the documentary, where the German POWs were standing in the blind spot by the compound fence where the guards couldn't see them, finalizing their plans for the escape. Behind them, sunset's pink light tipped Papago Buttes with fire. With Warren watching carefully, the actor playing the role of Kapitan Erik Ernst told his men what he expected of them that night. "Gunter, you will go first, and I will follow behind. Josef will bring up the rear. Once we are through the tunnel, we will immediately assemble our boat. If all goes well, we will be in Mexico by next nightfall."

The actor playing Josef replied, "*Jawohl*, Kapitan!"

But the actor playing Gunter did not look convinced. As Warren directed the camera closer, he asked, "What if all does not go well, Kapitan?"

Das Kapitan scowled. "Under my command, all things will always go well!"

Gunter looked up at the Buttes, stared at their fiery glow. "This land looks little like Germany, Kapitan. Its hardships may be more than we can bear."

Das Kapitan spit on the ground. "Fool! There is nothing a German soldier can not bear. Especially among weak people in a soft country. Although we will ride our boat south, we will keep our eyes toward the east—toward our dear Fatherland."

Above the three actors, a red-tailed hawk, its presence an unrehearsed gift of nature, swooped down to make its final kill of the day. It missed, and the rabbit it had set its sights on scampered safely into its burrow.

I saw Warren smile.

"That's a wrap!" he called, as the hawk rose back into the sky.

Epilogue

As the band at Phoenix Sky Harbor played a military march, the old man waited patiently on the tarmac, shielding his eyes against the morning sun. Although the drive up from Yuma had exhausted both him and his wife, they were uplifted to find that the ceremony had drawn such a respectful crowd.

Near his family stood several friends from Gemuetlichkeit, as well as a sprinkling of other civilians and military personnel from several wars. Yesterday's soldiers and today's, Germans and Americans, all standing shoulder to shoulder, united in purpose. He thought he recognized one of the old American soldiers as a former Camp Papago guard, but couldn't be certain. Most men changed shockingly with age. Of the identity of one old soldier, though, there was no doubt. The golf course millionaire! Regardless of the tragedies in that rich man's life, his clear eyes belied his age and he still fit perfectly into his old uniform. Clinging to his arm was the millionaire's flame-haired niece, the living memory of another woman from so many years ago.

Standing near her was the pretty blond detective he had heard so much about. Her tireless phone calls had resulted in this grand ceremony of farewell, Josef Braun's journey home to the son and six grandchildren Josef had not lived to meet. If circumstances had been different, he would have fallen on his knees in front of the pretty detective in gratitude, but as things were…

No, as his wife continued to remind him, the arms of INS were much too long. However—and here he hid a smile—he saw the pretty detective staring intently at him with the light of recognition in her eyes.

But she said nothing. She just gave him a big grin and looked away.

What a woman!

The only thing that even slightly marred the perfection of this day was the nosy film crew sticking their mikes and cameras into everyone's faces. Several times one of them had approached him. He'd given a curt refusal, then turned his head, because it would not do to have his face show up on a screen somewhere. Yet for all their intrusiveness, he could not dislike them, especially the handsome young director the pretty detective looked at with such love. After all, if there had been no film, this day might have never arrived.

The band's last note died away. In that short pause before the honor guard picked up its too-light burden, he stepped toward the casket. With soft reverence he leaned over and settled his age-spotted hand upon the glistening wood.

"Auf Wiedersehen, Josef," he whispered.

With that final farewell, Gunter Hoenig straightened his old submariner's spine and walked back through the Arizona sunlight to the people who loved him.

Author's Note

The Real History Behind the Book

On March 12, 1944, German POW Werner Dreschler of U-118 was found hanged in the shower room of Compound 4 at Camp Papago, a prisoner-of-war camp located between Phoenix and present-day Scottsdale, Arizona. Before death, Dreschler had been tortured; an autopsy found more than one hundred burns and stab wounds.

After seven POWs—all crew members of German U-boats—were arrested for the crime, Camp Papago became peaceful again, but only because the Germans were busy digging a one-hundred-and-seventy-eight-foot-long tunnel under the stockade fence. On Christmas Eve, 1944, twenty-five Germans (Eric Ernst, Gunter Hoenig and Josef Braun are fictitious characters, which brings *Desert Run's* total to twenty-eight) crawled through the tunnel and under the fence. They were led by Kapitan zur See Jurgen Wattenberg, of U-162, who had managed to smuggle a map into Camp Papago which appeared to show that a nearby river flowed all the way to Mexico. Upon exiting the tunnel, Wattenberg and his men soon discovered that in the Sonoran Desert, rivers are usually dry. Their plan to float to Mexico thus quashed, the POWs scattered across the desert. A reward of $25 per German was posted, but in some cases was not necessary, because several POWs surrendered within the first few days. Others stayed on the run until they were captured by local farmers, ranchers, housewives, and members of Arizona's Indian tribes.

The last prisoner was returned to custody on January 28, 1945. It was Kapitan Jurgen Wattenberg himself. For weeks Wattenberg had been hiding with two other POWs—and a bottle of camp-brewed schnapps—in a cave near Phoenix's famed Biltmore Resort. Eventually tiring of his rugged quarters (his companions had already surrendered), Wattenberg walked to downtown Phoenix and rested for a while in the lobby of the Adams Hotel, where he attracted the attention of a bellhop. Realizing the bellhop was growing suspicious, Wattenberg left the hotel and asked the foreman of a street work crew for directions to the local railroad station. Upon hearing Wattenberg's German accent, the foreman summoned the police, and what soon came to be known as "Arizona's Great Escape" was ended.

In contrast to the actions of the three fictional POWs in *Desert Run*, the real German POWs harmed no one during their weeks on the lam. Other than a few petty thefts of food and clothing, the only destruction they wreaked was in a Phoenix elementary school basement where two of them had taken shelter. In a jesting mood, Heinrich Palmer wrote the following words in a school textbook: "This is a nice house for a prisoner of war on his way back to Germany!"

While those twenty-five Germans were on the run in the Arizona desert, the wheels of American justice were slowly grinding on seven other Camp Papago POWs—the confessed murderers of fellow POW Werner Dreschler. On August 25, 1945, at Fort Leavenworth, Kansas, Helmut Fischer, Fritz Franke, Guenther Kuelsen, Otto Stengel, Heinrich Ludwig, Bernard Ryak, and Rolf Wizuy were hanged for Dreschler's murder in the last mass execution to take place in the U.S.

NOTE: Relations between the prisoners and their captives were so warm at Camp Papago that several former POWs moved to Arizona after the war. In 1985 others flew back from Germany for a reunion dinner and tour of the former camp grounds.

Several POWs still correspond with their old captors. Although an Oakland Athletics training field now occupies a portion of the former prison site, some of the German officer's quarters used at Camp Papago still exist and are in use in various locations throughout Scottsdale, Arizona, mere blocks from the author's home. They have become rental units, offices, and storage buildings for the Phoenix Zoo.

This former Camp Papago German officer's barracks sat behind a McDonald's fast food restaurant on Scottsdale Road for several years until it was purchased by a local historian. Along with other Camp Papago buildings, it is now being restored.

Sources

Wily Germans Elude Chase. Phoenix Gazette, Dec. 28, 1944

Arizona Walls: If Only They Could Speak, Judy Martin. Double B Publication, 1977

The Faustball Tunnel: German POWs in America and Their Great Escape, John Hammond Moore. Random House, 1978

The Crazy Boatmen of Arizona, Marshall Trimble. Crossroads, Vol. VII, No. 5. May 2000

"Flight from Phoenix," Robert L. Pela, *New Times*, March 8-14, 2001

Tour of Papago Park POW Camp Site. (Brochure) March 31, 2001

"Christmas Memories of POW Escape," Thomas Ropp. *Arizona Republic*, December 25, 2003

Papago Scout, newsletter of the Papago Trackers. No. 25. March, 2004

"Vet Traces POW Camp's Lore," John Leptich. *Scottsdale Tribune*, June 23, 2004

"One German POW's Story," Leigh Smith. *Borderlands*, El Paso Community College. September 24, 2004

"POWs in Papago Park," Tammy Leroy. *Phoenix Magazine*, December 2004

Also of great use were the memoirs of R. James LeGros, of Prescott, Arizona, a former guard at Camp Papago.

To receive a free catalog of Poisoned Pen Press titles, please contact us in one of the following ways:

Phone: 1-800-421-3976
Facsimile: 1-480-949-1707
E-mail: info@poisonedpenpress.com
Website: www.poisonedpenpress.com

Poisoned Pen Press
6962 E. First Ave. Ste. 103
Scottsdale, AZ 85251